D0192593

FOR SALE

WITHDRAWN

FROM

Lifeboatmen

Lifeboatmen

Simon Wills

First published in Great Britain in 2014 by
PEN & SWORD FICTION
An imprint of
Pen & Sword Books Ltd
47 Church Street
Barnsley
South Yorkshire
S70 2AS

Copyright © Simon Wills, 2014

ISBN 978 1 78346 288 9

A CIP catalogue record for this book is
available from the British Library

Printed and bound in England
By CPI Group (UK) Ltd, Croydon, CRO 4YY

Pen & Sword Books Ltd incorporates the Imprints of Pen & Sword Fiction, Pen & Sword Aviation, Pen & Sword Family History, Pen & Sword Maritime, Pen & Sword Military, Wharncliffe Local History, Pen & Sword Select, Pen & Sword Military Classics, Leo Cooper, Remember When, Seaforth Publishing and Frontline Publishing

For a complete list of Pen & Sword titles please contact
PEN & SWORD BOOKS LIMITED
47 Church Street, Barnsley, South Yorkshire, S70 2AS, England
E-mail: enquiries@pen-and-sword.co.uk
Website: www.pen-and-sword.co.uk

To 'B', my kind and loving partner,
without whose encouragement and support
this novel would not have been written

Prologue

10th February 1866

It was a late winter's afternoon, and a passer-by could hear Richard Stokes humming to himself while he went about his work. He was responsible for the harbour's navigation lights and had arrived at his usual time to tend to one of them. This lantern was of the bulls-eye variety, and carried upon a wooden post some five and a half feet high. The lightkeeper reached up, unhooked it, and lowered the heavy lamp onto the sand.

He lit the wicks so that he could examine the light's performance carefully. It was very bright even in the early dusk. He crouched in front of it, immune to the concentrated reek of burning whale oil, and his face was briefly illuminated in a manner which dramatically exaggerated and reddened his features so that he looked almost demonic: all nose, ears and beard. His breath came as surges of smoke in the cold air, adding to the devilish illusion.

Richard Sutton Stokes. That was his full name, although everyone called him 'Stoker', including his dear wife.

Stoker expertly extinguished the flames and rolled his neck as he straightened up, grunting when an ageing muscle twinged. He turned towards the weakening sun and over half a century of age was revealed in sharp relief. The effects wrought by time had been exaggerated by constant exposure to the elements, a meagre diet, and heavy use of pipe tobacco. His beard, confined below the level of his jaw-line, was thick, brown and wiry like his rapidly-receding hair. His deep-set, large grey eyes looked careworn but they also revealed something of his nature for his face spoke of a solid, stern, reliable character. He was a man given to responsibility, and his life was filled with it: husband, father, lightkeeper, and most recently coxswain of the lifeboat. Stoker took satisfaction in knowing exactly what was required of him in all these roles and in meeting the demands of each; in honouring what was expected. In short: he enjoyed a sense of duty.

Stoker paused and wondered how others saw him.

The sharp crunch of a foot on gravel behind him interrupted the lightkeeper's thoughts.

"There you are, Stoker," came a familiar voice.

"Hello Tom," said Stoker as they shook hands warmly. Tom Hart was an old friend, and the assistant coxswain of the lifeboat. A kindly soul, thoughtful, and well-liked. "What brings you out here then?"

"We were out on a duck-shoot this afternoon and I dropped Ben off in the cart. Wondered if you'd fancy a trip to the *Blue Boar* for a hand of cards."

Stoker was tempted. He could probably get away with it – no-one would know – but it wasn't the right thing to do. "I'd like that Tom, truly I would, but I can't. Still got three more lights to do after this one." He nodded landward, back towards the road. "Another time maybe."

"Pity," said Tom. "You sure you can't sneak away for a few hours?"

Stoker grimaced. "Wouldn't be right. Can't leave this half-done." He waved a hand towards the lantern at their feet. "Where d'you go on the duck-shoot?"

"Down Earwig Bay. It's misty down there this time o' the

year, and it gave us good cover. Got to do something these days to get food on the table, eh? I dropped a couple of mallards off with your Mary. She said I'd find you here."

"Thankee, that's very good of you Tom. Is the fishing still bad?" Stoker had once been a fisherman himself.

"Getting better, some say. It's the deep sea lot that seem worst hit." He sighed. "Still, Father always used to say every dozen years or so was a fallow year. Reckon that's about right – must be nigh on twelve years since the last lean patch."

Stoker shook his head. Poole was a fishing town and the long run of poor catches had hit the community hard.

"Things'll pick up soon," he said encouragingly. "Change in the weather once we hit March – that'll stir things up a bit."

"I'm sure you're right, Stoker." Tom ran his hand over his moustache. "Anyway, I must get going. If you're not coming, I'll look in on young Cain instead."

"Cain Matthews? Well, there's a thing," mused Stoker. "Taking that little hot-head to a card school. Is it some kind of test?" He chuckled.

"He'll have to watch himself, that's for sure," Tom observed. The young man in question was very outspoken: even his own mother used to say he'd argue with the Almighty. "Y'know Stoker we'll have to keep an eye on him in the lifeboat. Cain... well, he can be an awkward bugger. Following orders won't come easy to that one."

Stoker had to agree with his friend's assessment, but beggars couldn't be choosers. They had thirteen places on the new lifeboat and only thirteen volunteers, so that was that. And who knows how any of them would rise to the challenge.

Stoker smiled ruefully. "God help us."

Suddenly something caught Tom's eye. "Look at the sky." He nodded over Stoker's shoulder.

Stoker turned. From the seaward horizon was spreading an armada of tightly packed small white clouds studded into the blue.

"Mackerel scales – furl your sails," announced Stoker, repeating the well-known sailor's proverb which warned ships at sea to beware. The proliferation of little puffy clouds looked like the pattern on the flanks of a fresh mackerel, yet the axiom was often correct and usually indicated a significant change in the weather. A change for the worse.

"Looks like I ought to get going sooner rather than later," said Tom. "I'd better be off."

"Good luck."

Tom nodded, raised a hand, then left Stoker to it, trudging back to the road behind them.

Of course, Stoker had wanted to go with him. But the lightkeeper's role was well-paid because it was important. A wage of one pound per week was a good sum and meant that he and his family could own a cottage, yet it was a role that demanded diligence – no half-measures.

Stoker contemplated the good fortune that had brought him the role of lightkeeper when other families were struggling to put food on the table. That's why the duck hunt was popular. It would provide a free meal. He mused on this while he topped up the oil in the lamp. He'd had a hard life himself as a child, but like all children he'd just accepted his situation and taken it for granted that his parents would provide what they could. All the same, he remembered not having a pair of shoes until he was twelve, and that they rarely lit a fire even in the harshest winter because they couldn't afford the fuel.

Stoker's father had flitted from one job to another – fisherman, boatman, tidewader, even a spell with the customs service – but he never seemed to settle. He earned enough to pay the rent, but it was his mother's laundering and needlework that kept them fed and clothed. For a moment he saw his mother's eyes cast back at him from the reflecting surface to the rear of the lantern. Stoker had her same resolve.

The wicks looked straggly, and he pulled out a pair of scissors to trim the four elongated blackened ribbons down to size. The light from the burner was magnified by a nine inch lens at the front of the lantern that broadcast a bright white beam across the water at night.

He took out a cloth and polished the lens – front and back. The soot from the burner's smoke built up surprisingly quickly inside. Stoker's keen eye detected an irregularity in the thick glass and he bit at the margins of a thumbnail while he examined it carefully. His calloused fingertips ran over the warm lens and he frowned. There was a small chip on the surface – probably caused by a flying stone – but it had already started to crack slightly. Stoker tutted. Not serious, it would hold for a while yet; even so, he'd have to replace it soon as a precaution.

Ships depended on the lights to navigate the harbour safely, and they had to be protected at all costs. Stoker was responsible for four of them set around the harbour. It was a five mile walk to service them all – twice a day every day of the year and in all weathers. Safety at sea was vital to a seafaring community and there was no room for complacency. That was why he'd decided to volunteer as the coxswain of the new lifeboat, a decision helped by the fact that the lifeboathouse had been built here at North Haven, practically next door to Stoker's cottage. Thankfully, they'd not been called out yet, but it would happen sooner or later.

Stoker finished the polishing then straightened up again and rubbed his lower back; it had stiffened in the cold. He restored the lamp to its operating position atop the post, and lit it ready to act as overnight beacon.

Time to move on to the next light.

Chapter One

Cain Matthews had been sent on a mission by Tom Hart. A gale was in full force, and outside the protection of the harbour there were already ships in distress. They had to launch the lifeboat, but to do so they needed the assistance of the Poole steam tug. Cain's task: to talk the tug's captain into helping them. He wasn't surprised that the lifeboat was about to be called out, yet he was surprised that the assistant coxswain trusted him with the sensitive task of negotiating with the captain. Cain had been the first volunteer on the scene when the lifeboat signal went up, so perhaps Tom had had no choice. There was so much to do; the emergency was forcing everyone into unfamiliar roles.

As Cain neared the waterfront, the wind toppled one of three lofty chimney stacks belonging to the *New Inn* and it crashed onto the narrow street about seventy feet ahead of him. Despite the shriek of the gale, the thunderous hammer-blow of impact resounded above it all magnificently. Fine red Jacobean brickwork burst open on the wet cobbles and sent shrapnel flying in every direction. Cain's young reflexes threw him out of danger as if dodging a falling spar on deck: seamen have a good instinct for danger – at least the survivors do.

He lay for a second, sprawling in the rain-begotten torrent that Thames Street had become, and stared at the destruction. His heart was thumping with alarm. One tile off a roof could kill a man in this weather, but that chimney was eight feet tall and probably weighed four hundredweight or so. He stood and warily surveyed the destruction before him, squinting through the harsh elements. If he'd started out a few seconds earlier, run just a fraction faster… Cain grinned at his lucky escape; he was an adventurer.

He stooped to pick up his oilskin cap, swept his unruly hair back off his forehead, then pulled the cap on firmly. His face was serious again. Cain glanced aloft at the two remaining chimneys, balanced now like two men about to jump overboard. But there was no question of retreat: the longer way around would waste time. He swore out loud to the heavens then marched forward purposefully without allowing himself further time to consider the risks; Cain leapt over the rubble, and made his way towards the Quay.

The powerful wind howled down the once snug streets of the old town – buffeting the walls of houses in great gusts that boomed and shook. With curiosity and determination it probed every obstacle, frantically tearing and snatching at weak defences, and bearing aloft or casting aside all that it was strong enough to carry.

All along the coast, roofs were ripped open to expose the tender bowels of buildings, boats torn from their moorings, and towering trees effortlessly uprooted then abandoned with indifference. It was the beginning of the worst storm for generations.

The rush of adrenaline that had come from his brush with death had provided Cain with some temporary immunity to the cold, but soon he felt the biting winter wind chill his wet young body. He struggled to see clearly as the gale whipped the raindrops hard against his face. The force of the wind was increasing as he neared the waterside.

When he rounded the final corner to face the sea, a blast of air caught him and bowled him clean over, sending him tumbling into a tangle of oilskin cloak against the side of a building. He struggled up, and once more he realised he had been fortunate – he could easily have cracked his head open. He groped his way across the wind into a doorway which offered some respite while he gathered his wits.

Peering out, his senses were momentarily overwhelmed. Incredulity. The difference between the scene in front of him and what he had expected was hard to take in. The usual orderliness of Poole Quay had been replaced by outright chaos.

Before him was strewn a mass of timber. It had arrived yesterday out of season, and had been unloaded and neatly stacked in the afternoon. Now it was scattered around the quayside in great drifts of planking. There was a small punt with its back broken perched carelessly atop a pile of it right in front of Cain. Barrels, bags and bales of cargo lay scattered in confusion, many smashed or ripped open and the contents strewn randomly across the space before him. Canvas, rope, nets, two handcarts, a large shop sign and numerous other forms of debris lay where the wind had most recently thrown them. Here and there were parts of buildings: bricks, slates, even a door propped jauntily against a bollard.

No living things stirred amongst this confusion and yet the whole was moving – a jerky, unpredictable and violent movement animated by the wind.

And then as an awesome backdrop to this devastation there was the sea. The storm was driving huge swollen waves relentlessly into attack, hitting the exposed parts of the quayside with thunderous *whumps* like mighty mortars, before blasting into showers of snowy spray that smacked back – *thwack* – on the drenched stones.

Most of the ships lay huddled together at the western end of the Quay where there was a long sheltered stretch. There were many more than usual: they'd come into the harbour to

15

seek refuge. From this distance they were one giant jumbled silhouette of rigging undulating like a huge restless creature. Cain could not recall seeing so many ships at Poole before: all merchant ships, but many shapes and sizes, and moored close together, sails tightly furled. Tall masts crossed with spars shot skywards and seemed almost to caress each other as neighbouring hulls jostled nervously in the waves. If this kept up, some of them would undoubtedly suffer significant damage. Cain's expert eye judged that the nearest vessel already looked like she was taking on water.

He gathered his oilskin around him and sprinted across the windswept expanse towards the short stretch of the eastern Quay that was protected from the worst of the wind. There, as he expected, he found the steam tug, *Royal Albert*. Leaping aboard he grabbed the rail and thundered along the deck to the cabin.

———————

Another dark mass of sea rose up out of the gloom and slammed against the bows of the *Elizabeth*, breaking over the foredeck and submerging it in a menacing torrent of icy water. Captain John Back clung to a shroud as the ship lurched violently to leeward. His normally ruddy complexion was lightened by the cold, and his long wet greying hair was splayed out across his neck and back.

"She's falling away Mr Henley, keep her up into the wind," he ordered, shouting across the see-sawing deck to the stocky Mate at the helm.

"Aye sir."

Compelled to take in all but a minimum of canvas, the south-easterly wind was forcing them inexorably towards the shore despite their best efforts to beat away. And the angry sky suggested the storm was in no hurry to abate: if anything it was getting worse. There was an enormous strain on the ship in her current situation.

A loud crack from above and the main-topmast came crashing down amidships, bringing with it the only sail that had been set. The captain leapt aside just in time.

"Cut that lot away," he yelled.

Sailors advanced with axes to sever the rigging which held the tangle of wood and canvas to the ship.

"Over the side," the captain commanded. "Look lively!"

The seamen worked speedily and cleared the deck just as another unstoppable mass of freezing water swamped the bows of the *Elizabeth*. As they felt the deck plunge, every man instinctively stopped what he was doing and grabbed a sure hold to the ship. She was dipping her head into the huge seas as the storm continued to deteriorate. Wave after wave surged over her. The ship was struggling like a tired old woman laden with a heavy burden. Something was wrong.

"Mr Henley. Send below. See what water we've got in the hold."

"Aye sir." The Mate grabbed Seaman Reed and they hurried down the companionway.

Captain Back knew his ship and she wasn't behaving as he expected, even in these abnormal conditions. She had never been in weather like this since he'd been in command and it would test any ship, but she wasn't riding the waves and the swell: she was wallowing, slewing round too easily with the wind and late responding to the helm. That probably meant a serious problem somewhere beneath his feet.

It started raining hard; it came on suddenly like a tropical downpour, but was icy cold. The roaring winds whipped the rain drops at tremendous speeds and dashed them against whatever they encountered. They stung as they hit the captain's chilled skin. Visibility was now cut down to a few feet.

Henley reported back. His broad face held an uncharacteristic scowl.

"The hold's flooding sir. We've got about three feet of water down there."

"*Three* feet?" The *Elizabeth* was too old for this weather: her wooden hull was weak.

"And sir, the cargo's all over the place."

The captain cursed loudly. He couldn't help himself. So that was it: several tons of water and cargo rolling around. No wonder the ship felt sluggish.

"Mr Henley, call the crew to drop the best bower, then put two men to the pumps."

"Sir?"

In merchant ships the crew asked questions, something Back still couldn't get used to after his navy service where orders were orders. "We'll never claw away from this lee shore, not with all that shit down below slopping around," he explained. "We'll drop the starboard anchor, and aim to sit it out. If we can steady her enough we'll get someone below to see if we've sprung any timbers."

The best bower was the ship's heaviest anchor and weighed twelve hundredweight, but would it be enough to secure the ship?

On board the steamer, *Royal Albert*, Cain was hoping to persuade her captain to tow out the lifeboat. Cain was aware of his own reputation; he knew diplomacy was called for, but it wasn't something that came naturally to him. He preferred to tell rather than ask, and persuasion was harder still.

Captain Will Redmond listened to Cain, and sucked on the stem of his white clay pipe almost hidden amongst the black mass of his beard. He held the younger man's gaze as the heavy boat rocked. The captain was a big man, but the restricted space made him look even bigger.

"The thing is," said Cain, having quickly explained the situation, "we were hoping you'd tow us out with the steamer."

"Take you out in this!" The captain fairly choked on tobacco smoke. "Are you mad?"

"Steamer's built for this sort o' thing isn't it?"

"That may be, but there's the world of difference between being caught in a storm by chance and *choosing* to go out in it. And can you imagine what Mr Penney will do to me if I take the steamer out and anything happens to her?" The owner was notoriously protective.

"Ah! So it's old George you're afraid of then, not the gale?"

"Now that's not fair…"

"We simply can't get the lifeboat out there without your help." Cain attempted meekness, eyes bright, earnest. "Take us to North Haven, pick up Stoker and the lifeboat, and then tow us out the harbour *please*. Without the tug we've no chance – can't use oars or canvas in this." He nodded towards the window.

"But what's it going to be like out in the Bay, Cain? Just look at it in here, protected by the land! I've never seen anything like this in-harbour. Never. Outside, there'll be sea like you'd never believe. Mountains of it. Even the tug's not been tested in that kind o' thing."

"All the more reason to get out there soon as we can and save them poor souls that need us." Cain looked him squarely in the eyes: "we're their only hope, captain. We've had a message from Stoker – two ships gone under already and three more crying out for help. It's desperate."

There was a jolt as a large wave belted the *Royal Albert*'s side. Cain staggered, but the master of the tug was immovable. Will Redmond crossed his arms and leaned back, allowing smoke to curl out of the corner of his mouth. He scratched his beard with one thumb while he considered Cain's request.

"What about payment?" asked the captain.

"Come on…!" Cain was getting frustrated.

The captain held up a hand to stifle protest. "If it were my choice I'd do it willingly enough – you know that. But you know what Mr Penney thinks about people using the tug. No payment, no service: that's his line. Always has been." He held his pipe by the bowl and wagged the stem at Cain. "I've heard it enough times to have it ingrained in my mind."

"George Penney ain't about," Cain ventured, feeling trapped. "We could just slip out…"

"Oh, don't you worry." Will shook his head knowingly. "Foul weather like this! He'll be down here soon enough, fussing about, checking his property's not in no danger. Hang around and he'll be down, mark my words."

"People's lives could be at stake!"

"You don't need to tell *me* that. But," he wagged the pipe again, "emergency or no, it's George Penney that owns the boat, and it's him what has the final say."

Needless to say, this was enormously vexing. An impasse. Cain thought for a moment then tried again. "Won't he care that men could die?" he pleaded.

"He won't even look at it like that, you see. He's not like me or you. He's a man o' business and not a seaman, and there's all you need to know." Will took off his peaked cap and scratched his balding head, revealing a deep forehead scar. "Lookee here, I don't like this any more than you do, Cain, but I have me livelihood to think of, and Penney's a tough old bugger and that's a fact. I can't afford to go back to sea with this bloody leg o' mine if he gives me my marching orders, so I *have* to do what he wants."

"I see," said Cain. There was nothing more he could say now. He had to think of another way.

They both sat listening to the gale outside and watching the waves pounding the Quay.

"Look at that!" cried Cain as a fisherman's large round

crab-pot was bowled along the Quay as effortlessly as a screwed up sheet of newspaper. They both followed it until it pitched over into the sea.

Suddenly Will got to his feet and sighed loudly. "You're a bloody nuisance young Cain... disturbing a man's conscience." The captain had made a decision. "Right then, if we're gonna get this tug ready, we need to build up a head of steam. Listen to me though," he jutted his pipe towards Cain for emphasis, "when George Penney fetches up here – persuading him is *your* job."

———————

The rain stopped as abruptly as it had begun and for a short time the visibility was dramatically improved. On board the brig *Elizabeth*, Henley swore in alarm. "Holy Mother! There must be thirty ships out there, look!" He grabbed young Jack Cotten by the shoulder and pointed out across Studland Bay.

There they were: dotted in ragged array and all kinds of vessel. Henley could pick out schooners, fishing smacks, brigs, luggers, pilot-boats, a revenue cutter and, farther out, the huge bulk of a warship with a frigate to her lee side. All of them were at the mercy of the violent winds, and several were clearly already suffering damage and flying signals of distress.

Like someone drawing an almighty curtain, the rain suddenly came down again and hid it all from view.

Captain Back had ordered the *Elizabeth*'s port-side second bower to be dropped, so now she was secured by two anchors, like many of the surrounding ships. He had then retreated to his cabin to consult the Admiralty charts. The water ran down the captain's sleeves and made pools on the sheets in front of him as he pored over them. He tried not to think about the biting cold and refused to allow himself to shiver.

It was marginally quieter down here. A tiny respite in which to think. He could hear the wind and the sea, the strain on the ship's timbers, and the clunk-clunk-clunk of the crew working the pumps. Probably pointless, but it ought to be done. By his reckoning they were in the middle of Studland Bay, but how close were they to Poole Bar – the sandbank at the entrance to the harbour – and the associated and equally treacherous Hook Sands? Impossible to know for certain. They'd drifted too much in the storm and the visibility was poor.

That damned loose cargo made matters much worse, but it had proved far too hazardous to get below and make any attempt at securing it.

One of the young hands appeared with some hot coffee.

"We've had a brew-up sir."

"That's very good of you, Frost. Thank you." He sipped at it gratefully.

"D'you think we'll get out o' this sir?" the young man asked awkwardly. He was only twenty and very inexperienced.

"If the anchor cables hold, yes."

"Should we get the ship's boat ready sir?" He shifted uneasily from one foot to the other and back again. "Pardon me for saying, sir, but in case we need it?"

The captain looked up. Seamen asking him things again. "You've not been at sea long, have you Frost?"

"No, sir." Frost withered under the master's glare.

"Listen," said the captain. "Assuming we can even winch the ship's boat out in these conditions without it being torn off the davits and dashed to pieces – which I seriously doubt – we're too far away from the shore. It may not look a great distance to you Frost but in this weather, believe me, it's too far."

"S-s-sorry, sir," he stammered.

"Besides," the captain added, "venturing out in these seas in that wretched boat we have would be a death sentence for certain. Ship's boats are usually rotten in my experience and we'd all be drowned in no time. That boat is a last resort and only if the *Elizabeth* is sinking beneath our feet. If the worst comes to the worst I'll beach the ship, then at least some of us stand a chance of getting off alive."

Frost said nothing but gaped at him bleakly.

The captain realised that he had been too candid. A callow youth on a small ship in conditions like this needed encouragement. "Don't worry Frost, we're not there yet," the captain reassured him heartily. "I've been in *far* worse. Wait till you've seen the Cape!" He drained his coffee. "Let's get back on deck."

———————————

The grey-haired but spry figure of George Penney suddenly appeared from nowhere in a thick brown coat, round glasses splashed with rain. His slight frame looked too insubstantial to have withstood the stormy weather, but somehow he had struggled through it all to seek out his precious tug, just as Will Redmond had predicted. He barged past Cain as if he didn't exist.

"What are you doing, Captain Redmond?" he demanded in his high pitched voice, shouting above the wind till he almost shrieked. "You're building up steam!"

"They might need us for the lifeboat, sir."

"The lifeboat? In this? It's not safe!"

"If it was safe they wouldn't be launching the lifeboat, Mr Penney."

"Don't be insolent."

"I wasn't going to go without speaking to you, sir." Will hated his own forced humbleness.

"You want my tug to go out in this... this *monstrous* storm?"

Cain realised that all his ideas of pleading for the sanctity of human life, or appealing to this man's sense of public duty would be wasted. Will was right; George Penney was a tough nut to crack. A different tack was required. Something more creative. He had already decided he was not prepared to go back to Tom with a refusal.

"I was about to say," Cain cut in, "that the Lifeboat Institution will pay you five pounds for use of the steamer."

"Five pounds!" cried Penney and Redmond together.

Will had to just turn away. He stood staring fixedly out of

the window. *What was Cain playing at?* This fabrication could only end badly. He didn't want to be a part of it.

The owner turned to the tug's master. "Captain Redmond, will the steamer stand this gale?"

"Mr Penney, she's a tug: built for bad weather." Her captain reasoned that if she didn't stand the storm she'd go to the bottom and he'd be beyond Penney's reach.

"I see. Well, get this vessel ready and see that Cain and the lifeboat crew get to wherever it is they need to go."

Penney smiled at Cain, who seized the opportunity for a quick exit: "I'll go and raise the lifeboat crew now," he said, and hurried away.

Cain was certain someone would pay George Penney's fees – the grateful master of a rescued vessel or even the Lifeboat Institution. Or maybe Penney would be too embarrassed to ask anyone for the money when the gallant lifeboatmen returned. Maybe. Still, someone would pay and Cain gave it no further thought. The main point was that they had secured the tug's services and without it they could do nothing. Saving lives was more important; they could worry about the money afterwards. So much for diplomacy.

As soon as Cain was off the tug, George Penney turned to Will. "If there's any possibility of salvage, captain, you're to give that priority." A vessel abandoned at sea for any reason could be claimed as salvage and legally became the property of the finder. It was a potentially very lucrative business in stormy weather.

"Yes, Mr Penney, I understand you perfectly." Will gritted his teeth as Penney's motives became clear. Yet understanding was not the same as obeying.

On the *Elizabeth*, the captain knew there was nothing they could do now but wait and hope that they would ride out the storm. Below decks the pumps still clanked away unceasingly. Tiring work for all concerned, but they'd managed to reduce the water level in the hold by several inches which was more than the captain had expected. Yet it was impossible to do anything about the cargo: they were carrying coal and once it started to break free it had a dangerous life of its own. Great heavy sacks rolling around in the darkness in waist-high freezing water, and all lubricated by thousands of loose lumps of coal. Captain Back blamed himself – perhaps he should have inspected the hold more closely before they'd left Newcastle.

In the rare spells of improved visibility he could see many ships all around him, and all were in distress. Some of them, farther out, had cut their cables and trusted to finding the Solent and the relative shelter of the lee of the Isle of Wight, but the *Elizabeth* was too far into the bay to attempt this safely without a change in wind direction. At least three ships had already been lost. One – a brig – was a total wreck. Two others had been torn from their anchorage and sent hurtling past the *Elizabeth* out of all control. Although he had not witnessed their destruction he knew it was inevitable. To the east, he had glimpsed two more ships – schooners – desperately close to the sands of the Bar near the Harbour's mouth, where they would inevitably be pounded to pieces if they began to drag their anchors.

The wind had veered from south-easterly to southerly, making their chances of escape a little more hopeful perhaps but at the moment the dual anchors were holding the ship firmly.

Suddenly the captain felt the *Elizabeth* moving. He glanced along the deck – the port-side anchor cable had parted! The ship would swing more freely now, and suffer as a consequence.

"All hands brace…" the captain's bellow was cut short as the sea broke brutally amidships, swamping everything. And again. The whole world was water: above, below and all around. He heard the sound of breaking timbers but could see nothing through the profusion of spray. A third wall of water smashed over them, cascading savagely into the vessel, forcing her to lean over precariously into the raging seas. All the crew needed their wits about them. The sea could tear anything loose now and use it to kill or maim. A heavy fire bucket came hurtling across the deck towards the captain, propelled by an ominously large bolus of water: he instinctively threw up his right arm to protect himself and ducked while gripping the shrouds tenaciously with his left hand. He was only just in time. The bucket vanished over the side somewhere above him and the captain emerged from being deluged, gasping with the cold, coughing, his eyes and nostrils streaming.

The land was no longer visible, but they were riding comparatively easily once more, now that the ship had found her new mooring position, yet the unhappy *Elizabeth* was still battered mercilessly by the stormy waters at her single surviving anchor. The captain watched his brave crew emerging grimly from their various places of safety. Looking up he realised that the bowsprit had gone.

How many of the crew had survived thus far? The captain fought his way to the helm and the steadfast Henley. The ship was riding heavily and was gradually but perceptibly shifting position.

"We're dragging that anchor, sir." The pitching motion of the vessel was lifting the best bower clear of the hard sandy sea bed and every time that happened the ship was blown a bit nearer the crashing breakers on the sand. That anchor weighed nearly twelve hundredweight – a tribute to the almighty power of the storm.

"I know. It's only a matter of time now, Mr Henley." The captain was stoical. "When the cable parts, I want all men astern. We'll lash the wheel on a bearing straight for the coast, as best we can judge, and hope we run aground some place where we can scramble ashore."

"What about the pumps sir?"

"Keep them going for the time being." He cupped his hands to Henley's ear. "It gives the men something to do. It'll help to take their minds off our predicament, but get them up here the moment we're under way." All sailors dreaded the prospect of being trapped below decks to drown like a rat. "Is anyone missing?" he demanded, looking about him.

"No sir. Anderson and Frost were nearly swept away when we lost the port anchor, but so far we've kept a full complement."

"Well, that's a mercy at least." The captain turned as if to make his way forward, but then faced about. "Where's young Cotten?"

"Below decks sir, getting some rest. He almost slipped over the side earlier – given him the jitters." Jack Cotten, like William Frost, was not very experienced. "He's gone all shaky; not used to it you see, sir."

The captain approved of Henley's paternalism: they didn't have a single seaman on board over twenty-one. "Well,

Henley, try to keep him warm. These young lads can chill quickly." He paused. "There's a new boat cloak in my cabin," he added. "Take it and wrap him in it."

———————

Cain found Tom Hart with his brother, Sam. They were in conference with the harbour master – the appropriately named Mr Crabb. Tom's close-cropped brown curly hair, thick eyebrows and moustache were prematurely tinged with grey, but his eyes were alert and he spoke with urgency.

"We've got to get out there soon as we can," he heard Tom saying.

"More news?" Cain broke in as he reached them.

"A rider brought a new message from Stoker at North Haven Point. There's any amount o' ships in distress out there now: Studland Bay's crowded and another ship's gone down. Did you speak to Will about the steamer?"

"Aye, he's getting up a head o' steam."

"Good work Cain! I'm not quite sure how you managed that…"

Cain frowned and shook his head at Tom.

"…and I don't want to know either, it seems. We'll try launching another rocket to summon the rest of the crew, but they mayn't hear it in this weather so we might have to go door knocking."

"It'll take Will thirty minutes to get the steamer ready so we've time."

"Aye, Will Redmond's a good seaman and I don't know what we'd do without the steamer but I reckon it'll be a struggle to clear the harbour even for him. Let's hope we can get out there soon enough to still be of service."

Chapter Two

The *Antelope Hotel* was a typical brown brick coaching inn on three storeys with a tall-windowed eighteenth century façade, but parts dated back to over three hundred years earlier. A large plaster antelope surmounted a central first floor bay window, and an oversized gas lamp protruded over the street above the columned entrance.

The lifeboatmen had assembled in the taproom on hearing the sound of the signal rocket, and were crowded round the fireplace to catch the glow from the hearty crackling blaze that it held. This would be the first launch of the Poole lifeboat on a genuine rescue and the anticipation was visible in the faces of the men stood waiting. Very little was said. Cain noticed that most were too nervous even to smoke.

Tom Hart bustled in to join his crew and addressed them immediately in a firm voice.

"Now then," he said, surveying eleven faces concentrating their full attention upon him. "Many of us have never seen a gale like this, let alone set out in one. But we all know what we did in the practices and what we've got to do today." Their eyes were eager, determined, yet apprehensive. "I don't know what we'll find when we get out-harbour, but there are plenty o' ships in trouble round the West Side and we'll do what we can. The *Royal Albert* will take us to North Haven to pick up Stoker and the lifeboat, and then she'll tow us off into Studland from there."

At that moment Will Redmond's big frame appeared in the doorway. He waved to Tom over the heads of the lifeboatmen gathered before him: the steamer was ready.

Tom raised a hand to acknowledge the signal. "The tug's fired up and ready to go," he announced. "So let's take heart: we're in this together, and I know we'll all give our best."

A look of appreciation passed from Sam to his brother Tom as he put a hand on his shoulder. They had the same blue eyes and slim, tall build yet Sam was five years older, although few would have guessed. He lacked Tom's moustache, and Sam's untidy hair was more fair, but otherwise the brothers were very alike. They set off from the hotel at a quick march.

"Thanks Tom," said Sam, acknowledging his brother's speech to the crew.

"I felt I ought to say something," was the almost apologetic reply.

Once in Thames Street, which ran right down to the water, the lifeboatmen felt the cold air blast their faces, straight off the sea. They stepped cautiously around the tumbled elements of various buildings that the high wind had thrown into the roadway ahead of them, eyes cast heavenwards in case of new arrivals.

"What do you reckon to this then?" Sam cried above the wind, instinctively holding his cap on with one hand.

"A hurricane. Never seen one this bad, have you?" Tom had to shout above the wind.

"No. Even that spell I had down the Lizard – didn't see it like this." Sam turned to Bill Brown, an experienced local fisherman. "What d'you reckon it'll be like out-harbour, Bill?"

"You know it'll be worse than this!" he cried. "*Ten times* worse. The harbour protects us here but this lot's run all the way up the Channel, and away from the lee of the land – with nothing to stop it – it'll blow up giant waves like you'd never believe. Specially in deep water."

They marched on, leaning into the wind.

"Is the lifeboat up to it?" Cain asked Sam.

"What are you talking about!" exclaimed Sam with a look of surprise. "I wouldn't be heading out in it if I didn't think so. It's not the *boat* I'm worried about."

"How d'you mean?"

"Lifeboat's brand new – good vessel I'm sure – and what with the steamer to tow us, I reckon we're as safe as we've any right to be in this weather, all things considered. It's just…" he lowered his voice so that Cain could barely hear him above the wind, "there's a lot we don't know about putting to sea on a real call-out because we've never done it afore, just a few trials. We've been out in a fresh wind, sure enough, but nothing nowhere near like this…" He let the sentence hang.

As the Quay came fully into view, they were all lost for words by its extraordinary state. Tom Hart set his jaw and forged ahead as best he could, and the others followed. Cain glanced about him as they picked their way eastwards to the stretch of the waterfront where he had met Will earlier. The waves were still pounding the thick oak piles of the Quay to dramatic effect, and he could see the others, all stony-faced, as it began to dawn on them what they might have to deal with. None of the lifeboatmen really knew what they were letting themselves in for, but simply watching the raw power of this freakish gale as they advanced along the deserted, confused quayside was disturbing, even to these experienced seafaring men.

It was only a short distance from the *Antelope* to the *Royal Albert* and the twelve lifeboatmen were soon on board the steamer, together with Will Redmond's own crew of six.

———————

After an hour of being tossed around on the sole remaining anchor, the captain of the *Elizabeth* dared to hope that they might see the storm out, despite the sea breaching over her intermittently. There had been a lot of damage – bulwarks carried away, another yard was gone – yet the brig was still seaworthy.

Then suddenly the wind veered westerly, and the ship started to come about. He had to make a snap decision: stay where they were and hope to survive the storm, or run before the wind and trust to finding a safer refuge. In this weather they would never be able to weigh anchor fast enough by conventional means, but cutting the cable now and setting a small amount of sail could send them beyond Poole Bar and down towards the Solent and the protection of the Isle of Wight.

The problem with cutting themselves free was they'd have no anchor, so there was no dependable method of bringing the ship to a halt. Yet to stay where they were seemed to invite certain destruction if the storm did not let up soon, and the wind might just as quickly back away southerly once more.

The captain made his decision. The anchor cable was to be cut.

Once the order was given, the mate, Henley, darted below for a saw. When he reappeared, the captain ordered all hands to brace themselves. The mate paced purposefully forward, held the blade of the saw over the tightly-twisted anchor cable and stood ready to grab a nearby stay. He looked up to check that everyone was secure and then, after a nod from the captain, he started to cut through the taut, hard-laid hemp – one, two, three downward slices with the saw. Then as he started on the fourth stroke the yarns began to fray and suddenly the rope whipped apart with a crack, forcing Henley to fall back and shield his face.

As soon as she was free, the *Elizabeth* fell away with the seas, then came about briskly as the wind filling her stormsail forced her to respond to the helm. She quickly gathered speed and within moments began to charge headlong into the wind like a great bird, sending men above decks staggering backwards. Rigging, spars, blocks and tackle were cruelly torn away from her and crashed to the deck or trailed behind her clattering in the merciless raging wind of the storm.

Every man remaining on the *Elizabeth* clung desperately to whatever he could as the ship surged forward through the waves in full flight. Each prayed for a safe delivery. They had to miss the sandbanks to stand any chance of surviving. The captain forced the wheel as hard to starboard as he dared. The noise of the wind was deafening.

The *Royal Albert* steamed forward defiantly, her tall black-tipped funnel standing out proudly against the backdrop of the wild sea. They were steaming into the wind and the water was flying over the tug in clouds. Everyone on board was silenced by the ferocity of the storm and the expectation of what they would have to contend with once away from the protection of the land. It was slow work in the heavy seas, but eventually the steamer reached North Haven Point where the lifeboat was stationed in a building next to the home of her coxswain, Richard Stokes.

Stoker had been out on the headland with a telescope ever since sunrise. As soon as he realised the general predicament to which so many ships were subject he had hoisted aloft the distress signal, then borrowed a horse and rider from a neighbour, and sent the message into the town which Joe Crabb had brought to Tom.

As the steamer drew closer they realised that Stoker and his helpers had lost no time in preparing the lifeboat for launching. They could all see her waiting for them on her heavy four-wheeled launch carriage. She was the *Manley Wood*, the curious name derived from a Devonshire clergyman, the father of the enigmatic wealthy woman who had donated the boat. Thirty-two feet long, blue above and white below, and with stations for thirteen men – ten oarsmen, one bowman, a helmsman, and one station where a man could take a rest from rowing. She was the latest design and was said to have cost over two hundred pounds.

Stoker nodded grimly to his crew as soon as they stepped ashore.

Their reunion was not an occasion for conversation. Time was of the essence. They all knew what had to be done. Stoker and his helpers quickly assisted the crew into their bulky cork life jackets, up the wooden ladder and into the boat for immediate launching. Each man took his allotted place to ensure the lifeboat kept her trim when afloat. They sat on the thwarts, apprehensive, and almost identically dressed in the unofficial uniform: a tightly knitted navy blue jersey, oilskin coat and trousers, thick woollen hat, and knee length leather boots.

Stoker spoke briefly to Will Redmond to explain what he had observed during the morning, and to agree the tug's basic role.

Once launched, the steamer took up the lifeboat via twin fifteen-fathom tow ropes and made for the mouth of the harbour at her best speed through the angry dark water. Only then did Stoker talk to his men. He had a clear loud voice which they heard even above the wind.

"I've been watching from the Point four hours or more," he announced. "I know we can't see much from here, but I tell you now, when we hit the Swash Channel we'll see water like you'd scarce believe. Ferocious. Mountains o' sea. Never thought I'd see the like round here. It's not just the wind and the sea we have to keep an eye on, there are a load o' ships out there. I saw twenty-five, more or less, and they've had a lot carried away – at least three have gone ashore – so Cain," he called, indicating his position as bowman, "keep an eye out for wreckage."

Cain Matthews nodded briefly in acknowledgement.

"Twenty-five ships, Stoker. We can't go to all of 'em," cried Jack Fisher, his straggly hair jutting out sorely from the margins of his knitted cap.

"No," said Stoker patiently. "But they're not all in trouble. First priority: two schooners on the southerly edge o' the Bar. Near to wrecking."

"Ain't that one o' the pilot-boats?" interrupted Sam – he nodded to a vessel washed fully onto the shore.

"Aye," said Stoker. "The *Ranger*, ran aground about an hour ago, but they all got off safe."

Suddenly the heavens opened and the crew were deluged in a fierce downpour which hid everything from view save their immediate surroundings. Even Stoker had to shout to make himself heard above the roar.

Standing at the tiller Stoker was the only member of the crew looking dead ahead – the rest of the crew sat facing him – and he could see the violent conditions approaching them as they prepared to leave the protection of the harbour. He had his eye on the tug as she met the first of the rising heavier seas, and saw her thrown up high enough so that for an instant Stoker could see her starboard paddle revolving in the air, and when she struck the ensuing hollow she dished a sea over her bows that left only her stern showing.

"We'll be in the channel soon," he bellowed. "Brace yourselves." Already they could feel the lifeboat surging and bumping with greater intensity as the waves increased in size and strength. Then as they cleared the harbour the boat sheered and they shipped the crest of a large wave which swamped the boat with icy water to the level of the thwarts. They all knew the lifeboat shouldn't sink even when filled to the gunwales, yet testing the theory for the first time in this bitter tempestuous sea was truly terrifying. Each man clung desperately to the side of the boat, with water up to his waist, while the elements raged.

They were no longer sitting on that stormy sea; they were part of it, inside it.

But the lifeboat was fitted with a series of six relieving tubes at deck level which allowed water to exit. Each held a valve which only opened when water pressure was applied from *within* the boat and not when it gushed up the tube from the sea below. So they knew that the water would leave the boat, and it did so quickly, but none of them had been in this situation before, and it was a fearsome experience for all of them including the coxswain.

"Take heart!" roared Stoker. "There's more to come, and now we know she ain't gonna sink even if she fills right up." As if to prove the point the steamer towed the lifeboat straight into the path of another huge wave which curled over them and this time filled the boat to capacity. For a moment the men were up to their chests. Yet it was all speedily discharged and it seemed that the lifeboat had passed the ultimate test.

"Look!" Stoker spluttered through the water, and pointed ashore. "There's the *Devon*, she ran aground this morning. And there's another – *Sutton* – she were taken in tow by a pilot-boat but the cable snapped and she struck."

It was difficult to tell that either ship had once been a brig as both were so distorted: heeled over towards the land with masts reduced to stumps, and strangely squat and ugly without them. Like huge primordial creatures that had dragged themselves from the sea and stopped to rest from their labours.

———————

On board the *Elizabeth*, Captain Back felt sure he had made the right decision. Another hour in their previous position and the ship would surely have been matchwood. Now he stood behind Henley at the wheel in the driving rain, apprehensively clenching and unclenching his fists. They had to miss the Bar and the Hook Sands. He had taken the gamble that they had not already been blown too far inshore. The captain glanced aloft; the single stormsail seemed to be holding. A miracle that it hadn't been carried away already in this horrific wind. Henley had the wheel over to starboard, but the limited visibility and their drift in the storm meant that they were charging blind to eastward. If they hit anything at this rate of knots there would be no hope for them; the ship would be torn apart. The captain had placed a seaman forward on each side to look out for the sands.

Suddenly the torrential rain stopped.

"Ho there!" yelled Frost from forward. "Breakers on the port bow!"

The captain sprang along the deck to see for himself. Frost had a good eye. It was hard to discern the breakers amongst the mass of white-capped waves rolling shorewards, but he could pick them out now: only a couple of cables away and two miserable schooners being driven into them. Poor souls. At least on present course it looked as if the *Elizabeth* would miss the sands.

There were men up in the rigging on those schooners. For some reason many sailors believed that they stood a better chance of survival up there if the ship struck. Personally, the captain thought the rigging was a death-trap in such circumstances. On deck was the place to be – a springboard for leaping ashore or overboard if necessary.

As they drew level with the breakers, the captain felt the *Elizabeth* start a gentle shudder.

"No!" he screamed in rage and frustration.

Although Henley had the wheel over immediately, the keel was bumping along the most southerly margin of the sands. What misfortune! The sea was so rough that it had not been possible to determine precisely where the shallows lay. Captain Back cursed loudly, but as the words died on his lips, a towering wave broke over the side and charged across the decks, enveloping everything in its turbulent path. That brutal assault was timed perfectly: the sudden gush of extra water under the stern lifted her a fraction, she caught the rising swell, and the ship was knocked free before she could grind to a mast-snapping halt.

It had all happened in seconds.

The *Elizabeth* was on her way once more. The captain grinned with relief at Henley who clung to the ship's wheel, resolute but pale. If that was the end of the sandbanks, they were bound for the Solent now. Their prospects were better, although they were doing little more than staggering before the wind with hardly any steerageway. Nonetheless it would probably be adequate to ensure their survival as long as the wind held and that leak below didn't get any worse.

Without anchors, they would have to trust to riding out the storm and using alternative means of bringing the vessel to a halt when the time came.

"God help us!" muttered the captain.

———————

The steamer, with the lifeboat in tow, was now in the Swash Channel. This started at the mouth of the Harbour and ran south east, cutting through Poole Bar, with Studland Bay on the west side and the Hook Sands to the east. The Swash was not very wide, with little margin for error, hence the need for a pilot to navigate vessels unfamiliar with the area. The tug wallowed and tumbled into the furious sea. The speed of advance had slackened to a mere crawl. The waves struck her bows and flew high over the top of her funnel, blowing aft along her whole length.

After what seemed an eternity they neared the mid-point of Poole Bar. Stoker leaned out of the boat and pointed southwards.

"Look! There!" he cried. "Them two schooners I was telling you about – the *Pallas* and the *Augusta*. They've been driving since first light."

It was a desperate situation. Both vessels were clearly badly damaged and were close to destruction. They could barely see the hull of either ship on account of the ferocity of the water crashing all around them. Yet there were black shapes in the rigging. Unmoving. Clinging desperately. Men.

"Their captains chose a poor place to drop anchor," Sam observed to his brother.

"Aye, but they don't come from round 'ere," said Tom.

"Don't they have charts?"

"Surely, but in a storm like this, Sam, you gets thrown askew, and a ship moves so fast – you can't see the land, nothing. You thinks you're off Studland, when you're really off Bournemouth."

"What we gonna do, Stoker?" yelled Cain.

"The steamer'll take us closer in and then we'll row across."

"You sure we can make it?"

"We've got to try." Stoker waved both arms at the steamer and made a pre-arranged signal to indicate that the tow ropes should be slackened. "Right, unship the oars!"

Ten crewmen each took up one of the heavy oars, solid oak, twelve feet long, and held in place by a flexibly mounted rowlock. They slid them out quickly into the violent waters.

Stoker, at the tiller, watched as the tow ropes slackened off and the boat began to drift. "All together then... pull!" All ten oars took the weight of water between them.

"Pull!" Two or three strokes were needed to fully synchronise their actions.

"Pull!" They were almost in unison now.

"Pull!" That was it. Now they needed to build up a sustainable momentum to get the boat moving. This was the part that called for real strength and stamina as they could be at the oars intermittently for hours to come.

Stoker no longer needed to call the time – the men kept to the rhythm naturally as they were experienced seamen – but he could see they were struggling to make headway.

They kept it up for a full five minutes, although it seemed longer than that, but every man could see that even with a maximum effort, the best they could do was to hold their position. The sheer power of the elements was too much for them, and the rough seas constantly broke the synchrony of their strokes.

"All right, rest now!" Stoker shouted. "Well done lads. A great effort, but we ain't going nowhere in this." He signalled the steamer to take up the slack on the ropes and begin towing once more. Then he turned to the crew. "It's no good, we can't row out to 'em. Will said he'd tow us upwind of the schooners if we couldn't row across, then he'll cast us off so we can drop down and hook on to 'em with a line as we pass."

The steamer got under way again. The sea became more and more rough as they progressed up the Swash where the depth of water increased and they lost the remaining protection of the land. Time after time the sea broke over

44

them, but steamer and lifeboat struggled forward together stubbornly. There was a formidable swell running beneath the confused surface of the sea: when they rode on the crests of the waves they had a blurred vision through the spray and the rain of what was going on around them, yet they were just as quickly plunged into the troughs where all they could see were walls of water towering above them. They followed the steamer – vanishing and reappearing in front of them.

At their closest approach to the schooners they were about a quarter of a mile away and could see that great lumps of timber and planking had been ripped out of them. The waves breaking around the stricken ships were colossal: as they crashed, the stern of the nearest schooner was borne high for a moment before both vessels were enveloped in clouds of spray and hidden completely from view, even the surviving mastheads.

"They're in the breakers already," said Tom to his brother, Sam, nodding to port. "There's not much hope for them. Sea'll pound 'em apart in no time."

"Stoker!" cried Jack Fisher. "There's not enough water there even for us."

"It's breaking all around 'em," said John Wills. "They're aground ain't they?"

It certainly looked dangerous but Stoker thought the lifeboat was stable enough to get through it. "We'll be all right," he said. "The lifeboat don't sink when it's filled with water. We've seen that."

"Aye, but like Jack said, there's not much water there – we'll get turned over." Cain shook his head. He could see the risks and didn't like them.

"The lifeboat can't get turned over," objected Sam.

"Not can't, *shouldn't*," Jack bawled back. "Nothing's impossible in a sea like that. Look at it."

Stoker felt he was losing control. "We came out to save lives. We *have* to go down to those men. If we don't go there's no-one else. They'll die."

But the crew sat staring through the rain at the huge waves rising up and curling over onto the sands. Monstrous watery claws from the deep reaching out to clutch at whatever they could.

"What protection have we got against *that* lot?" asked Bill Brown, echoing the concerns of the rest. "We'll get flipped over like a pancake."

A resistance to oversetting sideways was provided by the lifeboat's heavy keel made of iron. This great weight positioned at the lowest position in the boat normally exerted enough leverage even in a heavy sea to prevent the boat upsetting. Even if the lifeboat did turn over she was rendered 'self-righting' by virtue of wood and cork in watertight compartments positioned strategically in the boat's design that would quickly force the boat to turn the right side up again.

The crew knew about these safeguards, and it all sounded fine in theory, but since childhood every one of them had been taught that in any perilous situation at sea it was imperative to stay with the boat and, if she went over, the chances of two or three of them at least being torn away was very real. It was hard for thirteen fathers, husbands, and sons to believe in the reputed properties of the lifeboat when they were staring danger in the face and had to trust their lives to it for the first time.

"We'll be all right. We're self-righting," Stoker declared with as much confidence as he could muster.

"Aye, but it's what happens afore we right ourselves again that's the problem," said Bill. He was the biggest of the lifeboatmen and could be very intimidating. "It won't be long afore the tide falls away and all that water from the Bay'll be sweeping over them sands. Once we're over, we could get drawn away from the boat and in this sea there's no hope of getting back."

There were nods of agreement.

"I don't like it, Stoker," Bill objected flatly.

"No, nor I," added Cain.

Stoker knew these men. They were all experienced seamen – friends – and he recognised the great danger of taking any boat into high, breaking seas. Nonetheless he felt personally responsible for the mission. "Well, let's wait till the steamer has towed us into position," countered Stoker cautiously. "Will Redmond knows what's required. Conditions may be better by then: wind might have died down."

There was obvious discontent in the boat, and Tom could see that having assessed the conditions close-up, the men wouldn't be happy to risk it.

"Stoker's right," he said. "Let's see what it looks like upwind. Tide turns in three quarters of an hour anyway so that might make all the difference."

Stoker caught his eye from the other end of the boat and there was thanks in the look he gave Tom.

Chapter Three

Once the lifeboat was in prime position, it was time for Stoker to reassess the situation. He cursed the slow progress that was eating away at the morale of the crew, and he feared that their resolve was waning as the time passed. The *Royal Albert* had towed them upwind of the schooners but it had been a painfully sluggish journey. The plan was to let slip the tow ropes and allow the lifeboat to be swept down towards the ships, which they would fasten onto using a grappling line.

Stoker had decided he would take no nonsense. There was no time for debate. He was the coxswain and he was going to assert his authority. "Right," he commanded. "This is our best chance. We'll drop down: Cain, you take the grapnel, and I'll have a reserve line ready in case you miss."

"Hang on there, Stoker," insisted Cain forcefully. "We're not sure this is safe."

"Well we can't just sit about, *Mister* Matthews, there are men out there. If we do nothing, they drown."

"I know that, Stoker," Cain bit back angrily, "you may be coxswain, but you're not bloody captain and we're not in Her Majesty's Service."

"Aye," said Bill. "It were too shallow by them schooners for my liking. I don't reckon we've got enough draught. Seas breaking right over 'em and all about 'em."

"What d'you reckon, Tom?" asked George King.

Tom couldn't decide. He could see both sides of the argument. He hesitated and before he could speak Sam cut in.

"Sea's fearful rough, and shallow, but I say put *yourself* trapped on one of them schooners…"

"Those men are dead already," cried Cain. "We'd never get close enough to 'em. They're in the breakers for God's sake – a bloody death trap. There's other ships out here that'll need our help, let's go to them."

"What are you talking about?" snapped Stoker. "We can't just leave 'em, Cain. Now come on, we're going in…"

"Well I ain't going in there to be rolled over and over, and drowned. I'll tell you that for nothing."

"Who says we're gonna get rolled over?" demanded Stoker.

"Are you blind?" countered Bill. "Look at it! Waves the height o' my house…"

"He's right," chipped in Cain. "No sense chucking our lives away."

"We're designed to *float*, not roll over," said Stoker defiantly.

"Aye," cried Cain, "in some bloody millpond in the Port of London, where those toffs tested it, but not in this. What's the matter with you, Stoker! Use your eyes."

"We're here to save those men's lives," shouted Stoker angrily. "There's no-one else out here but us."

Stoker glared at Cain through the spray, and Cain glared right back.

"P'raps we should wait for the tide to turn," suggested Sam, hoping to break the deadlock. "Only half an hour to go."

There was a grunting of approval from around the boat.

"They could be dead by then." Stoker was almost begging. He had not expected this resistance to his authority and was unsure how to deal with it.

The coxswain was enormously frustrated, and Tom could see it yet was betwixt and between: conscious of the mission but wary of the dangers. Tom knew that the longer they delayed the less chance there was of the schooner crews surviving. And Stoker was right: if the lifeboat did nothing those men would die. No doubt about it. He hated to see the skipper beleaguered, and he felt Stoker was looking to him for support. But he couldn't give it. He couldn't give it because for the past few minutes he hadn't been able to drag his thoughts away from his wife, Maria, and their six children.

He had not anticipated this response within himself – perhaps it was simply the extraordinary conditions they were facing – but in his mind's eye he saw his wife's reaction to news of his own death. He looked through the spray at his brother and had a fleeting mental image of having to tell Sam's wife that her husband had drowned. Poor Amelia, Sam was so devoted to her. But most of all Tom pictured his own little Isabel, just two years old. As the wind howled and the seas roared he couldn't make the images go away. It was too much to resist.

And yet it wasn't just his own family, he told himself. All of them in the boat were family men. Was it reasonable to risk the happiness of all these families to try and save men they did not even know? And with such little chance of success?

He tried not to give it a name, but somewhere within

himself, Tom knew this was fear talking. Whatever it was it unnerved him.

Crucially, Tom stayed silent when his support might have swayed the crew. Stoker had to capitulate.

"All right then," the coxswain barked. "All right. I don't like it, but if that's what you want. Like you say, I can't *make* you go." This was true, and if the lifeboat was to be of any help to anyone during the storm, Stoker needed their full co-operation. He threw up his hands in despair then signalled to the tug to pull them in. "Cain, you tell Will what you've decided."

The lifeboat was drawn up close to the steamer and Cain cupped his hands to hail Will Redmond.

"There's too much sea," he bellowed across the divide. "We can't do anything to save the schooner crews now."

From where he sat, Stoker could see Will's surprised expression and hated it. He'd think they were all cowards. But then Will Redmond was not in an open boat wet through and cold, he was on the steamboat. More importantly, on his vessel he was the captain and what he said, went.

"What do you want me to do?" Will shouted back.

Cain looked to the coxswain. Stoker loathed having no control over events. He sat smarting. "Tell Will to tow us into the bay out o' the worst of it. We'll try again in half an hour – at one o'clock, when the tide's turned."

———————

Running freely before the wind the *Elizabeth* raced joyously through the stormy seas celebrating her liberty, crashing headlong into the waves and ploughing the deep swells.

The captain was below decks with Henley showing him the charts. The ship plunged and heaved, and anything not secured was thrown with each violent movement. The captain's cabin was a mess.

"Due east carries us straight into the Solent," he said, tapping the broad area behind the Isle of Wight with his dividers. "What we do when we get there is anyone's guess, but the water'll be calmer and we can maybe set a sea anchor by furling a sail, or signal another vessel for assistance if we need to."

"I'll set about preparing a sail right away, sir." The sea anchor was a large funnel-shaped piece of canvas which would hold a ship to station remarkably well in a calm sea. In a storm the best that could be said was that it was better than nothing.

"If you would. Now how are the crew? No major injuries as far as I can see."

"Frost has a nasty gash on his leg, sir, from a falling spar. He's lost blood, but he can still get about. I've set him to the pumps so he can take a spell. The rest are all… well, in as trim a condition as can be expected, sir. Everyone's cut and bruised, tired, cold."

The captain nodded. There was an ugly contusion on Henley's cheek. "And the hold?"

"We're still about three feet in the well, sir, no worse. They're doing a good job on the pumps," he added with satisfaction. "But cargo's mostly shifted astern."

The captain nodded to register Henley's observations, but he was distracted by another matter. "Do you think that stormsail will hold?"

Henley snorted. "Course not, sir. You and I know it's a bloody – beggin' your pardon sir – it's a *wonder* that we've kept it this long. Sooner or later it'll be torn to shreds."

They were interrupted by a frantic knock on the cabin door.

"What is it?" shouted the captain.

Reed, one of the seamen, entered. "Sorry sir, but winds backed again now. South-westerly, sir."

The captain looked at Henley. "Thank you Reed," he said automatically.

A wind that would push them landwards while they were somewhere deep in Poole Bay. They'd surely never claw away from a lee shore in a storm of this intensity with the *Elizabeth* in her present condition.

He knew that he didn't need to spell it out for Henley. The captain threw his dividers across the cabin angrily. Fate took something away for everything she gave.

———————

It was one o'clock and the tide had turned but contrary to the lifeboat crew's expectations the weather in Studland Bay became worse not better. The wind had intensified and the intermittent bursts of torrential rain had changed to a constant feature of cloudburst proportions. The lifeboatmen sat hunched and dis-contented.

Cain seemed to think that the worsening conditions had vindicated their decision not to go to the schooners, and said as much, but Stoker realised that dropping down to them upon their arrival had been their best opportunity. Probably their *sole* opportunity. If only he could have convinced the crew to follow his lead earlier. There was absolutely no hope of reaching the schooners now. It was too late. Not that they could even see either vessel from their present position: they were only a mile or so away but even the men on the steamer could see nothing. He felt bitterly hollow inside at the thought that they had probably let the schooners' crews drown.

Stoker hailed the tug and asked Will to investigate the schooners' present position and to look for any other vessels more favourably placed that might need the assistance of the lifeboat.

While the steamer was away the crew again experimented with taking the lifeboat under oars. Even in the less violent waters of the inner bay, progress was very slow and demanded all their strength. Once they began to reach the more exposed sea, progress was simply impossible. Missed strokes were common as waves and swell abruptly carried the sea out of their reach. They strained at the oars and yet they were constantly forced back by the mighty waves.

Eventually Stoker turned the boat about and headed shoreward. His crew were hard men used to being soaked to the skin, used to enduring all weathers, used to taxing their strength to the limit but they were exhausted – from emotional over-stimulation as much as from their physical exertions – and they were all suffering from the freezing conditions despite the demands of rowing. The lifeboatmen had been out in the storm for four hours and none of them had had anything to eat or drink for nearly eight – their strength and determination was ebbing away. The slimly built young John Wills, in particular, was perished with the cold –

pallid, shaking, weak – and yet there was little they could do. Stoker fished out an old piece of tarpaulin to cover him.

"It's not much, Johnny, but it's another layer, eh?" he said. John accepted it gratefully and George King wrapped him as best he could.

Then Stoker remembered that there was a coastguard station in Studland Bay and decided to send a man ashore to see if there were any supplies that they could use.

They rowed the lifeboat shorewards until it touched the sandy bottom. Sam Hart eased himself over the side and waded twenty yards to the beach while the rest of the crew stayed behind in the boat.

Even this close in to the shore, the water was rough despite the protection of the land and the shallowness of the sea. Big waves slapped across Sam's back as he waded. He was thoroughly drenched and cold so it made no real difference, but he couldn't help picturing the clear placid waters of Studland in the summer when he and his family came here to play on the beach. Mother's blackberry and apple pie, warm sunshine, blue skies, Amelia's laughter…

Sam heard Stoker issuing orders: "If anyone wants to stretch their legs or take a piss now's the time to do it, 'cos we're going straight out again directly Sam gets back."

He trudged along the beach through the rain and reached the wooden coastguard station. It was strongly built, but it was a marvel to see anything standing in the teeth of the gale.

"I say," said a rich, lordly voice. Surprised, Sam spun round to face a man, dressed in a long black waterproof coat and matching sou'wester. He and his two male companions must have been sheltering behind the station. The man's neatly clipped white moustache and beard, and small round spectacles, made him look professorial. "Are you with the lifeboat?" he asked.

"Aye," said Sam uncertainly.

"I see." A knowing look passed from him to his colleagues. "When are you going to *do* something?"

"Do something?" Sam didn't like the man's tone. "What do you mean?"

"About the boats. The two boats practically run aground on the sands there."

Sam frowned. "Ah, the *schooners* you mean? The *Pallas* and the er…"

"The *Augusta*." The man had a telescope.

"Aye. What of 'em?"

"What I mean is, when are you going to actually rescue those poor wretches clinging to the rigging rather than sitting around out there?" There was no shyness in issuing the rebuke. "You did say you were with the lifeboat didn't you?"

Sam drew himself up, taken aback at this affront. "And who are you?" he demanded.

"My name is Alex Luckham," said the man imperiously, without offering a hand. "I'll come straight to the point. The lifeboat is funded by public subscription – I myself have given to the cause – and you don't seem to be doing much when there are clearly lives waiting to be saved. I've been standing here since ten this morning and no-one's done anything yet."

"What?" roared Cain. Sam spun round and there he was right behind him. He'd followed him up the beach and heard the last exchange.

Luckham did not even flinch. "I expect a certain valour from the lifeboat, not all this sitting around."

"Oh, so that's what the likes of you gives your money for is it?" Cain marched right up to Luckham, before Sam could do anything. "Payment so you can stand on the beach, safe in the lee of this hut with yer pals, and watch poor lifeboatmen go to their deaths."

"No, no. I'm only asking you to do your job." Luckham stepped away and held his hands up like a man at gunpoint. "And you are *paid* I believe," he added defensively.

"If we ever get back *alive*, Mr Whatever-Your-Name-Is, I will be given ten shillings!" Cain shouted angrily, waving a warning finger right in the face of the now not so assured onlooker. "Ten bob, for volunteering to go and risk me neck, but we don't get paid to throw it away on a hopeless errand." The gall of the man defied belief. "D'you know what it's like out there? Look at me: soaked to the skin in freezing water for hours with nothing to eat or drink and this is the worst storm in living history." He took a further step forward, forcing Luckham into a stumbling retreat. "Ten shillings! What's ten shillings to you, eh? A nice bottle o' wine to share with your rich mates when you're sat in yer bloody mansion playing chess."

Cain turned away from the man in disgust and tried the handle of the coastguard hut. It was locked, so he stepped back and with one sharp blow kicked the door in before Sam could stop him.

"Good gracious!" cried Luckham.

"Fuck off," said Cain hotly, and stepped inside.

Sam followed him in. "Cain…" he began with a warning tone.

"Don't speak to me," Cain demanded, casting about for supplies. There was no food or water in the hut, but Sam retrieved a large bottle of rum. That would do. Anything to give them a little warmth and comfort. They could be at it for hours yet.

As they left the building, Luckham raised his hand and opened his mouth to speak, but Cain stormed past without even acknowledging him and marched down to the water's edge, Sam in pursuit.

"Don't tell the others," begged Sam. Cain ignored him, so Sam grabbed his shoulder. Cain span round belligerently. "Things are bad enough," Sam insisted, "without some bloody landsman's interference."

Perhaps they were both angry because, deep inside, Luckham's words had struck a chord – *what had they achieved so far?* Sam shook his head to dispel such thoughts.

Just a few minutes ashore had allowed them to warm up a little and it was a shock to get back into the freezing water. They waded straight back to the boat.

"I got this," said Sam, handing the bottle to Stoker. "There weren't nothing else."

"Rum, by heaven!" cried George. "Well, that'll perk us up a bit, won't it, Johnny."

John nodded shakily. He looked dreadful. George put the

58

bottle to John's trembling lips. He took a swig then choked and coughed as the neat spirit caught the back of his throat. George tried again, this time allowing him a smaller amount.

"That's better," gasped John and he took another sip gratefully.

"Think of Katie Clacker, Johnny," said someone, naming a local prostitute. "That'll warm yer!"

There was a feeble cheer and John smiled weakly. George handed the rum bottle round the boat for everyone to take a swig.

"Only a nip now lads, make sure there's enough for us all!" Stoker made sure he was last to drink. He took a nip, then returned the cork immediately. A bottle of spirits in an open boat was not a good idea. "That's wonderful Sam," he said. "I feel ten times stronger already. Right, let's row out to our position so Will can find us when he gets back." He stowed the half-empty bottle in the locker by the helm and tried to ignore the several sets of eyes eagerly waiting for more.

"Is that all we're havin' Stoker?" demanded Cain.

"Aye, that's all the rations we got," said Stoker with finality.

"We could be at this lark for hours yet," agreed Tom. "We've got to take it sparingly, like medicine." He winked at Stoker when no-one was looking.

———

Henley was trying the best he could to keep the ship away seawards. The unwanted water ballast which the *Elizabeth* had taken on made her sluggish in responding to the helm, and the power of the stormy seas made any starboard movement of the ship's wheel beyond their present course all but impossible.

They had braced the foremast topgallant yard around, which held the stormsail, to try to carry the ship away from the land, but even storm canvas probably wouldn't hold for much longer. It was bowed out as taut as it could go, straining at the yard which supported it from above.

Suddenly one of the crew, Trump, on watch on the port side, sang out: "Pier dead ahead! Hard a-starboard! Hard a starboard!"

With great difficulty, Henley started to try to turn the wheel further to starboard but he couldn't do it; the ship would not respond. He pulled with all his might and, an inch at a time, the wheel slowly crept round, but he just wasn't strong enough to make a significant impression. The force of the water and the power of the wind were over-riding his ability to turn the wheel. Then, from nowhere, the captain was at his side and with Herculean effort the two of them gradually got the wheel turning a little more quickly. It cracked and strained as it turned and the ship started to creep a point or two further out to sea. Would it be enough?

Even as they wondered, something large and dark loomed on the port side as the ship sped past. It was the pier at Bournemouth, jutting out towards them in the poor light, less than four fathoms away. A very close shave. Were they really so near to the shore already? It was simply a matter of time now if they were this far in. The captain wondered if they would even round Christchurch Head. They had to pray for a favourable change in wind direction once more. It was surely the only thing that would save them.

On board the *Manley Wood*, the men were again at the oars, striking out from the beach into deeper water to await the return of the steamer. Struggling against the seas, they reached the spot where the steamer had left them and dropped anchor, making sure there was enough slack on the warp to find a hold as Studland Bay was mostly sand. The lifeboatmen had been gone for around half an hour and Stoker had expected to be able to see the *Royal Albert* as soon as they returned to their station. But this was not to be.

After about ten minutes alone at anchor the rain eased off. Less heavy now, but large semi-frozen drops of persistent sleety-rain. There was no escaping the wind and the driving rain, but the men huddled together amidships for warmth.

Tom clambered aft to where Stoker sat despondently, one hand on the tiller.

"Where've they got to?" he asked.

"No idea," said Stoker curtly, and rubbed his face with his hands. "Can't see anything from here."

"Do you reckon she's in trouble?"

"The steamer? Doubt it. Will Redmond knows what he's about. Besides, he would've sounded the foghorn, let off a flare rocket or something. Somehow he'd have let us know." There was a pause and Stoker continued in a low voice which only Tom could hear. "I should have made 'em go down after them schooners when we first got here."

"*Made* them? I'd liked to have seen you try. Cain is twice your size and half your age."

"I know, but I am the coxswain."

"That means nothing in conditions like this." Tom raised his eyebrows at Stoker. "You don't *employ* the crew and, like Cain said, this ain't the Queen's service. You can't dish out two dozen lashes for not following orders. All you can do is *ask* 'em to do things, which you did."

"Aye, but did I put the case well enough?"

"There's nought you could've said to convince Cain," said Tom. "Or Bill. You know them as well as I do. Don't punish yourself. We're in this together. Maybe we can get to them schooners yet, when the steamer gets back."

"Don't fancy their chances though in this, do you? It's worse than ever. I reckon they've had it."

Tom shrugged. "We don't know yet. Won't know till Will gets back."

Stoker did not reply.

There was a pause. Both of them sat looking eastwards to where the schooners were supposed to be, watching the sea relentlessly piling wave upon wave, whipped up white and furious by the gale.

"I still can't believe this hurricane, Stoker. I've never seen anything like it, let alone been out in it."

"Nor me. There was a bad storm in the twenties when I was a boy, but that were the last real brute I knowed of. Just our luck to get called out in it." Stoker shook his head. "This morning, afore the steamer got here, any number o' ships were torn from their moorings or cut their cables. Lord knows what became of them. And there's bound to be plenty more out here trying to weather the storm if only we could see. Still, it's been clearing a might over the last few minutes." He put his hand to his forehead to shield his eyes and surveyed the sea around them through all points of the compass. Suddenly he pointed due south of the *Manley Wood*. "Is that a ship just here? Look!"

Tom searched amongst the waves in that direction, and then he glimpsed it. "Aye, you're right." He caught it again as a wave raised the *Manley Wood* to give him a better view. "Is it one of our pilots?"

"It's a pilot boat all right, but an Isle o' Wight one I reckon." Stoker squinted at it, then pulled a small telescope from the locker. "Hard to use the thing in this weather," he said, steadying himself and protecting the end lens from the rain and sea splash with his right hand. "Aye, it's a pilot boat. From Cowes, I was right. The *Marquis of Anglesea* unless I'm much mistaken. Recognise her rig – I've seen her round here often enough. And just beyond her… looks like one of the Poole pilots… it's number eleven, *Figaro*."

Just as he was about to lower the scope, something caught his eye and he raised it again. It was the tug. "Here she comes!" cried Stoker to the crew. The steamer was making slow progress, and Stoker could make out very heavy seas all about her.

Eventually the tug reached them a full hour after they had originally parted company.

"Ahoy!" cried Stoker as soon as they were within hailing distance.

"Schooners have gone, Stoker," shouted Will across the thin stretch of turbulent water. "No sign of 'em." The wind was getting up again now and he had to bellow to be heard. "Sea out there... like the Atlantic... mountains of it... nearly didn't make it back."

Tom had been looking through the telescope. "The *Marquis* has just hoisted a distress signal," he said to Stoker.

"Pilot-boat astern," yelled Stoker to Will, pointing. "Distress signal."

Will went aft to look.

Stoker was enthused again: at last, action! Something the lifeboat crew could do instead of sitting about getting frozen alive.

"Right," said Stoker, addressing his crew. "There's a pilot-boat beyond the steamer, and she's in difficulty. We're gonna get Will to tow us over and then take the crew off to safety. Tom, weigh anchor and the rest of us need to be ready to take up the oars. Not you Johnny." Stoker ordered. "I think you'd better sit this one out. Take the end-thwart up here by me."

Will returned to the side of the *Royal Albert*, just as the lifeboatmen started to take in the slack on the anchor warp.

"Two of 'em in trouble," he cried.

"Can you tow us out?" asked Stoker.

"Aye."

Stoker turned to Tom. "*Marquis* first then *Figaro*," he said. But the assistant coxswain and another crewman were struggling mightily at the warp.

"What's up?" asked Stoker. "Is she foul?"

"No." Tom gasped. "Reckon not. Just this heavy sea…"

"Sam, give your brother a hand," commanded Stoker. "Get under way!" he shouted to the men at the oars. "It'll help Tom with the anchor. Pull!"

"No good, Stoker, we're not shifting it!" shouted Tom. "We got up the slack – about ten feet o' cable – but no more."

"Bill. Give the three of 'em a hand. The rest of us'll keep at the oars," said Stoker, taking Bill's place.

"Keep the strain on that warp! Pull… two-three-four… pull!"

With four men at the warp and the rest rowing, raising the anchor should have been an easy task, yet strive as they might they couldn't do it.

Will hailed Stoker from the steamer. He was waiting to throw him a towrope.

"Can't get the anchor up!" cried Stoker in exasperation.

Will looked in amazement. Stoker raised a hand telling him to wait. "Come on at the oars, keep going! Keep that warp tight! That's it."

"It's no good, Stoker," Tom insisted. "We're not doing anything."

"That's ridiculous," said Stoker. "The anchor only weighs eighty-five pounds. Here, let me try." He took Tom's place and heaved with all his strength in unison with the three others, but to no avail.

Tom tried putting the tiller right over so that the oarsmen would pull the warp in a different direction but that did not help. They tried rowing on one side only. Still the anchor did not move.

"We could slip the anchor and get the steamer to tow us over," suggested Jack.

"Lose the anchor! And then what'd happen if we needed to secure the boat?" scoffed Bill.

"Aye if we get parted from the steamer we're in trouble without an anchor," said Cain by way of confirmation.

"Can't the steamer go out to 'em?" demanded Cain.

"*We're* the lifeboat," protested Stoker defiantly.

"Aye, but he's right," said Sam. "If we can't go, and they can, let 'em try."

"They're closer than us too," observed John.

Stoker looked helplessly at Tom, who nodded sadly. This was beginning to turn into a nightmare for the coxswain of the *Manley Wood*. The crew were right nonetheless. If the steamer could get to the *Marquis of Anglesea* they had to go.

"All right!" cried Stoker, admitting defeat. He leaned out towards Will Redmond. "Will! ... can't get anchor up... can you go?"

Will waved a hand in acknowledgement and the steamer started away without them.

In the event it took twenty minutes of struggling to raise

the *Manley Wood*'s anchor and, once they finally broke it out, it came up slowly as if it was twice its normal weight. When they heaved it aboard, unmarked, the crewmen involved were exhausted.

So what had happened? Perhaps the long swell had removed the sand from around a large rock and the anchor had gone foul of it. The stormy seas made everything so much more difficult: each man had needed to stand to heave on the anchor cable, yet no-one could keep a sure footing so it had been impossible for any individual to use his full strength. Or was it simply that they were more weakened in their frozen state than they realised?

Stoker couldn't account for their difficulties, but fumed because of them. It was so frustrating and he took it all upon himself because he was the skipper.

They rowed with the wind for twenty yards or so, and dropped anchor again. The exercise had warmed them a little. By that time the steamer and the *Marquis of Anglesea* were out of sight.

The captain's hoped-for change in wind direction did not come and the *Elizabeth* surged on, pursuing her unsteady course. The heavy seas made it extremely challenging for the man at the wheel, and sporadic gusts of gale-force wind caused her stern to sheer towards the coast in a screw-like action. The tireless Henley fought with the wheel in an attempt to keep her bows out to sea, but the ship was dangerously close in now. The *Elizabeth*'s passage eastwards was faster than her motion shorewards, yet the move towards land was inexorable nonetheless. Could they do it – could they escape this trap? The captain didn't dare hope.

The seas were still tempestuous, and the wind still howled, but it had not rained for over an hour.

"Visibility's improving, sir," said Henley.

"Yes, I thought so too," replied the captain. "Although being able to see our fate rearing up at us isn't always an advantage."

"I don't know sir, a few seconds' warning lets us get prepared."

"If we hit anything at this rate of knots then no preparation on earth will help us."

"Is that land I can make out there sir?" asked Henley, pointing off the port bow.

"You may be right." The captain snapped open his telescope and focused it quickly. "Ye-s," he said cautiously, searching through the blurry shades of grey. "Yes. Land true enough. I can make out… a high cliff. Must be Hengistbury Head."

"Water gets shallow here, sir, quite quickly."

"I know," said the captain, closing his telescope. "I saw that on the charts. It would be just our luck to get stranded within sight of land but not close enough to get ashore. I feel the fates are against us, Mr Henley. They keep offering us hope and then snatching it away again."

"How far are we off, sir, d'you reckon?"

"Difficult to say in these conditions. Less than a mile. If we can round this headland we may make the Solent yet."

Suddenly the *Elizabeth* seemed to leap. It was as if in the middle of a waltz a dancer had abruptly introduced a most unexpected pirouette. It was so unexpected that the whole ship's crew was thrown off balance. The ship had hit something below the water, but she was still moving.

"What the devil…?" cried the captain, jumping to his feet.

Henley looked about him, shaken. "We're still on course, sir," he said.

The captain leapt to the stern rail and leaned over – no trailing wreckage. He checked the port side: no gaping hole.

Frost reported from the starboard side. "Nothing amiss here, sir."

What was it, a submerged wreck? A whale? Both unlikely this far in towards the coast; the water was too shallow. Had they struck a rock?

"Sir!" There was something in Henley's voice. The captain whirled round to see Henley spinning the wheel freely with one finger and shaking his head. "Helm's not responding sir. We've lost the rudder."

The captain held his head in his hands. They must have just clipped the top of Christchurch Ledge, hidden from view by the heavy seas. "I told you the fates were against us, Mr Henley. Perhaps we'll catch fire now as well, just for good measure," he reflected bitterly. "I think we've had everything else chucked at us."

With the rudder unshipped the *Elizabeth* became unmanageable. No anchors. No steerage. A lee shore. Destruction was inevitable. The wind and the waves would decide the details.

"All hands on deck Mr Henley! Lively now! Take 'em off the pumps and get everyone astern."

———————

In the past half-hour the crew of the *Marquis of Anglesea* had watched with mounting alarm as one by one vessels all around them had been forced from their anchorages by the intensifying storm. First, the pretty French barque *Hirondelle* with her captain screaming orders fit to be heard half a mile away despite the noise of the storm, then the lugger *Princess Mary*, the large brigantine *Solomon*, and finally two pilot-boats, the *Flora* and the *Agenoria*.

The appearance of the steamer caused the master of the *Marquis* to hoist an immediate signal of distress in the hope of his crew escaping with their lives, for the ship was taking on water. If they weren't blown out of control into Poole Bay, they would surely go down within the hour.

The prevailing conditions this far out in the bay made it impossible for the steamer to get very close. The waves were too high and the wind too strong. After several failed attempts to throw the crew a line, Will Redmond was pleased to see them preparing their ship's boat to navigate the short distance between the two vessels. He could see the *Marquis of Anglesea* listing already and knew there was little time left. Just as the crew left their vessel, her cable parted, and with a crack the two masts toppled over as she was picked up by the sea and driven away, missing the nearby revenue cutter *Gertrude* by only a few feet.

All four of the *Marquis*'s crew made it on board the steamer and then Will turned his attention to the other pilot-boat, the

Figaro. Although the ship was remarkably undamaged her master, having seen practically every other vessel within sight blown away by the wind, was keen to seek sanctuary. He requested a tow back into the harbour. Will took off the crew of four first, as a precaution, then towed the vessel into the harbour where he enabled her grateful master to anchor in Wych Channel under the lee of Branksea Island. The grateful master gave him every penny he had on his person – nearly three pounds.

Finally, as the *Royal Albert* struggled out of the harbour again to rendezvous with the lifeboat, she fortuitously came within grappling distance of the fishing smack *Goodwill* from Southampton which was out of control and being driven shorewards by the wind. Will steamed alongside, hailed her, and took off a frightened young lad who had been left alone on board before the storm.

Will remembered George Penney's warning and knew he should have taken the *Goodwill* in tow back to Poole, but he had promised to return to the lifeboat. It would be dark soon and he couldn't tow them both. He let the smack go adrift. A pity. She was a smart boat, well-made, but Will knew where his responsibilities lay, even though he had been concerned by some of the lifeboatmen's actions.

Chapter Four

Over thirty minutes of anticipation did not make the moment any less chilling. At two o'clock in the afternoon the *Elizabeth* ran aground, bows-on, with a terrifying crash as several hundred tons of speeding wooden ship smashed into the south coast of England. The whole foremast snapped off and crashed down across the foredeck, narrowly missing Frost, who had been flung forward by the force of impact. Standing rigging parted with loud cracks and the loose ends hissed through the air ready to whip or entangle the unwary.

The falling mast collided with deck timbers, sending huge lethal splinters spinning out in all directions. An uprooted plank caught Trump full in the face and threw him back violently against the wheel. The ship's boat was torn from its davits and rendered almost unrecognisable when it thumped heavily into the base of the mainmast. A heavy oak hatch-cover popped out like an enormous cork from a bottle and flew forward, scything through everything in its path until it crashed through the port rail.

There was a short, cruel, tremor as the remains of the ship were dragged along the seabed, turning the once-proud *Elizabeth* broadside onto the waves. Then she stuck fast to await her final demise as the cold dark sea of the Channel pounded eagerly against her injured hull.

The captain struggled onto all fours. The ship was heeled over at a bizarre angle and the steeply angled decks were a tangled mass of rope and wood piled up in confusion. He had hit his head somehow and didn't yet trust himself to stand upright. Even above the sound of the wind and the sea, he could hear the water gushing greedily into the hold. He saw Trump collapsed and crawled over to him.

"Trump," he called, shaking his shoulder. The captain rolled Trump over but his face was a mass of blood. He would die soon if no-one came to their aid. It was probably better to leave him unconscious for now. The captain started as a hand touched his shoulder.

"It's me, sir," said Henley. "Are you hurt, sir?"

"No. Thank you." He turned. Henley had already found young Cotten, mercifully also uninjured. "No I'm not hurt. But Trump, here, is in a bad state."

"We may not have much time, beg your pardon, sir. The ship will flood soon."

"You're right. At least we got everyone above decks before she struck, just the thoughts of being trapped below... You and Cotten check astern and I'll go for'ard. Get everyone to come back here."

They separated and the captain scrambled towards the bow. Despite the damage and the unusual angle from which everything was viewed, it was all familiar until he passed the stump of the foremast. A few yards beyond that it was different. It was different because the deck abruptly vanished beneath his wary tread: the planking turned into a gaping hole. With a gasp he pushed himself away from the craggy timbers that projected across the water.

"Cap'n, is that you?" came a voice.

"Aye. Frost?"

"Aye sir."

The captain heard Frost clambering over the debris before

he could see him.

"Are you all right?"

"Fine sir."

"You were hurt before we struck weren't you? Your leg?"

"It's nothin' sir."

"Very good Frost. We'll muster aft. Trump is badly injured I'm afraid."

"Reed is up in the rigging sir. What's left of it."

The bottom two-thirds of the mainmast still stood and, searching skywards through the entanglements above him, the captain could just make out the shape of a man clinging to the rigging.

"Reed!" cried the captain. "We're assembling aft."

"I'd rather stay here sir," came the nervous reply. Reed never said much but he was stubborn.

"Very well," the captain called back. "But if you decide to come down, you'll know where to find us. Are you hurt?"

"No... sir."

It was hard to determine which location was more perilous: the deck with its impending flood by the freezing waters of the English Channel, or the rigging with an icy gale force wind. But the captain had always been a 'deck' man. He'd been in a wreck only once before, but thought about it often. Perhaps he just liked to feel the solidity of the planking beneath his feet.

"Come on Frost, let's get back."

The two parties compared notes. Henley had found Anderson trapped under a mass of rigging but fortunately unharmed. They decided to stay where they were since it was out of the cold wind, although inevitably this part of the ship, like all the rest would soon flood with seawater.

For the moment, they huddled together listening to the rising water, the angry waves against the hull, and the groans of anguished timbers. The *Elizabeth* was dying. Hopefully the remaining crew would survive but that rather depended on the elements and the actions of people ashore.

———————

It was not until gone half-past five – over four hours after their last separation – that the steamer could return to the *Manley Wood*. The lifeboat crew were beginning to wonder if they would ever see the tug again. For the past hour hardly a word had been spoken and the crew were clearly drained. Too weakened, certainly, to row back to the Quay, even though the gale had moderated appreciably. Yet with the dropping of the wind came a further drop in temperature and Stoker began to worry about hypothermia. In fact he could feel himself longing to sleep but knew he must not, nor allow anyone else to do so.

He had decided that if the steamer did not come back within half an hour of sunset they would row back to the beach and make the best of it on land. They would have to find shelter.

In an effort to raise the crew's spirits he addressed them in as cheerful a voice as he could muster under the circumstances. "We'll finish off that rum now lads," he said, retrieving the bottle and handing it round. "Now, there's no point us hanging on out here all night; if the steamer's not back in half an hour we'll row ashore and get a fire going in the lee of them sand dunes to warm us."

When the steam tug did reappear the sun had just set, and the lifeboatmen had been exposed to the elements in an open boat since ten in the morning. They were numb with the cold, hungry, thirsty, tired, and dispirited by their fortunes which had prevented them providing the assistance which they had expected to render.

Will Redmond hailed them and informed Stoker that there were no other vessels within sight that needed assistance. After a brief exchange they decided that there was no further demand for the services of either vessel.

The lifeboatmen gratefully accepted a tow back to North Haven, to drop off Stoker and the lifeboat. Then the tug steamed on to Poole Quay to allow the crews of both the *Manley Wood* and the *Royal Albert* to return to their homes for much-needed food, drink, rest and warmth. Some of the lifeboatmen could barely walk when they finally got ashore.

It was seven o'clock in the evening.

———————

Henry Cutler had seen the *Elizabeth* run aground, and raced to the Christchurch Coastguard Station.

"A ship's run ashore near the entrance to the harbour," he burst out to the watchman.

"Wait here and I'll get the officer," the watchman replied

and he dashed away.

A few minutes later he returned with a lieutenant of coastguard. "What's all this about a ship ashore? What type of ship?" he demanded.

"I don't know," confessed Henry, "two masts, but it's smashed into the Bar and's breaking up. I've just come from Mudeford. There are men still on it, I've seen 'em moving."

"I'll come with you." The officer snatched up his hat. "Lieutenant Mansell," he said, offering a hand, which Henry accepted and shook.

"Henry Cutler."

Lieutenant Mansell turned to shout to one of his men. "Ben! I need you all at the harbour on the double. Robert, set off for Tuckton and bring the rocket apparatus down to me. I'll meet you there." He turned to Henry. "Lead the way," he said.

They half-ran, half-marched to the closest point of the shore where already a small crowd was gathering.

"Make way!" demanded Mansell, and pushed through. He pulled out a telescope and studied the remains of the ship: foremast gone, lower mainmast still standing, and a tangle of spars, torn canvas and rigging dancing under her lee. "Brig," he snapped. "What's left of it. You're right. There *are* men aboard."

The first thing Mansell and his crew of four attempted was to launch the coastguard galley. Henry had only a limited knowledge of nautical matters, but he eyed the very small, four-oared boat with suspicion. It would surely never stand up to the pounding sea which was roaring against the shore, yet he said nothing, deferring to Mansell's greater experience and official position. Mansell was in charge: the coastguard officer knew what he was going to do and the lieutenant was clearly not a man who liked debate.

Predictably, the boat was thrown about wildly before it could get very far from the shore. The breaking waves rendered it impossible to make headway despite a determined man at the tiller and very energetic attempts with the oars. Henry Cutler's fears were soon realised: the wind suddenly drove the boat beam-on to the breakers and a large wave smashed against the starboard side with a mighty smack which upset the boat and its crew into the shallows.

Mansell stumbled out of the water bedraggled, while his crew heaved the boat ashore.

"We'll try and get a line to her," he said, undaunted.

His assistant, Robert, struggled through the crowd with the chief boatman from the Tuckton Coastguard station.

"Good," said Mansell, seeing the rocket apparatus in its cart. "We'll need that. Come with me." He turned to the crowd. "Now," he commanded in a parade ground voice, "I must ask you to keep well away please. These rockets can explode and we wouldn't want anyone to get hurt. Ben, take people back to a safe distance."

Henry accompanied the coastguards down to the point on the shore where they judged they were closest to the stricken *Elizabeth*. She seemed so close, yet the short expanse of intervening sea was wild and menacing. They set up the rocket, with the line coiled neatly in a box which Mansell tilted towards the direction of flight, and then he established what he thought was the correct angle for the rocket to carry the line to the crew of the stranded ship.

"Anywhere between thirty-eight and forty-eight degrees, so they say," he said, half to himself. He crouched and looked along the projected line of flight. "That seems about right."

He lit the touchpaper and they both stood back. After a few seconds the rocket fizzed, sparked, then soared into the air with a loud bang that echoed off the land despite the high wind. The line whipped out of the box at a terrific speed, but fell short by twenty-five yards.

"We'll have another go," said Mansell. "Often need to try these things a few times."

The line had to be hauled in and coiled neatly on the shore for another attempt. He re-set the angle and launched the rocket a second time, but again it fell short. After the third firing he realised that the rope was never going to carry far enough. The onshore wind was preventing the line carrying to its full distance, and now that it was wet it was also heavier so the line was falling shorter each time. He tried once more, standing as close to the thundering waves as he dared. But it was clearly hopeless.

Henry eased past Robert and approached the lieutenant.

"Can't we take a bigger boat out to 'em?" he asked.

"Good God, didn't you see what happened to the galley?" exclaimed Mansell. "No boat from around here will stand up in this, it's far too dangerous. Look at the waves."

"What about one of the fishermen's boats, they have a broader beam don't they?"

"Not buoyant enough and too deep a draught, we'd never get close enough."

"We have to do something."

"I *know*," said Mansell, irritated. "We'll call out the lifeboat."

"The lifeboat? But that's in Poole, fifteen miles away."

"That's right, we'll send a telegraph."

"No, we *can't*," countered Henry, exasperated. "The telegraph station is closed on a Sunday, and I know for a fact that the operator's out o' town tonight anyway."

"You may be right, but I need to be sure. Ben! Send to the station-master of the telegraph office requesting that he call out the lifeboat. Give him all the details." Ben disappeared. "If you're right Mr Cutler it looks like we'll have to send a rider. Robert! Give Mr Newlyn at *The King's Arms* my compliments and ask for loan of a horse. Then ride round to Poole and deliver a message to Joseph Crabb, the harbour master. I'll write the message while you fetch the horse."

Robert raced off.

"I still don't see why we can't take a local boat out to 'em," complained Henry. "Why do we need the lifeboat?"

"Listen. We don't have a boat which can stand up to those great waves and even if we did it would take a huge effort to get there in any boat, let alone launch it. The lifeboat is shallow draught, buoyant, and resistant to rolling over. That's what we need; nothing else will do."

"Nothing? But we haven't tried anything else."

"I know what I'm doing," said Mansell curtly.

"It's so frustrating though," Henry persisted. "Knowing they're just a few hundred yards away shrammed to death, while we're standing around here."

"We're not 'standing around'!" cried Mansell indignantly. "I have developed a plan; now I'm carrying it out. Just leave it to the authorities please." Mansell turned his back on him and studied the ship through his telescope.

"Can't we put one of your rocket things in a boat and take it out just a short distance to get within firing range?"

"What do you do for a living?" he demanded without looking at Henry.

"I'm a fishmonger."

Mansell forced a sarcastic chuckle. "I see," he said derisively, lowering his telescope. "Well I won't sell fish round here, if you don't look after the safety of the coastline. Is that fair?"

Henry bit his lip. "I think it would be good to set some lights on the shore so that the men on the ship can see we haven't forgotten them," he said. "Give them hope."

"Yes, if you like," said Mansell dismissively, walking away. "Why not."

———————

Sam Hart promised never to take home-life for granted ever again. His wife Amelia had run him a deliciously warm bath, served him three dried herrings with potatoes and bread, and even allowed him a glass of the port she kept back for special occasions. It was so wonderful to be warm, dry and fed. He wriggled with comfort in the deep armchair that had belonged to his grandfather, warming his outstretched feet in the glow of the blazing fire. He ached all over like some ancient seadog.

It was clear that everyone on the lifeboat needed more experience. Today the crew had shown they had the stamina for enduring harsh conditions, but they lacked knowledge about what their boat could and couldn't do. Sam still didn't know for sure himself. What would have happened if they had gone to those schooners when Stoker wanted to? Would the lifeboat have turned over in the breakers? How quickly would she have righted again, if at all? And would any of them have lost contact with the boat in that confused sea? The very thought of it made Sam shudder.

At least the weather was beginning to moderate now. The wind still whistled outside, but the harsh booming of the gale was gone. Everyone said it was the most potent storm they'd seen – even old man Roberts and he was very old: over eighty. Many lives lost apparently. Most at sea, but a few in fallen buildings and other freak accidents.

His wandering thoughts were interrupted by a knock at the door. He looked at the clock on the mantel. Five minutes to eight. Who came visiting at this hour on a stormy night? Whoever it was, it couldn't be good news.

He shuffled to the door and opened it. There stood his brother.

"Tom?" said Sam. "What's this?"

"Sorry Sam," he said as he stepped from the pavement into the hallway. "I know we've all just got back, but Joe Crabb's had a message from Christchurch. They need the lifeboat."

Sam groaned, and closed the front door.

"I know, I know. I thought the same," said his brother sympathetically. "Just returned to the land o' the living, as it were, and here we go again. But it's serious by all accounts. A ship's gone aground within sight o' the shore, crew trapped on deck but no-one can get to 'em." Tom reflected for a second. "I didn't want to ask you, but there's no one else."

Sam sighed. "All right. I'm coming. Don't know how I'm gonna tell Amelia."

"Joe and I are rounding up a crew as best we can. Thought a signal rocket at this time o' the night wouldn't be considerate."

"It would be ignored, you mean!"

"That too. I didn't ask John Wills, he was so bad when we got him home, so Jack's asking his brother Frank instead." He looked pensive. "One problem though, the steamer's out of action. Will is overhauling her engine: it cut out a few times on the way back this afternoon."

"How are we gonna get there then?"

"A good question." Tom ran his hand over his moustache and mouth. "Joe was with George Belben when he got the message, and George and me went to the *Antelope* to borrow their brake, but it's out on loan. So George is going to that feller that runs the omnibus service to see if he can borrow the lot – horses and all."

"What if he won't give 'em you?" asked Sam.

"I put the same question to George and he said: 'I'm a bloody magistrate now aren't I? If he don't give 'em voluntarily then I'm commandeering 'em on the Queen's business!' " Tom laughed as he pulled out his watch. "I've a few more crew to round up, then we're meeting at the *Antelope* at half past eight."

"I'll be there."

"Thanks Sam. Could you go and meet George in case he needs a hand with them horses?"

"Right. I'll go now." Sam reached for his oilskin.

"And, Sam, I'm taking some provisions in case we're out all night. Must learn from this morning, eh?"

"Good idea. I'll see you outside the *Antelope* with the omnibus," said Sam, opening the front door for his brother. "I'd better go and tell Amelia." Sam shook his head. "She won't like it."

"Neither does Maria, if that's any consolation."

Chapter Five

What was left of the *Elizabeth* filled with water within an hour and a half, and soon the crew were standing up to their waists in cold sea; all except Reed who had stayed in the rigging in the teeth of the gale which, though lessening, was still fierce. They heard the sound of the rope rockets being fired and someone helpfully had put lanterns on the shore, but they couldn't see enough to know what was happening.

"A rocket line will never reach us in this wind, sir, we're too far away," observed Henley with a hint of contempt.

"Why don't they pull out to us, sir?" Frost demanded.

"I don't know," said the captain guardedly. "Perhaps there's something about these waters we don't know."

Frost seemed unconvinced: "A skiff could get out to us if she were handled right I reckon, sir. They'd have their work cut out for 'em no doubt, but all the same…"

"I hope they get a move on," Henley chimed in. "Stuck out here like this… What are they playing at?"

"Don't reckon they get a gale like this too often round 'ere," Frost observed, teeth chattering, "so they don't know what to do, most like."

"Maybe," said Henley. "Let's hope they make their minds up soon enough. We're only a few hundred yards off the land for God's sake."

The captain agreed with all that had been said, and wanted to add that they'd all freeze to death in no time if the shore party didn't get their act together quickly, but he bit his lip. Now was not the time to start raging; the crew needed encouragement and the captain knew he had to restrain his natural feelings and fulfil the vital role of leader. He must impart hope.

"I'm sure that those men on the beach will set out to us as soon as they can," he assured them confidently. "They've probably had to fit out a boat for the purpose. All takes time."

"When I was a nipper in Hull, sir," Cotten recalled, "my uncles and the other fishermen ran into a fluster when some ship stuck fast on the rocks. I remember it well – must o' been about ten at the time, sir. They took all of an evening squabbling over what were to be done and by time they'd settled on a plan – it were too late." He shook his head meaningfully.

Needless to say, this was not an inspiring anecdote. Cotten was clearly afraid, and this was prompting him to talk too much.

"Still, at least no rocks here, eh?" the captain came back with more spirit than he felt. "Just sand. I'm sure they'll be out to us in no time." He had to change the subject. "How are you bearing up Frost? How's the leg?"

"I'm fine sir, leg was aching but it's gone numb now sir – just like the rest o' me." He grimaced weakly, his young features pale and waxy. Frost was shivering more than the others. His whole body seemed to be shaking. The captain thought this was a bad sign – probably the loss of blood – but he said nothing.

"How's Trump?" asked the captain, nodding towards Anderson.

Trump had never regained consciousness after his accident, although the captain had tended his wounds as best he could. Each member of the crew had each taken it in turns to prop up the wounded man and keep his head above the water. Anderson had insisted on performing most of this duty. He was Trump's cousin and the strongest man on the crew. He was holding him in his arms now, helping to keep his soaking body warm and away from the bitter seawater.

"He's very cold sir," said Anderson. "I hope we get rescued soon, for his sake."

Henley swashed through the water to examine Trump. He was no longer breathing. Henley looked across to the captain, and then up at Anderson.

"I'm sorry George," he said to Anderson in a low voice, and then turned to the captain. "Trump is dead I'm afraid sir."

Poor Anderson did not know what to do. Overcome by grief, but unwilling to release the body of his cousin to free his hands, he simply wept, his great shoulders heaving as he sobbed in the cold gloomy dusk.

The captain waded over and gently took Trump's icy body from him. "Mr Henley," he said, as he moved away, "find me some rope and we'll tie him to the capstan to keep him free of the water. Let's go round the other side," he added, "so that, er, George doesn't have to look at him."

———————

"This is bloody ridiculous," said Henry Cutler to a man next to him as the wind gusted about them. The rider had gone off to Poole and the remaining coastguards had been

87

standing around on the shore talking for an hour or more. Henry had approached them twice with ideas for rescue attempts, but had been rebuffed with increasing firmness and told to wait for the lifeboat.

"I know. It's shameful," said his companion bitterly. "I can't abide it. That lot waiting about for someone else to do something while men just across the water are dying of exposure."

"How long d'you reckon it'll take for the lifeboat to get here?" asked Henry.

"Hours. Who knows in this weather? It's an hour's ride to Poole, then they've got to raise the crew, launch the lifeboat and get out here. They'd have to row – no sail could stand this wind on a small boat. I reckon we're talking eight hours, maybe more. Depends on the tide I suppose."

They both stood staring in angry silence at the coastguard cluster. One of them laughed out loud at some joke. That did it for Henry's companion who had been becoming more and more agitated.

"I can't take any more of this," he cried. "I just can't stand around waiting for that bloody lifeboat. I'm gonna do something meself. I'm going looking for volunteers."

"Well, count me in, friend," said Henry, conspiratorially. "I'm Henry Cutler."

"Sibley Derham." They shook hands. "I tell you what we're gonna do Henry: we're gonna stage a rescue ourselves. I'm not letting those men freeze to death out there within spitting distance of me own front door without trying to help."

"What d'you have in mind?"

"We want a bigger boat than that piss-pot they tried a couple of hours ago that's for sure, and with a shallow draught. Something with plenty o' beam should do the job in this sea and on that shoal ground, even though it's rough," said Sibley, rubbing his chin. "We could use my brother's boat. It's a lighter."

"That's one o' them cargo carriers I seen in-harbour?"

"Aye, they're flat-bottomed you see, like a barge, and we'd need that in this water – it may be rough out there but it's none too deep. Though we couldn't put her off as she is," he cautioned. "We'd need to put proper gunwales on her for a start otherwise she'd ship so much water we'd sink like a stone. That's a big job. Then we'd have to lighten her to bear up against that sea: get her more buoyant. We could pack some lightweight ballast along her sides to stop her pitching and rolling about."

"Sounds like you know what you're talking about, Sibley."

"Well, I've been at sea all my life and my uncle's a shipwright." Sibley reflected for a space. "Now we've decided what we're about, why don't we ask the coastguards to give us a hand?"

"Why on earth…?" Henry gasped. "You know they'll say 'no'!"

"But we'll need all the help we can get and they have gear and know-how we need. I'll admit they're bloody stupid, but we have to think o' those seamen out there: if the coastguard join us we'll get the boat ready and launched in half the time."

"Lieutenant Mansell's put himself in charge and he won't stand anything that doesn't fit in with his plans," said Henry, frowning.

"You may be right but I think we ought to try it leastways," counselled Sibley. "I know it goes against the grain, but we've nothing to lose. We just try to reason with him."

"All right then." Henry sighed. "But I don't give it much hope..."

They strode across the shingle, and Henry cleared his throat to attract Mansell's attention. "Excuse me," he began.

Mansell sighed and turned to face him. "Yes Mr Cutler," he said, as if it was a great effort to speak.

"Me and Mr Derham here have an idea lieutenant. We're gonna alter his brother's lighter, drag it down to the beach and use it to rescue the crew o' the brig."

The coastguard shook his head at Henry in apparent incredulity.

Sibley interjected with forced politeness. "It makes sense to pool our efforts," he proffered. "I know the lifeboat's on its way but we might just as well try something while we wait, and so we wondered if you and your men would lend a hand."

"We need help to prepare the boat," explained Henry. "Sibley here's a seaman and knows what he's about, but we got to make the lighter fit for the job, then lug her down here, and row off."

"How many more times..." began the lieutenant sternly.

"Will you just *listen*!" cried Henry, frustrated.

"Go on with you!" Mansell retorted angrily. "We don't want any of your help. You'll make matters worse by wrecking yourselves and then we'll have two crews to rescue. I've told you: wait until the lifeboat arrives. Now get away Mr Cutler... go and sell some fish."

One of the coastguards sniggered.

"Right," snapped Sibley. He'd heard enough. "Come on Henry!"

Sibley grabbed Henry's elbow and steered him away. Together they marched over to where a group of onlookers stood in the shelter of some trees, and Henry followed, incensed by Mansell's rudeness.

"Listen!" cried Sibley to those assembled. "We want to rescue those men out there, 'cos the coastguard aren't up to it."

"Haven't they called the lifeboat?" asked a man uncertainly.

"Aye, but how long will that take?" replied Henry. "It'll take hours. Too long we reckon. That lot out there'll be dead afore long."

"Speaking plain, the coastguard are a shambles," said Sibley. "Useless the lot of 'em and bone idle with it. They're over there jawing away right this minute: biding their time for the lifeboat, and we want to do something *now* afore them sailors on the brig are lost."

"We got a boat," added Henry, "but need a hand to make her ready. Everyone can help us drag her down here, and we need men who can use an oar to come with us and row off to the brig. Coastguard have refused to help us."

91

"*Refused* to help us, mind," said Sibley indignantly. "Refused to help save them poor souls out there. Did you ever hear of such a thing? Supposed to be seafaring men an' all." He cast a meaningful gaze over the faces before him. "Now, who's with us?"

A goodly number of arms shot up, mostly local fishermen. "Well done," said Henry gratefully, and eagerly shook the hands of each of the volunteers.

"Come with me," commanded Sibley, leading the way to his brother's boat.

———————

It was almost dark now, and on board the *Elizabeth* the crew's situation had become progressively more desperate. Up in the rigging Reed was ominously silent, despite attempts to communicate with him for the last half an hour. The rest of the crew were gathered almost immediately below and so none of them could see Reed clearly in the darkness. He was just a black distorted shape suspended above.

On deck, Frost lapsed intermittently into a stupor, yet apologised feebly to his crewmates every time he broke free of it.

The captain waded out into deeper water to try to get a better view of Reed. His body was too numb to even think of scrambling up the rigging after him. The wind had died down considerably now and he could even catch the sound of people talking on the shore. *Why didn't they come?*

"Reed!" he called hoarsely. "Reed!" Backing away towards the stump of the foremast, he hoped to get a better view. He moved round so that he was no longer looking at the shape from below and began to realise that the indistinct black outline was odd somehow, although in his mentally strained state he could not quite understand why. Yet once he saw the meagre moonlight fall fully on the crewman from the front, the reason was immediately apparent. Reed was hanging upside down, one leg tangled in a footrope. He was certainly dead – eyes open, mouth gaping, arms dangling stiffly beneath him. The captain looked hastily away. Poor man. Only a youngster, like Trump.

The captain's pity turned rapidly to anger as he questioned why they had not yet been rescued. It was so frustrating. Why? *Why*!

He checked the time. Inexplicably, the pocketwatch his mother had given him was intact and still functional. A minor miracle after all that had happened.

"Six hours!" he croaked quietly to himself. Almost a sob. They'd been stuck there for *six* hours. *What on earth could be taking a rescue party so long?* There were people on the beach, so why didn't they come? And the wind had died down dramatically now: still a strong wind, but nowhere near its former intensity.

Two crewmen dead who might have been saved. Hope was ebbing away. *Was he destined to die here?*

He had to compose himself. The crew were depending on him. He pulled himself erect and worked his way back to them with an appearance of calm.

"Men, I have been forward," he began stiffly. "I'm sorry to tell you that poor Reed is dead." They stared at him and no-one spoke. "He must have slipped in the rigging," he continued stolidly. "Obviously I should have liked us to cut

93

him down and give him some dignity, but I don't think any of us is capable of it."

They all thought they were going to die, he could see it in their faces. They looked lost. He had to give them hope, even though he felt none himself. It was his duty as captain.

"We mustn't give up," he said quietly. He cleared his throat and started again more confidently. "I know this is hard. Bloody hard. *I* think it's hard and my body's twenty years older than any of you! But we must all of us stand together and trust in God to spare us. The people out there on the beach, I'm sure, will be trying all that they can. When I was up forward just now, I could see them preparing some sort of boat." A lie! He was lying to them now, yet he had to instil hope even if it meant inventing it. "They've obviously not given up on us, so let's not give up on each other, eh? It's probably because the sea's shallow here and it will be very difficult for them to get a boat out to us in this rough weather."

They didn't really look any different, but maybe they felt a tiny glimmer of something inside. If so, the captain had done his job.

———————

Working as fast as they could, it still took ten men over three hours to get the lighter ready to launch. Fortunately most of the volunteers had been fishermen, so they knew what they were doing. When they were almost done – and against Henry's advice – Sibley decided to make one last appeal to Lieutenant Mansell for assistance.

Mansell had retired to his own home, and Sibley made his way up the hill to find him. He knocked on the door. There was no answer. He tried again. Still nothing.

Suddenly *that voice* rang out from somewhere above him.

"*What* do you want?"

Sibley looked up and there was the coastguard officer leaning out of an upstairs window.

"We got our boat ready: would you loan us some oars for the men to row out to the brig? I got nine men willing, but the oars we got ain't really big enough."

"No, no, no. The lifeboat will be here soon enough and everything is in hand. There's no need for you to risk your lives."

"Isn't that up to us?"

"Yes, but you're now risking my equipment as well and I'm not prepared to chance you losing it on a fool's errand."

Sibley knew there were at least three pairs of spare oars in the coastguard station, but Mansell had the key.

"What about lifebelts and lifelines?"

"Didn't you hear me Mr Derham? *No*. Come back at daylight if you want to help. The lifeboat will be here by then and, if not, we can try again with our galley. I'm quite prepared to consider loaning our equipment to you then if we are not able to make it ourselves."

"They'll be dead if we wait till daylight."

"Speculation. You know no more about that than I do. We don't even know how many men are on board, let alone their condition."

Sibley tried to stay calm. "Won't you at least give me a commission to use your men to launch our boat? It's very heavy and we won't be able to lift it by ourselves."

"Good," said Mansell and he slammed the window shut.

Sibley resisted the temptation to throw a brick through the self-same window, but stormed back to his colleagues at the boat, more determined than ever to take action.

"Henry!" he bellowed angrily.

"Yes," came the reply as Henry scuttled out of the shadow of the boat. "I'm guessing he said 'no'."

"That's right he did."

"What did I tell you …?"

"Is the boat ready?" Sibley demanded.

"This minute finished."

"We'll launch that boat ourselves."

"It's very heavy," Henry began.

"We'll launch it even if we have to drag the thing till our hands bleed. Come on!"

"What about the oars?"

"The ones we've got already will just have to do. Although I'm half-inclined to go down to that bloody coastguard station with an axe and break the door down."

At midnight the lifeboat crew arrived at North Haven Point.

"Come in all o' you," Stoker ordered. He was tired like the rest of them, but he was also one of the oldest and his age seemed to weigh on him. He had known they would come – at Tom's insistence the rider from Christchurch had been persuaded to make a detour on his return journey to inform Stoker of the situation.

His wife Mary sighed, glaring at the clean floor of the back room as the crew, all twelve of them, trooped in with their dirty boots and wet clothes. Thank goodness the children were in bed otherwise there wouldn't be room to breathe. She welcomed the lifeboatmen nonetheless. "Get round the fire," she said "you must be chilled to the bone."

"Now then," said Stoker once they'd all squeezed into the space round the fire. "What I was told was that a brig, the *Elizabeth*, has run aground on the sand in East Bay opposite Gundimore, about a mile from Christchurch at the harbour's mouth, a few hundred yards from the beach. The coastguard can see men on board but can't get a line to 'em. They want us to go in with the lifeboat."

"That's right," confirmed Tom. "But there's no help from the tug this time Stoker. Engine trouble."

"What d'you reckon about going under sail in this weather Tom?" asked Stoker.

"We'd never do it, Stoker," he replied. "Gale's eased since earlier, but canvas'd still get clean blowed away in this."

"I thought as much meself. Gundimore's a long way under oars." He scratched his beard. Christchurch was beyond the easterly point of Poole Bay.

"I don't mind saying that we're all tired, Stoker," said Cain.

"You don't need to tell me that!" Stoker came back.

"We all know Christchurch Bay," said Bill. "Nothing but banks o' sand that shift about. And you're on 'em afore you know, mind you. We got caught there ourselves a while back on a falling tide when we'd been up river – came out the harbour and near ran aground. We got through a channel – a 'latch' they call 'em Christchurch-way – which weren't there a month or two previous. The sands there shift about and in weather like this that brig never stood an earthly chance."

A low chorus of agreement.

"How are we ever gonna navigate out there alone and have any hope of finding 'em?" asked Sam. "Shifting sands, howling a gale, raining, and black as a wolf's throat. You can't see a bloody thing, begging your pardon Mary."

Mary threw up her hands and went into the kitchen.

Frank Wills was also candid: "You won't even see a tail light until we're right on top of 'em, not in this."

"I doubt they've even still got one," said Cain. "Mountains o' sea, gale o' wind – must be broke all to pieces by now."

"Same'll go for the hull soon enough in this if they're that close in," added Bill.

"Aye, well, we don't know exactly what we're dealing with

and we don't know how to find 'em, but we have to *try*," said Stoker firmly. "We'll pull out down East Looe and keep in sight o' the shoreline, feel our way round the Bay and hope they show a light or sound a foghorn and we can pick 'em up."

"That's a long haul Stoker in this," said Cain.

"It's all right hugging the coast, but we don't want to get caught on a lee shore like they done," warned Bill.

"I know," Stoker was patient. "We all scratch a living from this Bay and know our way about in all weathers. The sooner we get out there, the better we'll know what we're up against."

Tom wanted to support his coxswain, but realised sooner than Stoker that yet again the crew weren't going to be told what to do. Still he did his best to support him, perhaps out of guilt for not supporting him last time. "Tide's on our side," he observed.

"Aye, then let's set to it," ordered Stoker, pointing to the door.

"I don't like it," said Cain, raising his voice. "We ain't got the steamer, and we're worn out afore we start, every man jack of us, even you Stoker. We'd pull our guts out rowing that thing up into Christchurch Bay in a gale at night."

Stoker thumped the chimney breast with the flat of his hand. "I'm fed up with this!" he cried angrily. "We can't have a bloody debate every time we head out! There are men at Christchurch perishing. We *ain't* gonna just leave 'em like we did with them schooners this afternoon."

"I know, I know," said Tom peaceably. "You're upset about

this afternoon and so am I. We all are." There were nods around the room. "We went all the way out there with good intent, and didn't achieve much save getting shrammed near to death. But it weren't our fault: we did the best we could."

"We should have gone straight to them schooners when we arrived like I said," Stoker growled stubbornly, resisting the peacemaking attempt.

"All right, Stoker!" said Tom with some authority. "No sense having a set-to over that again. None of this helps them wretches trapped at Christchurch. Let's stay fixed on that."

"I agree with Cain," said Frank. "It's too dangerous to row over there – God help me it must be a dozen miles. And even when we get there we'd be picking our way round sand banks in the dark. No fear!"

"He's right," said Sam, reluctantly, "and we still don't know the lifeboat well enough, neither."

Stoker folded his arms and glowered at them all.

"It can't be helped, Stoker. The elements aren't in our favour." Sam put a hand on the coxswain's shoulder, but it was swiped away.

"Look at us. Just look at us, Stoker!" Bill insisted. "Bloody all-in, the lot of us. Apart from young Frankie here, we've been eight hours or more at sea in the freezing cold. Most of us just got home, had a bite to eat and put on some dry clothes afore we were called again. We're not fit to pull the skin off a rice pudding, let alone row all the way to Christchurch."

"Well, that's not good enough for me," the coxswain snapped.

Even Tom thought Stoker was now being totally unreasonable, and couldn't see how anyone could retrieve the situation unless the coxswain backed down.

"There's no other way to get to 'em, so we *have* to go," insisted Stoker. "Or at least we have to try. What'll folk say if we don't go?" he demanded. "Specially after this afternoon."

Then Sam piped up. "Can't we take the boat by road, on her carriage?"

"Don't be daft, that's bloody miles…" Bill began.

"No, he's got an idea there," countered Tom, recognising a way to break the impasse. "The boat carriage has wheels, and we've got a fine set of horses thanks to George Belben."

"The bloke at the omnibus won't like us taking his horses all out there," said one of the crewmen.

"Sod him," said Cain defiantly.

"And the road round the Bay must be clear 'cos that rider from Christchurch came along it all right," said Tom warily, sensing victory.

"We could be there in four hours I reckon," said Frank.

"Probably about what it'd take us to row there in the condition we're in," said Sam.

"At least that," agreed Frank. "Wind's not in our favour, and hark at it getting up again."

"But will that be soon enough?" demanded Stoker.

"Who knows, Stoker," said Tom. "We can only do our best, can't we."

"You said we had to try *something*, Stoker," Bill ventured. "This is something, and it's a lot safer than going out under oars."

"That's my way o' thinking," remarked Frank. "I reckon we should give it a go, Stoker."

Stoker sighed. "All right you devils," he said at length. "Are we *all* agreed on this then?" He looked around the room for any signs of dissent. There were none. "Good. Right, let's get to it. We'll unhitch the horses from the omnibus and use them to pull the lifeboat carriage to the road. Once we get there we can all sit in the boat and let the horses pull us too: save some strength for rowing once we get to Christchurch. Tom you take three others and put the omnibus into the lifeboathouse out o' the weather, after we get the boat out. The rest o' you help me hitch up the horses to the carriage and prepare the boat. Watch yourselves mind, it's slippy under foot – a load of weed's been washed up."

They filed out onto the cold, wet, windy headland, and Stoker led them to the boathouse. He and Tom drew open the doors and kept them open in the high wind, while the rest of the men dragged forward the lifeboat on its launching carriage so that it could be hitched to the horses. At night her gleaming sides made her look like a phantom boat.

"Now then." Stoker reached out, patted the boat, then barked his instructions. "Tom, you organise getting the omnibus inside; Frank and Cain keep the doors open in this wind while they're about it, and the rest of us'll get the boat ready. Hold the horses will you Sam! Tom, make sure we take the axes and plenty o' rope in case there are fallen trees on the road."

Manoeuvring the heavy omnibus into the boathouse was easier said than done. Bill Brown slipped as he pushed at one of the back wheels and cracked his head on the ground.

"I told you to mind yourselves!" Stoker shouted. "Bill, what do you think you're doing?" Bill leapt up and resumed pushing as if nothing had happened.

Once the omnibus was safely stored and the doors bolted, the six of them joined the others at the boat.

Tom gazed into the darkness. It was pitch black and out to sea nothing could be distinguished except flashes of white-crested breakers in the feeble moon-glow. The air resounded with the howling of the winds, and the thunderous roar of the seas dashing against the coast.

"Look at the size o' them waves," said Tom to his brother, nodding at the beach. "We'd never have got her off from here anyway, let alone set out in it."

It was one o'clock in the morning. The lifeboat was on its way at last.

Chapter Six

The slow, numb, trembling fingers of Captain Back fumbled at the small pocket in his waistcoat as he tried to retrieve his watch. He cursed quietly because it was so difficult. He was immensely tired and his whole body ached. Eventually he succeeded and held the watch up to catch the faint light.

"Midnight," he muttered to himself in disgust. "We've been here *ten* hours."

He could feel his physical strength ebbing away. And the mental strain was almost as agonising as the pain from his frozen and bruised body. Despair was welling up, yet he had to stifle it, take control of the situation somehow. It was clear that no-one was going to do anything to rescue them now. They would have to do something themselves soon before they were incapable of doing anything. But what? The sea was considerably less turbulent, and the wind was certainly no longer gale force.

They would have to try to get ashore themselves. It was either that or stay here and die like Trump and Reed before them. Yet they were all so weak.

Should he send one man to attempt it and hope to galvanise rescue attempts from the shore? Anderson could go maybe. No, that was not a good option. What if something happened to him? After all, it was more likely than not that he wouldn't make it by himself. If Anderson didn't make it then they'd be in the same position as now: not knowing what was going to happen to them and slowly dying of exposure, uncertain of rescue.

Action was better than inaction. They had to do *something*

and do it together. They'd find a large piece of wreckage and cling on to it – a hatch cover perhaps – and use it as a float to paddle themselves near the shore. If it was big enough they'd put Frost on it. He was no longer conscious and if they left him here he'd drown.

The captain cleared his throat. "I've come to the conclusion that no-one is mounting a rescue for us, for some reason. The sea is calmer now and yet we've not heard anything from the shore for hours." No-one batted an eyelid at this. They stood there staring at him dumbly. "Perhaps they think we're already dead, who knows," he added quietly. "But we're not giving up."

He explained his plan to them. There were no dissenters.

"Mr Henley, search about for long stretches of line to tie Frost to something that floats. Anderson, go hunt for some large piece of timber we can hold onto while we swim ashore. At least we can take off these bloody wet clothes."

Henley waded off. It was difficult to see anything now: it was so dark and the water was deep. He glanced up towards the shore. *What was that?* Something moving caught his eye. A dark shape against a dark background. Was that a boat? If it was, it had a very odd shape, and was already close in.

"Captain!" cried Henley sprawling and splashing aft. "Captain! There's a boat pulling out to us. About fifty yards away."

"We're saved!" cried Cotten with a catch in his voice.

There was a clumping noise a few moments later as the boat knocked against the *Elizabeth*'s deformed hull.

"Brig ahoy!" came a voice.

"Thank God!" replied Henley.

At last something could be done for Frost now. "Hear that Frost? We're rescued," said the captain hugging the limp figure reassuringly. But it was too late. Despite all their efforts William Frost had slipped away unnoticed during the excitement, and on the brink of being saved. Captain Back shook with emotion as he looked into those cold empty eyes, before gently closing them with one hand. Only twenty-one years old.

Sibley Derham clambered on deck. "How many are there aboard ship?" he asked.

"Four alive and three dead," reported the captain.

———————

Henry Cutler was returning from Susannah Stride's guesthouse where the *Elizabeth*'s survivors had been taken. He'd borrowed a horse and cart to transport them to their lodging and had rounded off his night's work by returning some of his tired fellow rescuers to their homes. He pulled his horse up sharply as the gleaming white outline of the *Manley Wood* rounded the corner. The lifeboat! In all the emotion of rescuing the poor men of the *Elizabeth* he had totally forgotten about the Poole lifeboat. He pulled up, jumped down from the seat of his trap, and ran across to the boat.

"Ahoy!" he called as he approached, causing the heads in the boat to swivel round. "The crew have been rescued," he declared proudly. "From the brig I mean. The storm abated, we got a special boat together to wear the shallows and managed to get 'em off a few hours ago." Then he noticed the lifeboat crew's blank faces staring at him. "I'm sorry you've come all this way..."

"I'm the coxswain," said Stoker wearily, clambering down from the boat. "Are you from the coastguard?"

"Good Lord no!" cried Henry. "Right bunch o' good-for-nothings they are. They stood about for bloody hours not doing anything so a group of us decided to do what we could ourselves, you see. And we were just in the nick o' time: three o' the crew were already dead and the others were shrammed right through, could barely walk. Another hour I reckon and..." He shook his head.

"I need to see the coastguard officer to report," said Stoker stonily.

"Of course," said Henry obligingly, a gleam in his eye. "Let me take you to his house in the trap. Hop on. His name's Lieutenant Mansell," Henry added as Stoker jumped up. "Awkward, officious little bugger. But it's only a couple o' minutes from here. Gee up!" He cracked his whip over the horse's bony rump and they sped off.

Henry started explaining to Stoker all that had happened, but Stoker could barely keep his eyes open and found it hard to concentrate; he nearly fell off at one point when they clattered round a sharp corner. What a waste of time this had all been. Two call-outs in one day. The first to spend hours afloat in Studland Bay for nothing, and the second to spend hours on the road to Christchurch for nothing. He was too tired even to be angry.

The trap stopped abruptly and Stoker shot forward, so that he nearly fell off again.

"Here we are," said Henry. He stepped down and walked to the front door on which he rapped loudly. There was no response. He tried again even louder. "Deep sleeper," Henry offered by way of explanation. He wouldn't have missed this for the world.

The window above them suddenly flew open.

"Get away with you, Cutler!" shouted Mansell. "I said *daybreak*. We'll try again when the sun is above the horizon."

"Sorry to disturb you, lieutenant," returned Henry politely, "but just to let you know we managed to take the crew off, as I told you we would, but I've brought the coxswain of the lifeboat here for you. They've just arrived."

Henry enjoyed observing the discomfiture on Mansell's face, made slightly more poignant by the fact that he looked ridiculous out of uniform in his flowing white nightshirt leaning over the street.

"Rescued?" repeated Mansell in surprise.

"Certainly," said Henry demurely, "as I said we would, and a few hours ago now while you were in bed. *Sir*."

The friction between the two men was obvious and Stoker had the sense to realise that whatever Henry's merits in rescuing the crew of the *Elizabeth*, he was now using the lifeboat coxswain to get back at the coastguard officer.

"With the crew saved, I take it we can stand down sir and go home?" Stoker proposed.

"Yes," snapped Mansell. "Yes," he repeated more mildly. "Thank you. Very, er, obliging of you to come all this way. Am most grateful to you. In the event I'm sorry that it, er, appears to have been a wasted journey."

Henry Cutler beamed up at the lieutenant angelically, but said nothing.

It was good that the crew of the brig had been rescued, but Stoker couldn't think about that. He couldn't even trust himself to speak. No words could express how he felt. Disappointment, anger, frustration, humiliation. All of these and more. If he said anything now he knew he would regret it.

A sense of futility washed over him. Stoker was tired, cold, miserable, and didn't want to become involved in the rivalry between Henry Cutler and Lieutenant Mansell. He turned away and walked back down the hill alone. Henry was calling after him for some reason, but Stoker ignored him. He just wanted to go home.

Chapter Seven

In his cottage at North Haven Point, Stoker studied the modest fire in the hearth. He stood as close to it as he could, warming his chilled hands while he listened to the wind sighing outside and the sea rolling against the shore. The house was quiet and the occasional crackle from the fire was a comforting sound. Mary was cleaning in the kitchen; three of his children were out to work, two more had apprenticeships; teenage Edward was painting the hall upstairs; James was at school; and little Albert was asleep.

The coxswain had required an extended rest to recover from the exertions of the beginning of the week. None of the lifeboatmen had had any sleep at all on Sunday night and so after their eventual return from Christchurch on Monday they had each retired early, yearning to make up the lost quota.

It was therefore not surprising that on Tuesday morning Stoker had slept late by a few hours. This was an event. It was the first time in his adult life, barring illness, that he had slept beyond six o'clock. Mary had tip-toed from the bedroom at first light to allow him to sleep on. But when he awoke and realised it was nearly mid-morning he had felt curiously resentful about the extra hours in bed – ashamed – annoyed that his body had demanded the additional time even though he knew he needed it. Mary had teased him about being a 'gentleman of leisure' which had exacerbated those feelings and made him irritable.

Around noon it had started snowing. Mary had kept him indoors and insisted he take it easy. He obliged – more for her sake than his own – but spent the time repeatedly mulling over the sorry details of the previous two days' events until he was sick of thinking about them.

That was yesterday. Now it was Wednesday morning. Today Stoker had woken at the normal time. He felt physically rested, but mentally he was still working at a rate of knots. He didn't want to think about the lifeboat anymore and kept pushing thoughts of it away.

It was still snowing. The white blanket outside was now quite thick – whipped into crisply demarcated little banks by the wind.

Stoker caught sight of his reflection in the mirror above the mantel. When he examined his features closely, the face that observed his with such interest was surprisingly lined. The eyes were tired – tired with age not with lack of sleep – his mouth straight and serious. Whiskers needed a trim, they looked unkempt. He hadn't studied himself in a mirror for a long time. Not a pleasant experience. He shook himself irritably, and frowned at the reflection. It made him look even older.

"Mary," he called. "I'm gonna check them lights."

"You can't go out in this Stoker!" she protested, bursting in from the kitchen drying her hands. "You need to *rest* – get your strength back after all that business with the lifeboat. Send young Edward to do it, like yesterday."

"There's nought wrong with me. Don't fuss." He patted her upper arm. "Any more rest'll kill me. Pig sick of rest."

Mary was not deterred. "Lookee there," she said, waving her hand towards the whiteness through the window. "It's bitter outside. Like the Arctic. It's not right, you know: man of your age running about in this weather..."

"Mary," he cut in authoritatively. "It's my job and you

know it. It's what Trinity pays me for." Trinity House in London was responsible for the safety of this stretch of the coast, and Stoker had looked after the navigation lights with utmost reliability since their installation in 1848. "If the lights can't be seen then ships'll run aground and lives'll be lost." Stoker turned away. "We can't have any more of that round here," he muttered.

She studied his back as he moved towards the door and shook her head. "It weren't your fault about Sunday," she called to his retreating form, then scuttled after him. "I know what you're like," she said, "I don't want you to keep trying to make up for it by pushing yourself all the time, as if you had a debt in God's book."

Mary was barring his way to the front door now. "It's not your fault," she repeated.

Stoker reflected for a space. "Why couldn't I make 'em see we *had* to go down to them schooners when we first got there?" He posed the question determinedly, tightening his jaw. And she noticed that he said this almost more to himself than to her.

"Well, you did ask 'em," she said. "Ain't that enough? You did your best I'm sure."

"Did I?" he protested. "The Regulations say they ought to do what the coxswain says."

"Is that so?" said Mary. "Perhaps you should take a copy with you next time to show 'em."

In his self-absorbed state, Stoker missed the sarcasm. "They didn't do what I wanted, and I'm supposed to be coxswain."

"I've heard enough o' this!" Mary's Cornish accent shone

through strongly when she was riled. "You're all *volunteers*, and some of your men know as much about the water as you do. You can't *command* them; you can only ask."

"I should've had the power to sway them, but they didn't trust me when I said we could do it."

"Respect is earned, so they say," observed Mary sagely. "They know you're a good seaman, but I reckon they figured you knew no more about the lifeboat than they did – you're all new to it."

"Maybe you're right." He sighed. "But because we didn't try it like I wanted, we still have no experience of a proper rescue you see, and so next time they'll just as likely refuse to go in as well. I needed them to see we could do it. We've not learned anything."

"Just how safe was it then?" she pressed him.

"Well, in the sea that was running it were touch and go, but we had to take the chance to stand any hope o' rescuing them seamen."

"So there you are then," said Mary, crossing her arms. "You wanted to take the chance, but they fancied it weren't safe – can't say I blame 'em for holding back. I were too afeared to step into the backyard myself that afternoon, let alone go out to sea. You were all in it together, so you had to listen to their opinions."

"I just wished they'd trusted me. Aye, it were dangerous, but somehow I knowed we could've made it. Galls me no end – seamen's lives lost, and we were there but practically watched it happen."

"Listen to me, Richard Stokes," said Mary sternly, waving a

finger, "you came home Monday noon after being out with that wretched lifeboat all day Sunday, all Sunday night, and Monday morning. It were the foulest weather we ever saw, and you were frozen half to death with nothing to eat for a day. I'm *not* gonna stand here and listen to you becalling yourself for it. Stop taking the blame for pity's sake!" she pleaded. "Hardly a soul would've had the courage to even set out in that hurricane. At least you tried."

He touched her cheek affectionately with the back of his hand. "Thankee Mary, I knows you're trying to help." Stoker sighed again. "It's all made worse by that infernal Christchurch business: dragging the boat all out there to be told we weren't needed. A waste o' time..."

"You think it's all your fault because you're the coxswain – the man in charge?"

"Aye. Course it is!"

"So, now you've worried yourself to death over it all, tell me: is there anything you could've done to have stopped it? Anything you could have done *different*?"

"About that brig at Christchurch?"

"About the whole lot – schooners, Christchurch..."

He thought for a minute. "Nothing, I suppose..." he admitted gruffly. "Christchurch were a pointless exercise, but it were either go by road or not go at all, and we couldn't not go."

"Well then, what's done is done. *Stop worrying*." She looked at him keenly, to see if this was sinking in. It wasn't. She knew he'd just have to work through it in his own time, like always. "It seems to me that all this can't be helped," she continued.

"It's a new lifeboat and a new crew: you have to learn, all of you, don't you? Including you. You got to get to know the boat, the gear; get to know each other. Most folks'd understand that…"

Stoker harrumphed.

"Why don't you come and sit by the fire," she invited briskly, taking his arm, "and I'll bring you a nice pot o' tea. I made a fresh loaf first thing…" She kissed him on the cheek.

"I need to go and check them lights first," he said, but this time almost apologetically. "I've not checked 'em myself since Sunday morning. Young Edward topped up the fuel, but they need proper looking after in this weather."

Mary pulled herself up to protest, but Stoker stopped her with an upheld hand.

"I know, I know, my love," he said quietly, "but it's in weather like this that they need most attention you see. Fierce wind or cold can break the glass, or Lord knows what else. Come on," he pleaded, "I'll not be long. You make me that cup o' tea when I get back. I'll need it."

"You're not a young man anymore you know."

"Thankee my love, I do know it, but what do you expect me to do? I have…" he shrugged and grasped for the right word. "I have me *duties*, and that's all there is to it. Got to be done."

She stood in front of him, arms crossed again, frowning. He gently edged her aside, gave her a peck on the cheek, grabbed his telescope from its shelf in the hallway, and went to open the door.

Mary reached out and stayed his hand.

"Take our Edward with you, will you Stoker, just for me?"

He smiled and nodded. "To keep an eye on the poor old man."

"Edward!" she bellowed. He duly appeared. "Eddie, go with your father to the lights, there's a good lad."

Mary quickly fussed over her son to ensure he was wrapped up to her satisfaction. Edward allowed her to do this even though he was sixteen years old because he knew she liked to mother him. Then with one last look at the fire, father and son stepped out together into the snow.

———————

Tom Hart walked to the *King's Arms* on the Quay and stomped his feet at the entrance to shake the snow off his boots. He had an hour before the departure of the *Ganymede*, and a pint of ale and a pipe would be most welcome in this cold. Might even get a few hands of cards in. Anything was better than standing around on the freezing deck forcing conversation with the ship's taciturn master.

He raised a hand to a familiar group in the far corner, but they didn't seem to see him through all the smoke. He pulled out his faithful pipe and began to stuff it with *Buccaneer Flake* from a pouch while he waited to be served. There were a few others waiting but Danny, the barman, was inclined to be slow.

In fact Tom had time not only to fill the pipe but to light it and take a dozen or more slow puffs before Danny finished serving the other customers. Yet instead of then turning his

116

attention immediately to Tom, Danny began cleaning behind the bar.

"Here Danny!" called Tom, thinking he had not been seen. Danny half looked up, then turned back to what he was doing.

Tom drummed his fingers on the bar, uncertain. He walked around so that he was as close to Danny as he could be.

"Have I got to help meself, Danny?" he asked jovially.

"You shouldn't have come in here today, Tom," said Danny quietly without raising his eyes from what he was doing.

"What on earth are you on about Danny Boy?" Tom replied, taken aback. "Come on, I needs a drink! I gotter take the *Ganymede* out in under an hour."

Danny turned and looked right to left as if about to impart some great confidence. "There's tempers flying about the lifeboat and the gale on Sunday. We had a punch-up in 'ere last night."

"A punch-up?" Tom stiffened. "What was that all about?"

Danny sighed and beckoned Tom to the more dimly lit end of the bar. "I don't want to get involved: I'm just saying what I've seen and heard. We had a group o' warehousemen in last night – regulars – few drinks inside 'em, words were said, one thing led to another. Couple o' your crew took a hiding."

"And were they there Danny – out in the hurricane – these warehouse boys?"

Danny shrugged. "I'm just saying be careful. I reckon you

ought to lay low for a bit till this has settled down. There's a lot o' people carping about the lifeboat – all over town, not just in taverns. The boss don't like it: don't want you in 'ere. Told us to turf any o' you lot out."

"So who are these people who know so much about the lifeboat and how it all should be done?" cried Tom resentfully. "Where were *they* when the call went out for volunteers to join the crew when the new lifeboat got here? Give me their names and I'll pop round this afternoon and sign 'em up since they're so plainly chock-full of seafaring know-how."

"It's not me that's saying it, Tom." Danny shrugged. "Like I said, I don't want to get involved."

"Well, you just tell any o' them fireside lifeboatmen to speak to me and I'll put 'em straight," said Tom loudly, slapping the bar with the flat of his hand. "Now then, a pint of ale if you please, Daniel." He was suddenly so loud that the whole inn could hear him. It was abruptly very still.

Danny moved reluctantly towards the tap.

"Belay there," commanded a voice.

Tom turned to face Alderman Wanhill, the town's chief magistrate, a rich and powerful man, and the owner of the *King's Arms* amongst much else.

"Mr Hart," said the Alderman, taking him speedily aside by an elbow. "I'm sure Danny has explained the situation. It's not to my liking but can't be helped. Could I ask you to leave the premises quietly without a fuss. Brawling is bad for business, I'm afraid. I'm sure you understand."

"I *don't* understand," said Tom, perplexed. "Just what am I being accused of here?"

"You're one of the lifeboatmen, are you not?"

"Aye. What of it?"

"If you really want me to spell it out for you…" he raised his eyebrows inquisitorially. "People in the town are upset over what happened. There've been a few scuffles. I don't want any more of that here. I'd just like you to leave quietly and not come back till this has died down."

"Well, I've heard none o' this," said Tom. "No-one's said ought to me about it. I come in here most days," he protested. "I'm not being chucked out on my ear 'cos of some bloody gossip put about by a load o' landsmen!"

He turned to speak to Danny again, but Wanhill caught his arm again. "They say you sat in your boat drinking rum while two schooners went down with all hands right in front of you." His voice was hard. "Men died and no-one likes it. Your job was to save them. That's what the lifeboat's *for*."

"And you were there were you, *Mister* Wanhill?"

"I didn't need to be: it's what's being *said*, and I notice you don't deny it. We're not having any more trouble in here. I had to call a constable last night, and I'd like to ask you again, politely, to leave."

"Like some bloody stray cur after a beating you mean?" he shouted. "With me tail between me legs? No fear, I won't have it, and I *demand* service!" He slapped the bar again.

"If you won't leave voluntarily, I'll have you thrown out," said Wanhill simply.

"You ignorant bastard," growled Tom, pushing Wanhill away. Danny stepped in between them.

"Please, Tom, I'd like to ask you to leave as well," said Danny. "We don't want a rumpus."

"I'm not going anywhere," said Tom, pulling up a chair and plonking down into it. "I'm a simple law-abiding man minding his own bloody business. A regular." He glared at Wanhill. "I've got nothing to be ashamed of."

"Go on," urged Danny. "*Please*. For your own good."

His eyes darted about him and Tom saw that a group was beginning to form near the bar. Tom knew many of the faces, yet he felt threatened.

Wanhill nodded towards the exit, and suddenly Danny and two other men grabbed Tom and started manhandling him to the doorway. He resisted as best he could but they were all young, strong men.

"Let go o' me you ruffians!" he bawled indignantly as they carried him out, struggling.

They set him down carefully on the cold slushy pavement outside and stepped back cautiously. Tom scrambled up and brushed himself down with his hands in front of the three men who stood behind him, arms crossed. He felt totally humiliated but it didn't deter him. He leaned towards the men and shouted past them to the dark figures he could see inside: "And where were you during the storm, Magistrate? At sea, or snug at home in your bloody great house?"

"The sooner we get this done the better," Stoker shouted to his son above the wind as they marched through the dense swirling flakes. "Watch your feet now, there's ice beneath the snow."

"Grace o' God, it's enough to bloody freeze you alive out here!"

"If your mother hears you saying things like that you'll be in trouble," Stoker warned. "And if you think it's bad for us here, imagine what it's like for them poor souls at sea." He pulled the collar of his oilskin up round his neck. "Wind's getting up again and it'll be a blizzard in no time, mark my words. Treacherous."

"Look at that snow piling up!" cried Edward, pointing back towards the cottage. "It must be three foot thick, yonder."

"I know. It's drifting. I sneaked out to shovel it away from the front o' the house first thing, while your mother was in the scullery, but it just comes back."

They strode forward leaning into the raw quickening wind, and picked their way between the banks of snow running like long white sand dunes.

"What do you need to do?" Edward coughed as snowflakes caught the back of his throat.

"See that the lights are still on for a start. They been going continuous now since Sunday, but we don't get snow round here too often so you can't tell what'll happen."

They trudged through the driving snow until they reached the first light.

"Here we are." Stoker squinted through the falling snow.

121

"Snow don't seem to be banking up in front o' the light at any rate." He talked as he worked. "Sometimes the cold or a stone cracks the glass." He examined the lens. "There has to be enough fuel, specially if it's burning round the clock like now, but not too much or the flame's drowned." Stoker peered at the oil levels and seemed satisfied. "When I first started, I learned the length of the wick's important: too short and the light's feeble and just burns out; too long and the flames go all smoky, the glass clouds up and dims the light."

The powerful lantern magnified the flame to broadcast a strong steady light across the water. On a clear night it could be seen over fifteen miles away.

"This one needs a new lens," remarked Stoker. "I noticed it were beginning to crack the other day, so I bought a spare with me." He looked up. "Thanks for coming with me, my son," he said.

———————

One of the lifeboatmen, Frank Wills, walked into Burdens the bakers, on Poole High Street. Jane, his wife, was pregnant and he refused to let her go out in the cold. Their first child. Not planned exactly, but they were both excited by the prospect so soon after getting married. She had been sick all morning, but had now taken a fancy to 'fresh new bread' and he determined to fetch some to encourage her appetite.

There was a small knot of women talking at one end of the counter. He saw one of them nudge another as he came in and they all looked up.

"Good morning, ladies," he said. There were weak smiles, but no verbal response. It was slightly unnerving. Frank cast his eyes around the shop in case he'd missed something.

There didn't seem to be anything out of the ordinary.

The young shop assistant, in her long white overhaul, disengaged herself from the group and stepped towards him. "Well?" she asked curtly, hands on hips.

"No 'good morning' then, Sarah?"

"It's snowing." She was blunt. "How can that be a good morning?"

"I see. Well, can I have that nice big cob loaf there and…"

"The loaf's taken."

"I'm sorry?"

"Put by for another customer," she said stiffly. "Now was there anything else?"

Frank paused. *What was going on?*

"What other loaves do you have then?"

"None I'm afraid. All sold or spoken for."

There seemed to be plenty on the shelves.

"Are you all right Sarah?"

She shook her head and sidled back to the group. One of the women tutted and also shook her head.

"I want to buy some bread," he demanded loudly to the group, restraining his temper but putting a commanding tone into his voice. "It's for me *wife* – she's *pregnant*. It's cold, she's sick, but she fancies some fresh bread."

He laid a sixpence down on the counter, and tapped his finger up and down on the coin slowly. Sarah walked over, silently wrapped up a random crusty loaf in brown paper, took up the sixpence and handed the bread across the counter to him.

"What's got into you lot?" asked Frank.

Sarah shrugged unhelpfully. Frank turned and stormed out past the short queue of customers behind him. Bloody rudeness! They'd never shop there again, that was for sure.

His march was arrested some thirty paces later by a loud female voice whose owner was not used to speaking softly. "Hold your horses, Frankie," it instructed.

He spun round. There stood the formidable Henrietta Greenham, landlady of the *Swan Inn*, clutching her shopping. She was a large upright woman with a bullish countenance, and she could be as tough as any landlady had to be, but despite appearances she was a tender soul. The *Swan* stood opposite Frank's father's house and Henrietta had known him since childhood. She'd come into the bakers behind him and watched events. Mrs Greenham pursed her lips and looked at him questioningly.

"What was going on in there?" asked Frank, bewildered.

"Frankie," she replied *sotto voce*, and glanced around her a little warily. "Come and walk me home." She led the way. "Carry me shopping will you my lad – I get so worried about slipping up in all this snow."

Frank relieved her of the load. "Is it some'it about me?"

She didn't reply immediately, choosing her words

carefully. "Everyone's heard about the lifeboat." She paused. "They're saying things."

"What things?" he demanded.

"Well, I don't believe 'em but they're saying things like you took ten hours to get to a brig at Christchurch and by time you got there some fishmonger had done the job for you." She grimaced, but persisted, "and that the lifeboatmen sat in Studland Bay drinking rum while ships went down all about 'em."

"That's all wrong!" Frank burst out. "The sea was too rough! And we did the best we could! Besides I didn't even go to Studland…"

"I know, I know. There's no need to tell me: I saw Tom Hart just now and he put me in the picture. He's livid."

They walked on a few paces, the hem of Henrietta's long dress swishing in the snow. "It's serious, Frankie. People are saying that you're all lazy… and worse," she said sadly. "And that just sets tempers flying. There's been trouble in town. I went to get George's pills this morning from the chemist and Tom Atkins was telling me lifeboatmen were in a couple o' brawls last night."

"Them people are bloody ignorant that's what they are!" Frank protested. "What does anyone know about the lifeboat unless they were in it? We're volunteers for God's sake, we did our best."

"Well, it's what's going around – and more importantly some folk believe it, so you ought to be careful. There've been complaints to the Mayor and all," she confided. "Gentry, they say. Specially one over Studland way. Up in arms."

He stared at her.

"I'm told there's gonna be something about it in the paper. Official-like."

Frank's heart sank. "We did our best, Henrietta. We honestly did. We couldn't have done nothing else."

"I'm sure you did," she said, touching his arm and smiling. "I believe you, Frank dear. I know your father, your brothers and I know you. I've knowed the Willses longer than I've been married, and Tom Hart's an honest man. Now I've got the real story from him I can go round setting the record straight. But people have got up a head o' steam, you see. There are folk saying you're a disgrace to the town and've let down the lifeboat people. I've heard some really nasty things being said, Frankie. Men spout when they're in their cups. I thought I should warn you."

———————

Sam Hart was not surprised to see his brother Tom at the door.

"Sam…" his brother began urgently.

"I know," Sam cut in, nodding. "I've already whacked a cheeky bastard on the Quay. Come on in. I've got Cain and Bill in the parlour."

Tom followed his brother down the narrow hall. Cain turned as he entered. He had a nasty split lip. "A trophy from Ben Greenslade at the *Blue Boar*," said Cain.

———————

Mary helped to towel Stoker dry as he stood naked in front of the fire.

"So, them lights was all in order, which means you didn't need to go out in the first place," his wife reproached him. "You come back all cold and wet for nothing."

Stoker refrained from speaking and just shook his head.

"I've got some good clean clothes for you here," she said. "I've had them warming by the fire. And that cup of tea for you on the mantel like you wanted. Lord above you're frozen! Not good for a man o' your age."

"Mary, don't fuss," he said simply. "I'm fifty-three and quite able to put up with a bit o' the cold. Anyways, you know it's all got to be done."

"Aye, but not so soon after what you went through on Sunday. Besides I don't see them folk in the town coming out here to help you," she said righteously, and rubbed his back with the rough towel. "They're all tucked up indoors in their nice warm houses; it's only us on this blessed spit o' land that seem to be worrying about it all. It's not as if you ain't got enough to do..."

"Mary, stop blethering." He pulled on his warm trousers. The heat was wonderful. Almost worth getting frozen for. Suddenly he stopped and put his hand up. "What was that?" he cried.

A noise muffled by the snow, but distinct.

"Horses! Mary, hand me the rest of them clothes."

He dressed speedily and made for the window as a black

four-horse carriage pulled up outside. Stoker bounded to the front door.

———————

"What have you heard, then?" Sam asked Tom.

"Wanhill the magistrate was in the *King's Arms* and had me thrown out." Tom told the tale to the mounting indignation of his audience. "Magistrate acting like bloody judge and jury. Said we were all drunkards, manner o' speaking."

"That Wanhill's a shit," growled Cain angrily. "There's no bigger shit than a self-made man, or so they say: you gotter be a certain sort to get there."

"And stay there," added Bill.

"Jack Fisher said the Mayor had a letter saying that we were 'disgracing the town' – that's his words," said Bill. "Some toff over at Studland complained so they say."

"What toff?" asked Sam, remembering their encounter with Alex Luckham.

"Lord knows, but he's mighty riled by all accounts."

"Nobody we'll know, that's for sure," added Tom, stuffing his pipe.

Sam fidgeted. "I met a gent when I went ashore for the rum," said Sam. "Alex Luckham. Cocky hound. Said we were lazy. No idea about the sea, of course."

"Nor have any of 'em," complained Bill. "That's what pisses me off. There's not a single seaman among 'em:

128

Wanhill, this Luckham character, Ben Greenslade, Danny at the *King's Arms*. What do they know about the sea save they live next to it? Sam didn't even know the bloke he clouted this morning, and I had a run-in with that Bart Walker from the school. What in God's name do he know about seafaring? Bloody schoolteacher!"

"What did you say to that Mr Luckham, Sam?" asked his brother suspiciously.

"Nothing," said Sam defensively, but he glanced at Cain.

Tom caught the glance and followed it. "Cain?" he inquired accusingly.

"He said we were just sitting on our arses," blurted Cain indignantly. "Bloody cheek, and I just didn't have time for it."

"What did you *say*?" demanded Tom.

"I told him to fuck off," said Cain, suddenly meek.

"You and your filthy mouth!" Tom shouted. "How many times must I tell you to mind your language. These so-called gentlemen..." He smacked the table. "It's just the kind o' thing to really get 'em going. No wonder he complained."

"We'd been in the boat for hours, doing the best we could," protested Sam, surprising himself by leaping to Cain's defence. "Frozen to death! And as soon as we step ashore there's some feller telling us to do better! What d'you expect us to say?"

"I expect you to be civil," demanded Tom. "Or to just ignore him. Bad language to that sort only ever makes matters worse."

"Oh, so it's all my fault is it?" cried Cain. "Who the bloody hell d'you think you are telling me what I can and can't do?"

"It's not your fault, Cain," said Bill. "Tom, go easy on him. We don't even know it were this Luckham character that wrote the letter. It's lucky for him that *I* didn't step ashore for that rum – I'd have bloody drawn him one off."

"But it's not just this Luckham bloke," said Tom, "it's others. It's all over Poole."

"And you're right, Bill," Sam affirmed, "none of 'em are seamen. Landlubbers all."

"What do we do about it then?" asked Bill, rubbing his jaw which was still sore.

"For a start, we avoid any more fights," commanded Tom, looking at all three of them meaningfully. "You know what it says in the Bible: we turn the other cheek. We explain it all to our families and our friends, and we go about our business as usual. If anyone says anything contrary, we give 'em the true account o' what happened straight and polite. If we can't do that, we *walk away*." He was watching their faces. "You got that?"

There were grudging nods.

"We need to let the rest o' the crew know what's going on," said Cain, "and Stoker." He recognised the wisdom of what Tom said, but would still rather have defended himself with his fists. Tom wondered if he could be trusted to behave.

Chapter Eight

The bulky figure of Rear Admiral Bartholomew James Sulivan stepped down from the carriage. He was a thick-set man in his mid-fifties, beginning to run to fat, and his dark blue naval uniform looked a little tight around the collar and middle. He had long narrow sideburns, but was otherwise clean-shaven, and his fleshy face was almost cherubic despite his years. The abundant gold on his uniform shone out through the falling snow. Stoker met him halfway to the house.

"Sir! This is a... a surprising pleasure, sir," said Stoker uncertainly. He wasn't sure if it was proper for a working man to offer an admiral his hand, hesitated, then did so.

"A pleasure to see you also Mr Stokes," announced the Admiral loudly, returning a firm handshake, "but our business is not so pleasurable I am afraid." He frowned, reacting as much to the swirling snowflakes as to the circumstances of his visit. "Let's get out of this filth before I say more."

Thoughts raced through Stoker's mind as he led the way back to the house. Admiral Sulivan's visit was almost certainly connected with the lifeboat, since he was vice-president of the Poole and Bournemouth Lifeboat Committee.

Stoker's rising fears were at least partly allayed by knowledge that, regardless of his rank, the Admiral was a remarkably thoughtful and benevolent man. He was well-liked and his ability to befriend many was aptly illustrated by the fact that he was a close friend not only of the radical naturalist Charles Darwin but also of many senior clergymen who detested Darwin because of his new ungodly

131

theories. Few men managed to successfully keep a foot in both camps.

Stoker took the Admiral's hat in the hallway, conducted him into the front room, then offered him the only armchair by the fire, which the Admiral filled snugly. Despite the feeble fire it was barely warmer inside the house than outside. Having only just settled, the Admiral hoisted himself to his feet again when Mary entered looking somewhat shy.

"Mrs Stokes!" he cried heartily, taking her hand and inclining his head. "I do apologise for calling upon you unannounced like this, and so early too. A dashed inconvenience for you I'm sure."

"Not a bit of it, Admiral," Mary replied, attempting a certain gentility which the occasion seemed to demand but wishing she'd had time to tidy up. "You are most welcome, sir. Can I offer you something to drink? A cup o' tea and some cake, sir, or maybe a glass o' port to keep out this bitter cold?"

"Mrs Stokes," he said jovially, "I think at this moment I'd give back Gibraltar for a hot cup of tea."

Mary smiled and nodded and retreated towards the kitchen.

"Ah... Mrs Stokes!" the Admiral called, suddenly remembering something. "Could I perhaps trespass upon your kindness for one thing further: would you mind taking care of my coachman?"

"Of course Admiral. I'll call him in and get him warmed and fed."

"Much obliged to you Mrs Stokes. Thank you."

The Admiral sat down once more.

Stoker had taken the opportunity of the distraction to hastily heap more precious coal upon the fire to make sure the Admiral was comfortable. He made a mental note to try to blag a sackful of the stuff next time he saw a collier on the Quay. As Mary departed, he pulled up an old straight-backed wooden chair to be closer to his important guest.

The Admiral took in the lowly surroundings: practically bare walls, no carpet except for a threadbare fireside rug, the limited and poor quality furniture. Yet he could not offend his humble host by refusing the best chair, the extra coal on the fire, or the offer of food and drink. Indeed the Stokes' kindness made his task all the harder. He steepled his fingers, prayer-like, resting his chin on his fingertips.

"Mr Stokes, I am sorry to say that we have a difficult situation with which to contend, and I regret intruding upon your home in this manner in order to address it." He sighed, then took the plunge. "You may know that in the town there has been some, er, criticism of the lifeboat since the gale of Sunday last."

"No, sir, I didn't know it," said Stoker, his heart sinking. "We're a might cut off here you see, sir. What have folk been saying?"

"I should state," began the Admiral earnestly, "that I, personally, by no means attach any credence to what I have heard, but this sort of thing creates an atmosphere in which anything could happen and it's up to us to discuss it, and to decide upon the most appropriate response." He cleared his throat. "Well, Mr Stokes, not to put too fine a point on it, there has been a number of complaints that the lifeboat did not fulfil the duty expected of it during the gale." He held up a hand to stifle Stoker's protest. "Specifically, that the lifeboat, though well-placed, did not go to the aid of two schooners which subsequently went down with all hands on Poole Bar; that despite being at sea in the vicinity it did not assist with the rescue of any other vessels in Studland Bay such that the *Royal Albert* had to attend to them; and lastly that the lifeboat took too long to reach Christchurch to rescue the crew of a brig and the delay caused three men to die of exposure while waiting."

The Admiral stopped and looked at him.

"Easy enough to say for them that weren't in an open boat in the thick of it," cried Stoker with bitterness, in his frustration omitting the obligatory 'sir'. "Who's putting these things about?" he demanded, his voice hoarse.

"We'll come to that, Mr Stokes," said the Admiral calmly. "Why don't you tell me exactly what happened first."

———————

Tom Hart stood by the fire in the Wills household. Frank and John Wills sat listening. They were very different in both appearance and personality. Frank was stocky, with long dark hair, a round clean-shaven face, and deep set eyes that gave him a meditative look. He was hardworking, yet sensitive in many ways. John, on the other hand, was wiry, with close-cropped hair and a handsome, bearded face. He was a notorious ladies' man, audacious, sociable, but inclined to be thoughtless.

"Joe were saying a brig and a screw steamer went down with all hands off St Aldhem's Head," reported Tom, "and a French brig ran ashore at Chapman's Pool."

John chipped in. "Round Pompey they had a dozen run

134

aground by all accounts."

"I can believe it," said Frank.

They were joined by their younger brother, Richard, who was still a teenager. "I just heard they lost the roof of the Priory Church at Christchurch on Sunday," he announced. "George were telling me. In the middle o' the service it were ripped right off! Imagine that! They all had to run out for fear o' being crushed."

"Aye, that's right," confirmed Frank. "A lucky escape for all concerned."

"I can't believe the damage down along Quay," John exclaimed. "And have you seen Hamworthy Road? Loads o' houses with no roofs on."

"Aye, a lot o' folks in the town are homeless," observed Tom, "and in this bitter weather too. But thank heaven so few have been killed."

"They've started finding bodies along the shore though," said Frank sadly.

"How many were lost in the Bay then, all told?" asked John.

"Don't rightly know," Frank's brow furrowed. "They lost all hands on them two schooners on the Bar for sure – that must be twelve men. Then three on the brig at Christchurch – the *Elizabeth*." He thought for a moment. "The steamer took the crews off the pilot-boats and t'other ships they got to in Studland. But we saw two ships run aground when first we went out-harbour: one crew saved so Stoker says, but the other all lost bar one. So I reckon that's at least twenty seamen, all told, and them's just the ones we knowed about."

John hunched further towards the fire in his familiar dark blue jersey. "Father says he can still remember the gale o' 1824, and people then said it were the worst they'd seen. On Monday I were down the Quay and them boatyards are chock-full o' cripples that limped in after the wind died down. Never seen 'em so busy there."

"Aye," said Tom, rubbing his face with his hands. "I don't mind saying I were never afeared at sea afore till we saw that water out-harbour on Sunday. T'was enough to turn a man's hair grey to look at it."

"And the wind," broke in John, "that bitter wind was like having your face gnawed by a dog. And seas like great cliffs all about us. I could scarce believe it, Frank. Waves higher than a house and wind enough to cut you in two. It were a struggle even for the steamer: she were knocked about something fearful."

"That's the swell you see." Tom shook his head in incredulity at the recollection. "Deep Atlantic swell, with all that wind behind it."

"What became o' the seamen they took off the *Elizabeth* then?" asked Frank.

"A good woman in Christchurch took 'em in," Tom revealed. "People gave food, and the Mayor himself paid the doctor to visit 'em."

"Poor devils," John muttered, shaking his head. "All them hours trapped in a wreck in a freezing gale. It's a wonder any of 'em survived. Still, least their families can count their blessings and that's a mercy. Them others… dreadful to think o' your husband or your son slowly freezing to death. Don't bear thinkin' about."

Tom nodded. "Stoker's upset we couldn't get to them two schooners on the Bar."

"He must be mad!" John countered with little sympathy. He still looked pale, and Tom wasn't quite sure he should be out of bed. "There's no way we could've fetched close enough to either of 'em in that bloody gale. Huge breakers ready to roll us over or smash us to pieces."

"The thing is, Johnny," counselled Tom gravely, "Stoker takes it on himself 'cos he were in charge of the lifeboat when lives were lost. It's natural. Like a general and his army: all the glory when you win, all the rap when you lose. It's gonna haunt him for a spell."

"But Tom, there was nothing we could've done," persisted John. "That's God's truth."

Frank couldn't have an opinion: he'd not been there. "What do you reckon, then, Tom?"

"Stoker reckons we should have dropped down to 'em as soon as we got upwind," said Tom, "and there's something in what he says."

"Nah, rubbish!"

"But we weren't to know the gale'd pick up by waiting," observed Tom. "Everyone said there'd be a lull when the tide turned."

"We could never have got to 'em even then," cried John. "Madness to think any other way. I can still see them breakers. Fearsome they were – never seen anything like it – and we'd all have been drowned: no doubt about it. If anyone's to blame it's not us nor Stoker, it's the captains of them schooners," he declared. "Lord knows what they thought they were doing getting caught against the Bar like that."

"Aye, Sam said that," observed Tom, "but it's easy enough to get caught out if you're not from round here. Who knows. They might've lost an anchor, read their charts wrong, had a load o' canvas blown away or anything. It don't take much in weather like that to find yourself in trouble. Just one bit o' bad luck. We can all get caught out on the water if things turn against us, specially if it comes out of the blue. I been in difficulty myself a couple o' times out there, and all of a sudden you think your number's up..."

Young Richard piped up suddenly: "What happened to you then, Mr Hart?"

"Hmm. Well, best not talked about." Tom liked to tease his audience. "Gives me the bibbers just a-thinking of it," he confided quietly, "even now." He fished out his trusty pipe and stuffed the bowl with fresh tobacco from the pouch in his pocket.

"We want to know all about it," said Richard. He pushed the door to, as if that invited a confidential atmosphere.

"Go on, Tom," encouraged John.

"Well, I don't know..."

Tom knew how to play his audience, and Richard always took the bait.

"Come on!" he urged. "You *got* to tell us now."

Tom smiled. Young Richard was so very eager about everything, and he did enjoy a good yarn. It was difficult not to succumb to his enthusiasm. "Oh well, all righty then." He cleared his throat. "It were years ago now anyway." He lit his pipe carefully and then drew in a few quick breaths through the stem to make sure it was alight. "Let me see now…" He leaned against the mantel to enjoy the pipe and the telling of the tale. "Must have been near enough '51 I reckon – I went out with Horace down into Earwig Bay." The room started to fill with the pleasant aroma of Tom's rough-cut tobacco. "We reckoned we could earn a few bob stopping off the Bay on low water. I was dead keen I remember but when we got to Patchins Point, Horace decided the tide would never go low enough to set the net across to the point at Shipstall. He was right, but I didn't want to waste our trip and I fancied picking some cockles, so we took the canoe right in, and while Horace was laying down the anchor I stepped off and waded over the flats when all of a sudden I thought 'this ain't right'. Something about the ground – it wasn't as hard as it should be, and afore I knew it I was caught in a quagmire!"

He surveyed his audience to gauge the impact. "There I was a hundred yards from the boat. The ground was all like jelly and I was held fast, good and proper, and I could feel myself being sucked right down into it. The more I struggled the worse it got. It had me legs right up past the knees in no time – right over the top of me boots an' all. I shudder when I think about it even now. Trapped I was. Couldn't move, and being sucked down all the time into all that stinking cold mud. God help me! 'This is it' I thought. 'The end'.

"I cried out to Horace and he got the boat over lively like. By this time I was terrified, shouting and raving like a lunatic. You should've seen his face – I could tell he thought I was a goner. He threw out the bottom boards from the boat all round me so I could grab one to lever myself out, but the best I did was stop meself sinking farther. So he threw a line and hauled me out. Great strong man was Horace as a young man. He took on the navy champion wrestler at Pompey and they had to call it a draw. Anyway it was hard work, but he dragged me up towards the boat, till I could clutch at some solid ground, then I scrambled over the mud on me hands and knees toward the boat – terrified I were gonna go down again – and he grabbed the arse of me trousers and pulled me into the boat over the transom. We were both done in I can tell you. Thank God the canoe's got such a shallow draft or Horace'd never have gotten close enough to reach me in time."

"Shit," said Frank quietly, filling the space at the end of the short tale. "You might have died."

"Don't I know it. I stood there thinking if Horace can't save me I'm done for, plain and simple." He shook his head. "And the worst of it is – and this gives me the real jitters – Horace nearly didn't go with me on account of Amy being bad. He changed his mind at the last minute and if he hadn't o' come with me I would've been out there all by meself: trapped and waiting for the tide to come in and getting drowned like a dog. I'd never have escaped alone. And it's that quiet down there – I could've hollered meself hoarse and none would've heard." He studied their dismayed faces. "There look! I got gooseflesh just telling you about it!" He rubbed his arms.

There was a stunned silence. "I stunk like a polecat afterwards I did. Horace took the canoe round to just below Gold Point where it's a bit stony and I washed myself down. It were a warm day and what with the row home against the flood I soon dried off. But there you are," Tom concluded.

Before any of his audience had time to react, there was a loud knock at the front door. Richard knew his place as the youngest, and obligingly went to answer it.

"Now, Frank, how's your Jane doing?" asked Tom during this interlude, brightening the atmosphere.

140

"Nearly six months gone now – would you believe it."

"And she's all right?"

"Aye, she still gets a bit sicky, you know."

"Don't let her do too much about the house mind, will you," counselled the older man.

"You try stopping her."

Sam Hart strode into the room.

"Have you heard?" Sam began.

"What's that?" asked Tom.

"We're all in trouble that's what. They're asking for an inquiry about the lifeboat."

The Admiral leaned back as Stoker finished his account and ran the thumb of his left hand under his chin a few times. He had not interrupted Stoker once.

"What's your own verdict?" he asked Stoker at length. "About the three 'charges' as it were."

Stoker hesitated.

"Come now Mr Stokes. Be *honest*," warned the Admiral. "If you can't be straight with me, then we're never going to be able to help each other. No-one knows I'm here, and whatever you say will be just between the two of us, you have my word."

"Well, sir, since you puts it like that, I'll set it out plain." Stoker gathered his thoughts for a second. "The schooners to start with: I wanted us to drop down on 'em soon as we arrived with the tug, but I couldn't persuade the crew to it. They thought the lifeboat wouldn't survive in all that white water and we'd be chucked clear and drowned." The Admiral's face was all attention, but carried no hint of judgement.

"I blame myself for that sir," Stoker continued, looking down, "for not having the where-with-all to convince 'em it were the best course to take, and that we'd be safe. But we agreed to wait a half-hour for the tide to turn, and after that the gale got so bad there was no way we could've dropped down to the schooners. No way at all. Never seen seas like that in me life, sir." He paused and looked out the window for a second. "All that business with our lifeboat anchor just drives me mad, sir, when I think of it – and I can't account for it neither – but we couldn't move that anchor and we tried everything we knew. I reckon it was right to send the steamer away by herself to rescue all them she could get to, and it was a blessing we did it when we did sir, because the *Marquis of Anglesea* broke her chains not long after."

"And what of the *Elizabeth*?" asked the Admiral, still impassive.

"The *Elizabeth* was a disaster, beginning to end," said Stoker flatly. "We did our best to get there as soon as we could – but we had no steamer and rounding up four horses in Poole took a while by all accounts. We couldn't put out under oars in that rough sea at night – specially in the condition we were in."

"From what I've read in the newspaper some considerable

fault lies with the lieutenant of the Christchurch coastguard." The Admiral folded his arms.

"Aye sir, that may be so." Stoker was wary of supporting that point of view based on the animosity he'd observed in Christchurch; he was also sensitive about criticism of the coastguard as his father-in-law used to serve with them in Polperro. "The way I heard it, sir, if the coastguard had helped Henry Cutler to ready their boat for a rescue, then maybe more could have been done. But I don't know, sir. We weren't there at the time."

"And to what do you attribute any failings of the lifeboat crew throughout all this?"

"Well we'd not done it afore, sir. It were our first time. We didn't know how the lifeboat would bear up in a heavy sea, and as luck would have it last Sunday were the worst storm anyone round here can remember. It were hard to be coxswain and tell the crew what to do when I only knowed what the Lifeboat Institution told me – about her not turning over, being self-righting and so on – and I believed it and passed it all on," he faltered. "But they're all seaman, you see sir: been on the water all their lives, and want to see for themselves first-hand what the boat can do afore trusting their lives to it on one man's say-so."

"I can accept that," said the Admiral, reaching into his breast pocket. "I think I might be the same." He paused, looking down at a piece of folded paper. "Can you read, Mr Stokes?"

"Aye sir, me mother taught me."

"Let me now show you this." He handed the folded paper to Stoker. "It is a copy of a letter addressed to the Mayor of Poole, from a Mr Alex Luckham, a gentleman who lives at

143

Studland. Read it."

Stoker sat and read it. It was an arrogant, inaccurate, and judgemental letter. It implied that the lifeboatmen were cowards, although it did not say so directly.

"This is going to be published in the *Herald* I'm afraid," announced the Admiral. "James Wood, the Mayor, is inclined to agree to this man's request for a public inquiry. Having heard your version of events I'm tempted to concur – just to clear the air if nothing else – for I am told that in certain quarters there is a lot of discontent about all this. In town, some of your crew have been treated badly I am afraid. No-one seriously hurt, but very unpleasant nonetheless: brawling, name-calling and such. So we must nip it in the bud." He checked the time on his pocket watch. "I assume that your crew will corroborate everything you say?"

"Aye sir."

"What do you think about an inquiry?"

"I must say I don't like the sound of it, sir, if I may be so bold – standing up there like a thief at the assizes – but I'll be guided by you, sir, if you feel that's the best way to settle it quick. I know we did the best we could, and we've done nothing to be ashamed of."

"It is vital that the whole community has confidence in their lifeboat," observed the Admiral. He stood and walked over to the window to watch the snow falling. "Would you be willing for me to share your account with Lord Osborne? He was the reverend gentleman who sat with me on the appointments panel when we asked you to be the coxswain here."

"I remember him well, sir. Aye, sir, please do what you

think is for the best."

"Thank you. Well, that's decided upon then. We will respond favourably to the request for an inquiry and try to organise it as soon as possible. Within a week if we can."

"Within a week?"

"Yes, we must nip this in the bud as I said. I'm bound straight for the telegraph station from here." The Admiral paused and looked his host in the eye for a moment. "You have been very honest with me Mr Stokes, so I will do so in return. The Lifeboat Institution is concerned that an incident like this could affect their fundraising – they receive no state aid as you know and depend entirely on public generosity. Further, the Mayor is of the view that a lack of confidence in the lifeboat might harm the sea-trading prospects of the town. He feels that ships might choose to dock elsewhere if they believed the lifeboat was unlikely to come to their rescue when necessary. I think he's wrong, but the important point is that *he* believes it – or at least says it." The Admiral folded his arms. "I also believe the Mayor is keen to apportion blame. He sees all this as a slight upon the town, and therefore upon him personally as its most senior civil representative."

"I see." Stoker suddenly felt the weight of the world upon him again.

"But I still believe it's in our best interest to take this forward and to do so quickly. Cauterise the wound, as it were. We'd need to call some of your crew as witnesses. Who would you recommend?"

"Thomas Hart, sir – the assistant coxswain, and his brother Sam would be fine choices. Good upstanding men, sir, well-spoken. Sam can read and write as well, sir."

"Good. We may need another, but I'll try to avoid it. Is there anyone you do not want to call?"

"From the crew? Cain Matthews, sir. He's hot-headed."

"Right. Anyone else we don't want involved?"

"That feller Luckham?"

The Admiral laughed at Stoker's little joke. "I wish we could Mr Stokes, I wish we could. But there is no doubt in my mind that he will most certainly be called. He will also, I am sure, play to the gallery as they say, and he will clearly use the opportunity to make a case against us as forcefully as he can."

Stoker was pleased that the Admiral had used the term 'us'; it implied that they were on the same side. He fidgeted on suddenly recollecting an issue that Will Redmond had kindly offloaded onto him.

"George Penney might be a problem, sir."

"Why is that?"

"He owns the *Royal Albert*, sir, and in despair when we needed the tug on Sunday morning, one o' my crew promised him five pounds. That's money we had no commission to pay him, and he'll be fuming when he finds out."

"Are you telling me that in the crisis of the storm, this Penney wanted payment for use of his steamer?"

"I am afraid so, sir."

"Even though he knew there were lives at stake?"

"Mr Penney's no seaman, sir. He's – what can I say – a

thrifty gentleman o' business sir," said Stoker tactfully.

"A penny-pinching profiteer," corrected the Admiral, eyes narrowing. "A scoundrel from the sounds of it, and certainly no gentleman. *George* Penney you say? Leave that with me. I will ensure that the wretched man *is* paid by one means or another. Perhaps I'll have a word with him myself. Anyone else?"

"Not that I know of, sir."

"Good. Now then Mr Stokes, not a word to anyone about my visit," commanded the Admiral. "And Lord Osborne and I will use our best endeavours to organise everything."

Chapter Nine

Late at night the same day, a rider came to Stoker's cottage with a short note from Admiral Sulivan.

"Mr Stokes," the note ran, "an inquiry is called for this Friday forenoon and is to be held at the Sailors' Institute upon the Quay. You will be called as first witness and should attend promptly for nine o'clock. From the lifeboat crew I have requested Thomas and Samuel Hart to attend and hope to avoid more. Other witnesses as expected. The Lifeboat Institution will send an officer down from London. I have booked rooms for him at the *Antelope*. Please present yourself to him on Thursday afternoon and render every assistance. Do not be concerned regarding Penney. BJS."

The Admiral had worked with extraordinary speed – an indication, perhaps, of how seriously he viewed the situation. For Stoker, it meant a sleepless Wednesday night, worrying about what might happen. He tried to brush it all off and make light of it for Mary's sake – he didn't want her to see how concerned he really was.

But she knew, said nothing, and felt powerless.

It was now Thursday, and as soon as it began to grow light Stoker slipped out of the house before the rest of the family was up. He'd decided to meet his old friend George King for the morning. It was an opportunity to occupy his time and take his mind off the inquiry; he also needed to visit Poole to speak to some of the crew and to meet the official from the Lifeboat Institution. George was a pilot and Stoker could hitch a lift into town with him when his friend piloted a ship into the harbour.

George and others like him were called on by captains unacquainted with the area who required navigational assistance. These days, taking a pilot on board was often a condition of insurance, so even those familiar with an area did not like to take the risk of running aground. Poole was not a busy port by the standards of, say, Liverpool, but nonetheless thousands of vessels entered the harbour each year – both British and foreign.

George was a quiet sort, but somehow always good company. They set out in his cutter to wait on Pilot Point for any vessels seeking passage into Poole from the Channel. It was a cold, crisp, clear morning: no longer snowing, but not likely to be warm enough to allow the snow on the ground to melt for some time. George went quietly about his business, and Stoker was too preoccupied with his own thoughts to exchange more than a few words with the hand on duty in the pilots' hut.

Despite the early hour, they didn't have to wait long for a tired-looking brig with heavily-mended sails to hove to and hoist a pilot jack at her fore.

From a distance Stoker had noticed that she sat rather low in the water, and it was even more apparent as he and George pulled alongside her. They scrambled up the ship's side. She was the *Susannah* and, as her master Nathaniel Weston explained, she was bound from North Shields to Teignmouth laden with 280 tons of coal. There was water in the hold and the ship needed urgent attention. Poole's shipyards, though much diminished in both size and prestige in the last fifty years, were still well-equipped to deal with the problem.

Captain Weston was a smartly-dressed fellow, with an

open honest face, and content to pay the stated pilotage fee without negotiation. They shook hands on the deal, and then Stoker ordered the hand to follow them in the cutter, so that he could get back home afterwards.

"Thank you captain," said George. He stood next to the seaman at the wheel and gave him instructions, while Nathaniel Weston went aft and chatted to Stoker. The heavily-laden, leaking *Susannah* made slow progress.

"She's a stubborn bitch at the best of times," explained Weston apologetically. "All this water we've taken on's only making her worse."

"I can see that," said Stoker. "How d'you come to take on water?"

"Hull's rotten as shit," said her master calmly. "Garboards have gone. This is her final voyage. Poor old lady. I was hoping we could get back this last time without needing attention. Just my luck: the owner'll go up the wall. I tell you, though, it were a blessing we missed the storms you had here at the beginning o' the week. Old *Susannah* would've sunk like a stone in weather like that. We were caught at the mouth of the Tyne by an unfavourable wind, then the Mate got sick and we had to call a physician. When we finally made sail we were running a full three days late. If we'd left to schedule we'd have been right down here in the thick of it. That's providence that is. Someone up there looking out for us."

"Aye, sounds that way."

"What a gale that was! I've heard such tales. We called in at Pompey and they knew all about it there I can tell you. But, mind you, they only caught the tail end of it. I bet you saw some sights round here. Dorset took the brunt of it they say."

150

Stoker gritted his teeth and hoped the subject of conversation would soon change. It did not. And it was not so much a conversation as a monologue. Stoker did not need to speak, in fact was not expected to, but he did have to listen: terrible conditions – who'd have thought it down here of all places? – a hurricane no less – lasted best part of a whole day – monstrous – so many ships wrecked – even a warship was crippled near Weymouth – dreadful that so many lives were lost…

"Why don't they have more lifeboats?" Weston asked suddenly.

Stoker was shaken from his determined indifference to the captain's ramblings.

"Don't ask me," he muttered.

"We need more lifeboats *obviously* – and if we need 'em, why don't Parliament buy us some? That's the way we should do it: get all we need in one fell swoop."

This seemed an unlikely scenario – the current Whig administration under Earl Russell was notoriously ineffectual and was widely derided, particularly in the Tory stronghold of Poole. It was unlikely to turn its attention to such a practical subject. But Stoker said nothing, not wishing to encourage him.

"The Lifeboat Institution does great work," continued Weston, "course it does – very well-meaning and all that – but they're a charity. The country needs more lifeboats and they just ain't got the money for it. It's poor baccy to rely on charity to buy something vital like lifesaving apparatus for men at sea don't you think?"

There was a gap. Stoker was forced to agree with a brief

nod and grunt.

"Great Britain," the captain proclaimed, "well, we're an island. We've the largest navy in the world – the largest merchant fleet in the world – we'll always need ships, and there'll always be gales, so why don't we have more lifeboats? What's a few thousand pounds to Parliament? That's all it'd take. Do you have a lifeboat here at Poole?"

Weston had stopped speaking again. Another response was required. Stoker reddened despite the cold.

"I think so." He smiled weakly. "I mean, aye. Aye, course we do."

"They were busy on Sunday night, I'll be bound."

"Expect they were," said Stoker as diffidently as he could muster, but clenching both fists tightly.

"Heroes," said Weston confidently. "All of 'em. D'you know they don't even get paid a retainer? Risk their lives for a few shillings whenever they're called out. I tell you I'd like to meet one of 'em who was out on Sunday. They'd have a tale to tell no doubt, eh?"

Stoker ignored the remark and, instead of replying, invented a reason to impart some unnecessary observation to George at the helm. Weston took a turn about the deck. Stoker was deeply uncomfortable. He'd told Admiral Sulivan the day before that the lifeboat crew had nothing to be ashamed of. Now he was denying them to a stranger.

Mercifully, Stoker's ruse of distracting the captain worked. When he returned he chose a different subject for discourse: the joys of the British countryside. Stoker was far happier with this line, and did all he could to encourage him – nodding and speaking in all the right places to keep him going.

Under George's direction the ailing *Susannah* avoided the fateful Poole Bar and Hook Sands to the east, and entered the harbour. There were various channels within the harbour but a vessel of this draught would need plenty of water beneath her keel. The Main Channel was scoured daily by the tide and this kept it deep enough for any ship. George carefully guided the *Susannah* past fir-clad Branksea Island with her Castle to port, followed by the Bell Buoy to starboard, then coursed the length of the Channel. At Stakes Buoy they ran north along Little Channel, past the Oyster Bank, to reach Poole Quay. The helmsman brought her neatly to a mooring just next to one of the slipways.

"I thought we might have needed a tug," said the captain.

"No, not in this light wind," replied George, who knew he'd been well up to the task without assistance. "Anyway it'd just be more expense to upset your owner."

"Thankee Mr King," said Weston amiably, handing over the agreed sum. "We'll get about our business soon as we can. Is there a yard here that you'd recommend?"

"Mr Meadus is as good as any – he has an agent on the Quay. Just ask."

"Obliged to you Mr King." Weston touched his cap. "If you're available when we depart, I'd be most willing to employ you for our safe exit. Can I leave word for you some place near?"

"Aye, at the *Lord Nelson*," said George, shaking Captain Weston's hand. "Leave a message for me there and I'll come if I can."

Stoker bid his farewells and stepped ashore once the gangplank was laid down and made for the Quay. He marched purposefully along the water's edge, yet almost immediately started to feel uncomfortable. He heard a couple of people whispering to each other as he passed; a man that he knew by sight didn't return his greeting when he hailed him across the street; another looked away as he approached.

He needed to see Tom, but he decided first to go and check on John Wills, who had been quite weak after the lifeboat returned on Sunday.

He made his way to the Wills household on Lagland Street, opposite the *Swan Inn*.

———————

"We need to speak to Stoker," declared Tom as he paced nervously back and forth across Sam's back room, Admiral Sulivan's note to each of them open on the table.

"Sit down Tom," prompted Sam. "You'll wear them boards out."

"What? Oh, aye, I'm sorry Sam. In a world of me own..." He sat down.

"There's no point worrying about this: there's nought we can do now. Just turn up to the inquiry, say our piece and leave. We've nothing to hide."

"It's not as simple as that. People are mighty upset by all this and we could get a proper dressing down. We need to work out what we're all gonna say in case they trip us up." He came back to the newspaper still spread out on the table. "I still can't believe that letter in the *Herald*! Who does this

Luckham bloke think he is? The lifeboat crew hauled over the coals by some jumped-up gentry – some farmer I dare say – who never set foot in a boat in his life I'll be bound…"

"I know," said Sam warily. He wanted to tell him to calm down but he couldn't bring himself to say it to his own brother. "Let's not… let's not worry too much about him for now."

"But it's all his fault! I tell you something, I'd string him up if I ever got hold of him that's for sure. Some toff complains to that idiot of a Mayor, and we have to go trooping along to an inquiry. What a carry on."

"Easy now, Tom. It's not a bloody firing squad." Sam looked at his brother curiously. It was not like him to get so agitated.

"I just can't get over it Sam. I really can't." Tom was up again and pacing. "We do our best in the lifeboat – risking life and limb to help people – and what reward do we get? Abuse. Treated like criminals."

"I know," said Sam again.

Sam had never seen Tom like this – tense, edgy, flustered – the very opposite of his normal character, and he didn't know how to deal with it. He stood up and stretched. "Tom…" he began. But Tom was clearly preoccupied and didn't react. "Tom!" Sam urged.

"Eh? Oh, aye, sorry Sam."

"I fancy a stroll," Sam suggested amiably. "Let's get outside for a bit. You coming? We'll go over Baiter and get some fresh air."

"What? And have all those folks gawping and whispering about us as we go? No fear."

"Well, put out in the boat then. Get away for an hour or so."

"No, no. I'm not going nowhere. I'm sure Stoker'll be down to see us soon enough. He'll have had a letter from Admiral Sulivan too, and we need to be here when he calls. Agree what we're gonna say at this inquiry."

"Don't let's get worked up about it," Sam advised him. "Just take it in our stride. What's done is done. We did our best, like you said. We just turn up and tell the truth."

"I don't like being put on trial Sam. Being judged by these... people." He spat the last word out. "I don't like being told that we're not good enough. That lot weren't even there." Tom waved a hand contemptuously at the open newspaper before him. "If the *Herald* can print this sort of stuff then what's to stop the inquiry deciding that we're cowards, or drunkards or whatever people are saying. I tell you one thing, we're never buying this rag again that's for sure."

"Who says we're drunkards?"

"Cain says they've got hold of the idea that you brought rum on board when we dropped you off to get vittles. They think we all sat around getting three sheets to the wind."

"Huh!" snorted Sam. "Lot they know. All seamen drink rum, Queen's navy runs on the bloody stuff."

"Right," came back Tom. "But this is what we're dealing with you see Sam: people who don't know what they're talking about. Don't know the sea."

"Well, fuck 'em, I reckon we…"

"Stop that foul language Sam!" Tom burst out. "It's like being here with Cain Matthews. His mouth got us into this mess with Luckham. I've had enough of it and I won't have any more d'you hear me?"

"I think I'll go for a walk," said Sam quietly.

"You do that," his brother snapped. Tom folded his arms and stood staring out of the window at the houses opposite.

———————

"Hallo Stoker!" cried Frank Wills, rising to his feet as John showed in the coxswain. "This is a welcome surprise."

"Well, I'm not sure how many homes round here I'd be allowed to step into." Stoker was mocking.

"Ah. So you know all about the goings-on then?" Frank sat, and beckoned Stoker to a seat beside him.

"I've seen Alex Luckham's letter," said Stoker, "and had some curses hurled at me on the way over here." A sigh. "No-one we know," he added.

"Never is, Stoker," replied Frank. "It never is. All sorts o' people have crept out o' the woodwork to sound off about all this. Don't understand it."

"It's all over town," John told him. "Cain and Sam have been in brawls, and a few o' the others. Even Jack Fisher, and you don't get more even-tempered than him."

"Tom was chucked out o' the *King's Arms*," revealed Frank.

157

"Throwed out?" Stoker was aghast.

"Yep. Beggars belief don't it," said Frank. "How long has Tom been going in there? Dozen years or more."

"That spiteful little bugger Wanhill had him hauled out onto the pavement in the snow," John explained. "Nasty bit o' work. He's the one that pushed poor old Cuppie over last year to make way when he were in a hurry. *Don't you know who I am?* and all that."

"It's lucky for him I weren't with Tom that's all I can say..."

"And we can't go in some shops – they won't even serve us." Frank sounded forlorn.

"Here's a way to treat good honest men in our own town!" said Stoker sadly.

"It's all just lies Stoker," John protested. "None of that lot were even out in it. None of 'em were *there*. They don't know what we were up against."

"Aye, some folk seem to have made their minds up about us already, Johnny, without even speaking to us. We need a chance to set the record straight, and perhaps we've something at hand that could help." He paused. "I came over to tell you there's an inquiry tomorrow."

"An inquiry?" said Frank, nervously. "That sounds bad. What for?"

"Well, I have it on good authority," said Stoker, remembering his promise to keep Admiral Sulivan's visit secret, "that it could be a good way to clear the air and let everyone know what happened. A chance to tell the tale from

158

our side. So I reckon it could work in our favour. Leastways that's what I keep telling meself."

"Will there be a judge, then?" asked John, eyes wide.

"No, no. It's not a court. It's just to get a true account o' what happened. There are no charges, but they're calling witnesses."

"Do Johnny and I have to go?" Frank ventured.

"No, Frank," said Stoker and he watched the younger man's obvious relief. "No, it's me, Tom and Sam that have been asked to speak on behalf o' the crew."

Frank looked thoughtful. "Will that Luckham be there?"

"Aye. Reckon so. I don't know much – just been told to turn up. It's on the Quay – at the Sailor's Institute – starts at nine tomorrow. Don't know what to expect to be honest, but it's a way to tell everyone what really happened out there."

There was a silence while this news was digested.

"I came round to check on you Johnny," said Stoker quietly. "How are you?"

"Oh, there's nought wrong with me!" declared John. "No need to worry on my account."

"Takes more than a storm to keep that one out of trouble," quipped Frank. "He slept for most o' Tuesday, but yesterday he were soon up and about same as ever."

"Well I had to be up to keep an eye on Pop Hayes," explained John. "We were owed some money: we picked two or three bushels o' winkles last week."

Frank offered Stoker his pouch of tobacco, which he accepted gratefully.

"Obliged," said Stoker and started stuffing his pipe. "I've heard that Pop's a bit of a rogue – will do you down if you don't watch him."

"You got to watch his type for sure, Stoker." John lit his own pipe. "They're all as bad as one another."

"We keep our own separate tally though," said Frank. "So there's no danger o' being caught out. Our Johnny keeps us all in order."

"One of the virtues of schooling you see, Stoker," John expanded: "maths and writing means we can't be cheated by old Pop Hayes."

There was the sound of the front door being opened.

"That'll be our Rich," said Tom, "I was wondering where he'd got to." Sure enough his younger brother entered. "Where've you been, our Rich? Thought you just nipped out for some milk."

"I met a gent looking lost near the station. He gave me a shilling to walk him to the *Antelope*."

Stoker laughed. "A shilling! Well I'll be blowed. You'll never starve."

"Said his name was Robertson. Captain Robertson. A proper navy captain too, in uniform and everything. He asked about you Mr Stokes," said Richard, nodding in his direction.

"Did he indeed. What did he have to say?"

"That if I saw you, I was to say that he desires very much to speak with you afore tomorrow, and could you meet him at the hotel."

"He must be the officer from the Lifeboat Institution," said Stoker by way of explanation. "I'd heard there was someone coming down from London. I'd better get off to see him then, get it over with. What's he like, Richard?"

"Grey beard and whiskers. Bit stiff and starchy. I'd say around fifty. Used to ordering people about that's for sure. Wanted to know all about the town and the Great Gale. Asked me what I thought o' the lifeboat."

"What did you say?" asked Tom.

"That me brothers served and we were proud of 'em, and that no-one should be running down the lifeboat till they've taken one out in a gale."

"Good for you!" said Frank heartily. "I reckon Rich has put the bait down for you there Stoker."

"That's right," Stoker smiled at Richard. "Now, Frank, John, I ought to go and see this captain and find out what he wants." He stood up to go. "I'll drop in to see Tom on me way over."

"I'll show you out," said Frank and he led him through to the hallway. As he opened the front door he turned to Stoker. "You know afore we had the lifeboat, no-one would even have set out in that hurricane on Sunday. And what's more without the lifeboat, George Penney would never have let his tug out either, so even more lives would've been lost." He clapped his hand on Stoker's shoulder. "I know you'll be worrying yourself sick over this inquiry tomorrow, but listen to me: no seaman worth their salt round here has an ill word for you. We all wants the lifeboat and we want *you* to run it. We're not having some gentrified landsman from Studland telling us how to do things. We're having the best man for the job and that's that." He shook Stoker's hand on the pavement outside the house for all the world to see. "This'll blow over soon enough! You'll get through it and our time will come. I know it."

"Thank you," said Stoker. The thanks were truly meant. Frank sometimes showed surprising maturity for a man in his twenties, and the encouragement was needed to buoy up Stoker's sagging spirits.

Fortunately, the Willses and the Harts all lived in Lagland Street, so it was a short march up the road for Stoker to call in on the assistant coxswain. He found Tom some few minutes later; Sam had not yet returned from his walk.

After Frank's morale-boosting words, Stoker approached this meeting with something almost like confidence. So he was all the more distressed to find the assistant coxswain in a state of obvious agitation. Tom paced the room constantly as they talked, running his hand nervously across his moustache and mouth, while he imagined the worst out loud.

"They're gonna have us out for sure," he predicted. "You and me – the men in charge – it's our necks, I've no doubt about it."

"You don't know that..." Stoker began, taken aback by the bitterness in his friend's voice.

"Course we do! Why are they having this thing at all?

They're looking for someone to *blame*. Make an example of us. You and me. Scapegoats. I ain't dared set foot in town or down the Quay for two days on account of all the bad feeling – folks staring at me, saying things behind me back, name calling. I've had enough of it."

"Tom…" Stoker began again.

"You know what? Poor Bill was walking along the Quay yesterday and some woman nabbed him and started wailing that because of him she'd lost her son – he were aboard one of them schooners. There's a thing to say to an honest man! Just come away from the coroner's she had. Dreadful. Weren't Bill's fault. Weren't anyone's fault. They're all looking for someone to blame mind you. You mark my words, Stoker."

"So you say." This was becoming a rant and Stoker needed to stop it.

"And I'll tell you another thing. Why have they got the magistrates involved – old Wanhill and the like? I'll tell you – it's 'cos they're gonna take it further. This inquiry is just the first part – oh yes, I worked that out! Get us to say our piece all unofficial like, and once they think they got it sewed up, they'll bring in a judge and jury and have us locked away…"

"On what charge?" demanded Stoker impatiently, interrupting him.

"Eh?"

"On what charge?" insisted Stoker. "Come on, Tom, you're getting carried away here. We haven't broken the law…"

"Well, I don't know. These lawyers… very clever… they'll dream something up if they need to. Whatever suits 'em."

Like Sam before him, Stoker did not know how to handle the situation. Despite their long friendship he'd never seen Tom so inflamed. He had to rouse him from the fret-filled world he was creating for himself.

"Let's not imagine the worst, Tom. It's just an ordeal to get through. Like being in the boat. This time tomorrow it'll all be over with." He spoke with a deliberate calmness to try to help his friend. "Now, I came over here because I've been thinking about something, Tom, and it's very important that you listen to me on this." He raised an index finger to hold his attention. "What I been thinking is that we must say that we *all* agreed it were too dangerous to drop down for them schooners when we first arrived."

"What d'you mean?" demanded Tom suspiciously. "Not tell 'em that you wanted to do different?"

"Aye."

"But why?" asked Tom perplexed. "You were right! You wanted to drop down straight away and that was the best chance we would've had."

"Because it sets us at odds with each other from the start. We need to say we acted as one, show a united front." Privately he was concerned that the coxswain alone might be exonerated and that would never do. The Lifeboat Regulations made it quite clear that the crew must do as the coxswain directed.

"But if we'd listened to you then we might have saved those hands," Tom protested. "If the inquiry goes against us, Stoker, you'll be blamed far more than the rest of us, you've got to say that you wanted us to go in. It might get you off the hook..."

"No," insisted Stoker firmly. "We've got to stand together, you see. That's what I've worked out. We can't let these people pick us off one-by-one. I want you and Sam to say that we *all* agreed *not* to drop down to the schooners. It's important."

Tom stood and stared at him. Then he sat down slowly, holding his head in his hands. "Stoker, this is all my fault. When you wanted us to drop down I should have spoken up to help you. But I didn't because... I couldn't stop thinking of Maria... the children... little Isabel... Sam's wife. I don't know what came over me. I wasn't myself. I were thinking I couldn't bear the thought of them getting bad news... Maybe me having to tell Amelia when we got back..." his voice cracked slightly as he turned away. "I'm sorry."

There was a silence. Tom sat disconsolately, looking at the floor.

Suddenly Stoker understood everything. "You've been carrying this around with you ain't you Tom? Taking all the blame yourself. But that's not on! There were twelve other men in that boat. We were all afraid."

"But I should have stood up for you..."

"And there was me thinking it was my fault because I were in charge," broke in Stoker gently, "and no doubt Cain's blaming himself for being such a surly bugger, and Sam for bringing that rum on board, and Johnny Wills for getting ill... The worst o' this business me old friend, is that it's made all of us feel to blame – as if we did something wrong – yet we did what we could didn't we? Leastways we did what we thought was best. What could we have done different? Can you think of anything 'cos I can't. We must learn from what happened but we mustn't blame ourselves now. It's pointless."

"But if we'd have dropped down when you said, then…"

"Then more than likely none of us would be here now, or you could be blaming me for Sam drowning, or he could be sitting there cursing me because you were dragged under never to be seen again." Stoker reached over to him and grabbed him by the shoulders. "I was *scared* too, Tom, I don't mind admitting it! More frighted than I've ever been in me whole life. But there's no sense blaming anyone for what happened. It's not your fault, it's not mine, we're a crew and we need to stand united at the inquiry. We must pull together."

"You're right. I'm sorry. I just worry that…"

"Perhaps we are all worrying too much," Stoker cut in authoritatively. "We turn up, tell 'em what happened and that's it."

"That's exactly what Sam said."

"Well, there you are then."

He could see he'd given Tom something to think about.

"Now," said Stoker, rising, "you're to stop getting yourself all in a lather about this old friend, you hear me?" He put a hand on Tom's shoulder. "I won't have time to come back later. I got to meet some bloke from the Lifeboat Institution. You'll have to tell Sam for me about what we're going to say: *that we all agreed not to drop down for them schooners.*" He paused. "You got that?"

There was a nod.

"Have you got that, Tom?" insisted Stoker.

"Aye." He sighed once more. "I think you're being very... noble about this Stoker. You could stand to be let off the hook if you told 'em what you wanted us to do."

"We all look out for each other, Tom, on land just like in the boat, eh? The crew is far more important than anything else."

Young Richard Wills was right. Captain Robertson was 'stiff and starchy' – very upright, grim and formal. A good summary. There seemed to be no chinks through to an unconstrained, softer personality beneath the solemn façade. He introduced himself to Stoker as 'Captain Robertson RN' just to make sure Stoker knew he was a proper captain. A naval officer. Not some master of a common or garden merchantman.

"Are your lodgings to your liking, sir?" asked Stoker politely.

"Satisfactory."

"I'm pleased to hear it, sir. Best the town has to offer. Now, sir, can I help you with anything for tomorrow?"

"It is imperative that I see the lifeboat today, if you would arrange that, Mr Stokes. I need to inspect the conditions of storage and so forth and to refresh my memory concerning the type of boat you have here, the equipment available and so forth. The boat is not housed in the town, I believe."

"That's right, sir. Of course I'd be most willing to accompany you myself to see the boat. The station is next to my cottage."

"At North Haven Point if memory serves me correctly?"

"Aye, sir. When would you like to visit?"

"I can go now."

And so Stoker arranged for Captain Robertson to see the lifeboat, taking a coach from the *Antelope*, for which the visitor mercifully paid the extortionate fare. On their arrival, the captain made it clear that he wished to be alone to inspect the boat and about thirty minutes later, on completing this task, the briefest of thanks heralded his rapid departure. At no time did Stoker manage to steer the conversation towards the next day's inquiry for long enough to elicit any advice from the captain. Despite what he'd said to Tom about 'just turning up and giving the facts', he really wanted some guidance from someone.

Stoker was left as concerned as he had been at the beginning of the day. The very word inquiry had an ominous ring to it. He had been called to a local court some years before to give evidence, and he recalled the bewilderment he'd felt on that occasion. Would this inquiry be like that? He still did not understand what powers the inquiry had or even how he was expected to behave. Would he have to take an oath? And as for its conclusions – he couldn't even begin to guess at them. He worried about letting the crew down, about what family and friends would think of him if he were held responsible for what happened. How would it affect his wife and children? Would the Lifeboat Institution take the lifeboat away? Would he be forced to stand down as coxswain?

Even if the crew were exonerated, would people think the inquiry was a whitewash?

Increasingly, a little voice inside was telling him that he couldn't win whatever happened, but he tried not to listen to that voice. Still, there were many possibilities and his imagination was, unfortunately, quite eager to explore them all in some detail.

Chapter Ten

A three storey, high-gabled building, the Sailors' Institute stood at the heart of the Quay. Although physically overshadowed by tall warehouses, it was an important meeting place for seafarers of all ranks and professions. Here they could rest amongst friends, negotiate business, eat and drink, or play cards, dominoes or draughts. It also held a comprehensive collection of nautical information to which seamen would otherwise not have had access such as copies of *Lloyd's List*, the *Shipping Gazette*, and sea charts whereby men might plan their voyages.

The Institute served the spiritual needs of this section of the community as well, since divine worship was held here regularly on a Sunday evening. In fact it was in the large room used for these services that the Poole Lifeboat Inquiry was now being held.

The President of the inquiry was familiar with this room, for he had preached here himself on more than one occasion. Nonetheless, Reverend Lord Sidney Godolphin Osborne shifted uncomfortably in his ostentatious high-backed chair. It was an official-looking chair – more like a throne in fact – that had been brought to the Institute from the Guildhall. No doubt its presence was intended to lend an air of solemnity and authority to the day's proceedings.

He closed his eyes for a moment. *An inquiry! What an absurd idea.* Admiral Sulivan seemed to think it would offer the lifeboat crew a chance to clear themselves, but Lord Osborne did not. The intentions had undeniably been good but he particularly regretted the Admiral's determination to get it all out in the open so quickly while passions were still running high on the issue. An efficiency born of the Queen's Service no doubt. If only the two of them had spoken sooner then he might have deterred Sulivan from rashly agreeing to the Mayor's proposal; but it was too late now.

He looked around the room at the other members of the inquiry panel, mostly engaged in polite conversation in groups of two and three.

There was no question that the Poole lifeboatmen were novices. They had never been on a rescue until Sunday last, and before then had apparently sat in a lifeboat only a few times to receive training. And training in a calm sea no doubt. Now they were effectively accused of cowardice, or at best incompetence. An unreasonable verdict from people with even less experience of sea rescues than the novitiate lifeboatmen.

Yet it *had* been a monstrous storm. A hurricane. The Great Gale, they were calling it. Nearly one hundred miles away in London it had wreaked havoc, but its most violent effects had been centred here in Dorset. The worst storm anyone could remember in this part of the world. Even thirty miles inland in his own parish it had been frightening and caused much damage. Only this morning he had read that the gale had toppled the forty foot dungeon tower of Corfe Castle which had been standing since the time of William the Conqueror, and it had ripped away the entire semaphore station at Portland. Who could blame men for being terrified in a storm of such magnitude? And lest anyone should forget, the lifeboatmen were *volunteers*. Coxswain Stokes was paid a meagre annual retainer, but the rest were only given a small honorarium when they were called out; precious little for risking their lives.

———————

In the hallway outside the inquiry room stood Stoker, arms folded. Face expressionless, mouth clenched tight shut. And inwardly? Squirming. Defensive, annoyed, anxious.

The many witnesses were waiting to be summoned in various locations, but Stoker would enter first and had been requested to wait here until called. He realised he had been picking at a fingernail and made himself stop. He fished out his pocketwatch. It had been his grandfather's and kept good time. It was a little after ten minutes to nine.

He looked around him, wanting the time to tick faster, and was surprised to see Richard Wills suddenly walk around the corner.

"Hello Rich," said Stoker, pleased to see a friendly face and happy for the distraction from his inner sense of unease. "What are you doing here?"

"I helped bring some chairs and stuff from the Guildhall this morning in a cart and Mr Wood said he'd give me half a crown if I'd stay on for the day. I've got to fetch people when they're called, and take everything back for 'em at the end."

"Right, I see. Well..."

"Sorry Mr Stokes, afore I forget," Richard butted in hastily. "Sam said to tell you that Bill Brown's been asked to bear witness, but that he knows what you said to Tom and not to worry."

Stoker nodded. Bill Brown – a bit of a loose cannon. Still, nothing he could do about it now. "So who's on the inquiry panel then?"

"Well, I don't know all of 'em, but there's Reverend Osborne, an admiral, that captain that I took to the *Antelope* yesterday, Joe Crabb, the Mayor... don't know the rest. There's a bloke that father's pointed out to me in town afore now – magistrate I think. Used to be Mayor."

"Not Wanhill?"

"Aye, that's him!"

Stoker swore under his breath. Wanhill's behaviour towards Tom in the *King's Arms* showed that he obviously had some fairly partial views on the subject of the lifeboatmen.

"Is that it?" asked Stoker.

"No, there are ten of 'em all told," he explained. "Oh, another one is George Penney."

Stoker frowned, unsure what to make of that news.

"They've whitewashed the walls in there and everything, tidied it all up – looks really clean." Richard suddenly started as he remembered something else: "They wants me to say that you should call Reverend Osborne 'my Lord', the Mayor is 'your worship', and everyone else is just 'sir'."

"Right."

"I'd better go in," announced Richard. "Good luck, Mr Stokes," he said, offering him a hand. He had large hands, and it was a strong assured grip for a young lad.

Richard knocked on the door and then entered at the distant call of "Come!"

Stoker was alone again and hoped he wouldn't be kept waiting too long.

Lord Osborne had already digested the scathing letters about the lifeboatmen sent to the Mayor. Alex Luckham was the principal detractor and his complaint had been published in the local newspaper, but the Mayor had received several others. The tone of all of them was distasteful: the privileged complaining that those of lower station had apparently not exposed themselves to sufficient danger. Almost as if their humble lives were worth so little that sacrificing them was of no concern.

James Wood, the populist Mayor of Poole, sat next to Lord Osborne wearing full mayoral regalia. Overly groomed, puffed-out chest, and a loud grating voice which made it impossible to ignore him, however much one might like to. It was an unchristian thought, but the word 'popinjay' leapt irresistibly into Lord Osborne's head. A few sharp letters of complaint from the local gentry and Wood had panicked and called an inquiry. He was rattled by the criticism which had been levelled at the local lifeboat, probably because he thought it might catch him in its glare. He might seek to apportion blame because it was the easy thing to do, rather than give the lifeboatmen a fair hearing.

Then there was Admiral Sulivan who sat with Lord Osborne on the Poole and Bournemouth Lifeboat Committee. He was in full dress uniform and Lord Osborne worried that all this trumpery might intimidate some of the witnesses: make it look like a court martial. Still Sulivan was a kindly soul – for a Services man anyway – and had acted with the best intentions: he honestly believed the inquiry would clear the air. Despite his own reservations about the wisdom of holding an inquiry Lord Osborne recognised that the Admiral had put considerable effort into arranging everything. At least naval efficiency meant it would probably all be over quickly.

There was more gold braid on show in the person of Captain Richard Robertson, also from the navy, who had been seconded from the Board of Trade to the Royal National Lifeboat Institution in London. Lord Osborne knew he was a stern officer – clipped speech, unemotional, no-nonsense. The RNLI were worried that the events in Poole would undermine the public's willingness to donate to the charity. Lord Osborne suspected Captain Robertson would give the lifeboatmen a hard time.

The inquiry panel also embraced various local men of standing in the community. All were keen to impress with their neat suits and white collars. Two in particular were important. One was Alderman Thomas Wanhill, a magistrate who ran a number of local businesses including a large local holding-merchants. A self-made man, shrewd, opinionated, and quite young to have achieved so much; in his later forties perhaps. The other notable was George Penney, who owned the steamer *Royal Albert*. Admiral Sulivan had appraised Lord Osborne regarding Penney and his profiteering, although he had found it all hard to believe. He did not want to know how the Admiral had achieved it but he had certainly cowed the objectionable Penney, who sat there compliantly, saying little. He looked uncomfortable. There were three other local businessmen on the panel, who now sat in a clique talking earnestly to each other in hushed tones.

Finally, there was Joseph Crabb, the harbour master. He obviously felt very out of place, and looked it. He sat bolt upright in his threadbare Sunday-best suit, and no-one had even had the courtesy to speak to him since he had arrived. He simply was not important enough. And Lord Osborne realised that this was the kind of indignity and prejudice that he wanted to avoid: the premature judgement of humble men by those with power and wealth. Men who wouldn't even dream of setting foot in a lifeboat. He did not relish the prospect of the lowly uneducated lifeboatmen being paraded in front of these local dignitaries to account for themselves – their clumsy, awkward manner being subject to close scrutiny in a formal hearing. It would be intimidating for them. Their reasoning and character would be called into question before the local lifeboat service had even had a fair chance to get started.

The harbour master saw that he was being observed and Lord Osborne smiled at him warmly, hoping to encourage him. Unfortunately, they were sitting too far away from each other to engage in conversation.

There was one last consideration. This was not a public hearing, but the Mayor had insisted that a reporter from the *Poole and South-Western Herald* be present. Lord Osborne had been introduced to the fellow, but he could not now recall his name. As a veteran in working with the press, Lord Osborne knew that reporters should not always be trusted. Sometimes a story was more important to them than the truth. He had made a point of referring to his own links with *The Times* of London, and even dropped the name of the editor casually into their brief conversation. ("My friend John Delane has remarked to me on several occasions that the duty of the journalist is the same as that of the historian – to seek truth above all things – and I am sure you would agree.") Maybe that would impress the local reporter, or hopefully even overawe him a little.

Lord Osborne opened his hunter pocketwatch. Four minutes to nine. He cleared his throat and all the other members of the inquiry panel instantly stopped talking and looked towards him.

"Gentlemen," he began. "Thank you very much for attending today. We have an important task before us, though one which none of us will anticipate with pleasure: namely to examine the conduct of fellow men in most demanding circumstances, and to determine if that conduct was wanting. I refer, of course, to the crew of the lifeboat, *Manley Wood*, during the Great Gale of Sunday last. The storm swept the whole district, as you know, and at sea played great havoc. In Studland Bay alone fourteen or fifteen vessels were either wrecked or blown out to sea and sunk. We may never know the true tally of lives lost." He cleared his throat. "The judgement of others can be a most difficult endeavour and I trust the inquiry panel will forgive me if I remind us all that we must be dispassionate. We must deal with the *facts*. We are not allowed the indulgence of visceral reaction, intuition, or emotional outburst. We seek the truth as far as we are able. And I ask God to bless us with the wisdom to arrive at a just conclusion."

"Hear, hear," said the Mayor quietly.

Lord Osborne did not even look at him. "I would like to suggest that the witnesses, before they are called, should remain outside and that once questioned should return to their various rooms and wait, in case we need to recall them. This whole subject has been debated with much passion and I fear there is a risk of argument or even intimidation if the witnesses congregate in one place before or after their testimonies."

"I think that is sound advice with which I concur," said Robertson, the RNLI man, with a formal air. There was a murmur of agreement along the length of the table.

"Finally," resumed Lord Osborne, "let us remember that this is not a court of law, and that, indeed, we have no legal status whatsoever. The lifeboatmen of course all serve their community as volunteers; they are not enlisted men. Likewise all of our witnesses appear today voluntarily, and whilst we should press them when necessary to clarify or explain themselves – and we should not avoid challenging them – this is *not* the place for an intense cross-examination or court martial." He deliberately looked the Mayor in the eye. "I will intervene if I think that witnesses are being subject to harsh or unfair treatment." He smiled. "But I am sure that will not happen. Now, Mr Wood has kindly provided the service of young Richard Wills, here, to usher in our witnesses, so unless we have anything further to discuss I will ask him to show in the first of them." Lord Osborne looked along the nine faces, first to his left and then to his right. No-one indicated that they wanted to speak. "Thank you. Richard, would you call Mr Stokes, the coxswain please."

Richard departed.

"I would like you to indicate by the raising of a hand whether you wish to ask questions," he instructed the panel. "After each witness we will confer amongst ourselves privately and we can recall them if we so wish for further questioning." There were nods.

Richard reappeared, ushering in Stoker, chin up, brisk pace, clutching his dark blue hat in front of him, and wearing a suit that he had borrowed from a neighbour as he did not own one. He knew it was too big for him, but hoped that would go unnoticed.

Lord Osborne welcomed him immediately and introduced himself as the president of the inquiry board. "Please take a seat, Mister Stokes," he said. He waved a hand towards the small chair placed in front of the inquiry panel so that Stoker was not left standing lamely in the middle of the room. The panel sat behind a line of abutting tables. The bright bare walls made the space seem much bigger than normal, and the fresh whitewash imparted a dank smell to the cold room.

"Thank you my Lord," replied Stoker and he returned a serious smile.

Lord Osborne was determined to establish an important point early on. "Now, ah, Mr Stokes, we know that you and your men had not been to sea on a real rescue before Sunday, but how often have you been to sea in the *Manley Wood* for training?"

"Some four or five times I reckon, my Lord." His mouth was dry but he kept his voice firm and steady.

"Four or five times, is that all?" Wanhill jibed.

Stoker bridled at the remark, especially from Wanhill, but he was determined to appear composed. "Well, we're all working men, sir, with families, and the lifeboat has only been here a short time. Them are the facts." Stoker folded his arms defiantly.

"And on how many of those times did you encounter stormy weather?" asked Lord Osborne.

"We been out two or three times in a heavy sea, my Lord, but nothing like that which prevailed on Sunday last."

Robertson raised a hand then cut in. "The point is: before Sunday had you ever been in a sea rough enough to fill the lifeboat?"

"No sir."

Robertson tutted and looked away.

"You have not often seen a sea that would?" asked Lord Osborne.

"Oh aye, my Lord, but there's been no chance to set out in a storm like that since the lifeboat arrived. Storms ain't common here, and a storm raging fit to blast out the church windows and blow down trees is a mighty rare beast in these parts. I've never seen a tempest like it."

"Quite. Now turning first of all, if we may, to the two schooners – the *Pallas* and the *Augusta* – the steamer towed you past them I understand?"

"Aye, my Lord. They were to the sou' sou-east of the swatchway – that's the Swash Channel on your map here." Stoker stood and pointed to the position on the large chart displayed on an easel to one side of the panel.

"And this was at what time?" demanded Wanhill.

"About twelve o'clock when we first saw 'em." Stoker returned to his seat.

"How did they appear, to you?"

"They were both lying at anchor with signals o' distress flying."

"Were they driving?" asked the Admiral.

Lord Osborne frowned at his naval colleague. "Driving? Could you explain that for me, Admiral?"

"I'm sorry, my Lord. Let me rephrase: was the wind pushing the schooners onto the sandbank despite them being at anchor?"

"I couldn't say for certain, sir," said Stoker. "The sea kept breaking so high that I couldn't see 'em well enough."

The Admiral continued. "And where were the crew of the schooners?"

"At that point we couldn't see whether they were in the rigging or on the deck."

Wanhill raised a hand to attract Lord Osborne's attention, who nodded to allow him to proceed. "The plan was for the steamer to tow you near to the schooners," stated Wanhill, "then row across when you were close enough."

"Aye, that was our plan," admitted Stoker cautiously.

"Then why didn't you carry it out? What stopped you?" insisted Wanhill, suddenly forceful.

"We were stopped by the heavy sea prevailing at the time, sir." Stoker countered Wanhill's belligerence with a calm civility, despite the quickening thuds in his chest. "We tried rowing the boat and made no headway, we kept shipping so much water. It were more than we could do to keep her head into the wind and we could see no possibility o' the steamer bringing us closer. It were too dangerous."

Robertson leaned forward. "Don't you think the boat had sufficient buoyancy to have stood the sea?"

"I don't know how she would have acted, but I don't think we should have got through it. The only other way there was of reaching them schooners was by dropping down from the steamer, but I don't think we could've got near enough to drop down to either vessel and take off the crew." Stoker paused as he realised he needed some justification for that statement. "As far as I could see, the schooners were already riding on the breakers."

"Which means what exactly?" asked Lord Osborne.

Admiral Sulivan stepped in before Stoker could speak. "It means, my Lord, that the schooners were in the shallows near the sandbank. There was so little sea under them that the waves were breaking on the sand all about them."

"I see. Thank you, Admiral." Lord Osborne nodded appreciatively. "So, the steamer towed you on past the schooners and anchored upwind as I understand it, and to the west of the Swash Channel. What was the time at this point, Mr Stokes?"

"We were at anchor at about half past twelve o'clock, where we waited half an hour hoping that when the tide turned things might ease a bit, but that weren't to be. We couldn't even see the schooners then."

"Why was that?"

"The lifeboat sits low in the water and there was mountains o' sea, my Lord, and it were raining so hard that at times we couldn't see more than two or three boat lengths. The steamer left us, went to see where the schooners were, and afterwards came back and someone on board the steamer said the vessels were gone. We'd stayed at anchor in Studland Bay."

"And there you stayed for the rest of the afternoon." Wanhill almost spat out the words.

Stoker looked down, but said nothing. He wanted to rage. To leap up and grab Wanhill by the throat. He tightened his jaw muscles and glared at Wanhill but knew he must stay silent and outwardly calm. Wanhill *wanted* to rattle him, and Stoker was determined not to rise to the bait.

Captain Robertson held up a newspaper and thumbed through it to the right page. "I'd like to return to the point where you first arrived and considered being dropped down to rescue the crew of the schooners. In the *Poole and South-Western Herald* of yesterday, the master and engineer of the steamer reported: 'We went out round the bar, and the lifeboat's crew said there was too much sea and that they could not do anything to save the ships' crews'. Was that said?"

"Yes, I believe it was passed along the boat," said Stoker guardedly.

"Was that *your* opinion as well, Mr Stokes?" demanded the Admiral.

Stoker looked at the Admiral very deliberately. "Yes, sir, it was."

The Admiral raised an eyebrow in surprise. He thought he had given Stoker the opportunity to exonerate himself.

"We discussed it and we were in agreement," emphasised Stoker. "Too dangerous."

The Admiral realised that Stoker had decided to support his crew and respected him for it. An honourable way to behave. Stand or fall together.

"Thank you," said the Admiral, sitting back in his chair, and Stoker knew that he had understood.

Lord Osborne consulted his notes. "And when the steamer returned to you it was at this point that a pilot-boat, er, the *Marquis of Anglesea*, hoisted a signal of distress and the steamer took up those on board."

"Let me ask you," Captain Robertson began, "if you were to windward of these vessels you could easily have dropped down on them, surely?"

"Yes we could've, but we could not get the anchor up then."

"It seems a very unaccountable thing that you could not raise the anchor," the captain observed suspiciously.

Wanhill sighed. "Did you make *any* attempt to get up the anchor?"

"Course we did!" growled Stoker, irritated by the implied accusation.

"Why could you not cut the anchor rope?"

"It would not do to leave the anchor there."

"You would rather let men lose their lives, than lose your anchor!" Wanhill exclaimed. *What a smug little bastard he was.*

"No," said Stoker, returning to his artificially patient tone with Wanhill. "I did not see any occasion why my men should risk their lives. We couldn't row the lifeboat, as I said, and with no anchor we wouldn't have been able to secure her either. We would've had no control over the boat. It would have been folly to expose the crew to that peril in such a fearful gale."

Wanhill opened his mouth to reply but Lord Osborne decided to intervene. "For how long did you wrestle with the anchor?"

"I would say we were trying to get up the anchor for a quarter of an hour or more, and in the meantime my Lord, the steamer took the men out o' the pilot-boat."

Lord Osborne produced a sheet of paper. "Now I have a list here of the crew of the *Manley Wood* from Sunday which I will read to you." Lord Osborne read out the list. "Including you, Mr Stokes, there was a crew of thirteen men. Can you confirm that those names are correct?"

"Aye, my Lord."

"Then you had six harbour pilots on board, the rest being fishermen?"

"Yes."

"Do you consider you have command over these men, or, putting it another way, do you think they would have done what they disliked to do if you had told them?"

"I don't know."

Lord Osborne had not expected that answer. "These pilots, in particular, are all intimately acquainted with the navigation of the harbour," he recalled for the panel. "What I mean to ask you is: would they obey orders from you, the same as any ordinary seaman would obey the master of a ship?"

Stoker decided simply to be honest. "I should give up to them and let them have their own way so far. If they settled what should not be done, I could not say it should be done."

"So, on the occasion of last Sunday, when a decision was made about not dropping down to attend the schooners, did you all agree – the six pilots, the fishermen and yourself – that you could not do what you did not do?"

"Aye, we couldn't see any chance of doing anything. We were unanimous on board on this point." Stoker could not help catching the Admiral's eye again, but he was impassive.

185

"When the steamer left you to look for the schooners the lifeboat crew rowed ashore. Why was that?" asked Lord Osborne.

"And when?" added Wanhill.

"It was about one o'clock when we went to Studland beach. The men were near perished and wanted something to drink."

Captain Robertson lifted his head from the notes he was making. "How many of your men landed?"

"One. Sam Hart, sir." Stoker decided it was best not to mention Cain.

"What quantity of spirits was brought on board?"

"I don't know, sir."

Admiral Sulivan raised a hand to catch his lordship's eye, who nodded. "Can I ask you whether you had ever been in a lifeboat prior to the establishment of the *Manley Wood*?"

"No sir, I had not."

"And when you say that you do not believe the lifeboat would have got through the breakers near the schooners, what do you think would have happened?"

"I believe that at the time in question, sir, the lifeboat would have rolled over and over in the seas."

"Have you not heard of the lifeboat station at Yarmouth?" asked Wanhill self-approvingly. "The boat there *regularly* attends vessels riding in a breaking sea on the outlying bank."

Stoker bit his lip. "No sir, I have not heard o' that, but I don't think the *Manley Wood* could have lived in the sea that prevailed on Sunday."

"I should point out, if I may," broke in Captain Robertson with unexpected support, "that the surf lifeboats used on the east coast are a larger and rather differently constructed boat to the one stationed here. They are specifically designed to meet the peculiarly rough shallow seas which prevail on that part of the coast. The *Manley Wood* has a deeper draught."

"I also think it is only fair, gentlemen," observed Lord Osborne, hoping to kill the issue, "that we all bear in mind that the crew of the *Manley Wood*, unlike the Deal lifeboatmen and others, are unaccustomed to such boisterous seas."

"I only wanted to show," said Wanhill arrogantly, "that from what I have read there was not more danger on Sunday than lifeboats usually incur."

Wanhill was surely being malicious in persisting with this point.

"But surely," replied Lord Osborne calmly, "it is only reasonable to admit that unpractised men can hardly be expected to do what practised men can accomplish."

Wanhill persevered in the tone and with the manner he assumed when he was on the Bench: "I simply wish to give these men full confidence in their boat..."

As if a bloody jumped-up magistrate – a seasoned landlubber – could inspire confidence in experienced seamen with mere words! Stoker resisted the temptation to shake his head at the man's audacity.

But Wanhill was still talking: "... and confidence is

something the lifeboatmen will need for the future."

"That is very considerate of you, Mr Wanhill," said Lord Osborne smoothly, "but could I respectfully request that we bring our attention back to the *present* time."

Then the Mayor picked up on the point. "Do you think, Admiral, that you would normally have expected a lifeboat crew to have behaved differently in the circumstances in which the *Manley Wood* found herself?"

The Admiral recognised the trap that was being created. "I would always expect an experienced crew to behave differently from a newly-recruited one. I'm sure Mr Stokes would agree with me there?" He raised an eyebrow towards Stoker.

"Aye, sir."

"Even I did not realise that the Yarmouth lifeboats were a different design to the one stationed here," admitted the Admiral. "An experienced crew riding breakers in a boat specially designed for the purpose is obviously a very different thing from the situation we had here on Sunday."

"I agree," said Robertson.

Lord Osborne needed to wrap this up quickly. "Does any other member of the panel have questions which they desire Mr Stokes to answer?" There were no responses. "Good. Thank you, Mr Stokes. We are obliged to you for attending. Could we further request that you wait outside in case we should need to recall you?"

"Aye, my Lord."

Lord Osborne waved a hand towards the door and Richard

Wills leapt up to open it for Stoker. He caught Stoker's eye as he did so. Whatever turmoil had been going on inside the man, outwardly he had remained in control. It had been a solid performance and Richard was glad that Stoker had managed to stand up for the lifeboatmen so well – he'd never been wrong-footed or allowed himself to get upset despite obvious provocation from Wanhill. Stoker smiled faintly but said nothing as he passed him by. He would have given anything for a stiff drink.

Chapter Eleven

"Richard," called Lord Osborne. "Don't summon the next witness yet. I think the panel must consider Mr Stokes's testimony in private." He nodded towards the door. "If you could wait outside, there's a good lad."

The newspaper reporter half-stood. "Er…" he began.

"Yes, you too, Mister um… Thank you. If you would." Lord Osborne smiled. "We will call you both back shortly," he assured them.

"I am glad we have time for discussion, my Lord," said Captain Robertson as Richard closed the door behind him, "for without wanting to prejudice the views of others, I feel we already know the essential cause of the events on Sunday."

"Simple inexperience?" offered Lord Osborne.

"Precisely so. The lifeboat was established in Poole a year ago and in all that time there has been no occasion to use it, save for a few experimental outings in calm or slightly rough water for training purposes."

"Still, I was surprised the coxswain expressed no particular regret for what happened," observed the Mayor.

Wanhill opened his mouth to add to this, but Lord Osborne headed him off.

"What stipulation does the Institution make regarding training?" he asked, picking up on Robertson's point.

"I have the regulations here," replied Robertson, thumbing through the papers in front of him. "Yes, the regulations state: *'The boat shall be taken afloat for exercise, fully manned, once during each quarter, sometimes in rough weather'*."

"I had no idea it was so infrequent," said the Mayor, and he looked to other panel members to gauge their reaction.

Robertson continued: "The lifeboat was stationed here in January 1865 and since then this crew has undertaken four or five training exercises – which is about what we would recommend – but they've obviously never been out in a real storm: the coxswain admits they'd never even seen the boat fill with water before Sunday. And with no experience of a storm, they were obviously totally unprepared for a gale of the intensity of Sunday last. A few trial runs in choppy water could never prepare them for that. They didn't know what to expect from the boat; how she would behave."

"I'm not sure inexperience is a good enough excuse for all that loss of life…" began Wanhill.

"We're not looking for an *excuse*." Robertson issued a mild, though earnest rebuke. "We're looking for *reasons*. In my view, inexperience is surely at the heart of what happened, but that does not necessarily excuse it, and it's certainly not the only matter for consideration when coming to our conclusions."

"I can accept that," conceded Wanhill. "One factor I would like to test with the other witnesses is this: did the coxswain make the decisions and the rest simply obey him, or was there really some kind of collective decision-making process as we have just been told?"

"We do need to know more about the principles behind the chain of command," acknowledged Lord Osborne. "I think the Regulations can help us with that as well, can they not, Captain?" he eyed the man from London.

"Yes, my Lord," Robertson answered, as he finished a note he was making. "The Regulations are quite specific; it is in section eight if you have a copy before you, but I shall read it out: '*As the efficiency of a life-boat depends on the good training and discipline of her crew, the strictest attention must be paid by them to the directions of the coxswain on all occasions connected with the service*'." He stopped reading and looked up. "So, it is very clear that the coxswain is in command and makes the decisions."

"Would they all know this?" asked the Mayor.

"Certainly," said Robertson. "A copy of the regulations is posted inside every lifeboat station. Yesterday I saw for myself that the Poole station has complied with this."

"I don't expect any of them can read," Wanhill asserted. "What then?"

"Coxswain Stokes can read," said the Admiral, "and for those who can't the regulations are read out to them when they volunteer and on at least one training session each year, so they should all be familiar with the contents."

"Thank you, gentlemen," said Lord Osborne, penning a few words to remind himself. "I will make a point of asking our next three witnesses about all of this." He reasoned that it was better for him to ask these questions of the lifeboatmen than the hostile Wanhill.

The Mayor nodded. "It is an important issue. Another vital factor, to my mind, is that the coxswain seemed to have little confidence in his lifeboat."

"And bravery is all about confidence," chimed in Wanhill.

"They have no *experience*," corrected Robertson firmly. "No significant experience with the boat, no experience of real rescues, and no experience of a storm of the intensity of Sunday last."

"Yes but, gentlemen, please!" cried Wanhill irritably. "Perhaps we are too keen to defend them! These are not landsmen. They are not ignorant of the sea and its ways, and it was their *duty* to try and save the lives of others. This was their acknowledged role within our community. Am I alone in thinking that they should have attempted *something* instead of just sitting there playing with the anchor and drinking rum!"

"Most decidedly," added the Mayor "and there is certainly blame somewhere – amounting to cruel negligence or a want of capacity – and we must root it out! Poole people will not be satisfied with anything short of a thorough investigation."

There were sounds of agreement from some of the panel.

"And what would this inquiry be saying now if the lifeboatmen had all drowned in the attempt?" prompted Lord Osborne.

"That they died bravely," protested Wanhill. "Doing their duty."

"Hear, hear!" cried one of the local men.

"In the event, such accolade would have been a poor consolation to their families, I fear," Lord Osborne noted gravely.

"Rather like the lifeboatmen in Yarmouth," added the Admiral, "which you threw at Mr Stokes as an example of how he should have behaved, Mr Wanhill."

"I'm sorry, I don't understand."

"I thought you knew." Lord Osborne was taken aback. "Four weeks ago, the Yarmouth lifeboat, the *Rescuer*, turned over in a heavy sea and twelve of the crew drowned, including the coxswain. Nine widows and twenty-two children all unprovided for."

There was a silence.

"Did you not know?" queried Lord Osborne quietly.

Wanhill had the decency to look embarrassed.

"I thought that was the point you were making to coxswain Stokes earlier, Mr Wanhill. That he should have led his crew in, despite knowing what happened in Yarmouth." Lord Osborne raised his eyebrows. "The *Rescuer* capsized in a heavy shallow sea when her keel hit a sandbank. A very similar situation to that in which the *Manley Wood* found herself on Sunday when contemplating a drop-down for the schooners."

"I should mention," said Robertson, breaking into an awkward lull, "that the *Rescuer* wasn't an RNLI lifeboat. The boat was ten years old, she wasn't self-righting like the *Manley Wood* and the crew weren't wearing lifejackets either, so it was a somewhat different situation."

"And men risk their lives every day in Her Majesty's Navy defending our country, isn't that so, Admiral?" blustered the Mayor, trying to assist the flagging Wanhill.

"But this is *not* the navy. That's the point," said Robertson emphatically, stabbing the table in front of him with an index finger and suddenly angry at the Mayor's stupidity. "Good Lord, sir, I should know! The navy is an experienced, disciplined service with paid officers and crew. The Lifeboat Institution is a *civilian* organisation manned with *volunteers*."

Now the Mayor was silenced too.

"I think we should have the next witness," said Lord Osborne tactfully. He had been wrong about Robertson. He was harsh, but he was also fair. He consulted his list. "It's Thomas Hart, the assistant coxswain. Let us hear what he has to say."

Richard was recalled and sent to fetch Tom, who duly entered. He was clearly very nervous and fingered the rim of his cap, which he held before him, almost obsessively. When asked to sit, he perched precariously on the edge of the seat, his face set into a strained rigidity and his features pallid. Richard had always liked Tom and willed him to be strong, for his stress was plain to see. Lord Osborne pitied him and hoped to keep his ordeal as brief as possible.

Tom's mind was racing and he felt like he wanted to turn round and run out. *It is very important to say the right thing. No slip ups.* He struggled to keep his voice calm, but knew he sounded nervy.

After a number of preliminary questions from the panel, Captain Robertson challenged him. "In your opinion, what opportunities for rescue did the *Manley Wood* have on Sunday?"

"I saw not the slightest chance o' the lifeboat being able to save life, sir. I wish I could say otherwise." Tom swallowed hard and then continued. "But, er, you see sir the two schooners were riding very heavy, and more than likely they struck at the same time as we arrived."

"I see."

Robertson did not sound sympathetic, so Tom continued, heart thumping: "At one point we could see men in the rigging under the remains o' the fore top-sail. That were very distressing, sir, to see them poor souls in such a wretched state, but we could not go to 'em for the sea was breaking all about and there weren't enough water there for the lifeboat." He stretched his collar a little with a finger. "We consulted amongst ourselves and decided to wait half an hour, 'cos we thought there would then be less sea and that would give us the best chance we'd have, but against our belief, sir, it got much worse and then..."

"How was the decision made to wait half an hour before trying to reach them?" Lord Osborne had to interrupt or else this witness would gabble away the entire sequence of events.

"We, that is the crew, consulted amongst ourselves while the steamboat was towing us and we decided it were no use trying to do anything at that point." Tom felt his own wet palms with his fingers. "The weather often changes with the tide, my Lord, and we all thought that the tide running hard with the low water at one o'clock might calm the sea down a bit."

"And how did the crew of the steamer react to this?" Robertson demanded.

"We hailed 'em and told 'em what we had determined on, and they accepted it."

"So, the steamer left you at anchor in the bay. Yet when the Cowes pilot-boat, the *Marquis of Anglesea*, hoisted the flag of distress could you not have got to her?"

"No sir we weren't able to do it, and I'll tell you for why." Tom cleared his throat nervously. "The steamer, you see, was then lying abreast of her. In fact she was nearer to her than we were: less than five hundred yards distance I should say. At that point myself and three more were trying to pull up the anchor of the lifeboat but could not, and..."

"Ah yes!" snarled Wanhill. "The curious business of the anchor."

Wanhill. Tom took a deep breath and tried to calm himself. A muscle in his face twitched involuntarily. "Try as we might we couldn't raise it sir, and that's a fact," pleaded Tom. "Even now I still don't know that we could've done anything different, even if we'd all taken the strain."

"Do you deliberately state," started Wanhill aggressively "that if all thirteen hands you had on board got hold of the rope they could not have weighed the anchor?"

"We tried to do our best," Tom implored. Even he thought it sounded plaintive.

"I don't doubt that," said Wanhill, waving a hand dismissively. He felt he'd made his point.

"Surely," broke in Admiral Sulivan, "if you wanted to get up the anchor you would have done better to have all the crew at the warp, rather than having half of them at the oars."

"The warp is a nautical word for a rope is it not?" asked Lord Osborne.

"Yes, my Lord."

"Thank you. Please answer the question, Mr Hart."

"There were three or four of us besides myself straining at the warp. The rest were pulling with oars to help the anchor break free from whatever held it, and to be sure we would make headway so soon as the anchor were up."

Sulivan caught Robertson's eye and shook his head slightly. Neither of the naval officers believed that the lifeboatmen had pursued the best tactic to raise the anchor, but both realised that further questioning on this point would achieve little.

"How many times have you been out with the boat?" Sulivan asked.

"Sunday made my fifth time."

"Were you never in service with a lifeboat before this?"

"No, sir."

Lord Osborne again: "I'd like to ask you about the chain of command, Mr Hart, when it comes to making decisions that affect the crew. Do you feel that Mr Stokes holds sway over you all?"

"Well, my Lord, to a point that is the way of things." Tom coughed. He could do with a drink of water. "Stoker, that is Mr Stokes the coxswain, sir, he takes the lead as it were but he knows that we're all volunteers and that's the way we're treated."

"So, for example, if the coxswain wanted you to pursue a particular course of action with which you did not agree, what would you do?"

"Er, I should put my view to the rest and we should decide between us."

"What if he asked you to do something which might endanger the lives of the crew?"

"Well..." Tom fidgeted in the hard wooden seat. "I suppose I'd ask him to think again, my Lord, if the rest o' the crew were of the same opinion."

"And finally, Mr Hart, the decisions that were made in the boat on Sunday, did they have the support of the whole crew?"

Tom had anticipated this question and had rehearsed a response in his head, but his mind suddenly went blank and he groped desperately for an answer. "Um, aye, er... that's the way it was my Lord. Aye," he said again. "That is, we all thought the same. No dissenters."

Lord Osborne studied him carefully for a moment. Tom thought he'd seen right through him. Then he smiled. "Thank you, Mr Hart. Unless there are any further questions I think we can let you go for the moment." Lord Osborne looked along the panel, then nodded. "Thank you for attending, Mr Hart."

This concluded Tom's evidence and he was ushered from the inquiry room obviously relieved, but a little dazed by it all.

When Sam Hart entered, he was asked to recount his role in events up until the point where the crew agreed not to drop down for the schooners. He had already decided that he was going to do exactly what he'd told his brother to do: simply turn up and say what happened. No upset, no nonsense.

"Why did you not even attempt to go to the schooners?" asked Wanhill.

"They were riding in broken water, sir, and there was no possibility of getting the lifeboat near 'em," Sam insisted. "Besides, I don't think the steamer could've got us back over the swatchway – there was maybe enough water but a heavy breaking sea. We couldn't have done any good. I've not seen such a sea in all my life, sir. I've been used to Studland bay for twenty-five years and never known the likes of it."

"But these boats will go through a broken sea," suggested Robertson.

"Perhaps so, sir, but not through as much as there was that day."

"Did it not occur to you that the lifeboat was designed to withstand those conditions?" Robertson pressed him.

"With respect, sir, whatever its design, in that sea on Sunday any small open boat would have turned over or been smashed to staves."

"Why did you go on shore?" asked Wanhill.

"Well, sir, after the steamer left us, we knew we'd have a wait. One o' the men were near exhausted and we went in to see if we could get some vittles."

"How long were you on shore?"

"About ten minutes, sir."

"And you came back with a gallon of rum. How much did the crew drink?"

"Beg pardon sir, but it weren't a gallon. It were a quart jar," Sam corrected him, "and then not full by the weight of it. But

200

the skipper, he didn't let us have much. Just a nip each, that's all."

Dwelling on the issue of rum was not helpful. Lord Osborne stepped in at this point to summarise the events which led up to the moment where the lifeboat anchor could not be raised.

Robertson raised a hand, and Lord Osborne gave way to him.

"I notice you use the standard anchor," said Robertson. "I saw it yesterday when I examined the boat. Do you know how much it weighs?"

"Eight-five pounds, sir."

"Eight-five pounds! Is that all?" expostulated Wanhill. "That's only one and a half sacks of potatoes. Can you lift a fifty-six pound sack of potatoes, Mr Hart?"

"I can sir, but lifting a dead weight on land is very different to hauling it in on the end of a warp at sea even in a calm – let alone in bad weather when it's fast to the bottom. Many o' you gentlemen struggle hard enough with a two pound bass on the end of a fishing line, if you don't mind me saying."

"That's true enough," said Lord Osborne, and he smiled at this man's artful ability to defend himself. He decided to assist. "And in a storm, the boat would be rocking and you all presumably would have been freezing cold."

"Thankee, aye, that's true, my Lord. A storm makes every task at sea much the harder."

"And at this point, and earlier when you had the option to drop down to the schooners – when crucial decisions were being made – was there ever any difference of opinion in the lifeboat as to the course you should adopt?"

"None, my Lord."

"Do the crew always obey the coxswain's orders?"

"We do if we see our way clear, but I wouldn't obey him if he ordered me to do something which would cost me my life."

"If the steamer had taken the boat in tow," asked the Admiral, "could the lifeboat crew have saved the lives of those on board the vessels in the inner bay – the *Marquis of Anglesea* and the *Figaro*?"

"Aye sir, but we could not get up the anchor."

"Why did you not slip your anchor?" asked Captain Robertson. He looked at Lord Osborne. "I mean *cut* the anchor cable?"

"If we could've managed the boat we would have slipped her anchor, sir, but in them conditions we would've had no control; there was too much sea running."

"Supposing you had slipped your anchor, could not the steamer have towed you up?" asked the Admiral.

"I question whether she could. It was as much as she could do to get back herself."

There were a few more questions. Minor details. Then suddenly Sam realised that Lord Osborne was thanking him and he was on his feet ready to leave the room. It had not been nearly as bad as he expected.

By the time Bill Brown followed as the last of the witnesses from the *Manley Wood*, the inquiry panel had exhausted their supply of original questions and, much to his relief, Bill's five minute appearance served simply to confirm some of the key points made by the three earlier witnesses.

Chapter Twelve

The next witness would certainly be more controversial, and Lord Osborne contemplated his approach. Alex Luckham was the main reason for the president of the inquiry's suggestion that witnesses should not be allowed to congregate in the inquiry room. For Luckham would certainly be outspoken and, since publication of his incendiary letter to the Mayor, he had naturally become the flag-bearer for local dissatisfaction with the lifeboatmen's conduct. There were only two prevailing opinions of the man himself in the community at large: champion of justice for the lost sailors or ill-informed rabble-rouser. Lord Osborne admitted to being intrigued by him, for they had never met. Luckham would be something of a challenge and needed to be handled with care. Manoeuvred subtly.

"Richard, could you ask Mr Luckham to join us."

A united front from the lifeboatmen, coupled with their well-attested inexperience, had made it difficult for the inquiry panel to be too critical of them thus far. Yet Lord Osborne feared that the arrival of Luckham could present a rallying call for adverse comment and analysis, and in particular enable Wanhill to take a stronger line and maybe bring some of the panel more squarely over to his way of thinking. However, Lord Osborne had read Luckham's rather unpleasant letter to the Mayor several times, and he suspected that if given enough reign he would show himself up for what he was.

"Thank you for attending today, Mr Luckham," he said as an immaculately dressed man entered. Luckham was in his late thirties but looked older on account of his grey hair and beard. The word to describe his whole demeanour was 'prim'.

"Please do have a seat, sir," instructed Lord Osborne, and Luckham obliged. "Now I would like to start by asking you to read the letter that you wrote to the Mayor on February 13th, if you will. The letter that was subsequently published in the *Poole and South-Western Herald*." He handed a copy across the table to Richard, who passed it to the witness.

Luckham cleared his throat. "Mr Mayor," he began, voice confident and cultured, slightly arrogant. "In a matter which much concerns the honour of your town, it seems right to address you as its chief magistrate. On all sides from landsmen, sailors – including some who were mercifully spared during the gale of Sunday last – I hear the most strong and decided expressions of *disgust* at the conduct of your lifeboat crew. As a landsman, perhaps, it does not become me to say whether any efforts to save the crews of the ships which were lost would have been successful, but of this I am sure, *not a single effort was made*." He looked up, to pause for effect, then continued. "The boat was towed into a snug berth and there remained whilst vessel after vessel, with flags of distress flying, broke adrift, and I fear their crews perished. During the time the lifeboat was under the cliff, I saw a single man put off from his own smack in a small boat and pick off a hand from another smack which was in greater danger than his own. If any inquiry is likely to ensue, I had far rather this should be treated as a private letter, but at the same time if any real object is in view and good to be done thereby, I am quite at your service to speak of what I saw. My only feeling is that such a matter as the loss of a number of lives, when to many persons it appears that there was a good chance of them being saved had an effort been made, should not be passed over without some explanation or inquiry. I remain, Mr Mayor, yours respectfully, Alex M Luckham."

Lord Osborne could see from the way that he read the letter that Luckham was still proud of it, and the Mayor, next to him, was nodding with such enthusiasm that it would have been no surprise if he had broken into applause at its conclusion.

"Thank you, Mr Luckham," said Lord Osborne, and hastily threw out his first question. "Where were you during the events that you witnessed?"

"I was near the coastguards' station at Studland during nearly the whole of Sunday last."

"Did you see the two schooners – the *Pallas* and the *Augusta*?"

"Indeed I did, my Lord, yes. A dreadful tragedy. They were almost a couple of lengths from the Bar Buoy."

Robertson indicated his wish to step in. "How did they appear to you?" he asked.

"Rapidly deteriorating wrecks sir, with a cluster of desperate men clinging to what was left of them. When the lifeboat passed by, the crews were all up in the fore-rigging. A most heart-rending sight if ever I saw one. I fancied I could almost hear their cries even on the shore."

This last touch of melodrama did not endear him to the Admiral, who detested sentimentality in all its forms. "When a ship is in the shallows it bumps when it hits the seabed," the Admiral informed him as he took over the questioning. "It looks like a jarring motion of the ship. Did you see that?"

"I cannot recall observing that, no."

"So how would you describe the sea around the schooners?"

"At times the sea broke completely over the ships – masts and all – so that I could no longer see them for a few seconds. With each wave, I prayed that no man would be washed away."

"Could you see any breakers?"

"I'm sorry, Admiral, I don't understand," Luckham professed.

"Were there any waves rolling against the sand bank?"

"I see, yes, I do recall seeing a line of them occasionally on the inside of the schooners."

"And what was your expectation of the lifeboat crew, Mr Luckham?" asked Lord Osborne.

On this cue, Luckham trotted out what sounded like a well-rehearsed speech.

"Lifeboatmen need courage, my Lord. I hope we would all agree that it is an essential part of the role and I expected to see it on Sunday last, but I regret that I did not. There was only the *appearance* of courage, an impersonation: they were dressed for the part in lifejackets, they were out in a storm in the vicinity of ships in distress, and they had a lifeboat. But they didn't *do* anything. They saved no lives and indeed did not make any attempt to save life as far as I saw. Perhaps they consider it acceptable to swagger around town with the title of lifeboatmen, but actual courage was lacking on Sunday and I cannot see how anyone could say otherwise. I would have liked to have seen the crew of the *Manley Wood* make an effort to save those men. I should have considered it a very gallant act."

"A gallant act because it was not without danger,"

observed the Admiral.

"Certainly, but no-one was better placed to help those poor souls than the lifeboat, and when they agreed to become lifeboatmen it surely was not without knowledge of the dangers they might face."

"But nonetheless," the Admiral pressed him, "you do acknowledge that there *was* danger."

"Of course. It was a *fearsome* storm. No-one would deny that. We lost ninety-nine large elm trees in Studland."

"Ninety-nine?"

"Yes, I counted them myself."

"Do you not feel, then, that the extreme ferocity of the storm is a mitigating factor when assessing the conduct of the lifeboat?"

"But they more than anyone else had the right equipment and were so ideally situated to help!" His voice rose to a little crescendo of protest. "From what I saw the lifeboat could have gone to the rescue of the schooners; it was just a question of travelling a short distance."

Captain Robertson leaned forward and caught Lord Osborne's eye for an instant.

"Tell me, Mr Luckham, would you consider yourself experienced in nautical matters?"

There was a short pause. "No, not experienced."

"Have you ever served on a ship?"

"Certainly not, I'm a gentleman."

"Ahem," interrupted the Admiral. "It may surprise you to know, *Mister* Luckham, that I am an admiral and also a gentleman. My fellow officer here is a post-captain and also a gentleman. Her Majesty's navy is filled with *gentlemen*."

Luckham coloured dramatically. "I am most dreadfully sorry Admiral, sir, I was not thinking, I, er…"

"So what *is* the extent of your nautical knowledge?" asked Robertson with calm persistence.

Luckham gritted his teeth. "Well, I have always lived by the sea…"

"Rather like everyone in this town," Robertson suggested dryly. "But you've taken one or two voyages I expect as well?"

"Yes," acknowledged Luckham sullenly.

Lord Osborne could barely restrain himself from congratulating Robertson. The captain had done exactly what he himself had wanted to do – to show up this 'gentleman' for the pompous, ignorant ass that he was. Yet Robertson had done a much better job of deflating Luckham than his lordship ever could. He tried not to smile. It was time to use Luckham's discomfort to force his exit before anyone on the panel gave him an opportunity to recoup his dignity.

"Thank you, Mr Luckham. It was so kind of you to come."

At this prompt, Luckham was on his feet automatically and, before he realised it, he was being led towards the door by Richard. He glanced sheepishly at the smouldering Wanhill as he passed.

The next witness was the master of the revenue cutter *Gertrude*, which had been anchored far out in the bay with a good view of the events. The captain believed that, with the assistance of the tug, the lifeboat might have gone safely to the rescue of the schooner crews either by being dropped down by the steamer or letting go their anchor. However, he did agree that in the circumstances of an inexperienced lifeboat crew unused to such heavy weather, waiting for the tide to turn was not an unreasonable decision and, further, that he would normally have expected that to have led to improved conditions.

After him came the chief boatman of the Studland coastguard station who described how vessel after vessel was driven from their moorings. Although he had not seen a lifeboat in action before, he did not think the risks which the *Manley Wood* crew faced on Sunday were any greater than a lifeboat crew might be expected to undergo. Yet under careful examination by Robertson it became clear that he had spent much of Sunday in the company of Alex Luckham and that this had perhaps shaped his views.

Then the master of the *Royal Albert*, Will Redmond, was called. He hovered in front of the panel waiting to be invited to sit. It was the only time that the witness chair looked in danger of being too insubstantial to hold the prospective occupant. However, Redmond nestled into it neatly enough when invited to do so. His employer, George Penney, gave him a barely perceptible nod of recognition.

"Now, captain," said Lord Osborne, smiling. "As someone who closely accompanied the *Manley Wood* throughout much of Sunday could I ask you to describe the sea and weather conditions for the inquiry panel as you experienced them."

"In the town there was great damage, my Lord, as you

know. In-harbour, the sea were rough, as rough as I've seen from the shore – mighty waves hitting the Quay even first thing in the morning. When we towed the lifeboat out-harbour, the wind blew fierce and bitter, and such a great heavy sea prevailed, that we could scarce see forward let alone make headway. Sir, I've worked in Studland for nigh on twenty years and I've never seen the like of it: great mountains o' sea, and the breakers on the Bar and the Hook were fearful big. It were raining most o' the time, but now and then it came a torrent, so to speak, so's a man could scarce make out the bow of the boat when standing astern."

Lord Osborne: "Could the lifeboat have gone out without the assistance of the steamer?"

"No, my Lord. Gale would have ripped canvas right off 'em, no question, and they could scarce have fetched the Stake's Buoy under oars it were that rough."

"Did you see the schooners?"

"Aye, my Lord. They were at anchor in broken water about three cable lengths from the Bar but being driven onto it."

"Do you believe that the lifeboat could have rowed to the schooners directly if you had towed them close enough?" Lord Osborne wanted an independent view on this point.

"The *Royal Albert* couldn't get close in my Lord, on account o' the heavy sea, but we could've gone closer in than we did maybe," Will Redmond reflected. "We acted on directions given by the lifeboat crew."

"You think the circumstances warranted the risk?"

"Aye, my Lord, but I'm of opinion that the lifeboat crew could never have kept at their oars if they'd attempted to row to the schooners themselves. They tried it for a space, but could make no headway despite straining at it for a good spell. The only chance would've been for us to have towed 'em upwind, then cast 'em adrift to be carried down to the schooners by the wind – and so sheer close enough to catch the schooners with a line – and that was our intention on board the steamer."

"But the lifeboat crew refused to do this?" challenged Wanhill.

"They desired, sir, to be towed into the calmer waters of Studland Bay, out of the worst o' the wind, and told us that waiting a half-hour for the tide to turn would give 'em a better chance of a safe rescue."

"Was there any way in which with the assistance of the steamer the lifeboat could have been placed in a position to save life?" Robertson demanded.

"I couldn't say for certain, sir." Will felt uncomfortable. He didn't want to criticise Stoker and his men, even though some of their behaviour during the gale had been questionable. He felt a certain loyalty to him as many seamen do, one to another, based on a sharing of experiences that no landsman can ever appreciate. "I feel bound to add, sir, that the gale were fearful enough to dishearten any man."

"You did not think it was a *hopeless* case, then?" asked the Admiral.

"The thought didn't enter me head, sir, and no-one on the steamer nor the lifeboat said as much to my knowledge. At a time like that we feel inclined to do anything to save the lives of our fellow creatures."

"Supposing," postulated Lord Osborne, "the lifeboat and

yourselves had acted in accord, could you by any possible means with the lifeboat in tow, have dropped down to the schooners, or done anything to save life?"

"I simply cannot say for sure and nor can any man, sir. If we had dropped the lifeboat down we might or might not have saved life."

"You don't say it was impossible to do so?"

"I don't say whether it were possible or impossible, I think it were a great risk to run."

Will Redmond was proving a surprising diplomat in the circumstances, but Admiral Sulivan felt he ought to probe a little deeper before someone else on the panel did. "Supposing you had been without the lifeboat; could you have safely steamed to the schooners?"

"I have every belief that we could when we first arrived."

"Were the schooners clear of the breakers on the bar?"

"They were *on* the breakers, sir, but outside the edge o' the sand."

"I understand you to say that it was quite possible for an attempt to be made to save life with the steamer, but there would have been great risk with the lifeboat."

"Aye."

"Could you explain your reasoning?"

"I believe the steamer to have been a more stable vessel in the prevailing conditions at the time of our arrival, sir, and, more's the point, we would've been able to make some steerageway. There would have been no possibility of navigating the *Manley Wood* in them waters – she would have been at the mercy of wind, waves and tide."

"You would have gone to the schooners yourselves if you had not been stopped?" asked the Admiral.

"We would've done our best."

"So I understand from what you say that it was a thing to be attempted?"

"I thought it was, until the lifeboat crew ordered me to tow them into Studland Bay."

"They *ordered* you…!" cried Wanhill.

"One moment," said Lord Osborne, holding up a hand, "for I fear this is important to avoid confusion. I wish to know who chartered the steamer. Did she go out for the purpose of aiding the lifeboat, or as a speculation on her own part?"

Will Redmond looked a little confused, so Lord Osborne decided to clarify his question. "I want to know, captain, whether you considered your first duty on board the steamer was to use the lifeboat for the purpose of saving life, or whether you considered you were merely helping the lifeboat as you were going out anyway, and had a right to let her go adrift at any time?"

Will remembered his conversation with George Penney and hoped he was about to say the right thing. "We were out to render service to the lifeboat, sir, we wouldn't have ventured forth otherwise."

Thankfully, at this point George Penney butted in. "My instructions to the men connected with the steamer were these: that whenever circumstances arose which, in their discretion, presented a chance of saving life at sea, they were to go out. I would be willing at all times to risk my property if my men will risk their lives."

There was a spontaneous round of applause at this, much to the disgust of both Lord Osborne and Admiral Sulivan, who knew more about Penney's true motives than the man realised. Will Redmond almost gasped at his employer's effrontery. Yet Penney clearly had no qualms about lying.

"Thank you, Mr Penney, we are all grateful for your generosity of spirit, sir," said Lord Osborne. He had to play along with the deception because Stoker's revelations had been conveyed to him by the Admiral in confidence. "I asked my question in the interests of the public. Captain Redmond clearly went out with the steamer to help the lifeboat, but it does need to be made perfectly clear whether he went out to assist the lifeboat into the best position, or with the general idea that if the steamer was more suited to undertaking the rescue that it should cast the lifeboat off and attempt rescue alone. There is also the case of *salvage*." George Penney straightened himself at this. "If the steamer crew saw a chance of obtaining three or four hundred pounds and the lifeboat was in tow, was it possible that the lifeboat might have been left by the steamer in order that she might salvage a vessel?" Lord Osborne glowered levelly at Penney. He already knew the real answer but wanted to make Penney squirm.

"My crew went out in order to render every assistance they could in saving others, and at all times I would expect them to put the interest of men's lives before financial reward... of course," said Penney sycophantically. "That is human nature. But it should be made clear that they are not lifeboatmen and they offered to assist those with more expertise, and so naturally defaulted to their judgements in all matters."

Very neat. Very clever. Penney was clearly smarter and more brazen than he looked.

Captain Robertson knew nothing of the meaning behind these questions to Penney, and innocently changed the subject by directing a question back to Will Redmond. "When the lifeboat crew decided to wait for the tide to turn, was it your opinion that it was not safe to leave the schooners for half an hour?"

"Well, I cannot say I formed an opinion, sir, but I felt we ought to have gone at once."

"So, if the lifeboat had gone down to the schooners when you first went out, could the steamer have brought her back?"

Will knew this was a crucial question, but although his feelings of loyalty made him content to be evasive to help the lifeboatmen, he had already decided that he was not prepared to lie. Even so he hesitated.

"Captain?" Robertson prompted. "Could you have towed the lifeboat back to safety if you had dropped her down on your arrival?"

"Aye, sir."

A most telling response from a very credible witness.

But Robertson had not finished.

"If after waiting for the half an hour, you had towed the lifeboat out for a second time in order to attempt to drop them down to the schooners, is it your opinion that you could not have got back again?"

"I will declare that we *could not* have got back again. We

216

had great difficulty in getting back ourselves. In the afternoon it blew much heavier. If we had been towing the lifeboat I'm in no doubt that a calamity would've been the result."

"Is it possible for a man on land to judge of the difficulties you had to encounter?" asked Lord Osborne, determined to once more emphasise Alex Luckham's lack of credibility.

"It is not sir, no."

"If you had a north country boat with men who had been long accustomed to lifeboat service in heavy seas, would you have taken them to the schooners?"

"Of course, my Lord, if they wished to go."

"You would have felt no fear for them?"

"No."

"Would you obey the orders of any man to take the steamer where you thought it would have led to her destruction?"

"No. Course not. I would've taken 'em anywhere as a rational man would've done, but not to destroy the boat."

Wanhill raised his right hand. "Regarding the other vessels seeking assistance on Sunday. We all congratulate you on the service that the steamer rendered them. If the lifeboat, unable to weigh anchor, had cut her cable and run to the vessels in the bay could you have ensured bringing her up again to safety?"

Another crucial question.

"If she'd gone to any o' the vessels in the bay near where we took off men ourselves, sir, we could've towed her back again."

The Admiral: "If she had drifted outside the boundary of Old Harry Rocks, could you have done so?"

"Oh no, sir, that is a different thing."

"And presumably there was that risk if the *Manley Wood* had no anchor of her own to secure her and you lost sight of each other."

"Aye sir."

Lord Osborne looked along the line of the panel to his left and right. There were no further questions. This concluded the testimony of Will Redmond, and Lord Osborne thanked him for attending.

The next two witnesses were the last: a pilot on board the *Royal Albert* and the steamer's engineer, John White. They largely corroborated the statements of the tug's master and earlier witnesses, and both agreed that the lifeboat's best chance for saving the lives of the men on the schooners had been to drop down on them as soon as they had arrived on the scene. Wanhill tried hard to make play on this, but Lord Osborne reminded the panel that the lifeboatmen had every reason to believe that the turning of the tide would have led to improved conditions, and that away from the turmoil of the storm, and with the benefit of hindsight, it was easy for others to identify a crucial half-hour opportunity in which a beneficial action might have been taken. However, by this time he had come to realise that there seemed little possibility of the lifeboat crew being completely exonerated.

Lord Osborne then advised the panel that before deliberating on their conclusions they needed to examine the conduct of the lifeboat crew in the evening as well. He reminded them that they had already been furnished with copies of the Christchurch inquest into the fate of the brig *Elizabeth*, which had taken place two days before, but he pointed out that there had been some criticism of the length of time taken for the lifeboat crew to get to their destination.

"I propose we recall Sam Hart," he said, "since I know he was instrumental in securing transportation for the evening. Then should we have any further questions, or require more details, we can recall any of the other lifeboatmen."

This suggestion was accepted.

Sam had been forewarned that he might be recalled. He was pleased that he'd taken it all in his stride on the first occasion, but in the intervening time he had spoken to Stoker and Tom, both still bridling over Wanhill's aggressive tactics. This time he felt less calm, and knew it was the wrong way to feel.

Lord Osborne begged him to be seated and thanked him again for his earlier account. He told him that his recall was not related to anything he had recounted so far, hoping, no doubt, that this would help to put him at ease. Then he asked Sam to describe the events of Sunday night and Monday morning.

Sam explained that the lifeboat crew had returned to Poole about seven o'clock on Sunday. About eight o'clock he had received a message from his brother that the lifeboat was needed at Christchurch. The steamer was out of action and George Belben had already tried to secure horses for them from the *Antelope* but without success. Sam had met with Mr Belben and they eventually secured horses and transport from the omnibus company, although this took some negotiation. They then rounded up a crew and took the lifeboat by road to Christchurch, leaving North Haven after midnight.

"Surely it would have been quicker to go by sea," asserted Wanhill.

"There would've been a great deal o' sea on Christchurch Ledge on an ebb tide, as the gale was still blowing. And besides it were dark, we didn't have the benefit o' the steamer to tow us, and the men had been out all day. We didn't think it was safe to go by sea."

"I have a letter here from George Belben," said Lord Osborne, "stating that, and I quote, 'It was unfortunate, but by no means the fault of the lifeboat crew, that horses for transportation could not be speedily obtained, yet no time was lost by the crew in getting the boat away. I myself assisted with obtaining horses'."

"The journey to Christchurch is a long one?" asked the Admiral.

"It's fifteen miles, sir," Sam told him.

"And what time did you reach Christchurch?"

"It was around half past five in the morning."

"Fifteen miles?" cried Wanhill, "and you honestly expect us to believe that having been notified that the lifeboat was required at eight in the evening that it was acceptable for you to take, what, *nine* hours or more to reach your destination? I could *walk* it in half that time! My wife could."

Even Sam was taken aback by the sharpness of this challenge. "Well, you see sir…"

"This is intolerable," continued Wanhill, ignoring Sam. "It is entirely *unacceptable* that a lifeboat should take so long to answer an emergency call. It's nothing short of a disgrace – sheer incompetence, negligence even," he sneered. "I don't know how you can stand and defend it."

The hardship which he and the rest of the crew had experienced during the Great Gale came back to Sam vividly, and suddenly a calm descended upon him. He felt like a prize boxer ready to deliver a telling punch.

"Mister Wanhill," he said in a surprisingly restrained, low voice, "would you ever consider serving with the lifeboat yourself?"

"Don't be ridiculous!" Wanhill almost laughed, despite an evident perplexity at the question. "I've no seafaring experience."

"That's right." Sam folded his arms. "And yet you think you can sit there and tell me how to behave when I've been at sea twenty-five years."

This direct challenge to Wanhill's authority left a spell-binding silence.

"How dare..." spluttered Wanhill.

But Sam got to his feet. "In the space of a day," he attested loudly, cutting Wanhill off, "the lifeboat was called out twice in a violent hurricane. We'd *not* been on a rescue afore, we'd *not* seen a storm like it afore, but we did the best we could, and that's all any man can expect of another. Yet I won't sit here and be told by some gent who lives behind a desk that I'm a bloody good-for-nothing when me and my family have had to fight all our lives just to earn an honest crust. You've never had to fight to survive, have you, which is why the likes of you don't serve with the lifeboat. Yet you expect us to."

"How dare you raise your voice to me!" thundered Wanhill.

But Sam had already turned his back on the panel and was walking out. It was an affront to Wanhill, but was only a restrained version of what Sam had really wanted to say and he could feel himself boiling inside.

"Mr Hart! *Mr Hart!*" the Mayor shouted after him.

Chapter Thirteen

It was predictable that Wanhill would be first to break the silence after Sam closed the door behind himself. "That was disgraceful!" he cried, indignant.

"I insist that Sam Hart is recalled," demanded the Mayor, "and made to apologise."

"No," said Lord Osborne calmly. "Mr Wanhill knows he brought that upon himself by insulting the witness. I told you all at the beginning that we had to be dispassionate. Our task is to work collectively to make an informed judgement about the whole chain of events, and not for individual members of the panel to start handing out personal criticisms to witnesses."

"I expressed my opinion, my Lord," retorted Wanhill. "I am sorry it was not to your liking."

"You abused the authority of this inquiry to insult a man of humble birth who was already intimidated enough merely by standing here." Lord Osborne was at his most stern. "I explained that this inquiry was not to be a visceral process, Mr Wanhill. I am ashamed for you. A magistrate of all people should not need to be told to keep his emotions – or prejudices – under control."

Wanhill maintained that he had no prejudices, but in vain did he wriggle for no-one in the room came to his defence, not even the Mayor. Wanhill flushed silently while the rest of the panel looked on. He realised he had overstepped the mark and would have to back down. Furthermore he knew that he could not – would not – stand up to someone who was so clearly his social superior. Lord Osborne was a county justice, the son of a lord, the brother of a duke, and a close friend to many eminent people. It would not do to upset him.

Lord Osborne dismissed Wanhill with an imperious wave of his hand. "Let us return to the matter at hand." He glanced at his pocketwatch. "I propose a ten minute recess to allow us to take refreshment, and then we will reconvene." There were nods. "Good," said Lord Osborne with finality, and they all stood.

Lord Osborne crossed rapidly to the reporter who had been busy scribbling down.

What was his name?

"I would like to request," he said quietly, "that you do not report that last exchange." The reporter was young.

"The editor wants it warts and all," he protested weakly.

"It would oblige me greatly if you would reconsider." His lordship smiled benevolently. "I think reporting Mr Wanhill's rudeness serves no purpose except, perhaps, to inflame the situation and we wouldn't want that, would we?" He watched the man wavering. "I understand that your editor thinks highly of you. I can use my influence with *The Times* to try to secure an interview for a position there perhaps..."

The reporter reflected for a second. "All right," he said, and he handed over his last page.

"Thank you," replied Lord Osborne, folding it carefully. "Now could I ask you to leave the room while we deliberate and I promise to give you a written statement for the *Herald* personally as soon as we are done."

The reporter nodded and departed as Admiral Sulivan

sidled up to Lord Osborne in a corner of the room.

"How do you think we will fare?" he asked quietly.

"I don't know, Bartie," admitted Lord Osborne. "I hope this recess will buy some time for bruised pride to heal."

"Wanhill?"

"Precisely." He sighed. "But to answer your question, I think the most we can hope for is an acknowledgement that our crew were inexperienced, yet I'm not sure we'll get away with that alone."

"I agree. But it will be a tough lesson for Richard Stokes if he's criticised personally by the inquiry. He changed his account to stand by his men. He said they all agreed not to drop down for the schooners when actually the crew wouldn't follow his instructions."

"I know. That says a lot for his character and proves to me that we didn't make a mistake when we appointed him. We must work to protect him as best we can." Lord Osborne rubbed his chin. "I'm no sailor, but when they couldn't raise their anchor even I think they should have slipped it to go to those pilot-boats, don't you?"

"Yes, I do as a matter of fact."

"Hmm." Lord Osborne ruminated. "I suppose it's an exercise in limiting the damage now: accepting some criticism of the crew as a whole, but doing our best to deflect anything levelled at the coxswain himself."

Admiral Sulivan nodded. "I suppose you're right."

Neither of them was happy with this conclusion, but both

knew they had to accept it.

Lord Osborne clucked his tongue. "I want to know what you said to Penney. He's been very quiet, mollified almost."

The Admiral permitted himself a small smile. "I paid him his five pounds and told him he was lucky to get it. I even said I would request the local lifeboat committee to pay him on future occasions, but that if I ever heard of him profiteering from the lifeboat again I would donate a navy tug and crew to the town as a personal gift and put him out of business."

"I didn't know you had a tug and finances to spare."

"I don't," the Admiral grinned. "But Penney doesn't know that."

"You didn't threaten to send a frigate in to sink his accursed tug then?" Lord Osborne's eyes twinkled.

"Competition in business was a far more vile threat!"

"Very shrewd I'm sure," said Lord Osborne. "Although I do find it irksome that when the inquiry is reported in the *Herald*, Penney will appear to be a most kind-hearted soul: all that nonsense about putting men's lives above the value of his steamer."

"Well, maybe it will be the making of him. And to my way of thinking there's a wonderful poetic justice to that, Sidney." The Admiral chuckled quietly. "The lifeboatmen all know what really happened, and it gives them a little hold over him in terms of his reputation that I rather like."

Lord Osborne shook his head. "So tell me, Machiavelli, how are we going to protect Richard Stokes's position?"

"I'm not sure," replied the Admiral, suddenly serious again. "I like the man, and he doesn't deserve to be treated badly."

"Let's go over it again while we've time then; see what room we have for manoeuvre. The key point for me is: should the crew have done what we know the coxswain wanted and dropped down when they arrived?"

"It could be argued either way. I've no wonder there was disagreement in the boat. I think they were most unfortunate that the weather deteriorated after they waited for the tide to turn. Most unfortunate. But a more experienced crew would have dropped straight down to the schooners on arrival, I'm convinced of it."

"And cutting the cable when they couldn't raise the anchor?"

"Well, you're quite right they *should* have cut their anchor warp as you said just now. There's no doubt in my mind that was a mistake, so I suggest we don't argue there. But as for the Christchurch end of things, it's clearly nonsense to blame the lifeboat crew for any part of it. You've read the papers – it was all the coastguard's fault."

"That's one saving grace at least. So we may have some scope to argue against blame for the schooners, you think?"

"Well, we should at least try it. I'll attempt to sow a little uncertainty – see if I can sway a couple of them – yet I suspect we may have to concede defeat. It all depends on what Robertson thinks."

"And we accept a reprove for not cutting the warp when they couldn't get the anchor up, but try to avoid any criticism being levelled at Richard Stokes personally."

"That would be my advice, yes," confirmed the Admiral.

"Good. Thank you Bartie. That's very clear. I am glad we have had time to discuss it. It's far more complex than I ever imagined."

"It won't be easy to get our own way on any issue now that Wanhill's all stoked up."

"I was hoping, as I say, that this recess will help him to simmer down."

"No, I think he's just making tactics, much as we are." He nodded to the opposite corner of the room where Wanhill stood deep in conversation with the Mayor.

"Well, let's not give him any longer than we need to," said Lord Osborne curtly, and then more loudly: "we must reconvene." He turned back to the inquiry panel and resumed his seat just as the harbour master returned and closed the door behind him.

"Our task now is to reach a conclusion," announced Lord Osborne as everyone moved back to their places. "Mr Crabb," he said, deliberately seeking out the most humble member of the panel. "You know the seas in this area well enough, and you know these men; what do you say? I would particularly value your opinion."

Crabb looked surprised, then honoured. "Begging your pardon gentlemen but maybe you ought to know that none o' these men have ever been out of Dorset." He wagged his finger towards the door. "I'm fifty-five and the farthest I've been away from here is Southampton, and that only the once. Poole and the waters within four hours' sail are all they know, and in forty years I never saw a storm like last Sunday. All very familiar, no doubt, to the Admiral and the captain here who've travelled – great gales are commonplace in the oceans – but not to me, nor to them." For someone who had said practically nothing for the past few hours, Crabb was surprisingly garrulous once he started. "They were most affrighted, that I'm sure: out in an open boat which weren't too familiar to 'em, with a great hurricane blowing fit to upset the boat. Yet as Tom said they still went out anyway, and they did what they thought was best." He paused. "Captain Robertson said they had no experience and that's what's at the bottom of this. I reckon, my Lord, it wouldn't be right to slate 'em for lack of experience when they've had no chance to get any."

It was a lot of words, but it reflected an important element of Lord Osborne's own opinion.

"Captain Robertson, what are your thoughts?"

"My Lord, we had three accusations, I think. One of them I hope we can all easily refute. Despite the voicing of certain, er, *frustrations* towards the end of the inquiry, surely we can all agree that the lifeboat crew did all they could to get to Christchurch. I think it is regrettable that it took them so long to get there, but I genuinely cannot see how they might have behaved differently. There is no emergency transport available to them if the steamer is not functioning and they had to beg horses without promise of payment. To add to that, I have here the jury's verdict from the inquest at Christchurch, which I know you have all seen, but I will read it out to you. *'The jury are of the opinion that the first two men of the crew of the "Elizabeth", Thomas Trump and William Reed, died from exposure and exhaustion, and that the third, William Frost, died from the same causes. The jury are also of the opinion that had the coastguard exerted themselves in the manner which they ought in assisting the fishermen to prepare their boat, so that they might have reached the brig at an earlier hour, the life of the third person might have been saved'."*

"I think it is fairly clear where the blame lies for that incident," concurred the Mayor. A Christchurch problem, not Poole's.

Robertson continued: "I suspect we will disagree over the details of the other two, er, 'verdicts'. For my own part I believe that a more experienced crew would have dropped down to the schooners as soon as the lifeboat arrived, and would have cut their anchor cable to enable the steamer to tow them to the pilot-boats. But we do have to reckon with the total lack of experience of these men, and I would like to see that taken into account in any written conclusion we come to."

"Do you not think," ventured the Admiral, "that waiting for the tide to turn was a reasonable compromise in the circumstances?"

"It was a compromise, sir, that only seemed necessary because of their inexperience," Robertson noted, "but even so I do have some sympathy with their decision."

"But ultimately it was a strategy that failed," countered Wanhill. "Shouldn't they be held to account for that?"

"That's right," agreed the Mayor.

"But we also have to consider the future of the lifeboat station here," said the Admiral. "If we totally discredit the lifeboatmen – which I personally feel is unwarranted – they would presumably all resign, or we would need to dismiss them, and that might deter anyone else from volunteering."

"Can we not simply sack the coxswain?" proposed

Wanhill.

"Make an example of him," added the Mayor.

"I don't think we can do that in isolation," warned Lord Osborne, "because this did seem to be a group decision. You heard Mr Stokes say – and his crew all agreed – that they decided what to do by *consensus*, and we should only be justified in getting rid of the coxswain if we feel that he alone made some grievous error."

"I don't think he provided sufficient leadership," countered Wanhill.

"That may be the case," the Admiral conceded, "but I would say the issue of leadership is connected with the whole crew's lack of experience and I agree with Captain Robertson's suggestion that whatever we conclude, that must form a part of it. We are looking to learn lessons, rather than condemn."

"Yes." Robertson was cautious. "But at the same time we must not lose sight of the fact that men have lost their lives."

"Precisely," the Mayor chipped in. "There is *blame* here somewhere. And may I say it's not the first time the lifeboat hasn't fulfilled its duty. In March last year the *Manley Wood* wasn't even launched when a ship was reported in distress near Old Harry Rocks…"

"The schooner *Richard* of Cardiff," Wanhill interrupted.

"And the lifeboat didn't go out to her," persisted the Mayor.

"I don't think this is the place to open up old wounds," said Admiral Sulivan wearily. "We looked into this at the time."

"The *Manley Wood* had only just arrived at the time of that incident," Lord Osborne explained, "and the lifeboat crew had not even sat in her once, let alone gone out in her. And besides, the coastguard, for once, had the situation entirely in hand and the seamen were all rescued." He allowed himself to sound irritated by the Mayor's interruption. "Let us return to the present situation. Captain Robertson, would you continue please."

"Thank you," continued Robertson. "However much we might feel that the circumstances for the lifeboat crew were difficult during the hurricane – impossible even – we must be wary of being too lenient for the sake of those who died and their families."

"Yes Captain, that is my view also," said Wanhill confidently. "And further, I agree with the Mayor's comment: I think the people of the town and the relatives of the deceased want to know who is to *blame*. I think they will demand to know who is responsible, and will want to be certain that it is not going to happen again."

"I would feel uncomfortable about going so far as to create a scapegoat," Robertson objected.

"And if we dismiss the entire crew," countered Lord Osborne, "we will be in an even worse situation, surely? We will effectively have to start again with an even more inexperienced crew." He knew this was a weak argument.

Then the Mayor unwittingly came to Lord Osborne's rescue by changing the subject. "I feel that we must make some mention of the good conduct shown by the men of the *Royal Albert*," he said. "Spare your blushes George, they do you credit."

Lord Osborne tried to remain impassive, but took up the call heartily as a distraction. "Yes, it was a commendable achievement by the steamer crew, and we should not overlook praise for their efforts. Nine lives saved all told."

The discussion continued for some time. Wanhill, with support from the Mayor, was adamant that 'someone had to take the blame' – they clearly wanted the lifeboat crew publicly censured. Against this point of view Lord Osborne and Admiral Sulivan continued to press for recognition of the crew's inexperience in uniquely terrible circumstances and to avoid any direct criticism of Stoker.

In the end it was Robertson's calmly reasoned middle ground which gradually won out. As self-appointed secretary he kept all the notes of their various conclusions, and with a masterful authority he chided extremism and leniency with equal firmness. Yes – the lifeboatmen made mistakes, but yes, they were inexperienced. Both factors were important and both had to be recognised.

Inevitably as the debate progressed, it became clear that despite the Admiral and Lord Osborne's efforts there would be criticism of the lifeboatmen on two counts. Lord Osborne felt that Robertson was more sympathetic to the crew than he made out, but perhaps he was a realist given the height of local feeling on this issue – better to offer limited criticism tempered with explanation than risk utter reprobation. At least they seemed to be winning the argument about not blaming named individuals or dismissing the entire crew.

After about forty-five minutes, when the beginnings of an uneasy compromise seemed to have been reached, the Mayor sent Richard to fetch a clerk from the Guildhall to draft their conclusions. When they returned the panel seemed in broad agreement on the appropriate wording. It was obvious that no-one, except perhaps Robertson, was entirely satisfied with their conclusions, but everyone had something of what he wanted and maybe that was all that they could have hoped for given the strength of feeling within the room and without.

Captain Robertson dictated from his notes for the clerk's benefit:

"The committee," he said, *"having had before them the crew of the lifeboat as well as the crew of the steam tug* Royal Albert, *the acting master of the* Gertrude *revenue cruiser, and the chief boatman of Studland station, and gone fully into an inquiry of all the circumstances connected with the loss of life that occurred off Poole Bar on Sunday 11th February, deeply regret that on the arrival of the lifeboat at the Bar, an attempt was not made to rescue the crews of two schooners then in distress.*

"Is everyone content with that form of words – 'deeply regret' and so forth?" asked Robertson.

There were nods from around the table. It was more harsh than Lord Osborne had anticipated at the outset of the inquiry, but he reflected that this was probably the gentlest criticism they could now expect.

"Can we make mention," suggested Joe Crabb, "that their decision to wait for the tide to turn was based on their local knowledge. I feel that gives 'em credit for something, even though in the end it didn't help as it turned out."

"Yes," said Robertson, and he began dictating to the clerk once more. *"But under the circumstances of a very heavy sea and violent gale, the men manning the lifeboat, from a long experience and local knowledge, formed their opinion that after low water the sea would become smoother and they decided to wait half an hour. Unfortunately, the wind and the sea increased, which rendered any attempt impracticable; shortly after, the vessels struck and went to pieces, and the crews were unfortunately lost.*

"Shall we move on to the second issue?" invited Robertson. *"The lifeboat anchored in Studland bay waiting a change, but the increased hurricane caused several small craft to drive. Signals of distress were hoisted on two of the vessels, and the crews were taken out by the tug, the lifeboat crew stating it was impossible for them to weigh the anchor.*

"The committee consider they ought, under the circumstances, to have cut or slipped the cable, dropped down on to the vessels concerned, and so rescued the crews..."

The Admiral interrupted. "I think we should add something like 'having the steam tug at hand to tow them back to their anchor'."

"Yes," said Robertson. "Are we all content with that wording?"

There was general agreement.

"So." He nodded to the clerk: *"having the steam tug at hand to tow them back to their anchor.* And now a new paragraph and I would particularly value your assistance with this section where we've agreed to make mention of their inexperience. *The committee desire to express their opinion that, considering the crew of the lifeboat had had no experience in the management of such boats, they are not surprised that in such a violent storm the crew should have shown...* should have shown what?" he asked them.

"Poor knowledge of the lifeboat," advised Wanhill.

"That is maybe a little critical."

"Maybe simple 'lack of confidence'?" suggested the Mayor.

"No sir, we cannot have that!" cried the Admiral. "A suggestion made in good faith I am sure, but in the Service 'lack of confidence' is a well-known euphemism for cowardice."

Lord Osborne had an idea. "Could I put forward: 'a want of confidence in the qualities of the lifeboat'."

"Yes, that is it!" said Robertson. He read back over the end of the sentence *"the committee… are not surprised that in such a violent storm the crew should have shown a want of confidence in the qualities of the lifeboat.* Now, new paragraph. *The committee also desire to express their entire satisfaction with the conduct of all those persons in charge of the* Royal Albert *tug."*

"And all we need now," observed the Admiral, "is a tailpiece about the *Elizabeth.*"

"I have my notes," said Robertson, and started dictating again. *"A resolution was also passed to the effect that it was so late before the intelligence of the lifeboat being required at Christchurch reached the authorities at Poole, that the lifeboat could not under the circumstances have reached the place in time to save any of the crew of the* Elizabeth *who were lost, and therefore no blame attaches to the coxswain and crew of the lifeboat with regard to this case."*

Robertson finished and sat back.

"Shall we give our clerk a minute or so for the ink to dry," said Lord Osborne, "and then determine if we are all satisfied with the final result?"

The paper was handed around and the panel read it in groups of three or so.

There was a general acceptance, if not contentment, concerning the accuracy and justness of the conclusions.

"Good," said Lord Osborne. He was suddenly rather tired. "Then it only remains for me, gentlemen, to thank you – all of you – for your time and hard efforts to do justice to a most difficult situation. Mr Mayor, thank you for your hospitality."

They all stood. Wanhill pulled out his pocketwatch and looked at it pointedly before making a rapid silent exit, as if he had some imminent matter of importance to attend to. He of all the inquiry panel was probably the least satisfied with the final wording.

Lord Osborne asked the clerk to make four copies of the document. He offered Robertson one for the RNLI, allocated one to the Mayor, one to the newspaper, and reserved the final copy for himself.

When the others were out of earshot, Lord Osborne leaned towards Admiral Sulivan.

"Have we let them down, Bartie?" he asked.

"Oh no! I don't think so," Admiral Sulivan reassured him. "I'm not entirely happy with the wording myself, but we've done the best we could. There was always going to be criticism, Sidney, and I suspect even the lifeboatmen themselves are prepared for that. We've done much to tone it down: if we hadn't been here, it would have been *far* worse."

"Maybe you're right." Lord Osborne sighed. "When the copies are prepared, would you be kind enough to ensure my copy reaches Mr Stokes tonight. I think it would be a courtesy for him to see it before it appears in the newspaper. I'm not sure how he will react – this paints a blacker picture than I had wanted."

Chapter Fourteen

"I must confess that I was not entirely content with the outcome," said Lord Osborne to his wife. He had returned from the inquiry feeling ill at ease. "If only we could have avoided an inquiry altogether," he complained, and not for the first time. "It is most unjust that our lifeboatmen should be publicly condemned so soon after the station was created. It will be detrimental to their future development: they will lose confidence and everything they do from now onwards will be subject to the utmost scrutiny." He looked away. "I did try to prevent it."

"I know, Sidney." Emily spoke patiently. "I'm sure you did everything in your power. I'm not sure what else you could have done."

But he was not listening. "Do you know," he said, "that some people are still not satisfied? Bartie says that there's been talk of more letters of complaint to the Mayor. What do these people want?"

"Why not come and sit here." She patted the chair next to her and smiled. "Shall I pour you a sherry?"

"What?" he muttered, distracted by his own thoughts. "Oh yes, that would be most welcome. Thank you, my dear; you are so good to put up with me in this foul mood."

"You must try not to feel responsible, Sidney. You take on too much. It will be your undoing. You are *one* country parson – very well-connected and the most resourceful man I know – but still only one man. You cannot take on everything."

"That fellow Wanhill was a perfect scoundrel at the

inquiry," he continued, undeterred. "He harried those poor lifeboatmen like a great hound, bounding after them to bite, bite, bite."

"Oh dear," said Emily, maintaining her sympathy. She knew that she simply had to allow her husband time to run out of steam. "Was Bartie not able to challenge him?"

"Not really, no, I regret to say." He sighed. "Although one of the lifeboatmen put him in his place in the end, and that was somewhat satisfying." Lord Osborne chuckled at the recollection. "He told Wanhill that someone who sat in an office all day had no right to judge a seaman with twenty-five years' experience, and I must say I enjoyed that. And he deserved it!"

"Thank goodness one of the men had the courage to stand up for himself."

"Yes. And at least we managed to stop them dismissing the coxswain, or blaming him for it all personally. At one time that looked a distinct possibility."

"Well, that's an achievement, surely?" suggested his wife.

"I suppose you're right," he conceded. "Bartie and I worked quite hard to put them off going down that track. And we managed to dampen Alex Luckham's ardour somewhat as well – although actually he did most of the damage himself."

"Ah, you mentioned him," she recalled. "The gentleman who wrote to the Mayor?"

"That's right." He reached for the sherry, which his wife had already poured for him. "But at the end of the day the facts were against the lifeboat crew, I'm afraid."

"You're running ahead of yourself Sidney, dear. If the facts were against them, then surely they *should* have been criticised? Was that not right?"

"Maybe. Perhaps I'm being too sensitive. But in the circumstances it all seems so unreasonable to me," he objected. "Everything was set against them: they'd never been on a rescue before, they were presented with the worst storm in over a hundred years and essentially didn't know what to do. How can you criticise men for that? They must have been terrified." He sipped at his sherry. "The fact is, between you and me, I think the Lifeboat Institution expects too much of these people. They build a station, supply a boat, appoint a coxswain and then expect the locals to just get on with it. We should be doing more to prepare them. Not just in Poole either. I think I'll have a word with Captain Robertson about it – send him a letter."

There was a pause while both took more sherry. A robin twittered outside – somewhere near.

"What is Poole like?" asked his wife, hoping to change the subject. She was not a good traveller and rarely accompanied her husband anywhere.

"Poole? Oh Poole is fascinating, my dear. You really must come with me one day. I know you detest to travel but I believe you would enjoy looking around. Yes," he reflected, "you *would* enjoy Poole. The town is rather dirty in places, I must be honest with you, but there are some delightful old houses and the Quay is a source of endless fascination. I sometimes sit and watch it for an hour or more. Vessels docking, unloading, setting sail. It's just like the Port of London in great miniature. But the main reason to visit Poole is the harbour," he said, full of enthusiasm. "For when the tide is full it takes on the appearance of a vast lake studded with islands. And right in the middle is the largest island, Branksea, which has its own houses, a quay, a delightful church and even a Tudor castle. It's a fine place to explore, for there are many birds and trees there."

Lord Osborne realised that his clever wife had succeeded in distracting him from his concerns. Still, he would write to Robertson about training for the lifeboatmen. That was a good idea.

———————————

Four days after the inquiry, Tuesday, and Stoker found himself in Lagland Street, standing outside Sam Hart's house. It was a dark-brick terrace lit up only by the gas lamp from the *Swan Inn* across the way – the *Mucky Duck* as it was known locally. Tom had suggested that the lifeboatmen should meet to discuss the inquiry. It was early evening and Stoker stood, about to knock at Sam's door, when there was a loud burst of laughter from the *Swan*, and then someone cut through it singing. It was *Jack Tar on Shore*. The clear, falsetto voice of an older man sailed high into the evening, and all was suddenly quiet while everyone stopped to listen. Stoker smiled to himself ruefully: seafaring men often found life on the land a less rewarding task than life afloat.

He'd had time to digest the conclusions of the inquiry, and the details had been in the *Herald* so everyone knew the verdict. It was not the vindication he'd wanted, but then it wasn't the mauling he'd dreaded. Maybe that was the best he could have hoped for.

The Admiral had been right. The inquiry had cleared the air to some extent – at least amongst ordinary folk. People had had their say, and everyone could now see all the facts. Some disagreed with the inquiry's conclusions, but that was inevitable and largely due to individual preconceptions. Those who had condemned the lifeboatmen thought the inquiry was too supportive; those who supported them thought it too condemnatory.

At least there was no more nonsense in the town. No more fights, verbal abuse. It had spoiled some long-held relationships, but perhaps there would be time for them to heal.

The singer reached his conclusion and the inn erupted in a chorus of cheers, tankard thumping, and applause.

Stoker knocked and was welcomed in by Richard Wills, who led him to the small, sparsely decorated front room. There, crammed in, were many of the lifeboatmen – Tom and Sam Hart, Frank and John Wills, Cain Matthews, Bill Brown, and Jack Fisher. All were smoking except Frank who, to quote himself, 'couldn't abide the taste of it'. The room had a low level fug of aromatic, brownish, drifting smoke hanging like a sea mist.

"Evening, Stoker," said Tom, waving his pipe at him. "Sit yourself down, my friend." He passed Frank his tobacco pouch, who handed it on to Stoker.

"Thankee, Tom," said Stoker, sitting. Suddenly he felt very at home. Amongst friends. For the past several days he had been alone – troubled, filled with angst, sometimes angry, although anger wasn't really in his nature. The ruminant emotions were more his line: guilt, remorse, melancholy. Now, somehow, the weight on his shoulders seemed a little lighter. Just being here with the other lifeboatmen made him remember he was part of a crew working together. A fellowship. A family. He was grateful to Tom for arranging the gathering.

"I'm sorry we've had to go through all this lot," Stoker began earnestly. "Inquiry, newspapers, all the jibing. Not easy for any of us. I always thought that wind and wave were gonna be our biggest challenge – but turns out that weren't the case."

"Aye" said John sourly. "What we went through with the boat was hard enough, without being called to account by all and bloody sundry."

"And you've borne the brunt of it, Stoker," observed Frank, nodding towards him. "You, and Tom here. And we're all grateful for that."

Nods and murmurs of 'aye' went round the room.

"We owe you a debt for standing up for us at the inquiry," said Bill. His big personality was touchingly mellowed by genuine gratitude.

Cain agreed. "Aye," he said, "the fact is, Stoker, that at the inquiry you could've said that *you* wanted us to drop down to them schooners and all of us refused. But you didn't, you stood by us and took the rap with the rest o' the crew."

"It was a decent thing to do, Stoker," said Tom quietly.

Stoker was embarrassed by the appreciation.

"Thankee," he said, face flushing slightly. "I reckon that what happens in our boat at sea is our own business, and we stand together as a crew when people on shore suddenly decide that they want to interfere."

"There've been more letters in the paper," announced Cain after a lull.

"Have there?" Stoker feigned surprise. "I can't say I'm bothered looking. Only upsets me." Actually, he *had* already read them, but didn't think it was healthy to be chewing over further criticism.

"Sam was about to read 'em to us when you knocked, Stoker." Most of the lifeboat crew couldn't read or write.

"They're bloody ignorant," said Sam, who had finished reading the letters to himself during the conversation.

"Well, read 'em out then," urged Bill. "So's we can judge for ourself."

"It's not gonna help – just get us all worked up," cautioned Stoker.

"I know that," said Cain. "But if folks are saying things, we've just as much right to know about it as you who can read it for yourselves."

"Go on then," said Stoker, shaking his head.

"There are two letters," Sam explained. "I'm sorry to say they're both... very bad." He looked up. No-one said anything; they were all sitting, expectant, so he held up the paper, shook it slightly, and started to read. "*Sir – I am almost ashamed to go into any of the neighbouring towns. Everywhere I go I am met with a 'tirade' about the gale of Sunday the 11th instant, and in common with the people of Poole generally, I am blamed for the loss of life on the day in question. Everybody seems to have formed the opinion that the lifeboat crew forgot their vocation. One man in my hearing reckoned them up as a 'fat and lazy lot', another that they would not have been afraid 'if a good salvage case had been in prospect'. I have done my best to explain how matters really stood, but all my explanations have been to no purpose, and I have been told that a lot of freshwater sailors would not have made a greater failure than the crew of our lifeboat. It strikes me, however, that the crew are not the only persons to blame in this matter. The lifeboat committee did wrong in allowing so many pilots to form the crew. If a lot of fishermen had been selected with, say, one or two pilots, I am of opinion that instead of the stigma which now rests on our port, valuable lives might have been saved and great praise bestowed on the seamen of our port, instead of blame. I am, Sir, yours truly, A Landsman."*

"Ignorant bugger's too frightened to use his real name!" stormed Cain. "Bloody coward. Shouldn't be allowed! We should write up and ask for his name."

"I told you this would upset you," Stoker reminded them. "I don't know why you want to hear it."

"Because we've as much right to know as you, that's why," retorted Cain.

"It's all bloody hearsay," said Bill. "A 'fat and lazy lot'? Who's he think he is?"

"Obviously knows you though, Bill," quipped John Wills.

"What?" cried Bill, standing up and smoothing his hand over his belly. "This slim figure like a royal princess?"

"Whoever saw a princess with a great gut like Bill's?" laughed Frank.

"It's all that beer you've been drinking yer royal 'ighness," said John.

"No," said Bill demurely. "*I* only drinks *champagne*."

It was good to hear everyone laugh, although Stoker noticed that Tom didn't join in. He suddenly realised that the assistant coxswain seemed isolated. Somewhere else. He threw him a smile but Tom looked away.

Stoker was hoping the crew had forgotten the other letter in the paper, but he had reckoned without Cain. Dogged and persistent Cain.

"We'd better have that other letter while we're all in a good mood," said Cain, folding his arms.

Sam appeared uncomfortable again. "You sure?" he asked. "It's all bollocks."

"No. I wants to hear it," Cain assured him stubbornly. No-one dared disagree.

Sam let out a deep breath and started reading, unhappy in his foreknowledge of the contents. *"Sir – Seldom has your report of any public or private meeting been awaited with such general anxiety as that which was excited on the occasion of the recent inquiry of the lifeboat committee, and in as few instances have your pages afforded so general a disappointment. The committee in their decision accord blame to no-one. To the number of perhaps twenty individuals are one after the other swept to a watery grave, while a splendid lifeboat manned by a physically efficient crew, and provided with belts, lines, and every useful alliance, is riding quietly at anchor in smooth water, not a mile to windward of the entire scene and no-one is at fault! It is doubtless often difficult to decide where misfortune ends and negligence or worse takes up the due; but here we appear to have a wider latitude than even the most forbearing usually accord."*

"Cheeky bugger!" cried Bill.

"Sh!" said Cain, and nodded for Sam to continue.

"That they should reject the evidence of Mr Luckham was

246

perfectly reasonable and in keeping. How could Mr Luckham expect that his vision was to be trusted by others when I am quite sure he could not trust to it himself? It must have been impossible for him to credit his own sight: twenty sailors consigned to a watery grave while the lifeboat sat a calm spectator of so appalling a scene."

"Oh, I might have known!" Frank burst out. "It's some playmate of that bloody Luckham."

Cain's head snapped round to glare at him, annoyed by the interruption.

"Sorry," mumbled Frank.

Sam resumed. *"It is said that our men are unaccustomed to the service. Had the surgeons who, in the Crimea, coolly dressed dangerous wounds under fire of the rifle pits pursued their professional studies under the influence of similar music? That there may be much in a knowledge of what a boat is capable of enduring is doubtless true, but there is far more in the hearty, energetic enthusiasm which makes the effort first, and balances the probability of failure or success afterwards. It is this, far more than to their training (although that may materially contribute), that the crews of our northern and eastern lifeboats owe their success, and without this all the training in the world will not avert, under similar conditions, a repetition of the scene of the 11th instant."*

Sam paused for breath. He hated being the conduit for someone else's savage criticism of his friends.

"It is an established physical axiom that the strength of a chain is only that of its weakest link, and this is often found no less morally than physically correct. On Poole and her nautical population the matter is, as it at present stands, a palpable and direct stigma. To leave the constitution of the crew in its present state, is to completely stultify the benevolence of the lady who presented the boat. I am Sir, yours, 'Inquirer'."

"Another one who won't give his real name," stormed Bill. "Not right. Give me a name and I'll call round and give him some'it to remember us by."

"I think that's why he chose to keep it secret," said Stoker.

"It lets him take a pot-shot at us without any come-back though." John was annoyed. "He knows who *we* are."

"But," Stoker maintained, "many folk'll think, like us, that it's some bloody toff who knows nothing about the sea."

"Right," agreed Sam, "a pal of our old friend from Studland trying to square things up after Luckham got such a rough ride at the inquiry."

"That pleased me no end to read how he'd been handled," said Stoker. "I reckon Luckham must've been mightily pissed off. Thought he'd strut in there, like a lord, say his piece, and have us lot in irons or something."

"What did they mean in that letter when they said the crew had to be changed?" asked Bill.

"We asked for volunteers last year and we're all that came forward," Cain snorted. "No-one else wanted to do it!"

"And all this about too many pilots on board," said Sam. "What's that about?"

"They don't know that pilots have got other jobs besides sitting about waiting for ships to steer," explained Frank.

"Frank's right," said Tom, speaking for the first time. "They reckon pilots ain't true seamen. They think we just take ships in and out-harbour in fine weather, and they don't know that most of us are fishermen as well. They've got round to thinking it's the pilots that let the side down. That last letter said as much."

"Bloody ridiculous," said Cain.

"I don't think it matters what they think," said Stoker. "It's what the group of us think that matters. Have we got a crew that's up to the job?"

"Course we have!" roared Bill. "It's gonna take more than a snotty letter in the paper to break this crew up."

"Well it may not be up to *us*, Bill," suggested Tom.

"I'd like to see anyone try just by writing a letter."

"A letter from Alex Luckham got the Mayor to hold an inquiry," Stoker observed.

"The Mayor's a prick."

"You're right." Tom drew on his pipe. "But it's not your opinion that counts, you see, Bill. Nor mine, nor anyone in this room. It's whether the lifeboat committee feel under enough strain to force a change."

"Force a change?" demanded Bill. "What are you on about!"

There were murmurs of discontent around the room.

"It can be done easy enough." Tom cut through the hubbub. "They hold the purse strings, such as they are. They own the boat leastways."

"But who's gonna volunteer for the lifeboat now," insisted

Sam, "with the reputation we got? No-one'd want to join us or take over from us. It's up to us to show 'em they're all wrong. Next call-out we'll do better. We'll show 'em!"

"Easy to say, Sam, but that might not be for months yet," warned Tom. "Meantime there could be more letters."

"Well, they *ain't* changing this crew." Cain folded his arms defiantly.

"All they have to do is move the lifeboat, you see," said Tom. "Lock, stock and barrel. Put it someplace else."

"Move it? But where?" demanded Cain.

"Oh, Wareham, Christchurch, Bournemouth…"

"Don't be so daft. They wouldn't do that." Cain paused, suddenly uncertain. "Would they?"

Tom had already realised that unless there was some sort of public blood-letting or sacrifice, the criticism of the lifeboat would probably continue. It was ironic that, unknown to him, he and Wanhill were in accord: the community needed someone to blame. Tom was determined that any reparation should not be at the coxswain's expense – after all, Stoker alone had urged the rest of them to go down to the schooners. Tom remembered his own reluctance to support the coxswain and knew what he must do. He had known since the inquiry, but putting it into action would be painful.

"I've been thinking," he said slowly, "that we need some *fresh* blood. It'd be good to get a few new hands so that we have more to choose from in future. That's not gonna be easy, as Sam were saying, but we can put a few feelers out and see if we can't get more fishermen on board maybe."

"He's right," said Stoker. "If that business over Christchurch taught us anything it's that we can't rely on the thirteen of us alone. What if some of us are ill when there's a call-out? We wouldn't have enough of us to man the boat."

"I also reckon," said Tom, feeling a way carefully with his words, "that it might be best for all of us if I stand down as assistant coxswain."

There was a shocked silence for a second. Then a sudden chorus of disapproval.

"What?" cried Stoker, who hadn't seen this coming.

"I'm sorry, Stoker, I've been chewing it over for a few days. I wanted to talk to you about it in private, but I reckon it's for the best…"

"You're leaving because of that bloody inquiry?"

"Aye, in part. I make no secret that I didn't like being stuck up in front of that cocky sod Wanhill to account for meself. The whole business upset me no end. I'm still angry now. But it's not just that. My joints played up something dreadful for days after we came back…" He was lying now.

"You can't do this, Tom," blustered Stoker, wrong-footed. "I… I won't let you!"

"Come on, Stoker," insisted Tom. "We've got to give these people a little bit o' what they want or they'll plague us to death. They don't feel they've got enough. There must be some changes or they'll say it's a whitewash. I'll go. Replace me with a fisherman if you like, or better still get someone new and promote 'em. Someone who ain't one of the hated breed of pilots." He couldn't resist a hint of bitterness, despite himself.

251

"I don't want you to go, Tom," said Stoker with something almost like tenderness.

"I know, old friend, and I'm not properly sure I'm doing the right thing, but we have to do something to stop the infernal carping."

"If you go, it'll look like it was your fault. Like we're giving you the heave-ho 'cos you're no good."

"It don't matter to me what people think, Stoker, as long as you all feel I played me part." He looked around him. "And I can still help out in loads of other ways. We've learned that we need to keep provisions in the boat, that we need a bigger list of volunteers and all their addresses – I can do that – and besides we need a contact for the lifeboat in town. Stoker, you live too far out – I can be your contact."

There was an awkward silence. No-one knew what to say.

Tom broke through it – determined to press his case. "I reckon this is for the best. And anyway I've made me mind up."

"Is this what you *want*, Tom?" demanded Stoker.

He dodged the question. "It's what's best for the lifeboat. That must come first. Come on, don't try and talk me out of it, me mind's made up."

Tom extended a hand to the sullen Stoker, but the coxswain wouldn't shake it.

"T'ain't right," said Stoker.

"Maybe," Tom replied quietly. "But you took a forfeit by

standing with us at the inquiry. This is *my* forfeit." He patted Stoker affectionately on the upper arm. "It's getting late, and I must go," he said, his voice suddenly brightening. "I'll see meself out. And don't you worry, Stoker, everything'll be all right. With me as chief recruiting officer for the boat you'll have more men than you know what to do with. You watch." Suddenly he just had to leave before the façade crumbled. "Good night, everyone," said Tom, raising his hand. "See you in the *Nelson* for cards on Thursday as usual." And with that he was gone.

They called their disconsolate goodbyes after him.

The conversation continued for a while, but it was subdued. Then one by one they made their own exits until Stoker was left alone with Bill Brown and Sam Hart.

"That took you by surprise then," said Bill at last.

"Too bloody right," cried Sam.

"Me too," admitted Stoker. "I don't know whether to thank him or thump him."

"Oh, you must thank him!" Bill assured them " 'cos he's right, you know."

"About what?"

"About everything. Them people – those 'letter-writers', whoever they are – they're men of station and they won't let go till they've got their way, or at least part of it. Enough change to make 'em feel they've made an impression. You'll have to give 'em something."

"It's bloody stupid!" Stoker thumped a fist into the palm of his other hand.

"I know it," agreed Sam, "but Bill's right. You must let Tom do this if we want to keep the lifeboat and get a second chance to prove ourselves when the next call comes."

"It'll need a good man to take his place. Oh, it's all too bloody convoluted for me," admitted Stoker. "I thought I was in this lark to save lives. No-one ever told me about inquiries and newspapers, bloody toffs and interfering mayors."

"It could be worse." Bill wagged a finger.

"Could it?"

"Aye, you could have saved the schooner crews but lost one of our *own* crew. Just one. You'd be feeling far worse now."

Wise words from Bill. And Stoker knew he was right.

"I just hope it's not gonna be like this every time we get called out." Stoker held his forehead.

"If you don't mind me saying," began Sam, "now we *know* the sea and the weather ain't the only danger, we're better prepared."

"What you need," said Bill, "is a break; time away from it. Something different. Why don't you come out with me in the skiff tomorrow?"

"I've given up being a fisherman, Bill."

"Maybe, but I think a change'd be good for you. We're only winkle-picking down Stone Island, but it's quiet there. What d'you think?"

Chapter Fifteen

Dealing with the fallout from the inquiry continued to be a strain, no matter how hard Stoker tried to pretend otherwise or rise above it. As coxswain he felt responsible; yet he was also angry that the lifeboatmen seemed to have been judged so harshly. He had been satisfied with his own performance at the inquiry, and couldn't understand why its conclusions had not been more favourable.

But most of all Stoker was upset by the departure of Tom. He recognised the honourable nature of Tom's decision – indeed, that it offered Stoker himself a measure of protection against being removed from his own position. However, he still resented the fact that a good man had effectively been sacrificed to appease those who were vocal yet ignorant.

He ran and re-ran the events through his head, analysing his own part in them. Stoker found the remorseless yet inescapable dwelling upon these concerns draining but couldn't stop. As the days passed, he was always tired yet sleep did not restore him. He wanted to focus on other matters – anything almost – but found it nearly impossible to give things his full attention. He felt hopeless and lacking in motivation; he was alternately angry and sad, exasperated and guilt-ridden. All these emotions churned over and over inside him even during the rare occasions when he wasn't thinking about them directly, and they threatened to consume him. Eventually he succumbed to a feeling of bitter helplessness. And from this despair was borne a passivity which concerned him, but from which he could not rouse himself. He was bored and annoyed by everything around him. There were no pleasures, opportunities or challenges any more.

The world retreated.

His geographical isolation on the Haven was both help and hindrance – it helped him personally because he didn't have to face the people of Poole every day, but it prevented him giving proper succour to his lifeboatmen or receiving any himself from others. Whenever he was in the town he made a point of trying to visit at least one member of the crew, but he knew he was poor company: he met them because he knew he ought to, rather than because he wanted to.

Mary was worried by his silences. He had rarely been angry with the children in the past, but now he was sometimes short with them – especially the older ones. Inconsequential matters irritated him to an extraordinary degree. She watched him thinking and dwelling – a pall of melancholia – and didn't know how to handle it.

He continued to read the local newspaper because he knew he had to be in touch with what was happening, but he opened each edition dreading further criticism, accusation, blame. There was a public collection for Henry Cutler and his 'intrepid group of heroes', as one paper dubbed them. A total of one hundred and forty-eight pounds, six shillings and sixpence was raised as a testimonial from the inhabitants of Christchurch and the neighbouring town of Bournemouth. The Mayor of Christchurch, John Holloway, was quoted in the newspaper report which described the award ceremony: he could not resist a jibe at the Poole lifeboatmen. *"When we contrast the conduct of these Christchurch men, who bravely went off at dead of night and in an unsuitable boat for the purpose of saving life, with that of the crew of the well-appointed lifeboat of a neighbouring town, I think the people of Christchurch ought to be proud that we possess such men."* There were cheers at this remark according to the reporter. Stoker noted with a certain rancour that the newspaper totally ignored the rivalry that had existed between the coastguards and Henry's group. Why had the Poole lifeboatmen been brought to book so publicly, but not the Christchurch coastguard?

Perhaps responding to the implied slight from Christchurch's Mayor about the courage of the men of Poole the people of that town held a collection for their own 'gallant and heroic' crew – that of the steam tug *Royal Albert*. As one newspaper correspondent noted: *"the crew of the Manley Wood lifeboat have each been paid for their services, but not a farthing has ever reached those who really did the work on that day"*. And to fully ensure that they were not outdone by Christchurch, the good citizens of Poole even petitioned the Lifeboat Institution itself for the steamer's crew to receive medals. In the event, medals were not forthcoming, yet the chairman of the RNLI awards committee, Sir Edward Perrott, wrote and thanked the crew personally and added five pounds to the town's collection. Stoker's stock and that of his crew fell even lower by implication. Their own parent body seemed to recognise that the untrained crew of a steamer had done a better job than the lifeboat.

To Stoker's chagrin there were, inevitably, further condemnatory letters published in the *Herald* and other local newspapers. All of them, as usual, anonymous. People queued up to peck at the wound, it seemed. *"How do the Poole lifeboatmen's consciences feel, I'd like to know?"* asked one reporter; *"that is if they've got any consciences."* People were dissatisfied with the inquiry which was branded as *far from satisfactory*. As Tom had predicted, there began to be calls to take the lifeboat away from Poole. One correspondent wrote that it should be stationed at Wareham, and that it *"be manned with hearts more brave and buoyant than those to be found in the still water behind North Haven Point."* Another letter used a report in *The Times* to compare an acclaimed action by the *Sisters Memorial* lifeboat in Llandudno, with the recent conduct of the *Manley Wood*. *"Both reaped the rewards of their self-devoting efforts,"* concluded the letter writer, *"the one in salvation from drowning of three fellow creatures, the other in saving a gallon of rum."*

Under a great deal of pressure, Lord Osborne convened a Lifeboat Committee meeting in Poole in March to recruit more volunteers. Tom Hart formally tendered his resignation at this point, as did George King who'd also become sick of all the attention, but six local fishermen joined the crew in the pilots' stead. It was not made public that these new recruits had all been the work of Tom himself, working behind the scenes, but Stoker knew. And so did Lord Osborne. Yet when Tom's resignation from the lifeboat became known the appetite for criticism gradually dwindled, and newspaper coverage petered out. The assistant coxswain had been sacrificed and journalists and locals alike began to move on.

It took a long time after the fear of further recriminations had passed for Stoker's own spirits to lift. For what seemed like a very long time he was dismal company: Mary suffered badly from seeing him fall so low, and he realised he had become a poor friend to all who knew him. Being a man of duty he baulked at the thought of being found wanting. He yearned to re-ignite the little fire that had once burned inside. So one day, Stoker was pleased to find himself seriously contemplating Bill's offer from a few months before to accompany him fishing. He would go and see Tom too. He had resolved to do something positive and was looking forward to it. That was a good sign.

———————

When he opened the front door John Wills had been surprised to see his brother Frank. He'd popped round to borrow a caulking iron and mallet.

"I'm sure they're in here somewhere," said John, as he

rummaged for the tools amongst the debris in the disorderly scullery. "How's Jane?"

"Oh, you know…" Frank started. He stopped and rubbed his eyes with his fingertips. "Sorry, Johnny, I'm tired. Baby's always ill – keeps us awake most nights. Difficult when you gotta be up early next day."

"What's wrong with him?"

"Lord knows. He just wails all the time. Won't settle."

"Ah! Here we are!" cried John, finding both mallet and iron. He handed them over. "What did the doctor say?"

"He's been twice, but he don't do nothing. Just says: 'keep him warm, make sure he feeds regular' but that's what we were doing anyway. Common sense. Can't keep calling him out every week if that's all he's gonna say – specially at three bob a time."

"Well, hope the baby picks up soon. I'm sure he will. He'll be a tough little bugger if he's anything like you." John squinted at the clock on the mantel. "D'you fancy sneaking to the *New Inn* for half an hour? You could do with a spell away from home by the sound of it."

"I can't," Frank pleaded. "I told Jane I'd be straight back."

"Oh come on, Frank! I hardly see you these days."

"I'd love to, but…"

"Jane won't mind just this once," John insisted. "We'll pop down the Quay with signs on our backs saying 'lifeboatman – kick me' and see what happens."

"That's not funny." Frank smiled despite himself. "You are such a bad influence, our Johnny."

"I know, but it's all part of me charm," John boasted.

"Is that what you tell 'em?"

"Tell who?"

"Your 'lady friends'."

"What are you talking about, my dear brother?" John put on an innocent-sounding voice, but he was grinning broadly. "What can you mean?"

"You know *very well* what I mean. You're getting a reputation, Johnny," said Frank sternly, "and it's not a good one."

"Tut, tut. My brother disapproves. Naughty me," he mused. "You jealous?"

"You don't care at all, do you?" Frank crossed his arms, unimpressed by his brother's carefree attitude.

"Does, er, Father know?" John ventured.

"What? No, I don't reckon he does, but…"

"Well, it's your job to make *sure* that he don't then. That's what brothers are for, eh?" He slapped Frank on the shoulder. "No point upsetting the Old Man – specially at his age."

"But he'll find out sooner or later. He's bound to…"

"Come on, this is getting far too grim!" said John in a tone that ended the subject. "You'll be telling me to start going to church next! I want that drink. Are you coming?"

———————————

Lord Osborne smiled at the sight of his assembled guests enjoying what he had to admit was a most remarkable meal. His new cook had worked wonders. Was this the sin of pride? Maybe. But surely the Lord allowed it in small matters. He caught Emily's eye and she beamed back. Her sister, Fanny, sat to Lord Osborne's right with her husband. Charles was professor of modern history at Cambridge, and a successful novelist. He and Lord Osborne had much in common: both were Anglican ministers and shared a keen interest in social reform.

Lord Osborne's sister, Mary, sat to his left with her husband, Lord Wolverton. He was a quiet man. Perhaps he needed to be, for Mary was rather outspoken.

The conversation dipped but Charles was ready to resurrect it. "Fanny tells me you're planning another great act of philanthropy," he noted, looking towards Lord Osborne.

"Well, we must all do something to help where we can." Lord Osborne was naturally modest, but pleased to be asked about his plans. "As you know I've striven for some time to try to persuade the local landowners to pay their labourers a reasonable wage…"

"Sidney, we *all* know about that!" chided Lady Wolverton. "Everyone who reads *The Times* knows about *that*."

It had been a recurring theme in his many letters, which had attracted great public interest.

"And you make far too much of it, Sidney," she continued.

261

"Many of these labourers you are eager to defend are often ignorant and slovenly, and with absolutely no aspiration to better themselves."

"Mary, really!"

Charles butted in diplomatically. "Am I right in supposing you have had no success with the landowners?" he asked.

"Regrettably, no progress whatsoever, I am afraid," he confessed, "but I have found a new solution, at least for some of the poorest families. I'm encouraging another group of them to live in Australia."

"Australia!" exclaimed his sister. "Where we deport the convicts. But these labourers of yours are honest men?"

"Yes, of course," said Lord Osborne irritably.

"Then I doubt that they will look favourably upon being shipped out to live with a group of felons! Sidney, have you really thought this through, my dear?"

"Mary," he began patiently. "Australia is a new world – a place where people have the chance to start again. To begin a new life. There's a wealth of land and the climate is very tolerable, so they say. Besides, those whom we sent out some years ago, with but one exception that I ever heard of, have done so well that the great majority possess property and position in the colony far beyond what could possibly have been anticipated if they had stayed here."

"Well, I would not want to live there!"

"Mary, you have no *need* to emigrate. You have everything you require here in England. But these people – these labourers – have nothing. Nothing at all. It's nigh impossible

262

for us to even begin to appreciate their wretched existence. Their possessions are pitiful. All they have is each other and the clothes that they stand in." He sighed. "So I have booked passage for some of them to leave the country and to continue our experiment to determine if their lot would be a better one by starting afresh elsewhere."

Lady Wolverton appeared to digest this but said nothing.

Charles nodded. "It seems a sad reflection on our times that it is better for an honest man to take his family halfway around the World to some distant colony than to be employed in his own country."

"Quite," agreed Lord Osborne.

"All the same," Charles continued, "I expect it is a miserable experience for some of them to leave their community even though they may have lived in hardship. Most of them will never see their families and friends again. I would much appreciate hearing the outcome of your little experiment, Sidney. It has certainly been a most enterprising solution to the problem and I congratulate you on its originality."

"Thank you. I have found it impossible not to be moved by their appalling circumstances and I was determined to help at least some of them if I could. I am afraid that I do become rather irate when we discuss the situation: the abuse of the poor by those with wealth and position. Almost as if they count for nothing – little better than slaves."

"Sidney…" his wife touched his elbow and smiled, hoping to calm him.

"But it's not just in agriculture that there is a prejudice against those of humble station," maintained Lord Osborne. "I have recently been called upon to assist with an inquiry into the conduct of the lifeboatmen at Poole during the Great Gale and had an insight into the lives that seafaring men lead as well."

"Good gracious!" cried Lady Wolverton. "Did a lifeboat really go out in *that*? They're not very big boats are they – I've seen them – how on earth did they survive?"

"Well, the lifeboat is a lot more sturdy than one might believe from its appearance."

"All the same," she continued, "Sidney, dear, they deserve a medal just for venturing forth!"

"I agree, but there are comparisons to be made between the poor who work on the land and those who live off the sea. The men who serve with the lifeboat, for example, are all very poor – fishermen, harbour pilots and so on. In agriculture a small number of landowners have the power to force labourers to work for a pittance, and I observed a similar abuse of power concerning the lifeboat just recently. The crew of the Poole boat were called to account based upon the complaints of a landed gentleman. This was someone with no seafaring experience, yet because of his social station his letter of complaint to the Mayor resulted in a public inquiry. Lifeboatmen paraded out for a good ticking off."

"Was the complaint justified?" demanded his sister.

"Their behaviour was perhaps not exemplary, but the weather was most extraordinary, as you yourself noted, and I don't believe the criticism of them was fitting so soon after a lifeboat had been stationed at Poole."

"Oh, now come along, Sidney, you must give us the full story," Charles enticed him, placing his cutlery neatly on the plate in front of him. "It sounds fascinating."

───────────────

Stoker made his way down the wide road between the dark three-storey terraces to Tom Hart's house. He rented of course. Few working men could afford to buy their own house, but the rents were affordable and Tom's landlord was more reasonable than most. He knocked at the door, noting the beautifully polished brass handle: Maria was industrious, and kept a good clean house.

Tom himself opened the door in his rolled-up shirt sleeves and brown serge trousers.

"Afternoon," said Stoker, smiling weakly.

"Hello Stoker!" cried Tom, surprised but clearly delighted. He shook his hand warmly. "Bless my soul! Come on in. Didn't expect to find you standing there." He led the way down the narrow hall. "How are you? Not seen hide nor hair o' you for blimmin' ages. Was beginning to wonder if you'd gone on a long sea voyage or something."

"I know."

"I'm here solo. Let's have a smoke and a yarn by the fire."

"I had to cut myself off for a bit, Tom." It seemed a feeble explanation now. "Come to terms with it all, you know…"

"Don't you go apologising to me, Stoker," he warned. "You been through a trial, and no mistake. A lot o' men would've buckled under it all, or gone off to live as a hermit or some'it."

"A hermit? Mary would never let me get away with that.

She'd be forever coming to clip me beard or iron a shirt for me. I'd be the smartest hermit in England, that's for sure." Stoker let out a deep breath. "Some days I get so screwed up about all this," he confided quietly.

"And by time you get to the end o' the day you're cursing yourself for dwelling on it, but you can't help it."

"That's right." Stoker appreciated his friend's insight.

There was a silent space disturbed only by the slow quiet ticking of the clock on the mantel.

"Hope you don't mind me asking, but have you given any thought yet to your next assistant coxswain?" asked Tom. It was still a tender subject.

"A bit. I mean Sam's the obvious choice, but he says 'no'. Can't say I blame him. He felt it would be hurtful to you – I expect he told you – and I asked Frank too but he don't want it 'cos of the baby being ill." Stoker paused. "I'm not sure who else to ask. Why? Did you have someone in mind? You're not going to suggest Cain now, are you?" He grinned.

"Well, that's not so far off the mark. What about Jim Matthews?" Tom suggested.

"Jim? Cain's brother? He's nought but a boy! He can't be much over twenty I reckon."

"I say if you're good enough you're old enough, and I tell you what: he's strong as a lion that lad. Frank reckons he's the toughest man in Poole. Seen him pick up Fred Young and carry him over his head… "

"Well, if we could get him we'd have no trouble recruiting anyone else, that's for sure." Jim was one of the most popular men on the Quay and very different from his more truculent brother. "Everyone likes Jim. D'you think he'd be interested then?"

"Don't know, but I can ask him on the quiet if you like," offered Tom. "He only lives over East Quay Road – above the *King & Queen Inn*."

"What about Cain?" asked Stoker.

"How d'you mean?"

"Will he mind – us asking Jim?"

"You think Cain would feel he's been passed over, do you?" Tom expressed amazement. "He'd never want the job *surely*! That bugger would quarrel with a stone. He'd be no good at all…"

"No, no. I mean should we ask Cain to speak to Jim?"

"I can't see Cain making a good case now, can you?" Tom raised his eyebrows.

Stoker wondered if he was dodging his own responsibility if Tom helped him seek out a replacement. But on the other hand, Stoker wasn't sure he was prepared for a rejection and Tom knew Jim much better than he did.

"Maybe you could speak to him then," agreed Stoker. "Sound him out, like you say. Would you mind, Tom? It's very good o' you."

"No trouble at all. You need someone fit for the job and everyone'd be pleased to work with Jim. What's more he'd be a good right-hand man. Give the crew confidence and back you up."

"I think you got a good idea there, Tom," said Stoker, offering him his baccy pouch. "The more I think on it, the more I reckon Jim'd be a good asset."

Tom started stuffing his pipe. "Thankee, I reckoned so too." He handed the pouch back so Stoker could fill his own pipe, and then they both lit up and sat back enjoying the aroma of the burning tobacco.

After a few minutes of silent enjoyment, Tom turned to Stoker. "What we need is a victory to set the record straight. Pull off a good rescue, and then all this'd be behind us. Forgotten."

"Aye, I've been longing for a way to prove ourselves but all we can do is bide our time. I *know* we can do it, and it's not easy waiting for God to give us a second chance."

Chapter Sixteen

The early morning light showed a dark sea in dramatic contrast to the low, chalky clouds. A lone fishing vessel ploughed with determination through the chopping waters, the thick reddish-brown sails billowing out with a gentle rumple as the boat tacked in the gathering wind. The waves slapped against the hull and sent sprays of salt water into the faces of the two fishermen and their companion.

It was mid-August but it was still surprisingly fresh this early in the morning, for the sun had not yet fully risen. Even while it ebbed away the remnants of night seemed to exert a smothering effect on nature – maintaining all life in dormancy. It was remarkably peaceful.

Richard Wills had a narrow serious face with keen blue eyes and his brown hair was matted down by the sea spray that had blown over him. Although only a youth he already had the frame of a powerful man. He was strong and knew it. His large hands – 'like great dinner plates' his father used to say – were particularly noticeable. He surveyed the deserted sea about them, then he returned aft to talk to Bill Brown, standing at the tiller of the *Ursula* with Stoker. There was a satisfied murmur from the rigging, the smack of the waves. A gull squealed by: a courtesy call – he knew there'd be no scraps yet.

"Shall I take the tiller?" asked Richard at last, breaking into the tranquillity.

"No, no. Not yet." Perhaps Bill observed the young man's disappointment: "Later on," he conceded. He wanted him to know that he called the tune on his own boat. Richard had worked with his father since the age of ten, and he was now fifteen, but his father's boat was laid up for repairs so he'd sought employment from Bill. And Bill was glad to have him – a good strong lad who knew his way around the harbour – but when the ebb tide was running this hard he trusted his own hand on the tiller more than anyone else's.

"Reckon it'll be a fine day, when the sun's pulled this mist away," Richard observed.

"Aye," replied Bill after a space. He was not keen on early morning conversation. There was a further space of a few minutes, then: "Rich, take your hands out o' your pockets." It was important to always have your hands free on deck – you never knew what might happen.

Richard did as he was told. "There's a nip in the air," he protested.

"Aye," said Bill again. He looked a veritable bulwark of old England, standing there in his heavy black jersey: a sturdy though portly figure. Quite formidable on first sight, Bill actually had a very fatherly disposition. He straightened his cap, while Richard leaned against the transom of the *Ursula* folding his arms tightly to warm himself a little.

Standing at the back of the boat left Richard fully exposed to the wind and he wanted to go forward where he'd be protected from it, but he couldn't show weakness in front of Bill and Stoker. Stoker was strangely silent, pent up. Like a bottle with the cork rammed in tight.

"D'you know," said Stoker, turning to Bill suddenly, "that George Penney sent Will out with the steamer the day after the Great Gale looking for salvage?"

"I do know it," said Bill, disappointed that the subject had been broached at all after so many months. "Still that's his job,

270

I suppose. But I thought you were coming out here with us to get away from all that?"

"It were one o' them schooners," said Stoker looking distant. "The *Augusta*. She'd not gone under. Took two ballast barges alongside to re-float her and then the steamer towed her in."

"Mr Meadus's shipyard took her, at Hamworthy," Richard announced. "I seen her come in."

"Her master was washed up at Christchurch, you know," Stoker informed them quietly. "William Nathan Bryant was his name."

All three of them studied the bottom boards in silence for a space.

"It's good to have the water to ourselves," Bill broke in heartily, forcing a change of subject. "You won't see it this quiet very often. When was the last time you went out fishing then Stoker?"

"Oh, not for a long while." Stoker used to be a fisherman himself, but the lightkeeping role no longer allowed time for it.

"How long?" Bill insisted.

"Last time I went out was – well, with you I reckon and that must be three years ago at least."

"Get away, is it really three years?" Bill was genuinely surprised. "Three years since you did a *proper* day's work then." Bill grinned.

Stoker knew what his old friend was trying to do and

appreciated it. "I miss the variety," he mused. "You never know how much you're going to catch, or what you'll catch."

"Aye, there is that. But with your big family, a regular wage for the lightkeeping is a boon. Some days I come back from fishing with next to nought, and I still got to feed a household somehow." Bill nodded to Richard. "The sooner we get working the sooner we'll warm up," he assured him.

"I know." He'd been trying not to show that he was cold.

"And I thought I told you to wear a hat, Rich."

"I forgot."

"Well no wonder you're cold. Look in that locker there, you'll find an old one o' mine."

Richard obediently went forward. He came back wearing a red knitted cap. It was dirty and smelt of fish but he didn't care.

Bill needed something to distract Stoker; take his mind off his troubles. He could already see him beginning to mull once more. He mustn't be allowed to keep turning it over and over in his head, for that was the first step in a chain of events which rapidly turned inwards into self-pity and depression. He had to help him break the cycle. Break it once and it would be easier to break next time.

"Here, Rich," said Bill loudly, "you take the tiller and keep her in the channel in the hardest o' the tide, and I'll get the gear ready. Stoker'll tell you a thing or two no doubt." Richard didn't need instructing, but it would give Stoker something to think about.

When Richard went out with any of the fishermen he was

usually given the job of clearing the decks, ready for when they fished in earnest, so today he enjoyed the freedom of standing on the stern platform handling Bill's boat. That sense of liberty was only slightly marred by having Stoker stand alongside, but he liked Stoker and resolved to make an impression. He kept course resolutely towards the mouth of the Harbour, alert for possible danger. Bill busied himself doing all the jobs that he would usually ask a youngster to do: cutting up the bait, cleaning out the boxes where the catch would go, clearing the decks of clutter, checking the rig; a sharp knife and hatchet put ready in case of emergency.

Stoker was impressed at Richard's handling of the yawl. He noticed how he gave the buoys a wide berth: it was easy to go foul of them with little steerageway on a hard tide. The youngster did not ride the helm but gave the boat freedom to run with what wind there was, before adjusting her bearings from time to time. Stoker could see that Richard was an excellent seaman even at this young age, and exuded a certain confidence.

Stoker warmed to the lad and told him tales to pass the time.

"That channel back there – Rum Row," said Stoker. "Did Bill ever tell you about the narrow squeak we had there?"

"No," said Richard, intrigued.

"Ahoy there for'ard!" called Stoker. "What's this then Bill? You not told this lad about our capers aboard the *Fortuna*?"

Bill looked up. "I knew I should never have brought you out here." He shook his head. "Go on then…"

"Ah well," began Stoker, "it goes like this you see. When me and Bill were a lot younger we went out with old Jacob

Norris, God rest him. Now Jacob had a terrible old boat called the *Fortuna* – rotten as shit – but I didn't know it and neither did Bill, but old Jacob hadn't two pennies to rub together, as they say, and we offered to give him a hand to go spratting." Stoker bent his knees a fraction to see past the bulge in the sail. "Just port your helm a fraction, that's it, so's we give Aunt Betsy Buoy a wider berth. Now, where was I? Oh, aye, well, we made fair way under sail and got out abreast Half Diver when we sprung a leak. Now when I say 'leak' I don't mean some pissing dribble but a great spurt o' water suddenly just shot up through the planks near the mast-step like a bloody whale. I dived down and stemmed the flow with a bit o' rag.

" 'What's going on, Jacob?' I said.

" 'Oh not again,' says he.

" 'Not *again*?' says Bill.

" 'Same thing happened last week,' he says!"

"Well then," said Bill, taking over the story, "I felt around and all the planking was soft as a pear. Me pocket knife went straight in it, easy. So ginger-like, I stuffed the hole as best I could and we stayed off the rotten timber while Stoker and I kept bailing out, and Jacob puts the tiller over for Rum Row."

"It were touch and go," continued Stoker. "Water gushing in like there were no tomorrow, everything awash and I thought we'd had it. But as luck would have it the tide was rising and it edged us over toward Summerhouse Lake. There's no water there to speak of – you could see the seabed – and just as we were getting into the shallows the keel struck, the whole bottom gave way, and she stove herself in on the sand."

"The *sand* mind you!" emphasised Bill. "I ask you. She were that rotten that a sandbank finished her off. It's a wonder that me or Stoker didn't just fall through her as soon as we stepped aboard at the Quay."

"What did you do then?"

Stoker resumed the narrative. "We just had to jump overboard. Water came right up to our chests – bloody freezing cold day – and we waded up to the beach at Elm Park. The shallows go out there for about quarter o' mile and it took us twenty minutes more or less. I thought old Jacob were gonna freeze to death in it and had visions o' me and Bill having to carry him. But we got ashore and there was Jacob blethering about his 'lovely boat' when he'd near killed us all."

"How d'you get home?" asked Richard.

"We had to *walk!*" cried Bill. "Wet through as shags, the three of us."

By now they were outside the harbour and racing through Long Channel. Bill went forward once more.

"Keep well outside them channel buoys, Rich," said Stoker. "This tide's still running like a train." He stroked his beard. "I remember my father telling me a West-Indiaman went ashore just here near the harbour's mouth. Over fifty years ago it must be now. Mr Sturt – he were member of parliament then – he owned Branksea Island and he took 'em all in, fed 'em, dried their clothes and gave 'em rest. They lost the ship, but thanks to Mr Sturt they saved the cargo and crew. The owner were so grateful he sent Mr Sturt a fine horse."

They passed across Studland Bay and headed towards Old Harry Rocks.

"Right," said Bill. "I'll clew that sail in, you stay on course Rich, and keep an eye out for the float."

The lobster-pots were laid in a line of ten with each end weighted. Their location was marked with a knot of corks bobbing on the surface holding an upright cane topped by a piece of coloured sailcloth. Richard kept his eyes peeled wanting to spot the float first. "There!" he cried as he spotted the tell-tale piece of orange cloth, "just outside of us." He knew this was the lower end of the string, so he let the *Ursula* run towards it and with a cry of "Coming about!" he brought her up into the light wind. The boat virtually stopped and it was easy then for Bill to pick up the float with the boat hook.

"Heave ho," he sang out as he hauled the line in, hand over hand, allowing it to coil neatly on the deck next to him. After about sixty feet of rope the first lobster-pot came into view. The pot was the shape of an inverted pudding basin and was made of locally cut withies woven together. It had a single funnel entrance – or swallow – which allowed a lobster to enter but not to escape, and it was kept on the seabed with three large pebbles. The first pot was empty.

Richard helped Bill lift the pot on deck. Stoker re-baited it ready to be put back in a different location.

"Keep clear o' them lines, Rich," called Bill, who warned him every time there was rope in the bottom of the boat. It was important that this safety message was ingrained into young fishermen as second nature, so they'd never catch a foot in a turn of the rope when it was going out and be dragged overboard.

"Aye." Richard carried the pot aft. "I'll stack them pots over here as they come in."

"That's right." Bill continued to haul on the rope. "Good lad."

A second pot came up, this time with a lobster inside. "Here we are!" Bill cried. "Take a look at that Stoker – there's a fine one!" He pulled in the pot before Richard could reach him to help.

"Well I never, I didn't think we'd get anything today. That joker must be at least four pound." He reached in and skilfully pulled it out through the swallow. "Tie up them claws, Rich."

Richard fished into his pocket for the short lengths of string he'd cut the night before just for the purpose and took the dark blue animal expertly from Bill.

"Reckon he's getting on for five pounds," said Richard eagerly. "Look at the size of that clumper claw!" The two asymmetric claws of the lobster were known as the pincher and the clumper, and the clumper was always bigger. He soon had them tied and handed the lobster over to Stoker for examination.

"A beauty," said Stoker appreciatively. "Not seen one this size for a while."

"Nor me." Bill grunted as he heaved on the rope again, and Richard put the prize lobster into one of the storage boxes which was kept forward.

Bill continued pulling and more pots started to come up – three, four, five – with a lobster in each.

"Take a spell," Richard suggested. "I'll get these others in."

But Bill rarely allowed Richard or any of the other young

fishermen he took with him to do the hauling even if it was getting too much for him.

"No, no," said the older man. He had been feeling the strain of the haul, but was now determined to show he was up to the task. "You just catch hold o' that tiller and make sure we drive beam-on to the end float."

Pot six held two small lobsters. They'd been fighting during their confinement and one of them only had one claw remaining. Bill tutted as he pointed it out to Stoker. Pot number seven held one lobster; pots eight and nine were empty. The tenth pot was the last pot and Bill struggled heartily to pull it out of the depths.

"Saints alive! We've got something heavy here and it's not a lobster, that's for sure," he gasped as he pulled. Without asking, Richard went to Bill's aid and they both tugged hand over hand taking the strain between them. "Reckon we caught on some wreckage down there or something…"

Stoker wanted to help but knew he'd risk getting in the way. Besides, a sixth sense told him Richard wouldn't like it. He came over to look all the same and together they watched as the pot came up into view through the icy clear water.

The sea thrashed as the occupant of the last lobster-pot tried to resist being drawn away from his watery home and into the world of air.

"Bloody great conger eel!" cried Bill, breathing hard as they heaved the pot into the boat. "Talk about a tight fit, you couldn't fit more eel in that pot if you tried."

They stood and looked at the pot crammed with sliding thick grey eel, squirming in the restricted space.

"He's almost as thick as my thigh," observed Bill, catching his breath. "And that great head looks far too big to have even got in the pot to start with. He had to work to squeeze himself in there and no mistake."

"Why on earth do a fish that size ever go in a lobster-pot in the first place?" asked Stoker.

"Well, congers like the taste o' rotted fish just like lobsters," Bill explained. "They smell it from a long way off and go looking for it, and they like small spaces, you see. Like to get into little holes where they feel safe: they live in gaps in the rocks and the narrow places."

Stoker was sure he was right, but wanted to ask him how he knew all this, but there was no time. Bill barked out the orders. "Right Rich, you can have the joy o' trying to get him out when I've finished taking up the rest of the line here and that end float. Watch your fingers mind, a bite from him'll give you sores, blood-poisoning and all sorts." He turned to Stoker. "Jack Fisher got bit once and had a hand the size of a football for near three weeks. Couldn't work, it were that painful."

"I remember it," commented Stoker. "Near lost his hand, Isabel told me. Thought they'd have to get a surgeon down."

The rope was in and so was the end float.

Bill let the sails fill with wind and carry the boat forward. "We need to get off a bit afore we put that lot back down again, Stoker," said Bill, nodding to the lobster-pots.

Meanwhile Richard studied the conger. Bill was right: the head looked far too big to have passed through the funnel of the pot in the first place. It had stopped thrashing and lay coiled – still and sulking – and certainly in no mood to

279

co-operate with any attempt to remove it from its new home, but Richard knew what to do. He found an old piece of sailcloth and wrapped it round his hand then, dashing in quickly, he grabbed the end of the fish's tail and pulled it out through the swallow. The eel twisted momentarily, then surged out of confinement backwards. It was a trick that Richard had been shown before but it was the first time he had performed it with an eel this size and, surprised by the rapidity of the fish's movement, he was caught off-balance and tumbled backwards releasing his hold on the eel's tail, which went slithering across the deck into a grey figure-of-eight against the side. By instinct Richard twisted as he fell and broke his fall by landing painlessly on his right shoulder.

Stoker laughed. "Are you looking for a job with the circus, our Rich?"

Richard found it hard to laugh at himself, but grinned back at him as best he could. "Well he's out anyway," he said.

"So I see," said Bill. "What are you gonna do now then?" Bill was testing him.

"Can we sell him?" Richard suggested.

"Not on your life. No-one'd eat that rubbish. Tastes like a mouthful o' earth. Dreadful."

"Put him back then?"

"What? And waste that valuable bait? There's nothing prawns and crabs like better than a tasty slice o' conger meat."

"Shall I put him in one of the boxes?"

"Aye, but you'll have to kill him first otherwise he'll be out o' there in no time at all. Great eel like that'll live for hours and we can't have him gallivanting round the decks getting under our feet and making everything slippy."

As if by way of demonstration the eel detached itself from the side of the boat and starting wriggling strenuously amidships making a plaintive low barking noise. Stoker stared incredulously: he'd never heard a noise like it.

"It speaks!" cried Bill. "He's issuing you a challenge, Rich. Now imagine him doing all that wriggling around in the middle of a gale, or if we trod on him unexpected while we was working. We'd be pitched overboard."

"Well I never," said Stoker. "I never heard a fish make a sound afore in me life."

"They don't all do it, Stoker. Only the big 'uns like this twister, and then only on occasion."

Richard was silent. He didn't want to have to kill the eel. Killing and gutting ordinary-sized fish was fine, but this creature was bigger than some people's dogs. He didn't fancy cutting into it.

Stoker studied the conger for a space. It seemed even bigger now it was fully uncoiled and moving freely. "No wonder our ancestors thought there were monsters in the oceans when they pulled out brutes like this," he observed.

"How do we kill it then, Mr Richard?" demanded Bill.

"Don't know. Cut his head off?"

"With the hatchet, you mean?" Bill laughed. "Lord almighty, I'd like to see you try! No, no. Let me show you something. Take the tiller and keep us on a heading for that

281

buoy over there." Richard did as he was asked. "That's it."

Bill went forward and carried on speaking with his back to Richard and Stoker. "This is something that your Granfer showed me when I were a lad, God rest his soul." He started rummaging in the locker. "Here we are!" he cried, turning round again. "You need something heavy like a cosh. I picked up this iron tholepin down Baiter a few years ago: comes in handy sometimes. Now watch this."

He marched purposefully to the conger eel and in a swift movement turned it over and before the creature knew what was happening he struck hard once with the tholepin on a small vent on the underside. The eel straightened immediately and gave a harsh shiver as if suddenly cold then relaxed. It was dead.

"How's that then?" said Bill, looking up.

Richard and Stoker gaped in amazement. Richard was relieved he hadn't had to do it himself.

"Now you've seen it, you won't forget it neither, will you. Great creature like that with a secret weakness if you know where to find it."

They had reached their destination and in no time the baited lobster-pots were sent back to the sea floor. The *Ursula* headed westerly and soon Old Harry Rocks loomed up large on the starboard side. The high chalk cliffs had a thin green capping of vegetation but it was barely visible and against the backdrop of the pale clouds they looked taller, more imposing, as if reaching up to merge with the white heavens.

"Good lad," said Bill with a nod to Richard at the tiller. "Now we've got a dozen crab-pots to haul up," explained Bill to Stoker, "ten prawn pots and we're done."

"Aye," returned Stoker.

Bill spotted the first float and called out to Richard. "Put the conger in yon box and swab that deck down: get rid of all that eel slime. Stoker'll take the tiller."

Richard was surprised by the great dead-weight of the conger as he carried it to the box and slung it there unceremoniously. Its two vacant clouded eyes glared back at him and the jaws gaped, revealing its ranks of needle teeth. He dipped a bucket over the side and threw seawater against the planking to wash away the slime. Just to be certain he ran a brush over the area.

The crab-pots were the same as those for lobsters, except that they were baited with fresh fish. They were easier to pull in because the water wasn't as deep. It was a good spot as the first five pots all had crabs in them, but as Bill was pulling up the sixth he suddenly yelped and grabbed his right shoulder, letting the rope slip until he caught it with his left hand.

"What's up, Bill?" cried Richard as he and Stoker rushed across to join him.

"Don't know," he grunted. "Pulled a muscle, I think." He did not realise that this pain was arthritis caused by years of wear and tear on his shoulders. The constant hauling was virtually pulling his frame apart.

"Here, let me," said Richard, grabbing the rope.

"No I'm all right…"

"Just to take the weight off you for a moment," Richard suggested, and held the rope while Bill massaged his shoulder.

"Come astern with me," said Stoker, winking at Richard over Bill's shoulder.

Bill grimaced as he rolled his shoulder trying to work the shoulder into a pain-free position. "Just what I needed," he growled.

"Let Rich pull them last few pots up," whispered Stoker. "He's dying to show you he can do it. Look at him." He nodded over toward Richard, still keeping the strain on the rope.

"I'll get these in, Bill," he said, and didn't wait for approval, just started hauling.

"All right," said Bill cautiously, making his way back. "Handsomely now! Don't pull too hard in case the rope is caught on the rocks, and always keep two hands on the rope. Watch yourself when a swell comes under the boat: you need to brace yourself otherwise you'll go arse over head when we slip down the other side of it."

The next pot came up and housed a crab and a lobster. Richard seized the pot before Bill could interfere and transferred it to the deck. "If you take the lobster out Bill, I'll get ready to bring in the next one." Did he see the small smile that played on Bill's lips for a moment as he gave the older man his orders? If he did he showed no sign of it. Richard took the weight of the line in one hand then passed Bill the pieces of string from his pockets to tie the lobster claws.

And so they progressed with roles reversed. Richard was sorry for Bill's pain, but he enjoyed having the opportunity to drag the pots up from the depths himself. He always knew he would. Constant rowing about the harbour had hardened the skin on his palms and he felt no discomfort. Hauling was hard work, but the effort was easier if he maintained a rhythm. Even so Richard began to sweat as the sun was now higher in the sky.

The rope fell neatly into its natural coils beside him as it came on board. Richard stopped himself yelling out as a sharp piece of shell embedded in the lay of the rope dug into his hand, but he managed not to give this away.

The next pot held the second surprise of the day.

"Well I'm blowed," said Bill as it came into sight. "A bass in a crab-pot. I've never seen that afore. A stroke of luck! There's your tea, Stoker."

Richard smiled as Bill gleefully seized the large shiny silver fish, skilfully removing it from the pot while avoiding the spines in its gills and along its back, and carried it aft to show Stoker.

Richard made nothing of pulling the last few pots and they were rewarded by six particularly large crabs.

Bill stacked the empty pots and Richard re-baited them in the interim while they sailed to their new destination a few fathoms away. The two older men stood on the stern platform while Richard set the pots back into the sea. Bill was pleased to see that he had learnt well for they went over the side without fouling, and Richard took great care in keeping clear of the rope as it snaked past him.

Bill gave instructions for getting under way again to retrieve the prawn pots. Stoker took the tiller while Richard raised the foresail and Bill cleared away all the bits of seaweed and other detritus which had collected on the planking. They were past Old Harry now and following the base of the imposing chalk cliffs towards Ballard Point. Despite Stoker's experience, it was natural for Bill to take the tiller here as it required skill to negotiate from one prawn pot to the next. They were laid individually, each one marked with a float.

Richard picked up the first one with the boathook. These pots were large tightly netted boxes with a narrow funnel entrance baited with fish in the centre, so only small creatures that ate carrion could enter to dine. In practice most of the catch were prawns. He quickly hauled the short line until the pot came to the surface. The water boiled out as it left the sea and Richard held it to the boat's coamings, allowing it to drain fully via the gulleys, before heaving it on board. The pot was brimming with prawns. The small crustaceans struggled feebly in their prison, making a characteristic rustling noise which sounded like a small crowd quietly chewing soft food with their mouths open.

Bill never ceased to marvel that the cycle of the prawns was so faithful: they spawned in Studland Bay, then migrated when very small to the harbour which acted almost as a nursery. They grew quickly in size and then around August time dropped out again into Studland Bay.

Once on board, Richard released the trap door in the bottom of the pot and emptied the contents into a large box before handing the pot to Stoker for baiting. Then it was put overboard in a different place and they set off for the next pot. Gradually they worked the whole series of pots until the last one was back in position ready for tomorrow.

Richard could hardly contain his enthusiasm throughout and Stoker delighted to see it. Richard didn't even feel tired. It was exciting to be in control of the haul and with each full pot he had become more and more pleased with their morning's work.

"Look at that, Bill!" cried Richard surveying the boat neatly stacked with their catch. "Better'n yesterday!"

"Aye," said Bill. "A day's work," he noted with a conservative satisfaction. He glanced towards the horizon. "About half-nine I reckon. Let's get on home afore this weather turns on us," he said, eyeing some small clouds way out to sea. "Them messengers tell me we might have a blow directly."

The tide was in full flood and when Richard set the foresail the *Ursula* dipped her nose into the sea and glided towards the channel. She was soon racing along at a fair speed, charging clean through the waves as if they were not there, the sail taut and so full of wind it never flapped once. Perhaps this was the fastest she'd ever travelled. It had been a long time since Bill had felt exhilarated by his own boat slicing through the elements like this.

"We're making quite a lick!" he cried above the wind and the waves. "Pity we can't come back like this every day. We'll be home in half an hour easy."

Richard smiled. He had hoped to steer the boat himself, but seeing Bill's great pleasure he hadn't the heart to ask. Another day perhaps. Instead, while Bill chatted away merrily to Stoker, Richard sat on the thwarts to attend to a task he had always liked. The very first time that he had been in the boat with his father, aged about seven, he'd been asked to sort through the prawns for him: 'Everything that's not a prawn goes over the side' his father had instructed. Richard liked the job partly because of that happy memory but also because he never knew what he might find.

"Watch your hands, Richard!" called Bill; he couldn't resist giving him instructions, even though he'd done this job hundreds of times.

Even an experienced fisherman had to be a little careful about diving his hands into the boxes because of the sharp needle-like spine on the head of each prawn. Then there were bullheads – small fish with an array of sharp spikes around their gills, head and fins. There were always plenty of them mixed in with the prawns. Nonetheless Richard dug his tough hands into the prawn boxes with impunity.

He started by pulling out small pieces of green seaweed and then found his first real intruder amongst the packed prawns – a squat lobster. They were like lobsters – with two claws – but much smaller: the body no more than two inches long. The body was squashed and greenish-brown as opposed to the blue-black of a real lobster. No-one seemed to know if you could eat them. Richard had asked often enough but never got a straight answer. Over the side it went, and there were plenty more where he came from, plus an even greater number of crabs of all sizes and colours. There were dog whelks too, not unlike winkles and about the same size.

Richard continued raking through the mass of feebly struggling translucent prawns. There was a small flatfish – hard to tell what kind – but a perfect flatfish in miniature just an inch and half long. And, there, a short red eel – a ling – five inches or so and very soft, plus several small silver fish. Pollack perhaps? Far too small to eat anyway. Over the side they went. As soon as they hit the speeding water they zipped downwards towards the sea bed. There was something intensely pleasurable about this little task. It was a fascinating little world in which anyone could easily become quite absorbed.

What else was lurking in the boxes amongst the prawns? Some brightly coloured wrasse, a blenny, a few whelks, stones… and right at the bottom a white prawn. It was identical to its grey vitreous brethren in all respects apart from its colour. He showed it to Bill.

"Aye," Bill said. "A 'miller'. Not seen one o' they for years. Mighty rare. They go red as you like, when they're cooked. You ever seen a miller, Stoker?"

"Can't say I have," he replied.

And then Stoker realised he hadn't thought about the inquiry, the letters in the paper, or anything to do with the lifeboat for a good five hours. Besides, he was looking forward to that bass for his tea.

Chapter Seventeen

Tom Hart did not forget his promise to sound out Jim Matthews concerning the vacant position of assistant coxswain, but he bided his time – waiting for an appropriate moment to bring it up. He saw Jim around the town often enough, but didn't want to ask him about the lifeboat when he was in company or distracted by other matters. Sooner or later, Tom reasoned, the right occasion would present itself.

Sure enough, one evening he spied Jim walking alone across Baiter Field and Tom hailed him and went to work, expertly whetting Jim's appetite and preparing the way for Stoker. He knew Jim liked a challenge – physical or mental – and that was the line he pursued. By the time they reached his lodgings above the *King & Queen Inn* on the Quay, Jim was so stirred by the prospect that he determined to speak to Stoker about the position at the earliest opportunity.

So, a few days after this encounter, and when his mind was preoccupied with something completely different for a change, Stoker was delighted to find himself accosted by Jim in the smoky atmosphere of the *New Inn*. Jim had a darker complexion than his brother Cain, a thick mop of black tousled hair, and his perpetual smile contrasted with his brother's habitual scowl. He was wearing a thick grey jumper but his strong physique was still very evident.

"How are you then, Stoker?" asked Jim.

"Oh, well enough Jim. Well enough."

"Tom was telling me about the lifeboat," said the younger man, leaning against the bar next to Stoker.

"Aye," replied Stoker noncommittally. It was a while since he'd seen Jim. Now he saw him up close again perhaps he *was* a little too young for it.

"I spoke to Cain too," Jim continued. "They were both saying that you could do with a few extra hands."

"That's right," the coxswain affirmed. "I'm looking for strong men who can handle a boat. Men who can sit out a gale all day in the bitter cold, and who know the sea." His eyes narrowed as he scrutinised Jim.

"Well, I'd like to be counted in, Stoker, if you think I'm up to it."

It was all said so honestly, and without guile, that Stoker was forced to laugh and instantly he changed his mind about this young man's suitability.

"Up to it?" roared Stoker. "You're from one of the oldest fishing families in Poole, and the strongest man any of us know! Course we'd have you aboard any day o' the week."

Jim beamed in response. "Thankee," he said.

"Let me get you a beer. Harry!" he called, "two more pints here, my friend!" Stoker glanced about him. "The thing is Jim... you know what we went through in the, er, inquiry and all?"

"Aye – know all about that."

"So you know it's no bed o' roses. That lot's behind us now, but we gotta be sure it won't happen again. We need a crew that'll stick together – that knows the boat, knows the waters, knows each other. Kind of a family to my way o' thinking." Stoker lowered his voice. "I want people from round here to be *proud* of the lifeboat and know she can be relied on, but we've got some ground to make up."

"What happened last time – how do we know it won't happen again?"

Stoker was slightly disconcerted by the question. "Well, knowing we'd be all over the paper again with more o' them bloody letters is a big enough spur to betterment, I can tell you," confided Stoker. "We've all been through the mill on that account alone. But now we need something to aim at: fear of failing ain't enough when we're out there in a gale. We need to be ready for anything." He stopped as two beers arrived on the bar. "Well done, Harry," said Stoker, laying down a sixpence and handing one of the drinks to his newest recruit.

"Thankee, Stoker," said Jim as he sipped at the top of the pint to stop it slopping out of the tankard.

"Come on," said Stoker, "let's go sit over yonder in the corner."

They made their way to a quieter part of the inn by a window.

"Your good health," said Stoker, holding his tankard up.

Jim did likewise. "And yours." He took a big gulp.

"Supposed to be haunted," said Stoker, nodding around the bar as they sat down "but I never seen nothing, have you?"

"No. Load of old rubbish." Jim looked impatient and brought the conversation straight back to the matter at hand. "What d'you reckon you need, Stoker, to get a crew fit for the job? That's what I want to know. Be honest with me now. How big a task are we up against?"

"Well, the main thing is sussing out the boat herself – to know she ain't gonna capsize on us, break apart, sink – we got to get used to handling her in all weathers. It was want of that which held us back afore. The inquiry said as much."

"And what about the men? Are they up to it?"

"Surely!" said Stoker, surprised. Jim was like his brother Cain in one respect – he was very direct. "Aye, no problems there."

"Not even with my brother?" Jim grinned.

"Well, you know Cain…"

"I do, and I reckon he'll have far too much to say as usual."

Stoker sat back and smiled. "Aye, he does."

"He needs to know who's boss, Stoker," warned Jim. "Make no mistake; otherwise we'll never get a thing done. Good man at heart, but *contrary* – and you know well enough what I mean."

They both took a long drink.

"Look at that!" hissed Jim, glaring out the window. "Is that Molly Roberts?" Stoker looked and saw John Wills in an embrace with a woman in a dark street corner.

"Aye. That's another stick to beat the lifeboat with." Stoker sighed. "Everyone knows Johnny's on the crew. Him and his goings on. He ought to be more careful." He drew the raggedy curtain to hide the view.

There was a burst of laughter from the bar, and Jim downed most of his remaining beer.

"Are they strong enough?" asked Jim, returning once more to their original topic. "The lifeboat crew: are they man enough? Rowing in a storm's not like rowing in-harbour."

Stoker valued the opportunity for an honest assessment. "They're strong enough, and tough enough, but it's the boat they're worried about and learning how to handle her in a heavy sea. It's different to any boat I've ever been in – there's no boat like your own, is there – and staying out in a gale on purpose goes against nature for anyone with an apeth o' sense."

"Hmm," said Jim, and fished out his pipe. "Have you got another bowman aside Cain?"

"No, we ain't had a big enough crew for reserves, but Tom's gonna help us with that."

"And does Cain practise throwing that grapnel? Oftentimes you're only gonna get one chance to hook on to a ship."

"No, I've never seen him do it. I asked him but…"

"What d'you think about doing more training?"

"We need it, for sure, but it's finding time – we're all family men, got a living to make…"

"If we don't do the training we're gonna fail again," insisted Jim, "or some of us are gonna get killed."

"Aye." Stoker was beginning to feel inadequate as a leader. Jim's observations were correct, but Stoker doubted his own

294

ability to bring about the necessary changes. Perhaps he lacked the personality to persuade others, but he could see that Jim would carry much more authority despite his relative youth. There was just something about him… Stoker watched him finish his beer.

"What are you gonna do about replacing Tom?" asked Jim, interrupting Stoker's thoughts. Jim knew that Stoker was thinking of asking him to take that role, but it wouldn't do to presume. "Tom said you were looking for someone."

"Aye. I need someone I can trust you see, Jim, and someone the rest o' the crew will look to. We've been through hard times of late and we need some fresh blood to inspire us, give us all a gee up." Stoker studied him again and then took the plunge. "I reckon you'd fit the bill, Jim, if you fancy taking it on."

Jim smiled. "I reckon I will if you're really offering it me."

Stoker reached across the small table and shook Jim's hand. "Good," he said. "Good. I know you're gonna help us turn this thing around." He gave him a suspicious look. "Did you know I was gonna ask you?"

"Well, Tom dropped a hint," revealed Jim. "I've been thinking about it for a few days. Lifeboat's so vital, Stoker, and Lord knows you went through a lot 'cos of that Great Gale – don't know how you took it all on – but I want to be part of it from now on; want to help you put new life into the lifeboat; make it work; get ready for the next call-out. Tom told me you needed a victory and he's right."

Stoker actually felt elated. Genuinely happy. He knew he'd found someone who could help him achieve his goal.

———

Lord Osborne and his wife stood watching the ship packed with their local labourers meet the horizon.

"Bless them all," he said quietly. "Launched on a sea of adventure to lands where their industry and honesty may gain a life denied them here. God speed little ship." Lord Osborne's eyes were watery. Was it emotion, or the effect of staring into the wind for so long? "They will be infinitely more contented over there than back here in England," he said. "I feel sure of it. Australia offers them a wonderful opportunity. A chance to escape the trap of poverty in a new land away from greedy landowners."

"Yes, I hope you're right," Emily said wistfully, then looked at him and smiled. "No, I *know* you're right. It's just that at a personal level it all seems so very wrong. I know it was the only solution we could come up with, but ripping these good people out of their homes like this..."

Lord Osborne nodded. "Did you hear the little girl asking her mother if she could go and play with the neighbour's kittens? Even here in Poole they were thirty miles from that neighbour; in Australia they'll be thousands of miles away." He sighed. "The children do not understand what it all means."

"I have always thought it must be a dread and bitter moment when they bid their final farewells to aged fathers and mothers," said Emily sadly. "In a short time their children, their grandchildren, quitting them and in all probability for ever. A monstrous upheaval for the whole family..."

"And all because wealthy men refuse to pay labourers a reasonable wage for an honest day's work on the land," he observed. "A sad motive for so many, at such mental cost, to leave their homes and take a long sea passage to a far distant country." He let out a long sigh.

It was the young and middle-aged who went. Just before their departure Lord Osborne had fallen into conversation with two young men who were about to embark. He had felt compelled to apologise that their mother country had treated them so badly. One of the men said: "I tell you what it is, sir: we are starving each other here. We be too thick in our place; the best of us can't earn enough for bread for our children and ourselves, let alone clothing and the rent. When we be gone 'twill be better for they we leave behind."

Emily broke into his thoughts. "I was talking to one of the young women – her name was Betsy. I asked her what she had managed to pack – a silly question and I felt ashamed the moment I asked it for they all have precious little, but I wanted to be interested – and she called her husband over and they showed me a great tea-tray, with pictures of a wagon with large white horses. It was the chief ornament of their cottage wall: the very tray they bought for their wedding tea-party. 'We had to sell all else' she said, 'but we both would like to save this more than any other thing we possess'."

Suddenly, provoked by her own account, Emily burst into tears, and then they both were holding each other while the tears fell. It was the insight into these people's poverty and hardship, coupled with joy at their liberation. Husband and wife knew they had transformed the labouring families' lives by helping them to start afresh, but both bitterly regretted the necessity of their intervention and despaired of the many others who would never receive help.

———————————

There were some initial rumblings amongst the lifeboat crew against the appointment of someone as young as Jim Matthews to the position of assistant coxswain. However, these feelings soon dissipated once Jim took up the position and the crew were able to see for themselves his disciplined approach to duty. He was a natural leader with a deceptively easy-going manner, a calm confidence and a surety of purpose which leant him authority.

It was some time before the lifeboat was called out again, and this gave Stoker and Jim plenty of opportunity to establish the new leadership and put the crew through their paces. Stoker felt reinvigorated, and was determined that the lifeboat and her crew would pass the next test with flying colours, whenever it came. With Jim's help he was able to get the men to do things that they would never have done for the coxswain alone. This renewed enthusiasm coincided with an unexpected letter from Captain Robertson at the RNLI offering to assist them with a training exercise.

Stoker and Jim leapt at the prospect of help from a navy captain and on the day in question they were gratified to witness a fine turn-out from the crew. Following Captain Robertson's instructions the lifeboatmen took him from North Haven to the Quay in the *Manley Wood*. He made sure that they all heard him congratulate Stoker on the crew's efficiency in launching the lifeboat and their ability to handle it at sea. The manner in which he paid compliments was honest and the crew could tell that he was not used to giving them freely.

When they reached Poole, Robertson had arranged for the lifeboat to be hauled up out of the water by one of the dockyard derricks, and then he ordered her to be dropped into the sea, keelside-up, from a height of about fifteen feet. The crew watched as the lifeboat almost immediately righted herself. Then the captain stopped up the reliever valves and the crew pumped seawater into the lifeboat until she filled to the brim. The boat sank low into the sea but she didn't sink, and as soon as the valves were unblocked the boat rose miraculously out of the water to float merrily on the surface. Two dramatic and memorable demonstrations of the lifeboat's capabilities.

The captain split the crew into teams and set them to race with each other as they took it in turns to row between two points while he stood and timed them with his pocketwatch. Jim was very competitive and his team always won. Then they practised pulling drowning men out of the water. Captain Robertson showed them the safest way to load survivors into the boat to maintain its centre of gravity and how a packed boat could overbalance if this was not carefully attended to. He made them all practise throwing the grapnel and demonstrated the best technique for accuracy and distance. They even took the boat out in shallow water and deliberately capsized her a few times so the crew could practise scrambling back on board fully clothed. Finally the captain gave them advice on how to survive in the harshest conditions, including how to prepare a sail to make a roof over the boat to afford some protection during a long spell at sea.

It was a very thorough preparation and at the end of the day's training, all the crew had learned to be more confident in the boat and each other.

After the inspirational training provided by Captain Robertson, Jim made each of their regular exercises an opportunity to encourage his crew to excel and demonstrate their prowess. He challenged, cajoled, nagged, pleaded, joked and bullied. He employed every trick, but he got them to do what was required. He knew how to get each man to give his best. Their *real* best: not simply what was good enough, but their finest effort. They were tough men, but Jim made them tougher. Together they swapped warm evenings indoors for cold, dark training nights at sea. They stayed at the oars when they might otherwise have given up; with Jim at Stoker's side they obeyed his directions without complaint or issue.

Jim was smart. He may have had a sibling's advantage in sussing out Cain, but he rapidly learned how to handle everyone else too. He even used what he knew to tease them when giving instructions and they all just laughed it off. It was a revelation for Stoker, but obedience to the chain of command was essential – no matter how and why it came about – if the lifeboat was to become as effective as it needed to be. Stoker wondered that he did not resent Jim. But he couldn't. There was no cause for it. Jim's genial good humour, his ability – for he seemed to be good at everything – and perhaps most of all his respect for Stoker made any jealousy impossible. More than anything else Jim was fiercely loyal to 'the skipper' and he always deferred to the coxswain even on the odd occasion when Stoker suspected he did not agree with him.

The management of the lifeboat was now a combination of Stoker's knowledge, practical skills and experience together with Jim's motivational and leadership abilities. It was a formidable partnership which united the oldest member of the crew with the youngest, and it revitalised the whole. There was a true camaraderie: the family that Stoker had been looking for.

But it was no longer simply a bare crew of thirteen. Tom continued to make a major contribution, just as he had promised. His determined recruitment drive saw ten new men join the lifeboat service in a matter of weeks – all local fishermen. Tom sought them out one by one: the brave strong hearts of Poole. He selected them all himself, finding them by reputation and recommendation, and choosing the right moment to approach them. Whatever it was that he told them it always worked, for Stoker never heard of a soul refusing him. Maybe Tom was right – perhaps he had found a role more suited to his natural talents.

Jim evidently had decided that the training was to become a personal mission. He made the whole crew row for long periods without a break to learn about keeping their rhythm and getting used to the motion of the boat in different conditions. Mile upon mile until they ached. They went out in storms to build up confidence and to get to know how the lifeboat would behave. It was a shock for the new recruits when they found the boat filling with water for the first time, but with what pleasure did Stoker watch the 'old hands' give them reassurance! They were forced to endure the cold and the wet, and they shivered yet never complained: after all, Jim and Stoker never did, so how could anyone else? Jim even made his brother Cain and the stand-in bowman practise throwing the grapnel until their aim and distance improved. Someone who could handle Cain – that alone was a boon.

New crew members, new leadership, new skills and new spirit. All of this meant that when the call eventually came to launch the lifeboat for real, everyone was certain that they were up to the task. But would it be enough?

Chapter Eighteen

Stoker saw the incident himself. He had taken a stroll down from North Haven to Poole Head as he often did, and had the perfect vantage point to see all that happened.

A large brig was cruising towards him at a fair rate of knots in a rapidly rising south-southwest wind. Even without his spyglass he could easily pick out the large ensign of Prussia with its majestic black eagle set against a white background. She was a beautiful ship – all her woodwork black and white – proud and invulnerable; very clean with sharp lines. Through his glass he could make out the name on her bows: *Antares*.

The captain had clearly decided to head for the harbour's entrance, but unaccountably did not request a pilot. Almost unheard of for a foreign ship. Stoker could see what was going to happen before disaster struck, and yet was helpless to prevent it.

The ship had far too much canvas set and was making such headway that she would never be able to safely navigate the relatively narrow Swash Channel. The Hook Sands were to her leeward but having raced into the Channel at a great rate of knots she quickly came too close to its shallow margins and was in imminent danger of grounding. The order was given to put the helm down, but at a crucial moment the main-boom sheet fouled the wheel just as the vessel turned towards the wind. The seamen worked frantically, but the *Antares* was losing way, broadside on to the wind. Her sails flapped uselessly, but the wind continued to push the vessel north-eastwards.

The crew started to get the ship round, but scarcely had

this begun when she struck the sands and ground to a juddering halt. She was lucky not to lose a mast – and that was probably only because she had been reduced to such a slow speed – but the image of beauty and invulnerability was now totally shattered. Stoker watched the crew being thrown into confusion as rigging and canvas were transformed from order to chaos. Little black ants crawling all over the place. Stoker was too far away to hear their cries, but he could imagine what it was like. The ship slewed around with the wind and was pushed hard and fast into the deep sand. Soon they'd need assistance.

Sure enough, minutes later, up went a flare, and then immediately afterwards another one just for good measure. Stoker sighed and hurried back home to light his own flare and hoist a signal flag to call out the lifeboat. How could any ship's master worth his salt cruise into a bloody great sand bank in broad daylight? It defied belief. Why on earth hadn't he taken a pilot?

Still, perhaps this call-out would be an opportunity for the lifeboat to make amends. To show the town what he and his crew were capable of. Something positive.

In the daytime when the weather was good the lifeboatmen could be with Stoker in as little as thirty minutes. He hoisted a signal flag to alert the crew that they were needed, then ran indoors to let Mary know what was happening. It was a shame his son Edward was not home otherwise he could have made himself useful. Stoker quickly rounded up a few neighbours and between them they opened the lifeboathouse doors, then hitched two horses to the boat's wheeled carriage. It was a straightforward matter to pull it out of storage. He checked the boat regularly for damage or wear but while there was time he gave the *Manley Wood* a quick inspection to be sure. Nothing to worry about.

Re-entering the lifeboathouse he assembled the lifebelts for the crew. All one size with three adjustable leather belts to fit anyone – one belt for the waist and one for each shoulder. The flotation was provided by large pieces of cork – a circle of blocks around the abdomen and another around the ribcage. They were effective up to a point, but nothing provided truly adequate protection if a man went overboard in a very heavy sea.

The North Haven lifeboathouse had been sited at the mouth of Poole Harbour to allow an easy launch either into the Harbour or outside it into Poole Bay. The Hook Sands were located in the Bay so Stoker's helpers led the horses eastwards towards the beach.

Frank Wills was sitting in his back yard mending a fishing trawl when he heard the sound. The loud 'pock-pock-pock' of a rocket. That was the signal that the lifeboat crew was needed. Who could need the lifeboat in this weather? A strong breeze sure enough but not a gale. Frank turned his eyes heavenwards, and saw the storm clouds gathering. Looked like a gale was on the way through. He dropped his nets and ran next door to leave a message for Jane with a neighbour.

Six-month old Francis Junior was still ill, and Jane had taken him round to her mother's. At his last visit the doctor had taken Frank aside and told him that in all probability their son would not live more than a few months. Poor Jane. He hadn't told her what the doctor had said. It was dreadful knowledge, but he simply couldn't bear to see her so distraught. She was expecting their son to recover. Who knows, perhaps he still would. A miracle maybe. But he had to try to put all that to the back of his mind now.

Cain Matthews was on the Quay talking to Will Redmond. He was just thinking about sneaking off to the *King's Arms* for a pint of ale when he heard the rocket. Cain was supposed to be helping his father paint the house. Abandoning thoughts of home, ale, and painting, he reversed direction and ran westwards along the Quay towards the *Antelope Hotel*. He was so close to the rendezvous point that he thought he would be first to arrive, but when he got there Jim was already waiting.

John Wills bolted out of bed. "Sorry, Maggie. That's the lifeboat rocket. I've got to go, my love." He whipped on his trousers and turned to give her a kiss.

"Johnny! Can't you stay with me?"

"You know I can't." He fumbled with the buttons of his fly.

"Charlie's away until next Monday," she explained, "so I hope you'll come back here later... when you've finished in the boat."

John struggled into his shirt.

"I've got a nice meat pie for tonight if you're back in time," continued Maggie. "Real nice beef. No rubbish."

"Where did I put them shoes?" he cast around the floor, refusing to allow himself to be drawn into further commitment.

"Johnny," she whined. "You ain't listening to me."

He smiled. "Am I better than your old man then? Better than Charlie?" He wiggled his eyebrows suggestively.

"Stop it, you're making me feel guilty."

"Oh I wouldn't. He's in the navy and he'll be getting his fair share I'll be bound – whenever his ship docks – so it's only fair that someone looks after you ain't it?" He winked at her.

"Suppose so," she mused, but Maggie didn't like this line of conversation, and pouted.

John spotted the toes of a pair of shoes poking out from under the bedside chair. "Ah! There they are." He grabbed them and thrust them on.

"Well you be careful, Johnny, and make sure you come straight back here when you're done to let me know you're safe and sound. Then I can give you a little reward if you're good." She fluttered the bedclothes a little.

"Maggie, I'm always good. You know that." He kissed her peremptorily. "Now I must be off."

"But will you come back here afterwards?" she called as he ran out. He didn't reply. "Don't go out the front door, the neighbours'll see…"

She heard the front door slam.

"Bugger."

———————

By coincidence, Sam Hart was with his brother when he heard the signal rocket. They looked at each other knowingly for a second.

Tom dived into the scullery and came back moments later with an oilskin bag. "Here, take this."

"What is it?" asked Sam.

"Ship's biscuit and some sweet tack mother made. You might need it. I tried storing it in the lifeboat, but it just goes all soft. I been keeping it here, nice an' dry. There's enough for all o' you."

"Thankee," said Sam, abashed. "Come with me and see us off."

"No, no, can't do that. It's Jim's calling now. Wouldn't do to have me hanging round. Wouldn't be right. You'd better get off."

"Thanks, Tom." It felt odd to leave him behind, even now.

"Good luck, Sam." He smiled ruefully. It had been the right decision to stand down from the crew, but at this moment it was tempting to think otherwise.

At the *Antelope* a four-horse brake stood waiting for the lifeboatmen. The first ten men to turn up were guaranteed a place – the full complement being made up by the addition of Stoker, Jim, and Cain (as bowman). John Wills was the last of the ten to arrive.

"Off we go!" commanded Jim as soon as John had swung

himself up. The driver cracked his whip, sending the brake shooting forward. It clattered up the High Street, largely deserted as the wind continued to grow in force, and once free of the confines of the town it rapidly gathered further pace.

"We'll be there afore we know it at this rate," cried Sam excitedly.

"Aye," said Jim. "A good set o' horses. Fresh. They ain't been used today."

"Landlord were gonna palm us off with some worn-out old rubbish," Bill told them, "but Jim here stepped in, calm as you like, and said: 'No, we'll take the best you got: lives are at stake.' And that were that. No arguing."

Sam grinned.

The driver was urging the horses on ever faster, and the speed was such that they were all thrown together whenever the brake rounded a corner. They reached North Haven in less than thirty minutes, where they were directed to a launch site on the south east shore overlooking East Looe and facing outside the harbour. They could all see the ship in distress on the Hook, barely three-quarters of a mile off shore.

"Bloody foreigners," said Cain as they climbed out of the brake. "Look at that! Don't know their port side from their backside. What a lash up."

Stoker and his helpers were ready for them and the crew were in the lifeboat and launched within minutes of their arrival.

The coxswain had had plenty of time to come up with a plan, and before they got under way he explained his intentions.

"Right!" He called them to attention. "This brig, it's the *Antares*; Prussian. She ran aground an hour or so ago. We're gonna slip down East Looe Channel under canvas, then row up to 'em. When we fetch close, we'll tie on to the leeside of her stern, get aboard and see what's to be done." He stopped and scanned the faces in front of him. "How's that?" Stoker raised his eyebrows, seeking approval.

"Right-ho, skipper," called Jim and suddenly came nods and calls of agreement all around the boat. No dissent. Not even a whisper. Stoker's heart swelled.

"Good," said Stoker, taking the tiller. "Unsheet that sail!" he ordered.

The *Manley Wood* swiftly made the end of the East Looe Channel. The water was choppy and the wind fresh, but the conditions excited no concern for the crew, and as the sail came down Stoker put the tiller over and the lifeboat turned across the wind. Then the coxswain gave the command to unship the oars.

"Let's show 'em what we're made of!" cried Jim to give the crew encouragement as they began to pull, even though there was not far to go. "I want them Prussians to think it's an express train racing up to 'em. Pull! Come on! Put your backs into it you buggers!" he growled. "That's it. Show a load o' foreigners what we can do." He kept up this encouragement throughout, even though he took an oar himself. No-one wanted to show Jim that they weren't up to his standard.

Not surprisingly the lifeboat made the *Antares* in no time at all. For the last few fathoms the lifeboat had to turn into the wind, but they were then to some extent in the lee of the grounded ship which afforded them some protection. Cain tied them onto the stern of the *Antares*.

"Well done, lads!" cried Jim. Now even he was breathing hard. "Bloody good work. Reckon we'd outdo a frigate the rate we were going."

"Well done," said Stoker. The efforts of his crew made him more proud and pleased than he could say. "Well done!" he repeated more loudly. "Up you go then, Jim," he shouted, seeing him looking keenly aloft.

Jim clambered up the ship's side and as soon as he got near the aft rail he was grabbed and helped aboard. Sam Hart followed along behind him.

A tall powerful-looking man in a green jacket with his back to them was shouting orders as the crew heaved a broken spar over the side. His loud, guttural German sounded harsh. He spun round as a member of his crew reported the lifeboatmen's presence on deck.

"Hello," he said, stepping towards them. His face was deeply tanned, his brow creased in concern. He shook hands with both of them.

"Hello, Ludolph," said Sam. "I wondered if it might be you. D'you know Jim Matthews here?"

"No. I have not met before." His English was good but overlain with a heavy Teutonic accent, and his voice was hoarse from shouting.

"Jim, this is Ludolph Röpke."

"Aye, I've seen you on the Quay," said Jim.

Ludolph had jumped ship a few years earlier, settled in Poole and married. He still served in the merchant service for

310

cargoes bound between the Baltic coast and southern Europe.

"There is no danger for now," said Captain Röpke. "We have secured everything, but there is the water below. Two feet in the hold maybe. But a lot for this ship: she is always so dry, you know. We have pumps working."

Jim was curious. "What happened?"

The captain grimaced, and scratched the back of his neck. "We, er, I made an error and here we are, we pay the price. I have been this route many times and was thinking that maybe we did not need a pilot…"

"Ah," said Jim. All was now clear. "Wanted to save a few bob, eh?"

"The mate, he is the owner's son and he puts that idea in my head it is true – 'we do not need any pilot, you can do this yourself'. The wind was getting up and we hit the sand. I am so sure the Hook was more to the east last time."

"Aye well, it moves around a lot you see, er…captain," said Jim. He couldn't remember the man's peculiar foreign name. "Sands are a *completely* different shape now to what they were a year ago. When was you last here?"

"About a year I think." The captain contemplated for a second. "Almost one year – January '66 was our last time."

"Oh well! Since then we've had the Great Gale. Of course we have. Shifted everything about that did. Nothing's the same now – channels, shoals, sands all moved about a bit."

There was a slightly awkward pause while that information sank in.

"Sounds like you need a new mate," suggested Sam, hoping to help the captain save face.

"I know it!" The captain thumped one fist into a palm. "He's a bloody fool and I want to be rid of him." He nodded towards a short, swarthy man, leaning against the side. "I am more foolish for listening to him." He shrugged. "Do not worry, he speaks no English. None of the others also. I am the only one."

"You were lucky not to have more carried away when you struck."

"Yes. It is not so serious, but the wind is stronger now, and it could be bad for us if we stay, I think."

"Aye. D'you reckon you could kedge off?" asked Jim.

The captain frowned in incomprehension.

"Could you use an anchor to warp her off… drop an anchor and pull at the cable to move her?"

"Ah! Yes I understand. That is *kedge* in English? I must remember. But no I do not think that is possible. We are stuck too hard here. Look!" He took them back to the rail and they looked over the starboard side. "Also the water, it is too deep and violent, and so fast."

Sam was inclined to agree with him. They were right on the margin of the Swash Channel and the wind was increasing in intensity.

The three of them started as with a loud crack like a shotgun the mainstaysail burst suddenly from its frappings and flapped wildly about the space between the two masts. The captain shouted orders at the mate in German and it was

312

rapidly secured.

"What we need," prompted the captain as he eyed the skies nervously, "is a steamer to pull us away. Can you take me to get one?"

"Aye I reckon we could," said Jim, rubbing his chin. "But if we're gonna go, we ought to go now. This wind's getting up and you don't want to be here any longer than you need to."

He called over the side and explained the situation to Stoker who agreed to transport the captain to the Quay to seek assistance.

Within a few minutes the two lifeboatmen were back in the boat along with the captain of the *Antares* who stood aft with Stoker. The lifeboat cast off, the mainsail was raised and the wind filled it immediately, carrying her along the port side of the *Antares* and down the Swash Channel towards the harbour's mouth.

"What are you carrying?" asked Stoker, turning to Ludolph.

"Corkwood. Bound for Portsmouth. We were taking timber from Greifswald to Lisbon two weeks ago and now we take the cork from Lisbon to Portsmouth."

"Not sure I fancy all them long spells at sea you have to put up with. A year away from home!"

"Well, it is maybe not the best life for everyone. It pays for my family at least."

"Didn't you marry Bill Stone's daughter?" asked Stoker.

"Louisa. That's right," confirmed the captain.

"I thought so. Didn't think there could be too many other Prussians living in Poole." The lifeboat bumped as it forced its way through the rougher water at the harbour's mouth. "Quite a character was Bill in his youth," continued Stoker. "I haven't seen him for ages. Deaf as a post last time I met him. Is he all right?"

"Yes, yes. But still most deaf. We must all shout."

"He used to tell a good yarn too. Did you ever hear him tell the tale of the prank he played with the horse and cart?"

"No, I never heard that story." Ludolph frowned as he tried to recall. "Louisa, she always tells me these things but I don't think I heard that tale."

"Well," said Stoker, "Bill used to work with an odd cove called – let me see now, er… called Andrews, Harry Andrews. Now he was a rag and bone man. Used to come round same day each week and no matter what time o' the day you saw him he were always half-cut. No idea where he got the booze from or how he could afford it: never had two ha'pennies to rub together. But that's by the by. Anyway, one night he got home roaring drunk on the cart, waltzed into the house and left the front door open. So Bill Stone was passing, and sees the chance for a bit o' mischief: he unhitches the horse, leads it through the door into the front room, opens the window and then puts it back in the harness so it's all hitched to the cart again." Stoker laughed at the captain's astonishment. "Well, next day, Harry gets up, wanders downstairs hung over and there's the horse staring him in the face *inside* the house!" Stoker started to laugh again. "And the best of it is, when Bill found Harry next morning, he were trying to work out how the horse had *jumped* through the front window still hitched to the cart!"

Ludolph wheezed with laughter. "A horse in harness jumping through the window…?" he wheezed. Many of the crew nearby had heard the story and were laughing as well. "Yes, I have heard many tales about this Harry Andrews," continued Ludolph enthusiastically. "Was he not also the man who fired a gun up his chimney?"

"Aye!" cried Stoker. "That's the one! Said he couldn't afford a chimney sweep, and too lazy to do it himself properly, so one morning, drunk as a lord, he used a shotgun. A *shotgun*, mind you! Stood in the fireplace and let it off. What a noise that must have been! Brought the whole street out. And all that black just raced down the chimney all over him. Bill said the room was like you'd got great sacks o' soot and thrown them onto everything. And I mean everything. Inches thick. Just smothered it all was."

They both laughed.

"What made you settle in Poole then, Ludolph?"

"Well, it was not the plan. I jumped ship from the *Neubau* to the *Swallow* at Copenhagen and she was bound for Poole. I found good work and then I met Louisa and then I stayed."

"Do you reckon you'll ever go back to Prussia?"

"No. It is too…" he struggled to find an appropriate word, "too unhappy there. There is war often. You do not understand here, where there is never the fighting on your own land. We have just had the war with Austria – only seven weeks – but it was not right to fight them: they are the same… er" he sought again for a suitable word, "they are the same family, the same blood. We called it the *Bruderkrieg*: a war of brothers."

"Did you win?"

"Yes for sure. Chancellor Bismarck only makes this war when he knows we can win."

"But why does he do it?" Stoker was mystified.

"He wants one big German country" Ludolph explained. "To bring all the brothers together, but I do not think it will work, and it needs much violence to make it happen. It is too much."

"Wants Prussia to be the top dog, eh?"

"Top dog?"

"Wants Prussia to come out on top, be the winner? Have this big country, but Prussia runs it all?"

"Of course. That is the reason for everything. But I have family there, friends. It is a concern, you see? I fear for them. Prussia is hated by many; no-one knows what will happen."

Stoker could appreciate the captain's unease but could think of nothing supportive to say in response, so said nothing. Britain was fortunate to be protected by the sea, he reflected. On the continent of Europe soldiers could just march across a border and invade a neighbouring state. He'd never thought about that before. It must be very unsettling.

Ludolph broke the silence. "Thank you for coming out to us."

"Don't worry about that – it's what we're here for," said Stoker proudly. His lifeboat was about to land the master of a stricken vessel at the Quay so that he could save his ship and men. That act meant he would have to prepare a report for the RNLI in London: *Manley Wood lifeboat, Poole. SSW gale. Brig*

Antares of Greifswald, landed one man.

Their first successful rescue. A small victory, but a victory nonetheless. Stoker was thankful after all the waiting. The Admiral would be glad to hear of it; so would Lord Osborne. He would write to inform them straight away.

Chapter Nineteen

Ludolph Röpke managed to secure the services of a tug. Stoker took him to see Will Redmond in the hope that using the *Royal Albert* would help to diffuse any remaining tensions between George Penney and the lifeboat. However, the *Antares* was wedged very firmly into the sand and it took several days of laborious effort for the steamer to break her free, before towing her to the safety of the Oysterbank just off the Quay. The brig suffered greatly from its beating by the wind and waves and needed extensive repairs.

However, ship, crew, and cargo had all been saved, and the captain of the *Antares* was very grateful for the assistance that the lifeboat had rendered. Just before returning to sea, Ludolph visited Stoker at North Haven to thank him once again. The owner's son had even authorised him to pay the lifeboat crew ten pounds as an expression of gratitude. Stoker ventured to suggest that the captain might like to write to the Mayor expressing his satisfaction with the lifeboat's conduct, and this he did. It was a most complimentary letter yet nothing ever came of it: no acknowledgement from the Mayor, no mention of the incident in any of the local newspapers. Admittedly it had not been a dramatic rescue – there had never really been occasion to suspect that anyone's life was in serious danger – but Stoker had hoped his men would receive some public encouragement.

No appreciation was given locally – the lifeboat's involvement was not even mentioned in the *Herald* or the *Dorset County Chronicle* – although to Stoker's satisfaction the *Antares* rescue was mentioned warmly in several other newspapers from outside the area. Captain Robertson's doing, perhaps?

Yet Lord Osborne kindly penned a private note to the coxswain congratulating the crew on their achievement and Stoker decided he would make a point of reading it aloud to the assembled men at the next training session. That was one small consolation.

However, perhaps the more important outcome was that the crew themselves knew they had achieved something – a positive action by the lifeboat after so much criticism many months ago. All the same, Stoker now realised that the lifeboat would have to achieve something truly extraordinary in order to receive formal absolution from the wider community.

———————

Frank Wills sat staring at the small bundle wrapped in white. Jane's heaving sobs downstairs came in surges of desperate sadness and yet there was nothing he could do. Helpless. Powerless to prevent what he'd been told would happen and unable to ease his wife's pain. He'd known for months. The doctor had warned him this day would come. Yet he'd decided not to tell Jane so that she did not lose hope, and to spare her the erosive effects of foreknowledge. How on earth would he tell his father? He'd kept the fatal illness from him too.

His sister was with Jane now, trying her best to comfort her, and Frank needed to be down there too. He'd just wanted one last moment alone with his son.

He bent over and kissed that tiny cold forehead, and then all at once the tears and the pain came, breaking over him like a wave. *Why?*

———————

"How are your lifeboatmen then, Sidney?" asked Lady Wolverton.

"I do beg your pardon?" said Lord Osborne who had been distracted by his wife, Emily, talking at the same time.

"Your lifeboatmen," she prompted. "You were telling us all, the last time we visited, that there had been some sort of inquest in Poole."

"Inquiry," he corrected. "Yes that's right, Mary. Well they have had one call-out since, but nothing really to test their mettle I'm afraid. I'm not as up-to-date with the situation as I should be as I've been away in Ireland for a while. I'm sure that Bartie can give us a fuller account," he said, nodding towards Admiral Sulivan.

"Yes, just one call-out," he confirmed. "They landed the captain of a Prussian brig who took his ship right into a sandbank in broad daylight for some unaccountable reason. So I suppose that counts as lives saved, albeit indirectly."

"We came across a wonderful little ditty about Poole the other day," announced Lady Wolverton. "Now what was it? 'If Poole was a fish-pool and the men of Poole fish, there'd be a pool for the devil and fish for his dish'. It doesn't say very much for the local inhabitants, Sidney, now does it."

"Yes, yes, I've heard that old rhyme before, many times," Lord Osborne waved a hand dismissively at his sister, "but it was written centuries ago, when the town was a den of pirates and smugglers. Now it's quite a respectable place."

"People do not often change as much as we might believe," contemplated Lady Wolverton. "Did the coxswain of the lifeboat keep his position in the end?"

"Oh yes. There was no problem there."

"You said that he lied under oath to protect his men didn't you, darling?" said Emily.

"Well, they weren't under oath, Emily, but he did lie to protect them, yes. He told Bartie privately that he'd ordered the crew to drop down to pick up the crew of two schooners and the men had refused to obey him. But when we asked him about that at the inquiry he said it was a group decision to hold back. Wanted to protect them, you see."

"I say, that's most frightfully honourable really, isn't it," Lady Wolverton opined. "It's so easy to be caught out by working people sometimes. It's not really what one has come to expect, but it is good to be agreeably surprised from time to time."

"They're all humanity, just like you and me, part of God's creation."

"Oh Sidney, do stop!" his sister chided. "God loves them, of course, but believe me my dear they are *not* like you and me!"

"What makes you feel they are so different?"

"The squalor for one thing, many of them are indolent, and they are so uneducated – most of them can't even read."

"You can hardly blame them for being uneducated!" Lord Osborne protested. "Most of them have never had the opportunity."

"I'm not *blaming* them. I know you're a rector, my dear,

and you have a duty to say all these good things – even believe them perhaps – but you said they were like us and I'm showing you that they are not." She patted him on the back of the hand.

Lord Osborne refused to back down. "The only difference between them and us is money, Mary."

"Does *breeding* count for nothing in Dorset these days then?" This provoked low laughter and smiles from the other guests. "And they may have next to nothing, yet they still continue to produce offspring. Why do the poor insist upon having so many children?" she demanded of the dining room at large. "They can't possibly support them all. Oh Sidney! How can you really believe that they are anything like us?"

"You are right, Mary, they do have nothing. It is almost impossible for us to understand what that really means. *Nothing*. No food; very rudimentary, cramped and cold quarters, and only the clothes they stand up in. Perhaps *we* have too much."

"Too much! Good Lord, don't say that, we have barely enough to pay the servants. We don't want them getting ideas that there's money to spare." This brought another gentle chorus of mirth from around the table.

"And what if, by some accident of birth, you'd come into the world as the daughter of a fisherman, or an agricultural labourer? What then?"

"Now Sidney, don't be vulgar, we are not going to have a sermon…"

"It's not a sermon. I would like to show you what these people are up against in their daily lives." Lord Osborne loved his sister, but was disturbed by her lack of social conscience. "So what would you do as the wife of a fisherman?"

"For one thing I would keep a clean house. Cleanliness is next to godliness. There's a new schoolmaster in the village. He and his wife keep a wonderfully tidy house I'm told. Now, they do have some ideas above their station but the fact is that they are respectable. They have two children, they're clean, the head of the house is gainfully employed, and they are polite and mannerly. I'd be just like them."

"Know your place, you mean?"

"If you put it like that, Sidney, yes."

"And could you do all this as a fisherman's wife on ten shillings a week?"

"No, don't be ridiculous."

"What if that was all that you had?"

"Well, Sidney, then I'd have to persuade my husband to catch more fish!" This brought laughter again.

———————————

The card game was euchre – universally pronounced 'yooker' – and was a new but popular form of evening entertainment amongst the men of Poole. Bill, Sam, Cain and Jim sat in the Sailor's Institute studying the hands that Bill had just dealt.

Euchre was played with a short deck of cards – nines and above only – plus a joker known as the 'Benny'. The Benny was ranked the highest card irrespective of which suit was

323

trumps and this was then followed by the jack of the trump suit ('right bower') and then the jack of the other suit of the same colour ('left bower'). The rest of the cards followed in their natural order. Each player was dealt five cards, leaving a further five undealt as a kitty, and when four people played they played as two teams of two.

"Off you go then, Jim," said Bill as he turned the top card of the kitty face up. It was the queen of diamonds. Each player now had to decide in turn if he wanted diamonds as the trump suit. If he did, then Bill as dealer had to pick up the queen and add it to his own hand after discarding one of the cards he had been dealt. This was called 'ordering up'.

"Nope," came Sam's partner, Jim, rejecting the chance to order up.

"No," said Cain.

"No," from Sam. He wanted spades. Right bower, ace and king of spades, plus two hearts.

"She's over," said Bill as he turned the queen face down, rejecting diamonds himself. Now each player on his turn could call for any suit to be trumps except diamonds as long as with his partner's help he could win at least three of the five tricks.

"Nope," said Jim again.

"Make it a spade," from Cain.

He'd chosen Sam's preferred suit. Sam wanted to grin, but kept his features composed. This could be good.

Jim led off with the king of hearts, Cain took it with his ace and everyone else followed suit. A pity that the opposition got

324

such an easy first trick but depleting the hearts could prove useful to Sam in the long-run.

Then Cain led the Benny. Sam threw in his ace of trumps with a disconsolate 'tut', hoping Cain would think it was his only trump, Bill played the nine, and Jim discarded a small diamond. Those discards should have given Cain a clue that all might not be well, but he either didn't consider it or trusted to luck too much. He played the left bower. Sam snapped it up triumphantly with his right bower. Cain himself tutted this time, but was still confident he would win as he held the queen of trumps and the ace of diamonds. And diamonds had not been led yet.

Then Sam played his pièce de résistance – the king of spades.

"How many bloody trumps you got there, Sam?" asked Cain, annoyed, and tossing in his queen.

"Enough," said Sam, knowing that Cain didn't have any left. Out came Sam's last card: the little ten of hearts. Cain cursed volubly. Sam watched with pleasure as both he and Bill discarded valuable aces. Cain and Bill had not made their contract.

"You're down!" cried Sam with emphasis, thumping the table. Cain hated losing.

"Well bugger that!" Cain retorted. "I had Benny, left bower, queen o' trumps and two red aces and I couldn't scratch a measly point."

"And I had two trumps and the ace and king o' clubs to support you," said his partner Bill. "I were sure you were gonna lead clubs on that last round, but I never got a look-in."

Sam knew what Cain's mistake had been. He'd been greedy in playing that left bower; he'd hoped to win all the tricks and score more points. If Cain had played the ace of diamonds instead he'd have won because Sam would have been forced to use up one of his trumps to win it. Cain wouldn't have got all the tricks but he would have taken three of them, which was enough to score one point. As it was he'd given penalty points to Jim and Sam. The first team to reach nine points won the round and they played as many rounds as they could. Often it went on late into the night.

"Bloody ridiculous," said Cain. "If you can't win with a hand like that, I may as well pack it in and go home."

This seemed to mark the beginning of a change in fortunes for Sam and Jim. They had been trailing all evening; now they took the next three games to win the round convincingly.

Bill shuffled the cards then handed them to Jim to deal. He started stuffing his pipe. "I hear we got a full complement on the lifeboat crew now," said Bill.

"How's that then?" asked Cain.

"Tom's been working on getting us the right sort and we're up to twenty-six."

"Enough to man us twice over," observed Cain.

"That's right," Sam acknowledged. "It'll be first-come first-served now when we get to the *Antelope* on a call-out."

"Aye," said Jim. "And that's the way it should be. Just in case people are ill we've got other men we can turn to, or if we get called out twice in one day we've got a fresh crew to take over. Tom's been doing a good job there – I don't know where we'd be without him."

"You've been doing a good job yourself, Jim," said Sam, smiling wryly. "Bullying us lot."

"Ah! You bring it on yourselves. Must keep you fat blighters knocked into shape."

"We still need a proper rescue," asserted Cain. "Not some brig on a sandbank 'cos her captain hadn't a clue what he was doing. We gotta show them halfwits in the Guildhall and over Studland that we're better than they think we are. And I wanna be there to see it."

"There'll be plenty more chances," said Jim confidently. "You mark my words. They didn't put a lifeboat here for nothing."

———————

"How old do I need to be to join the lifeboat, Mr Hart?" asked Richard Wills. He shifted round to find a more comfortable position on the mooring bollard where he sat on the quayside. Tom Hart stood next to him puffing intermittently at his pipe, waiting for the ship in front of them to finalise preparations for setting sail. The Danish barque *Johannes* was a ship he'd piloted twice before and he knew the captain didn't like to hang about.

"Well, my son," Tom replied, "I don't rightly know." He stroked his moustache. "There's nothing about the age o' crewmen in the regulations. Why? Are you interested in joining us, Rich? We don't just take anyone, you know." He chuckled.

"Course I'm interested!" said Richard indignantly.

Tom touched his cap as he saw the master of the ship approaching them rapidly from the direction of the harbour master's office. The captain returned a casual wave-cum-salute to Tom, then shouted something up to a seaman on deck in Danish.

"We will be under way in five minutes," he told Tom, reverting to English, and then stepped aboard.

"I got to take this one out," Tom explained, and started to knock his pipe on the back of the bollard to empty it. "I must tell the truth, Dick, I reckon you're a bit young for the lifeboat yet. Give it two or three years, I'd say. There's no doubt you'd be strong enough, if half what Frank and Johnny tell me is true."

Richard thought he must have looked very disappointed because Tom quickly added, "But I tell you what, if your father's minded to allow it, why don't you come and help launch next time we're called out and then you can see what it's all about."

"Aye, I'd like that!" cried Richard enthusiastically.

"I'll let Stoker know then. But make sure you ask your father – and I'll check with him, mind you!" Tom started up the gangplank. "Don't just turn up at the *Antelope* and expect to go without his say-so."

Chapter Twenty

Even though he was extremely tired, Captain Fabian Addler strode proudly along the deck of his brig, checking once again that everything was in order. The *Contest* was not the largest merchant ship that ran out of St Peter Port on Guernsey, but she was one of the most elegant and was practically new. Less than a year old. It was only a short voyage to London, but the captain was determined not to give the ship's owner, Mr Lelean, cause to regret his decision to appoint him as master. Addler had been on his feet since five in the morning paying attention to every detail concerning the ship and her voyage, and it was now nearly eleven at night.

Cape La Hogue, the last remnant of the French coast, had disappeared astern two hours ago and a fresh breeze had sprung up to replace the lighter winds they had experienced near the coast. Now they were making fine progress. It would be wonderful if he could bring the *Contest* back home to Guernsey in record time. He stopped and smiled at his own enthusiasm. He was letting himself run away with fanciful ideas. Even so, as he resumed his pacing of the deck, the new captain was still determined to go all-out to impress the ship's owner in order to repay his trust.

Addler checked their bearing once more: north east by north on the starboard tack, going at about five knots. Before retiring he studied the heavens carefully in the moonlight; standing amidships he braced himself against the motion of the ship and surveyed the horizon through three hundred and sixty degrees. All was clear. Then he went below, leaving a message with the boatswain to call him at midnight.

One hour's blessed sleep.

It was all too short. One hour later, there was a knock at his door and Corbet, a very experienced seaman, entered at the captain's summons.

"You asked for a call at midnight, sir."

"Thank you, Corbet," said the captain, rising to a seated position on the edge of his bunk. "How are we making?"

"On the same tack sir, wind's easterly. We're making a little over five knots."

"Good. I'll be on deck directly." He heard the bells chime for middle watch.

The captain consulted his charts. He rubbed his eyes, but made himself check the *Contest*'s progress carefully. Another hour at most on this tack and then they would alter course for the Isle of Wight. He could hand this task over to the ship's mate and then retire to catch some more sleep.

On deck once more, he was surprised not to see the mate who had charge of the watch.

"Where is Mr Martel?" asked the captain.

"Er, he's down below, sir," said Corbet. "Checking the cargo, sir."

The captain did not consider that anything needed checking in a six hundred ton cargo of granite slabs, but appreciated the extra care the mate was taking. And Addler himself was so dreadfully tired.

"Very well. Give Mr Martel my compliments when he comes on deck, and tell him to hold our current course for an hour, then bear for the Solent and call me at the morning watch. I've written the course on the slate." It was a simple enough instruction, well within the competence of a ship's mate.

"Aye sir," returned Corbet.

"And Corbet," he added, raising his eyes aloft to the sails and rigging that sang with the wind, "call me if the wind gets up."

"Aye sir," Corbet repeated.

Now the captain could at last retire for a few hours' much-earned rest.

———————

"What are you mulling over?" asked Mary, watching her husband's distraction.

"Oh nothing." Stoker smiled reassuringly. "Just thinking how pleased I am that Jim Matthews is part o' the crew. He's worked a miracle Mary, and that's a fact. Don't know what I'd do without him."

"I'm pleased to hear it. You *deserve* a good and loyal crew."

"I miss Tom though," he admitted. "It's not right the way he were treated…"

"Stop it, dear," she chided him gently, "not afore bedtime – it'll stop your sleeping. Tom took his own decision. No-one made him step down."

"I just hope all this new-found effort can soon be put to good purpose." He yawned. "I want to see us do something that'll make them buggers like Luckham sit up and take notice."

"Whatever you do my dear, you do it for yourself not for the likes of him." She smiled. "I'm sure it's just a matter o' time," said his wife assuredly. "But don't you go taking no risks out there. You got nothing to prove to that Mr Luckham, nor to me or anyone." She kissed him lightly on the cheek. "Come on now it's time for bed."

"I covered for you," said Corbet in the darkness.

"Wassat?" demanded Martel, screwing up his eyes to focus on the source of the speech behind the lantern. The light seemed far too bright and he waved it away.

"I told the cap'n you were down below checking the cargo."

"Thankee, Silas," said the mate, struggling unsteadily to his feet. "You're a good sort and no mishtake. Have I told 'e that afore, my friend?" He clapped a strong hand on Corbet's shoulder. "A very good sort."

"Cap'n says to change course and bear easterly in an hour, but he's written it all on the slate."

Corbet asked himself if it was an error for him to cover up this breech of discipline: the mate drunk on duty within hours of the *Contest* leaving port. The captain was so tired and the course was easy enough. Better to say nothing this time, especially since it didn't do to upset the second in command – the mate had a lot of power over the crew. But if it happened again – well, then he would do something. Corbet had given Martel strong coffee and hidden his bottles of rum. He'd sober up quickly enough.

Martel suddenly lurched. "A bit rough up top is it?"

"No," hissed Corbet, rankled. "It's *you* that's moving not the ship. She's steady."

"Aye. Aye, well let's get on deck then. Wouldn't want the cap'n to miss me, eh?"

"He's turned in. Let's get you up there – the fresh breeze'll do you good."

The fist came out of the blackness of the night as John Wills rounded the dark corner of Paradise Street. It caught him square on the jaw sending him careening backwards. He expected to feel his head crack against the cobbled street, but two strong arms grabbed him from behind to hold him upright as he fell. They held him while the fist of the first man returned with expert savagery to his solar plexus, taking the wind out of him. Another thump to the head, and the whole world was whirling around him, spinning. There were more punches to his tightly held body but somehow he couldn't feel them anymore. He struggled feebly. Then they let him drop to the street at last.

"You stay away from Amy Piper," snarled an angry voice. "Or next time we give you a proper hiding and drop you over the Quay after."

He recognised the voice. It was Amy's brother.

Footsteps echoed off the backstreet warehouses as the two men left him sprawled in the road.

John's head was swimming, and he knew he couldn't stand. He'd look a right mess tomorrow. Yet he thought he'd been *so* careful. He'd have to say he'd walked into something, or fallen off a ladder…

———————

The captain of the *Contest* was thrown violently from his low bunk in the darkness and landed on the floor of his cabin. He awoke perhaps a fraction of a second before he hit the planking, but personal injury was not his immediate concern. *The ship had struck something!* He leapt up, heart racing, as he heard the resounding crash of splitting timber above. He sprinted on deck in his nightshirt to confront a scene of utter chaos. Foretopmast down. Ropes and timber strewn about, and the thundering and beating of the useless canvas made the masts buckle and jump like fishing-rods. There were men running and shouting, and in the midst of it all the mate whirling around yelling incoherent orders.

"Mr Martel!" screamed the captain. "What have you done to my ship!"

The mate was obviously dumbfounded and gawped at the captain, glassy eyed, presumably from shock, but he wasn't the most quick-witted man at the best of times.

"We've run aground, sir," reported a seaman.

"Run aground!" the captain's voice was a shriek. He grabbed Martel by his lapels. "How did this happen, you idiot? No ship runs aground in fair weather sailing from Guernsey to London." He spat the words out in incredulity. Then it dawned on him. "You didn't alter course, did you! You let us sail onwards on our old tack! Whatever have you

334

been doing, not putting the ship about according to my orders?"

Martel burbled something, looked ashamed and bewildered, lost, but said nothing more.

"Get out of my sight! You're dismissed," the captain commanded angrily, and pushed him aside. "Get below." There would be time to deal with him later. "Corbet!" he snapped, "you're now acting-mate. Where are we?"

"Too dark to know for certain, sir. Sandy bottom though and there's land to westward. Could be Hook Sands, sir, I reckon."

"Hook Sands!"

"Mouth o' Poole Harbour, sir."

"Yes I know where they bloody well are. What's the damage below?"

"Don't know, sir."

"Well get someone down there immediately. *Don't* go yourself," the captain restrained him. "I need you here. Then secure all that canvas before it beats itself to shreds. Get a crew aloft. I'll organise two hands to start cutting that foremast away."

What a bloody mess! How could this be happening? His first voyage in command.

The captain leapt nimbly over the wreckage on deck to reach the port rail. It was still night-time, but he thought he could just make out land on the lee side. He stared down at the outer hull below as he walked forward trying to see the waterline, but the darkness and the waves breaking on the Hook blocked his view. That wind was decidedly fresher than it had been a few hours ago. *What was the time?* His watch and his clothes were in his cabin. He realised he was still in his nightshirt, bare-footed. The captain grabbed a seaman by the shoulder.

"Jones!" he cried. "You and Spencer: free that foretopmast and pitch it over the lee side."

Jones nodded dumbly.

"Look lively!" barked the captain, and Jones scurried away.

Corbet reported back.

"We've taken on water, sir, but not too much – no more than a few inches in the hold."

"Have we sprung any timbers?"

"None reported, sir."

"Good. Now, I'm going below to change and I'll be back in *one* minute. Make sure Jones and Spencer get that mast away and secure all sail. Then we'll rig up a warp so we can try and kedge her off."

———————

Bill Brown was not in the habit of entertaining conversation during the first hour or so of the day and neither of them had uttered any sound since leaving the Quay. Richard Wills spoke when he felt that Bill was in the mood to reply.

"Why've we come out so early, Bill?" asked Richard.

"There's a fresh wind working up." Bill narrowed his eyes against the cold breeze as he nudged the *Ursula*'s tiller to port.

"How d'you know?"

Bill turned to him and smiled. "Here," he said, beckoning. "Feel that little puffing wind in your face?" Richard nodded. "Little parcels of something a lot stronger to come. And lookee here," he pointed to the horizon. "See they little scudding clouds yonder? I've shown you that afore. Always a sign we're in for a strong wind down-along. No mistake about it."

"But how d'you know?"

"Ah!" he smiled. "Experience. When you've been out here long enough you sense bad weather. We're in for a blow right enough and we'll have to be smart about it this morning. We'll haul in every one o' them pots double-quick and take 'em home. Can't afford to lose no more, and some of 'em need repairs at any rate."

"Why ain't any o' the other boats come out then?"

"Because they're not as smart as Bill Brown." He beamed with self-assurance. Bill was always right. Or at least he believed he was. Even when he was wrong it wouldn't be his fault.

"Will we catch much today?"

Bill shook his head. "Doubt it. Wind's all wrong: easterly. End o' the season too." His catches had been poor in the last month – they always did tail off as winter approached – yet this month's prices were the same as at the height of the season. It was a buyer's market. "Never catch much this time

337

o' the year," he added, "but I'd sooner take all them pots back empty than lose any."

During the past six months or so he had lost only three pots, but now it was November and it was vital not to lose any right at the end of the season since his reduced income over the winter would make it difficult to replace them. Effectively, pots lost now meant reduced ability to catch at the beginning of next season, and therefore less future income, so it was important that as many pots as possible survived for the following year. Over the winter they would all be carefully repaired.

Captain Addler stood and studied the mess that was once his beautiful ship. There was more order than an hour ago, but compared to when they left port the transformation was still a shock. Corbet gave his formal report after a thorough inspection of the hold and a roll-call of all hands. No major damage below the waterline and no-one was injured or missing, thank God. One of the hands was a joiner and he had patched up a couple of minor leaks below the waterline and the pumps had soon shifted the small amount of water they had taken on board.

The captain had to try to move the vessel off the sandbank as soon as possible. There was now thick cloud cover and the wind was fresh. If a storm blew up they'd be pounded to pieces. That heavy cargo didn't help because it was pressing the hull down into the sand, yet even in this poor light he could see that there was deeper water just a few fathoms to starboard.

The lack of major damage below meant that perhaps she wasn't stuck too fast and so he might be able to sail her off since the tide was rising. Set against that was the fact that the *Contest* had run into the sand bows-on at over five knots, so she surely must have been driven in deep; also her sailing ability had been reduced by loss of the foretopmast.

The captain decided to set a spread of canvas including a forestaysail with a jury-rigged jib from the bowsprit, which was fortunately intact, and brace the mainmast round so its sails could take the full weight of the easterly wind. The addition of the boom-mainsail might help too. It was worth a try. If this failed, all other options would require considerably greater effort.

Once set in motion the canvas filled as taut as a drum skin. The masts and spars creaked with the strain, but the *Contest* did not budge. If it didn't work soon he couldn't risk maintaining it or he'd have more carried away.

The *Contest* stubbornly refused to move. He soon realised this approach would not be effective and set the men aloft to furl the sails.

The sun would not be up until a quarter to eight, but there was already a glimmer on the horizon.

The next best option was to attempt to kedge off. It was most unlikely to work with a ship carrying this weight of cargo, but it had to be attempted. He sent an anchor out in the ship's boat and the crew pitched it over the side fifty feet away. They would have to kedge her off stern first, which was not ideal, but there was no other option. It was a frustrating experience because the anchor would not bite so when the crew hauled on the warp it simply came back aboard. On the fourth attempt the anchor did find a hold and the captain set the crew to the capstan to take the strain.

It had no effect. The ship would not budge.

So he tried again with an additional anchor at a different angle from the first. Taking the strain on both was also unsuccessful. He needed a full crew to do this and even had to call the disgraced Martel up from below to assist. However, this strategy did not work either: the *Contest* was stuck hard and fast. It was getting colder too, and they all noticed it despite the physical demands of their work.

As the captain was trying to decide what to do next, his thoughts were interrupted by a cry from a sharp-eyed seaman.

"Sail ho!"

"Where away?" demanded the captain.

"Port beam, sir," came the reply.

The captain squinted into the gloom. It was seven o'clock, and the light was grey and dim to starboard, whereas down in the west from whence the vessel approached it still seemed to be night. He could just make out a small craft – *a pilot-boat!* – skipping across the waves towards them. There must be just enough light now for the *Contest* to be seen from the shore.

———————————

"Hello, what's going on there then?" asked Bill as they entered the Swash Channel.

Richard looked up from his deck-scrubbing chores to follow his gaze. There on the Hook Sands was a large brig silhouetted against the lightening sky to the east. As they drew towards the windward side the sea made a clean breach over the ship from behind. There was a pilot cutter under her lee.

"Looks like George King were up early," observed Bill seeing, his familiar pilot-boat. "Let's fetch up closer and see if they need a hand." He put the tiller over and ran up to within hailing distance.

"Ahoy," he called up, when they were close enough.

George poked his head over the side of the brig. He may have resigned from serving with the lifeboat, but he still felt a responsibility to help fellow seafarers in difficulty.

Bill waved a hand. "You all right there, George?"

"Aye," he cried back. "Stuck fast, but not much damage so far as I can see."

"Anything we can do?"

"No thankee, Bill. Me brother's gone away for a tug – see if we can't tow her off. Bit worried about this lot," he pointed at the clouds above them.

"Aye, reckon you got a few hours yet though," Bill advised.

"Looks like we got more company." George nodded astern of Bill's boat.

Bill and Richard turned to see the Studland coastguard boat drawing closer.

"I'd better get out your way, George," said Bill. "Good luck!" With that, he brought the *Ursula* into the wind and headed away across Studland Bay.

Chapter Twenty-One

Frank Wills craned his neck as he sought his brother, John, amongst the crew packed into the *Antelope*. He hadn't seen him for over a week and was hoping that the lifeboat signal ten minutes ago would reunite them. He was definitely missing. *Lazy bugger*. Or maybe it was some new woman. Frank sighed inwardly and hoped not. John's pursuit of the fair sex was more than simply youthful exuberance. Why couldn't he at least *try* to be more discreet? Father knew all about it now and was understandably very upset – angry and ashamed. He belonged to a generation where this kind of behaviour was simply unthinkable, and he was determined to bring his son under control. Not an easy task. John was such a free spirit. Perhaps he had already become bored with the lifeboat in the same way as he seemed to quickly lose interest in everything else.

But Frank was brought back to more immediate concerns when he realised that Jim Matthews had already started to address the assembled crew, and was describing the stricken vessel which was the object of their current call-out.

"…and she's called the *Contest*. Now unlike the old *Antares* we went out to last time, which were on the west side of the Hook, this one's on the east side. George King's aboard her, and they don't know for certain that they need us yet, but this wind's getting up and I reckon they'll want us out there soon enough on account of it. So we're gonna get to North Haven just in case; then we'll see what's what."

"We taking the steamer, Jim?" asked Cain.

"Nope. The ship's so close-in we won't need it, and they're using the tug to try and pull the brig off anyway. Right! Let's be about it." He clapped his hands, then rubbed them together on account of the cold.

Jim stepped aside to let the men through the doorway behind him, and when he did so he caught sight of a skulking figure towards the back of the room as the crew filed out to go aboard the brake. "Tom!" he cried, and edged his way past everyone to grasp his hand. "Good o' you to come and see us off."

Tom Hart nodded and smiled. He hadn't wanted to be seen. "I bought some rations for the crew," he said. "Sam forgot 'em." He handed over the oilskin bag. "It's nothing much but you never know how long you're gonna be out there, Jim."

"You're right, thankee, Tom. And I been meaning to thank you, my friend, for all you've done in getting more men to join the lifeboat. You're a one-man press gang! We got more men than we know what to do with here – I had to send some home."

"Better too many, eh?"

"Oh aye!" Jim leaned back to peer through the doorway. All the men were waiting in the brake. "Now then Tom, I got a bone to pick with you. We meet in the *New Inn* of a Thursday, how come I ain't seen *you* there?"

"Well, I'm not part o' the crew no longer…"

"Listen. You're our recruiting sergeant. We wouldn't *have* a crew if it weren't for you. So next Thursday I want to see you there – we owe you at least a pint for this lot." He held the bag aloft and smiled. "Thankee for this." He clapped him briefly on the shoulder, and then strode out to jump up into the brake.

Tom heard Jim announce: "Tom's got us sorted with vittles." Then the brake lurched and clattered off. Tom smiled to himself.

———————————

The coastguard boat, which had come out to the *Contest* earlier to nose around, soon disappeared when the coastguard realised there was some serious work to be done. Frankly, George King was pleased to be rid of the smothering influence of officialdom. His brother had secured Will Redmond's services at the Quay and shortly afterwards the steamer *Royal Albert* appeared at the harbour's entrance and made her way slowly up the Swash Channel.

At about this time the sun poked above the horizon – it was difficult to pinpoint the exact moment as thick clouds were building to the east.

Captain Addler was certainly aware of the accumulating cloud and paced his deck nervously. He judged that they probably couldn't afford to remain where they were for much beyond midday. The sea was already pounding hard against the *Contest*'s windward side, making the whole ship tremble as if she would go to pieces like a stack of cards. *Still, new ship should be strong.* At least that's what he kept telling himself. *New ship! What a bloody shambles.* He'd never live this down. Never. End of his career most likely. Mr Lelean would dismiss him for certain.

The captain consulted with George King, still on board the *Contest*, and they decided that the pilot would assume temporary command of the brig to enable the best attempts to be made to free the ship using the steamer. Will Redmond came on board and together he and George agreed a plan.

Twin towropes were taken astern of the *Contest* to the *Royal Albert* and, once firmly secured, the steamer took up the strain in an attempt to pull the ship out the way she had gone in. After ten minutes pulling and no movement, George could see that further effort was wasted and signalled to the tug to desist.

They had a second option – to take the tug around the other side of the Hook into the wind to the west side of the brig and try to pull the ship over the sands while the tide was still high. It was unlikely to free her, but towing the vessel into the shallows could have a protective effect in the increasingly likely event of a gale. If the ship stayed aground in her present location on the margin of deeper water she'd be beaten to pieces in no time at all by the rough seas. As they were contemplating this, George's brother appeared leading a lugger out of the harbour. The lugger had brought thirty-six labourers from the quayside who could assist in offloading the *Contest*'s cargo so that she might be floated or towed off more easily. But which to do first – pulling with the tug, or offloading? There would probably not be time to do both on this tide.

Given that all other attempts to move the ship had failed it was decided to tackle the cargo first. The lugger brought the labourers up and they scrambled aboard the brig. The lugger had to return to the Quay as she was not suited to heavy weather.

Granite was clearly not the most easily manoeuvrable cargo, and this was going to be hard work.

"How much granite are you carrying?" asked George.

"About six hundred tons," reported the captain.

345

George let out a low whistle of surprise. "Well," he said, "I reckon we oughta get a hundred ton over the side as quick we can, then try again with the steamer afore the tide falls away." The captain nodded but suspected the pilot had underestimated the ease with which the cargo might be moved. However, he was very clear about his priorities. The cargo was precious – and there'd be hell to pay with the customer when he found out what they'd done with it – but the ship was even more precious and had to come first.

In the event, moving the cargo proved an incredibly slow and frustrating task. Without the facilities of a dock, everything had to be done manually with blocks and tackles. After two hours they had shifted a mere fifty tons and it had been exhausting work for all concerned. *Would it be enough to make a difference?* George looked at his watch – ten o'clock. They could attempt one last pull with the tug before the tide dropped away too much, yet the wind was very strong now and a gale was clearly imminent. He consulted with the captain. George proposed launching a rocket to request the lifeboat to attend them in view of the conditions. The wind was whipping up and the waves breaking on the Hook had increased in size dramatically in the past half an hour. A sudden further deterioration could leave them all stranded, or worse. The lifeboatmen had already been alerted to the fact that they might be needed and were in position at North Haven awaiting a signal.

The captain reluctantly agreed to George's proposal, but was uneasy about the decision as it seemed to indicate the possibility of abandoning ship – something he would never countenance, unless the *Contest* started breaking up. He did not believe that the ship was in danger and assembled his crew to make clear that the lifeboat was simply a precaution to stop the labourers becoming stranded.

Once the captain had explained the situation to his crew,

George waited until a wave had broken over the ship, steadied himself, then lit the taper of a rocket. After a few seconds the blazing missile shot high in the sky, exploding into a red star with a *pock!* It hung momentarily in the dark cloudy sky before being swallowed up.

Then a rope was passed from the bow of the brig to the steamer, now in position to the west of the Hook, and Will Redmond ordered the *Royal Albert* to take up the slack and pull the newly lightened brig. George was not confident of success, but to his surprise there seemed to be almost immediate movement as the towrope tightened in front of him. The vessel groaned as she slipped and scraped forward with agonising slowness through the sand. There was a huge stress on the ship's timbers but the rope was holding. Will Redmond maintained a steady, even speed to avoid unnecessary strain and hoped to keep the ship moving for as long as possible. Inch by inch the *Contest* crept forward into the shallow water which would hopefully protect her from going to pieces in the coming gale. Then, suddenly, with a crack and snaking hiss the towrope parted. Almost simultaneously the heavens opened and a heavy squall of cold rain descended on the scene.

They had previously decided that half past ten was the cut-off time for the steamer's efforts and the *Royal Albert's* captain duly brought his vessel back around the Hook.

Bill was pleased – he'd managed to retrieve all his fishing pots – although his prediction of a poor catch had proved correct. As the fishermen sailed back through the harbour's mouth, making for home, they passed the lifeboat heading out towards the *Contest*. Bill saluted his comrades, and Richard recognised his brother Frank sitting forward next to Jim.

Richard remembered Stoker's promise to let him help with the next lifeboat launch. He had missed the opportunity – just his luck.

Bill smiled grimly at the lifeboat crew. He hoped that they would finish with the brig soon because he sensed the gale wasn't far away now.

———————————

Jim handled the tiller expertly to bring the lifeboat safely alongside the *Contest* where George stood leaning over the side waiting to explain the situation.

"How many you got on board?" demanded Jim.

"Forty-six," George came back.

"Lord Almighty!" Jim exclaimed, taken aback. "D'you want us to take them all out now?"

"No, we been trying to get the ship off. We need to pitch a load o' cargo over the side to lighten her. Can you stay in case we need you?"

Jim looked at Stoker, who gave a curt nod.

"Aye," Jim shouted back.

George waved a hand in acknowledgement and disappeared to organise a safe method for offloading more of the granite.

"What do we do now then?" asked Cain.

"We wait till they need us," growled Stoker, sensing dissent.

"We could be here all bloody day," Cain complained, scowling. "Don't fancy it in this bitter cold."

"We're here to fetch the wreck when she needs us, and fetch it we will if we have to wait a week," said Jim stoically.

"Aye," said Frank.

This was enough to silence Cain for the moment.

But it was very cold and the swell and the waves were building. The rain, although it had been appearing to ease, suddenly intensified so that no-one could be heard above its roar on the boat and the surrounding sea. All around was grey sea, grey rain, grey cloud.

Then Sam had an idea. "Why don't we rig the foresail over us for shelter?" he shouted to Stoker. "Like Cap'n Robertson showed in that training."

"Aye, but we're already soaked right through," grumbled Cain.

"But it'd keep the wind off," cried Stoker, taking up the idea, "so we'll be warmer." Remembering the last time they were at sea for a prolonged period, he privately thought that giving the crew something to do would be beneficial for morale.

"It won't be an easy job in this wind," warned Cain.

"You *are* a bloody awkward bugger!" said Jim. "Does anyone else want to be out in the pouring rain when they could be in the dry?"

"Let's just get on with it," ordered Stoker.

The crew turned to and took down the foresail aft, which they stretched across the sides of the lifeboat, tying it to the cleats to make a roof. It was no easy job for the wind was so wild that it kept getting under the loose sail and threatening to carry it away. The sail flapped and bucked and billowed, frustrating all initial attempts to bring it under control. Indeed, Stoker was later to recall: 'Wrestling with that canvas were like fighting a steam engine'. Eventually, however, the deed was done and there was a certain satisfaction to be gained from triumphing over the elements.

When the roof was up, eleven of the crew snugged away underneath it, and two men stood on the after-grating thwart keeping a look-out with life-lines around them. Jim volunteered for first watch and insisted on volunteering Cain as well.

The lifeboat carried a binnacle and the lamp in it gave out a weak ghostly glow under the sail to illuminate the jumble of arms and legs sprawled in the bottom of the boat, one upon another. Sometimes a man would complain that another was lying on his leg or that he had cramp, and then maybe someone else would howl out that his arm was squashed and feel the burning pain as the blood rushed back into a dead limb, but as time went on and the temperature dropped further the cold seemed to take away all feeling and the protests diminished. Stoker realised that this presented a danger in itself, in that some of them might slip into hypothermia unnoticed, so he made a point of speaking to everyone regularly by name and ensuring that each one answered him.

As the seas flew over the boat, the water filled the sail that stretched above them and bellied it down upon the crew, giving them less room so that some had to lie flat on their faces, but when this became too much of a problem, Stoker led them in getting up and making one heave with their backs under the sail and so chucking the water off. The sail did an impressive job of keeping out wind, waves and rain.

After an hour Stoker changed the men on watch, and called Cain and Jim to seek the shelter of the sail while Frank and Sam took a turn outside. The crew of the watch eagerly sought sanctuary within the confines of the huddle, and even Cain now appreciated the value of it.

When two hours had passed and it was time to change the watch again, Stoker began to be concerned about two of his crew – Luke Allen and Ned Thompson. They were both relatively new recruits and this was their first attendance on a real rescue. More importantly, neither man was heavily built and reduced body fat offered much less resistance to the cold. They were both pale and shivered uncontrollably. Stoker watched them carefully and concluded that they were not in immediate danger. He caught Jim's eye and nodded towards the two men meaningfully. Jim studied them, then turned back to Stoker and shrugged as if to say 'what do you expect?'

Frank and Sam returned to the huddle and two of the crew assumed the vigil in their place.

Stoker began to question his motives in standing out to sea near the *Contest*. Yes, they had been asked to stay, but how much of his willingness to accept this was based upon his own determination not to fail? And they must not fail this time. They couldn't afford to return to North Haven to warm up if it meant that lives in the brig were put at risk while they were ashore. What would people say if they did that?

Then Stoker had an idea.

"What say we break out the rum?" he asked.

There was a strengthening chorus of 'aye' from under the sail. "And we got Tom's supplies too," Jim reminded them.

When he opened the locker it was full of water. He rescued the bottle of rum and passed it round. Everyone partook. The biscuits had turned to a mass of pulp despite careful wrapping, but the second parcel within Tom's oilskin was still sealed. Stoker opened it to find some sweet oatcakes: sticky, sugary, and smelling of butter and oats.

"Look at this, lads!" he cried. "Now here's something to bless Tom's wife for." He handed them round and enjoyed seeing everyone's profound contentment while they munched away. There was enough for one each, including the two crew on watch, plus a few spares. He looked at Luke and Ned, and handed them another oatcake each. "Here you go," he said. Then he gave the remainder to Jim. "Keep an eye on these," he said. "Gold dust."

———————

Throughout the morning and afternoon the crew of the *Contest* and her labourers had worked tirelessly in the cold to jettison the granite cargo. They were able to lift only small loads now because of the high winds – winching it from the hold and then dumping it on deck to be pitched overboard manually. It was far too dangerous to try to hoist the stone out over the sea directly using blocks and tackle in case the wind got hold of it. By one o'clock George estimated they had thrown a total of one hundred and ten tons over the side, but now they had to rest. The workforce was exhausted and the wind was raging such that the use of pulleys had become too perilous – the heavy loads were being buffeted by the gale as soon as they left the safety of the hold and threatened to break loose. At great risk the *Royal Albert* again ventured to the other side of the Hook and managed to tow the brig a little further westwards. The reduced weight had made a difference.

After a decent rest and some hot food from the ship's galley, George once more mustered his forces. Although blocks and tackle were now far too hazardous to contemplate, between them they began to lift some of the lighter slabs from the hold by hand, one at a time, and toss them over the side. It was backbreaking work since even the smallest slabs, at two feet square, weighed almost sixty pounds and required two men to manhandle them through the ship and up onto the deck. But it was all they could do in the prevailing conditions, and in many ways the physical effort was welcome as a means to ease the effects of the biting cold wind. Everyone helped – even George and the captain himself.

More than once George looked over the side to see the lifeboatmen continuing to dodge about in the heavy gale and a tremendous sea with a grim determination to do their duty. It was a marvel to see that little boat in such a great mass of stormy water and to know that thirteen men had been in it cold and soaking wet for three hours without the benefit of physical exercise or hot food to warm them. In her new shallow water berth the *Contest* had stood up to the conditions much better than George had anticipated and unless there was a dramatic deterioration, perhaps it was fairer to send the lifeboatmen back now to revive themselves fully. They'd surely be in no fit state to row their boat otherwise and the men on the brig might well need them in due course.

––––––––––

It was drawing on for half past one o'clock in the afternoon and some of the lifeboatmen were groaning with the cold and

353

pressing themselves against the thwarts with the pain of it. The crew voted for another nip of rum and the coxswain made no objection. The liquor went around. They lay in a heap hugging each other for warmth and Stoker, noticing that both Luke and Ned seemed to be dozing, prompted Sam to help him.

"Give them two a prod would you, Sam? Don't want 'em slipping away under our noses."

"Luke!" said Sam and jostled his shoulder. "Luke!" he tried again. Then the others nearby joined in, determined to rouse both their comrades from stupor. It took much effort of shaking, shouting, and pinching to awaken them.

"Are we nearly there yet, Gracie?" asked Luke. "Fetch me some more hot-buttered toast." His lips were dark, his face pale, and he spoke without opening his eyes properly.

A couple of the men laughed, thinking it was a joke. But Stoker knew it was serious. Once men became delusional then it was time to head back to dry land and warmth. He wanted to stay, but he was taking no chances with his crew. He scrambled over to the two men and, assisted by the rest, he rubbed the men's limbs vigorously to increase their circulation, and he gave both of them a sip of rum. Slowly they came round, but they were very drowsy and clearly no longer competent to function as part of the crew.

"Right!" he said. "We've got to furl that sail and it's time to strike out for the *Contest* and see if they need us. If they don't we're heading back to North Haven and a nice warm fire."

The sail was drawn in and it was a shock for all those under it to be exposed to the full ire of the gale once more. The wind shrieked past them as the boat rose and fell dramatically with the swell. At least the rain had eased for the

354

time being.

When they unshipped the oars they moved like old men, fumbling, unco-ordinated, weak. The crew groaned as one, when their cold, aching muscles took up the strain. It was a feeble first stroke. Luke and Ned were still semi-stuporous despite the crew's best efforts and could not row at all, so Cain gave up the bow to one of them while the other perched next to Stoker at the tiller. Encouraged as always by Jim their successive strokes became stronger and then stronger still – "take it easy now lads to start", "work your way back into it", and slowly they built up a more powerful rhythm which could carry them through the deepening swell. They may have been incapacitated for a while but their spirit was not broken.

Bit by bit, the *Manley Wood* was pulled closer to the *Contest* and eventually the assistant coxswain was able to hale them.

"Ahoy!" shouted Jim, standing up in the boat. George came to the rail. "Are you gonna abandon ship?"

"No, we're all right here for now. Tide's falling away so I reckon we're safe for a few hours. Reckon you should go back and we'll run up a flag if we need you."

"We'll come back afore nightfall," Jim promised, "and see how you're placed."

George nodded to show that he understood and Jim sat down again.

"Give way all!" Stoker commanded and they took up the strain, moving the lifeboat slowly landwards, every man eager for the shore. *Warmth! Hot food! A fire!* The anticipation was a greater stimulus to their efforts than anything Jim might say by means of encouragement and he knew it and kept quiet.

355

Chapter Twenty-Two

As the *Manley Wood* neared the shore, many of Stoker's neighbours ran down to the water's edge to help beach the lifeboat. Once this was done, the crew's first priority was warmth. They struggled up the foreshore like invalids, uncertain of their strength and footing. Luke and Ned had to be carried, they were so weak, but as soon as they reached Stoker's cottage his wife, Mary, and their eldest daughter, Louisa, were able to wrap the stricken pair in thick blankets and give them sips of hot sweet tea to revive them.

The rest of the crew accepted the Stokes' hospitality gratefully and gathered around one of the two fires which Mary had kept blazing in anticipation of their return. She had no fresh garments to give them and so they huddled together in their wet clothes, as close to the hearths as they dared, waiting to dry where they stood: half of them in the front room, half in the back. The heat seeped into their frozen bodies; it was such a delicious relief to be ashore. Yet it was clear that they all had to be fed as well and so Mary opened her pantry to the lifeboatmen. There was barely enough food to go round – some bread, cheese, salt fish – but she shared with them freely what little stores she had, and it was accepted with such gratitude that Mary felt her eyes prickle to look at them.

Their aching weakness gradually abated, and enfeebled men slowly grew strong again as if revived by some magical potion.

Nonetheless, Stoker could not afford to take any further chances with his two most severely affected men and he sent a message back to Poole requesting Tom to round up fresh members of the crew for the next launch. It would probably be colder then, and the weather almost certainly worse.

Sunset was at half past four so unless the brig signalled for the lifeboat sooner, he planned to venture out again at about four o'clock.

All afternoon the crew and labourers on the *Contest* toiled, and by the time the sun neared the horizon another fifty tons of valuable granite had gone into the stormy grey water. The ship was still stuck fast but George was determined to continue unloading for as long as they could – every little reduction in weight might help them in the end. The high tide should offer them an opportunity to refloat the ship if they could get her light enough, and if she stood up to the storm. George knew the gale had not yet reached its height and the eventual intensity of the elements was the biggest single factor which would determine their fate. The difficulty now was that the brig was taking on more water and so he had to have some men constantly at the pumps.

Captain Addler met him amidships.

"I can't thank you enough for all you're doing, George," he said. "Getting her into the shallows will save the ship I've no doubt about it."

"Aye, and if we can lighten her enough, we may float her off on the high tide at midnight – take her right over the sands if we're lucky – but we got to keep the men working: get rid of as much o' this granite as we can." George paused. "If this gale picks up we can't stay aboard you know…"

"I'll *not* abandon ship," the captain said stiffly, "unless there's no other choice. This is rough weather but we can sit it out. I've seen much worse. Soon as we step off her the *Contest* can be claimed as salvage and I'll not have that."

George pursed his lips. The captain was right: they probably could sit out the storm if it stayed at its present intensity, but George knew that at this time of the year it could only get worse – maybe much worse – but how soon and how much worse was in God's hands. These early winter gales were often the fiercest of the season – bringing winter back with a vengeance. George decided to say nothing more… for now.

"I don't know what the owner will say." The captain gazed into space for a second, unfazed by a cascade of sea spray which smashed down on the deck next to him. "I had such high hopes. Practically brand new ship; now look at it."

"You insured?" asked George, leading the captain away from the weather side.

"Aye. Four thousand pounds for ship and cargo, but I don't reckon it covers us for chucking the cargo into the sea."

"It's a hell of a load o' granite, what were it all for?"

"For the floor of some building in London – a bank I was told. Imported from Italy. Must've cost a small fortune. It was for John Mowlem, a builder. He's going to be fuming."

George raised an eyebrow in response to the name and the captain picked up on the apparent recognition: "You know him?"

"Not met him, but know *about* him. Local man, builder. Comes from Swanage. Done very well for himself by all accounts. He's been repairing bridges over the Thames – t'was in the paper."

There was a dull thud and then a muffled scream from below. George and the captain raced to the head of the companionway. From below there were further cries of anguish.

"What's going on here?" demanded the captain, unable to see because of the press of men in so confined a space.

"A slab slipped, sir," cried Corbet from a few feet below him. "It's trapped one o' the men."

"Clear a way there!" shouted the captain and he herded men up on deck so he could get to the scene.

Scrambling down the wooden stairs, the captain came upon a young labourer propped up against the ship's side and nursing a bloody left arm. His face was screwed up in agony and tears of pain streaked down his grubby face.

"What happened?"

"Lost our footing, sir," Spencer explained. "Dropped the slab and it crashed down the companionway out o' control and caught this young 'un against the side, sir."

"I thought I told you to leave the bigger slabs below," reproached the captain. "They're too heavy."

"Didn't know, sir. Sorry sir."

"Corbet! Why are you moving these bigger pieces?"

"We had to move it to get to the rest o' the cargo, sir. It were in the way so we thought we may just as well take it up."

"Good God, it weighs two hundredweight at least! It's a mercy someone wasn't killed!" He shook his head at Corbet. "For the bigger slabs see if you can break 'em up first before moving. They're not very thick – a few hefty cracks with a sledge hammer should do the job. Get some o' the labourers and see to it, Spencer."

"Aye, aye sir."

"Now then, young man," said the captain, turning to the unfortunate labourer. "I reckon we need to get you some place warm, and a good measure of rum inside you." Rum was the seaman's antidote to all things medical. "Corbet, get this man's arm bound, set up a cot and blankets near the galley, and serve him a double measure. Give him hot soup too if he'll take it." He gave the acting-mate a stern look. "No more accidents, Corbet," the captain commanded.

———————

Even above the howl of the gale the lifeboatmen at North Haven heard the clatter of horses' hooves outside as the brake came to a halt. Stoker peered through the window at the driving rain and made out two men scampering towards the house, protected by a sheet of tarpaulin. No doubt the replacements for Ned and Luke that Stoker had asked Tom to seek out. Stoker made for the door, but at that moment it opened and in stepped Jack Fisher and John Wills.

John Wills was hardly the best choice – he'd been shrammed almost to death in the Great Gale so his ability to withstand the elements was open to question. However, he seemed to get on well with the crew – even the older ones – despite his amorous escapades, and some of the younger ones even secretly envied his reputation. Tom must have been hard-pushed to secure replacements at such short notice. He had probably opted for experience over brute strength and both these men had been with the lifeboat since the beginning. As John turned into the light of the fire Stoker saw he had a nasty black eye.

"Thankee for coming, lads," said the coxswain warmly to break the silence occasioned by their arrival. "We needed two skilled seamen." He shook them both by the hand. Then he guided John aside as conversation in the room resumed. "You sure you're fit for this?" he asked quietly.

"What?"

"Your face."

"I fell off a ladder few days ago," he lied. "Took a knock. S'nothing. All alright now."

"Oh," said Stoker suspiciously. "Be more careful next time."

John's brother Frank overheard the exchange and was not convinced by John's explanation either. As Stoker turned away, Frank sidled up to his brother.

"What really happened then?" he demanded in a low voice.

"I fell off a ladder," John repeated through gritted teeth.

"Haven't seen you about much."

"Was gonna say the same about you."

"I hope you're not…"

"Me life's me own," he declared with emphasis and turned away to speak to someone else.

But it was now four o'clock. The predetermined time for the lifeboat to return to the *Contest*. Stoker came to stand next to Jim by the hall door.

"Reckon we must set to it," he announced.

"Aye," Jim agreed. "All hands!" he called to rouse the crew roasting around the hearths in both rooms.

The lifeboatmen dutifully assembled before them.

"We're going out to the brig now to see what's what," explained Stoker. "They may want us to take some or all o' the crew off."

"How're we gonna do that, Stoker?" asked Frank.

"Well, Jim and I reckon the safest way would be to take 'em out ten or twelve at a time. Any more and the lifeboat could capsize, so we only take more if it looks like the brig's going down."

"That's four trips out then," calculated Cain.

"Aye." Stoker nodded. "We'll chance a stretch of canvas maybe, what d'you reckon Jim?"

"We can try it and see what we get away with: would do us good to save our strength for the oars later on."

"That's settled then. So we fetch up close to parley, but if we need to take men off we'll anchor to windward first then row up."

"What about the steamer?" asked Sam.

"Reckon she'd be a hindrance in this," said Stoker. "Easier for us to get out there under sail and row back. Steamer couldn't get us close enough – too shallow. If it gets any worse we'll need her help, though, so we can dump the men we rescue aboard her to save coming back here every time."

They had to launch the lifeboat in-harbour because the waves rolling on the south east side of North Haven Point were already too high. This meant navigating a length of the Swash Channel after leaving the protection of the harbour in order to come under the lee side of the *Contest*. The deep water here was a challenge to the crew. The swell surged and ebbed, lifting the lifeboat high and dropping her down, while the waves breaking over her port side drenched the crew in icy sea every few minutes. Nonetheless they used the sail when they could, tacking back and forth to catch the wind, and resorting to oars only when essential. In this manner, they eventually caught up to the *Contest*. George was waiting for them.

Jim had to stand precariously amidships and yell at full volume to be heard. "What do you want us to do?"

"Still need to lighten her," George came back. "Get her off at midnight on the high tide."

"D'you want us to take men off?"

"No. We'll show a light if we need you."

Jim opened his mouth to reply, and a split second before it happened he knew he was going to be pitched overboard. The bow of the lifeboat rose abruptly as a wave suddenly crashed around the stern of the *Contest*, taking the whole crew by surprise. Jim reached out, flailing into nothingness as the lifeboat bucked and threw him backwards over the starboard quarter. He hit the water headfirst and instinct stopped him gasping at its icy temperature as the sea swallowed him up. His heavy sea-boots weighed down his legs as he tried desperately to kick out and propel himself upwards; his oilskin ballooned around his body hampering his movement. He was struggling with all his might to break the surface when the swell lifted him and pushed him upwards so that his head reached the air for just an instant. He gulped a desperate deep breath before he was pushed down again, kicking and thrashing at the sea all around him. In that brief space he had already been dragged fifteen feet from the boat. He struggled to get his boots off but his oilskin was tangled and twisted all around him. He knew he was slowly sinking despite his lifejacket – *he had to get those boots off*. He fought the rising panic as his lungs and throat burned with the craving to exhale. The boots were made of leather and tight-fitting: not designed for speedy removal. He tore at the buckle of his left boot for agonising seconds. Suddenly it came free, then his right more easily; he ripped the boots off and, kicking out with all his might, he felt himself moving. *But was it in the right direction?* He was disorientated. All around was blackness and cold but he kept kicking, hoping to find the air. His head was pounding, his chest was heavy. *His poor mother.*

As soon as Jim hit the water, his brother Cain knew what to do. He thrust off his boots, trousers and oilskin, and dived over the side. It was a curious thing, but Jim couldn't swim. Many seamen couldn't. Better to drown straight away when the ship goes down than to be left struggling in the water for hours facing a slow death. At least that was the conventional wisdom. But Cain could swim, and swim well. He struck out just as Jim's head bobbed out of the water a few yards ahead of him. The water was icy and treacherous; he could feel the swell tugging at his body.

After his brief re-surfacing, Jim went under again as a big swell dragged him down despite his life jacket. He was pulled into darkness then suddenly propelled upwards so that he burst out of the waves again gulping in lungfuls of air, gasping and coughing, swallowing sea water too as his chest rasped in protest. He could see nothing – his eyes were full of cold, salty water. He flailed out with his arms to try to keep himself at the surface. Then something happened. *What was it?* He wasn't moving properly.

"I've got you," gasped a familiar voice. "Bide still."

Sam threw out a lifeline and the crew reeled them in.

"Keep a strong grip on him now," urged a voice.

Jim was hauled up forcefully into the lifeboat, cracking his shoulder hard against the side as three of the crew pulled him out with all their strength.

"Thank God," said someone as they helped Cain back on board.

"Sit down all o' yer!" Stoker ordered. "Or we'll have another one overboard."

Jim lay exhausted in the bottom of the boat. Coughing, spluttering, and utterly spent like a half-drowned animal. Pumped full of adrenaline but barely able to move. He felt himself slipping away into blackness.

———————

The sun had been down for an hour by the time the lifeboat made it back to North Haven. Jim had recovered his wits before they reached shore and thanked Cain and the crew with a feeble yet heartfelt appreciation that only a man saved from certain death can know. He had already made it known that his accident was not going to stop him returning to the

Contest with the lifeboat if they were needed.

Once ashore, the lifeboat was secured and the crew made their way back to Stoker's cottage. Mary had anticipated all their needs. She had maintained both fires – and once again the lifeboatmen stood around them dripping and hoping to dry quickly. While they'd been out she and Louisa had toured the neighbours, borrowing all the towels and bedclothes they could. Mary had them all ready to dry and cover the wet lifeboatmen. And inevitably she had hot cups of tea waiting.

"Louisa, you keep out o' the back room and the front room. I'm getting 'em all to strip off in there so we can dry their clothes and give 'em something hot."

In the middle of all this came a loud knock at the door and Louisa ran to open it. It was one of Mrs Kittle's servants from nearby Heathside House.

"Hello Martha," said Louisa.

"Afternoon to you, Louisa. Can I have a word with your mother?"

"Who is it, Louisa?" Mary called from the kitchen.

"It's Martha," Louisa reported, as their visitor stepped into the hallway.

"Sorry to barge in on you like this, Mary, but it's old Mrs Kittle. She's been watching the wreck on the sands there and seen the lifeboat going to and fro. She's got me to cook you a couple o' gammon joints to feed the men. I'm getting Beth and Susie to bring 'em over to you, but just thought I ought to warn you in case you were cooking yourself."

"Oh Martha! That's so very kind!" said Mary. "I was just

thinking 'how on earth am I gonna feed this lot' cos we ain't got much and they do so *need* a proper hot meal. I must come with you straight away to thank her."

"No," Martha protested, holding her back. "She's quite clear that you're not to stop what you're doing, but says she hopes this'll help to spare you another job. You got enough on your hands, Mary. She says I can stay here and help you serve it an' all."

"Well, let's not tell the men and we can take it in as a surprise. They've worked so hard, Martha. Been out in it for hours and so wet through and cold – every one of 'em like ice. Jim got washed overboard and near drowned, and two of 'em had to be carted back to Poole this afternoon in no fit state to carry on."

"I know! We saw someone go in. Is he all right? Mrs Kittle's daughter has a big telescope and was describing it all to us and when she said one of the lifeboatmen's gone in old Mrs Kittle she screamed she did. 'Oh merciful God' she said 'save that man!' And as soon as he were back in the boat she made her mind up. 'Martha' she said 'we're gonna make them men a fine supper to warm 'em through. Run to the larder for them gammon joints and cook 'em for Mrs Stokes'."

"She's a lovely lady, Martha."

"She is. And always so generous. We all set to in the kitchen – her daughters helped me peel the spuds and all. You've got gammon, spuds, turnips and carrots coming over. Enough to feed a blimmin' army. I hope you can eat it all."

On board the *Contest*, it was now nearly five hours since

367

sunset. The workforce was on its last legs. George King's determined efforts had resulted in the shifting of perhaps a further twenty tons at most. This made a total of some one hundred and eighty tons for the whole day – almost a third of the total cargo – but the crew and labourers were now so exhausted that further effort was simply impossible.

Every man aboard was aching from top to toe and since nightfall the air temperature had dropped markedly to well below freezing point. The darkness also seemed to have ushered in a more spirited wind and it was whipping the sea up to a frenzy. The gale made it feel even colder, but the most worrisome problem was the mighty waves now crashing against the hull of the *Contest*. Each one sent a shaking rumble throughout the whole ship, and there were three or four of those every minute. It was dark and they could no longer see the land save for the faint lights on North Haven Point which marked the location of the lifeboathouse and the coxswain's cottage.

––––––––––

Will Redmond was shown into the back room where the lifeboatmen were crowded in, talking quietly amongst themselves. Stoker and Jim sat on chairs in the corner furthest from the fire discussing their plans; Frank, John, and Cain were on the floor by the longest wall, and the rest stood around the fireplace save for Sam Hart who was on watch duty outside. Twelve men plus a blazing fire made the room very warm indeed, although not uncomfortably. Having cruised around in the steamer for ten hours, Will appreciated the heat.

"Hello, Will!" cried Jim, looking up, and he and Stoker stood to greet him.

"You're still with us then," observed Will, nodding at Jim.

"I am thanks to Cain."

Cain looked away, abashed, as if he had not heard.

"Bravest thing I ever saw, Cain Matthews," said the steamer captain quietly.

"Anyone else would've done the same – I just got me boots off first."

There were smiles at this – Cain's self-effacement went down well. Yet so very different to the Cain Matthews that most of them thought they knew. Even Jim had been amazed at his brother's courage and now stood next to him proudly.

Will nodded in appreciation – admiration even. Cain had never before been the object of such positive attention and respect from his fellow men and Jim realised that his brother did not know what to do. Others in the room, recognising this unexpected shy modesty, liked him for it.

"You fit now then?" Will asked, turning back to Jim.

"Aye," Jim replied heartily. "Now that Mary's fed us and got us dry again. Ready for anything."

"Well, I thought we ought to meet and plan for later," said Will. "Wind's getting up and the brig's taking a pounding. Sea's breaking clean over her bow – she's lucky not to have had anything carried away."

"We were just talking about it, Will," Stoker informed him. "We got Sam on the headland keeping an eye out for a light in case they call for us. Won't be long I reckon. It's a gale o' wind now."

"You gonna try towing her off again, Will?" asked Jim.

"If we get out there on the top o' the tide, would be worth another go if it's not too rough: there'd be a few more feet o' water under her and they've shifted a load more o' that granite."

"I reckon they might call us afore midnight at this rate." Stoker looked grave. "We've got – what? – three hours to go yet till high water and it's getting worse by the minute."

"I don't know why we couldn't have taken some of 'em off earlier," complained Jim. "It's gonna be a devil of a job taking forty-six hands off now in this, let alone if it gets any worse. Maybe we ought to go out to 'em anyway in half an hour and try to persuade *some* of 'em to leave at least."

"Would you try towing 'em again if we went out that soon, Will?"

"Well, we could give it a go, but I reckon if it gets much worse we gotta forget the ship and think about saving lives. You can hear her now out on the point trembling as the sea smacks against her. She's jarring against the sand and she's gonna shake herself all to pieces if it keeps up."

At that point a heavy gust of wind rattled the windows of the cottage to emphasise the point.

"It's these gusts what do the damage," said Jim. "Least it's not raining."

"No, there is that," agreed Stoker, "but it's dark and we'll scarce see a few yards all round the lifeboat which means we'll have to go up the swatchway, we can't risk East Looe in this – too narrow."

Jim looked at Will. "You'll give us a tow out?"

"Oh, aye," the captain confirmed. "I suppose we just have to sit and wait." Will got out his pipe and started to fill it.

"Have you eaten, Will?" asked Stoker. "We had some fine gammon earlier, and there's plenty left."

"Gammon eh? For all o' you? That's mighty kind o' you, Stoker. I reckon they're paying the lifeboat coxswain here too much!" he said with a twinkle.

"No, no. We were given it all by old Mrs Kittle." Stoker jerked a thumb over his shoulder.

"I was pulling your leg." Will smiled. "Can't say I've given much thought to food these last few hours, but now you mention it, I wouldn't mind a bite to eat. Keep me going for a bit."

Just then Sam burst in.

"She's showing a light!" he cried.

Chapter Twenty-Three

The *Contest*'s clanking pumps were no longer able to keep pace with the influx of water; remaining spars were ripped away one by one in the darkness; all the ship's boats were gone, and the sea broke so viciously across the decks that even the lee side was no longer a sanctuary.

Once he'd decided it was no longer safe to remain on board it still took George King more than an hour to persuade the captain of the *Contest* to abandon ship. In the end it was the sea itself that lent the most convincing force to George's case by dramatically carrying away the whole port rail. George and the captain were on deck at the time: one minute the rail was there, the next it was hidden by a huge plume of white water. Then it was gone.

The sea was pounding incessantly now. Bigger, more forceful and more frequent waves. A relentless assault. They'd be lucky to get off alive.

As Will Redmond had predicted, the priority now was no longer the ship. It was to save the men on board.

George made the prearranged signal to summon the crew of the *Manley Wood*, yet even as the decision to abandon ship was made, an enormous wave cracked against the bows and snapped off the jib-boom leaving it flapping loosely like a broken arm. Within ten minutes of showing a light to call for the lifeboat's assistance, the whole bowsprit was gone. They never even heard the timbers crack above the roar of the wind and the waves; the water simply took it. The disengaged forestays hung forlornly like vines looking for a hold, whipped about by the wind. The loss of the bowsprit put the *Contest* in danger of losing her damaged foremast as well, since the stays served to help keep it upright. The captain had re-secured them after the loss of the foretopmast. Maybe its reduced height would offer the mast a measure of protection.

"George, you and the labourers are to go first," insisted the captain. "Especially that lad with the broken arm. I'd like you to go with him, and make sure he's safe."

"I thought maybe I should stay here to help..." George began.

"No. I think you've done all you can – for which much thanks – but let's be sure you get home safe to your family. How many can the lifeboat take?"

"Well, I couldn't say for sure. She'd probably want to take no more than a dozen at a time."

There was a long pause while they both watched the sea.

"Do you think," ventured the captain at last, "that we could ask the steamer to try towing us off *one* last time?"

George smiled. Most captains would rather lose one of their own limbs than lose their ship. He knew it was probably a waste of time in a sea this rough, but there was always a chance, and this captain – despite his earlier apparent capitulation on the subject – evidently had still to be wholly convinced there was no alternative to abandoning his ship. "I reckon we could have a go, towing up the swathway, but I'm not sure in this heavy sea that it'll do any good. I'll put it to 'em when they gets here."

Plunging bows under as she came along, the steamer towed

the lifeboat through a blizzard of spray. The towrope veered out a long way too far astern of the steamer for the bigger vessel to act as a break-water to the smaller one, so the heads of the seas blew into and tumbled over the lifeboat repeatedly. The air was full of water and scarcely was the steamer and her charge atop the height of a swell than they were rushing like an arrow into the next hollow.

In quieter seas the tug could have used a shorter towrope and her bulk would have given the smaller boat some protection, but in heavy weather the towrope had to be long to prevent the line from 'snatching'. Snatching produced an alternating taut and slack effect, which was abrupt and unpredictable, and which would have given the lifeboatmen an even rougher ride.

With the steamer as close to the brig as she dared, the lifeboat was cast free and the crew, who already had their oars unshipped, rowed the *Manley Wood* up against the biting wind. It was a tough haul. The lifeboat carried a warp to the *Contest* before seeking a relatively secure berth fifteen fathoms to windward of the brig's starboard side. Then Captain Redmond initiated the *Royal Albert*'s final attempt to tow the *Contest* from her sandy confines. The warp from the brig's port bow was secured to the steamer's stern and they tried to pull her over the Hook. The cable tightened and, as earlier, Will allowed the tug to take up the tension gradually as he steamed slowly north-west up the swathway, but the stubborn deadweight of the brig coupled with the pressure of the tide and the wind behind him put too much strain on the rope and with a sudden snap it parted. The brig had not budged an inch.

George King shook his head as he watched the steamer moving away after its unsuccessful mission. He looked at the captain who sighed heavily then, cupping his hands to his mouth to ensure he was heard above the wind, barked out the final order: "All hands prepare to abandon ship!" Corbet took up the cry and ensured it was passed along. The men began to assemble aft. The bows were now almost permanently awash with sea, breaking over her with ever-increasing force and even in the darkness the white water charging across the ship could be clearly seen from the stern.

Stoker could see what was happening and commanded that the lifeboat's anchor warp be paid out so that they could drive down to the lee side of the vessel's stern. Once in position, Stoker bellowed up at the ship's crew.

"*One* at a time!" he ordered.

As agreed on shore, Sam and Frank crouched amidships, secured by lifelines, and ready to receive the men as they clambered down a rope which was dangling over the side. The rest of the lifeboat crew sat ready at their oars in case they should need to make a hasty retreat. They were to take twelve on the first trip.

First came George King. It was a nerve-wracking descent. He was used to climbing up and down ropes, but not in these conditions: his heart pounded, but he made himself take it steady. The wet rope and wet sides of the ship made it easy to slip – especially with numb hands and a high wind – and the lifeboat was never still. She was carried up and down, but could also be pushed away from the side of the brig leaving nothing but sea beyond the end of the rope.

"We got a lad with a broken arm," George panted as soon as he was safely on the lifeboat. "They're gonna lower him over the side."

"Any other wounded?" asked Stoker.

"No, just him."

They could already see the young man's feet twirling around above them as he began to be lowered. He was buffeted against the ship's side repeatedly as his descent continued. They heard him cry out as his injured arm cracked against the hull. Without warning the lifeboat bucked just as he was within reach, sending it away from the brig for a second, and the youth shrieked for divine intervention as he suddenly saw no boat beneath him.

"Don't worry lad, we're still here!" cried Frank, reaching up. He grabbed the boy's right foot and guided him down into the boat: face as pale as a sheet and shaking with the shock of it all. "You're gonna be all right now," Frank reassured him as Sam untied the rope.

In quick succession, more men made their way apprehensively down the ship's side and into the safety of the lifeboat, but just as the twelfth was aboard a huge sea thumped against the aft hull of the *Contest* and the lifeboatmen heard the brig judder loudly.

"Pull away!" ordered Stoker, and the crew heard the alarm in his voice as they rapidly took up the strain.

"Pull!" Jim yelled. "You! Get down in the boat!" he shouted at the latest arrival, worried he was going to pitch overboard.

There was no point going back now for a few more. "Make for the steamer," Stoker commanded. He looked over his shoulder. The *Contest*, which had held position for so long, was moving, and slowly began to slew broadside on to the wind and seas. That meant she was now going to take a heavy beating along her whole port side. They were going to have to act quickly or there might not be any ship left. It also meant that the next trip would be far more dangerous because the waves were starting to break with a new ferocity around her stern.

Jim was encouraging the men in his usual fashion. "Come on!" he roared. "Let's show 'em what we're made of! That's it, lads. Pull for England now! Let's be hearty, boys! Pull!"

The rescued men sat silent in the middle of the boat, grateful to be off the ill-fated brig. And George King marvelled at these lifeboatmen – these friends and former crewmates – who'd been so cruelly vilified during the Great Gale. *Were these the same men?*

In only ten minutes the *Manley Wood* had fetched up under the lee of the steamer which had stood off into deeper water to the east of the Hook. Cain secured the lifeboat properly to the steamer's side before allowing any of the rescued men to disembark. They struggled up the *Royal Albert*'s high side and were hauled aboard by Will Redmond's crew. It wasn't easy – everything was a battle in these conditions: the men were understandably keen to gain the security of the larger vessel, while the sea was determined to try to force the steamer and lifeboat apart.

"Have a care," Will called to Stoker. "She's come across the sea now – there'll be a regular surge o' water round her stern."

"I know, we saw it," said Stoker glancing back. From here the ship was a phantom, barely discernible. A silhouette against the white water cascading about it and over it from behind. The light of the feeble full moon barely amounted to anything as it was obscured by cloud.

"Good luck," said Will. Cain cast them off and the lifeboatmen set to rowing out to the ship once more. It was very hard work because they had to row against the cold wind. The crew all sat with their backs to it, which reduced their personal discomfort, but Stoker at the tiller had the wind and the sea in his face. He squinted through the spray from the waves crashing over the bows and kept the lifeboat on course.

On board the *Contest* the crew and remaining labourers could hardly believe that so small a vessel as the lifeboat could meet such a sea and survive. Yet as she came back on her second trip she rose like a duck to the great roaring waves which came towards her, draining every drop of water from her bottom as she was hove up, and falling with terrible suddenness into the following hollows, only to bound like a living thing to the summit of the next gigantic crest.

"We'd be safer lashed to a mast than out in that little thing," shouted someone.

"Lashed aboard here you'd be as safe as the bowsprit was afore it were broken away," shouted the captain. "Now listen to me, all of you, it's not safe to stay here. I've been below and there's several feet of water in the hold – when the ship moved we must have stove a plank in somewhere. We're *all* getting off. Me and the crew are going last, but I want all you labourers off the ship double-quick when the lifeboat comes alongside."

Crew and labourers alike could all see that the captain was concerned. There was a new urgency to his orders.

A mighty wave smashed against the hull and they felt the ship judder beneath their feet once more. The waves pounded away sending deluge after deluge across the foredeck and huge white icy-cold cascades that splashed over everyone standing astern.

"We're going to get smashed to pieces here," the captain was adamant. "So we have to go. Mr Corbet, set knots in that rope over the side to help the men get down as quick as they can."

Far aloft in the darkness there was the sharp report of the main topgallant sail breaking free from its frappings. The loose canvas thrashed about noisily in the wind, beating the mast as it was rapidly rent apart by the gale. In no time at all the sail was nothing more than tatters.

With great difficulty, the lifeboat made it to her anchorage. The crew was exhausted.

"Don't worry," Jim assured them. "We can take a spell in a bit while we get them men on board, and then we'll have the wind behind us when we head back."

As before they reached the stern of the brig, and a man started to descend. The brig's crew had rigged up their knotted rope to climb down which made it easier.

The first labourer touched the deck of the *Manley Wood*, helped by Jim and Sam's willing hands.

"Now go forward and sit down," Sam instructed.

"We're going to pieces!" insisted the labourer. "Water in the hold and ship bumping on the bottom. How many men can you take at once?"

"I reckon we could take twenty," said Jim, looking to Stoker for approval. He nodded.

"I'd rather take a load of 'em now," announced Stoker above the waves. "This lot's only gonna get worse by time we come back again."

"Aye," said Jim. "If we take more of 'em this time, then

we'll only need to come back once."

"Get forward," insisted Sam to the labourer, "and keep low in the boat." This time the man obeyed. The lifeboatmen shuffled along their thwarts to make as much room in the centre of the boat as possible.

A second man came down the rope.

"Watch out!" shouted Cain, on look-out at the bow.

Everyone crouched low in the boat as a huge wave crashed around the stern of the *Contest*, sending the lifeboat bobbing up and down like a cork. When it passed, Sam sent the labourer forward and they prepared to receive the next man.

And so it went on. Every two or three men, a wave broke and sent the lifeboat plunging up and down or careening away from the ship's side. The lifeboatmen patiently got back into position and then waited for the next man.

After what seemed like an eternity Jim stole a glance about the boat and saw it almost full. "How many?" he called to Stoker.

"Twenty-one!" the coxswain came back. "Room for three more I reckon, no more."

Three more came down. *Had they taken too many?* The lifeboat was heavily laden and sat so low in the water.

"Give way all!"

As the lifeboatmen strained to pull away from under the *Contest*'s lee, an almighty wave breaking off the sandbank curled right over the boat and swamped it to capacity. The oarsmen kept at it, knowing they couldn't sink, but the labourers shrieked and cried in fear.

"We can't sink," bawled Stoker.

But it made no difference. They were terrified.

Over and over again the lifeboat was buried, but as regularly did she emerge, with her crew looking fixedly ahead concentrating on giving their steady, strongest efforts with the oars, and Stoker watching the steamer with a face of iron.

Bit by bit they crept closer to the *Royal Albert*, the regularity of the oar-strokes making their mark with a dreadful slowness through the swells and waves. Jim kept up his encouragement so that even his own men were amazed that he had the strength and imagination to do it. "Keep going you rascals! Pull your hearts out boys! Show me what you're made of! We'll have a tale to tell, eh!"

Sam looked down at his hands as he tried not to think of the biting cold. They were white like wax, but gripped the shaft of the oar as if part of it. He found the rhythm of the rowing a great stimulation – no-one wanted to break that rhythm and impair their progress. Back and forward again, back and forward; like a clockwork toy.

Two of the labourers near him were gibbering uncontrollably like frightened children, clinging desperately to the thwart beneath them with both hands. Sam had no time or energy to comfort them. He knew he had to stay focused.

A wave curled over them once more and, acting as one, the lifeboatmen automatically slowed their rhythm while the water surged across them; then they resumed. They were used to the deluges, but many of the labourers looked like they were in shock – pallid faces distant and rigid.

Frank stole a glance at his brother John: he had a look of strength and determination he'd never seen before. Then he looked at Cain. His heroism in saving Jim had been a revelation to everyone, yet he was staring dead ahead, jaw set, just like all the others. One purpose.

Eventually they made the steamer's side and the lifeboatmen collapsed at their oars, while the labourers clambered out – some effusive in their thanks, others silent as they reflected on their ordeal. But whether the rescued were vocal or not, the lifeboatmen could do nothing but ignore them. They knew they had to go back, and they could all see that the conditions were even worse than last time.

Stoker reached into the locker by the tiller and fished out a bottle of rum. "Time for rations," he announced. "I reckon we earned 'em."

The bottle went round and each man gratefully took a nip. Despite their extreme physical exertions, every one of them was shaking with the cold. They were soaked through to the skin in icy water and the bitter wind was howling with ever-increasing intensity. The rum would keep the cold at bay for a while, and they really needed respite, but Stoker knew that a rest risked men catching a chill or even refusing to go back. He had to keep them at it while their bodies were still able to convince their minds that they could do it.

"I've got an idea," Stoker announced. "If we get Will to drop us down the swatchway a few fathoms towards the Bar Buoy we can row across the wind instead of into the teeth o' the gale. It'll be a longer trip out, but I reckon t'will be easier."

"Reckon you're right," said Cain. "And we'll have the tide behind us too as we go up."

There were signs of agreement from all round the boat, so

Stoker made his request to Will Redmond, who carried it out.

"Now then lads," shouted Jim as they were about to cut themselves loose from the tug. "Remember this is the last time we're gonna have to do this. Once we're there, coming back's a lot easier than going out."

The lifeboat was set free and the crew set their jaws and rowed with all their strength. The wind was harder, there was more sea, but rowing across the wind with the tide pushing them made all the difference. It required each man to give every ounce of his strength and they all needed to keep in time as a few missed strokes would send the boat running away in the direction of the wind away from the brig, and that could not be allowed to happen.

With an almighty effort which sapped their strength they made their anchorage and slipped down from it to the brig's side once more. In the intervening time the *Contest* had lost the remains of her foremast which leaned over the port side towards them sorrowfully, rigging trailing in the water.

The waves were breaking around the ship so regularly now that timing the men's descent from the deck to meet the lifeboat had become virtually impossible. Men frequently had to climb halfway down and stay there, dangling above raging seas, while the lifeboat fought her way back to position before they could complete their journey. Fortunately, the remaining ten men comprised the ship's crew and as such they were well used to scampering through a ship's rigging, so this situation was not as perilous as it might have been if there had still been labourers left aboard. Eight of the seamen made their way down to the lifeboat including the wretched Martel and to all concerned it seemed to take an age.

Even to these experienced seamen the size of the waves came as a shock once they were in the lifeboat. They appeared large enough from the deck of the *Contest* – seas towering higher than the brig's hull before crashing down on her – but from the considerably lower platform of the lifeboat they seemed gigantic and the ship's crew were cowed into a fearful silence, eyes downcast as if in a trance. The lifeboatmen sat there – steely, determined and apparently unafraid. *Who were these men who could accept this danger with such* calm?In truth they were afraid but had learned to repress the fear; to accept it as a normal, if unhelpful, reaction, and then ignore it. And they had learned to trust in their own boat and its coxswain.

Eventually Corbet, the last seaman, began his descent, leaving the captain alone on deck. Perhaps having waited so long for his turn, he was even more anxious than his predecessors to get to safety – determined not to be left behind. Whatever the reason, he seemed to be in a particular hurry. A few knots from the top of the rope, his right foot slipped on the wet side of the ship and he fell just as a wave dashed the lifeboat away from the brig's side. For a split second he flailed in the air, but by a miracle one hand found the rope and grabbed onto it as his feet hit the water. He crashed hard against the hull as the lower half of his body entered the icy water, but he still clung on tenaciously and brought his second hand to the rope as the waves swung his sore, stressed body back against the side and held him in their freezing caress. The *Manley Wood* made it back to her position and Jim and Sam grabbed Corbet and hauled him aboard, gasping with shock and relief. But there was no time to lose.

Jim pushed the frightened man to the bottom of the boat. "You were lucky!" he said. "Sit amidships." He pointed to a space on the thwart next to Frank. Corbet was too shocked to reply but did as he was told.

Captain Addler left the ship last of all, as was his right and duty, and made his descent uneventfully. He nodded appreciatively to Stoker at the tiller and found a place amongst his crew, who all sat heads hanging.

Then began the lifeboat's worst journey. As they left the protection of the *Contest*, the seas raged after them with such force that they leapt right over the boat; the air was filled with water flying high over them in broad sheets which fell with a roar like the explosion of a gun ten or a dozen fathoms ahead. The boat shipped water time and again as the oarsmen maintained their steady stroke under Jim's expert encouragement. Despite the wind at their backs it was hard going. The swell kept taking the water out of reach of the oars so that strokes were missed and the regularity so important for progress was thrown into confusion. With endless patience Jim kept up a stream of bellowed instructions to the exhausted men as they had to reacquire their rhythm again.

"Pull! Off we go! Pull! Keep it steady now! Pull! That's it. Easy, easy, keep it going!"

Sam wondered if he was the only one who could no longer feel his feet. They were numb with cold and felt like dead weights. They would burn mercilessly once the blood started to re-circulate. His heavy wet trousers chafed against his thighs and he knew they were being rubbed raw. He'd probably get water welt which often festered for weeks afterwards. But it all simply had to be tolerated; there was nothing he could do.

Cain wondered that he hadn't collapsed long ago. It was bitterly cold and he never knew he had this endurance in him. With each merciless stroke of the oar he told himself that it would just be one more. Then just one more again. He just had to keep going. Did the others feel the same? He could not let them down. He would not.

John, sitting next to his brother, worried that he would not have enough strength to keep pace with the other men. *Was he strong enough?* He was determined not to show weakness, but how much longer could he keep this up?

Even Jim could feel himself beginning to tire, but he knew he must not show it. His back, neck and shoulders ached with exertion. But they couldn't give up, or start to flag, they had to keep at it or die. It was as simple as that. If they stopped now they'd be swept out to sea on a cold, stormy night and they'd all be dead in no time. "Pull!" He roared at them hoarsely. "I *know* it bloody hurts! Pull! Come on, just a few more fathoms now. Pull!"

They were all soaked through to the skin of course, and had been for hours, but it was no use thinking about the discomfort of cold and wet, any more than their aching bodies. There was a job to be done.

Eventually by some miracle, by an incredible combination of strength, determination, leadership, but above all courage, they made the side of the *Royal Albert*.

The crew of the *Contest* climbed gratefully onto the steamer.

It was now half past one o'clock on Sunday morning. All the lifeboatmen were silent. Totally spent. Each knew he'd given everything. *Everything.*

Stoker sat back silently with his men as the lifeboat was hooked on to the *Royal Albert*'s towrope.

And how did the coxswain of the lifeboat feel? It was a difficult sensation to describe – not one emotion, but many. He was pleased with the successful rescue of forty-six souls, proud of the performance of his men, grateful that they had had the opportunity to prove their worth and had passed the test.

He surveyed the lifeboat, still shipping heavy seas, and realised he now knew the affinity for her that all skippers felt. She was a good boat; she too had proved herself.

But more than any of these things he was relieved. He knew it marked the end of their prolonged and testing probation. No-one could look down on the crew with disdain any more, disparage them in public. All talk would be of the lifeboat's achievements, not of its shortcomings.

But did that mean he wanted credit, or expected acclamation?

No.

He knew only that his crew could now continue to undertake the duties which befell them as lifeboatmen unencumbered by a need to make amends for the past. The burden had been lifted. Freedom and the future had arrived together.

Notes on Historical Accuracy

All the people and incidents in this story are real. Some of the events seem extraordinary, and yet these actions of the Poole lifeboat and Christchurch coastguard in 1866-67 are all recorded in contemporary sources. The dramatic rescue of the crew and labourers from the *Contest* turned out to be the biggest saving of life from a single vessel by any lifeboat in the whole of the UK in 1867, so in the end it proved the best imaginable means of silencing the Poole lifeboatmen's critics.

However, although I have adhered closely to the facts, all authors have to employ some licence in converting an historical account into a novel. In particular, the real events involved a very large cast of characters, and there was a plethora of people with the same or similar names, so sometimes I had to omit individuals for clarity. For example, there were two men in Poole called George Penney: one the owner of the steamer *Royal Albert*, the other secretary of the Lifeboat Committee. I made a decision not to mention the second one. Similarly, the captains of two prominent ships in the story were called John Back and John Blackler, so I changed the latter to Addler. Nicknames were common in Victorian Poole and I often followed this real-life trend, so whilst the nickname 'Stoker' is a complete fabrication by me, Thomas Matthews was known as 'Cain' by his contemporaries.

Four of the ships involved in the Great Gale were the *Elizabeth* (of Exeter), the *Elizabeth* (of Teignmouth), the *Eliza* and the *Ela*. I felt these names were too alike and would cause confusion so although the *Elizabeth* of Exeter kept her original name, the other three became *Devon*, *Augusta* and *Figaro* respectively.

Inevitably I had to shorten the lengthy original account of the inquiry, so I omitted similar questions repeated to different witnesses, and I sometimes had to re-order or edit exchanges to provide a clearer narrative. The story still closely reflects the original proceedings, although Will Redmond's testimony is a composite of his own and that of three other witnesses.

A difficulty with reconstructing historical events is the lack of surviving detail: even the newspaper report of the inquiry was criticised at the time for omitting key facts. Furthermore, no-one now knows precisely why the mate of the *Contest* let her run aground or why Tom Hart left the lifeboat service, for example, because it was not documented at the time. Yet I hope the explanations that I have provided for some of these mysteries are credible. Where contemporary sources offered conflicting information I have pursued the line which seemed most reasonable, although inevitably this is a personal opinion.

I created a small diversion from reality when I brought Jim Matthews into the story. He was in fact already serving as a member of the lifeboat crew when he was appointed as assistant coxswain – he wasn't a newcomer. I also decided to omit describing a fruitless launching of the lifeboat that came two days before the *Manley Wood* attended the ship *Antares*. My most significant deviation from history was the brief description of Lord Osborne's sending of agricultural workers to Australia; this actually happened a number of years before 1866, but I included it here as a practical illustration of his renowned compassion for the poor.

Although contemporary records can often capture an element of a person's character, the detailed behaviour, motivations, and actions of long-dead persons clearly require imagination. I hope my attempts to do this have created engaging and believable personalities. Fortunately, I had help here from my late father, Peter Wills, to whom I owe a great debt for his unflinching encouragement. He was a powerful exponent of the Dorset tradition of oral history, and passed on to me many stories of the characters of old Poole and of the lifeboat. He was in a good position to do this, because his grandfather was Richard Wills who appears as a young lad in this book but who later became one of the most charismatic and heroic coxswains of the Poole lifeboat.